Praise for Pamela Red...

Suburbanist...

"A delightfully lighthearted story.... Funny, sexy, and heart-warming." —Fresh Fiction

"Engagingly told, funny, and real, *Suburbanistas* will capture the hearts of readers." —*Booklist*

"Redmond's writing just keeps getting better, and her stories are an absolute delight.... A wonderful book."
—Dorothea Benton Frank,
New York Times bestselling author

Younger

"Beautifully written ... a tale that will strike at the hearts of women of all ages." —*RT Bookclub*

"Funny and touching." —*Publishers Weekly*

Babes in Captivity

"Through her women characters, Redmond tells realistic and intriguing stories that will enthrall, and ultimately, surprise readers." —*Booklist*

"A breath of fresh air.... It's delightful to read about women attempting to find out what really makes them happy, without throwing away their families to accomplish it."

—BookLoons

***The Possibility of You* is also available as an eBook**

THE POSSIBILITY
of YOU

PAMELA REDMOND

GALLERY BOOKS

New York   London   Toronto   Sydney   New Delhi

Gallery Books
A Division of Simon & Schuster, Inc.
1230 Avenue of the Americas
New York, NY 10020

First Gallery Books trade paperback edition February 2012

GALLERY BOOKS and colophon are registered trademarks of Simon & Schuster, Inc.

For information about special discounts for bulk purchases, please contact Simon & Schuster Special Sales at 1-866-506-1949 or business@simonandschuster.com.

The Simon & Schuster Speakers Bureau can bring authors to your live event. For more information or to book an event contact the Simon & Schuster Speakers Bureau at 1-866-248-3049 or visit our website at www.simonspeakers.com.

Designed by Renata Di Biase

Manufactured in the United States of America

10 9 8 7 6 5 4 3 2 1

Library of Congress Cataloging-in-Publication Data

Satran, Pamela Redmond.
    The possibility of you : a novel / by Pamela Redmond.—1st Gallery Books trade paperback ed.
        p. cm.
    1. Women—New York (State)—New York—Fiction. I. Title.
PS3619.A82P67 2012
813'.6—dc23   2011043159

ISBN 978-1-4516-1642-2
ISBN 978-1-4516-1643-9 (ebook)

To my grandmother
Bridget Agnes McNulty Goudie,
who did it all for me

AUTHOR'S NOTE
AND
ACKNOWLEDGMENTS

It's ironic that a novel about how momentary chance encounters change the course of women's lives began with a momentary chance encounter that changed mine.

One day I happened to click on a link to the Ellis Island website, where I discovered a feature that lets you look up the records of relatives who may have immigrated through that New York port. Typing in the name of the Irish grandmother I grew up with—Bridget McNulty—yielded in an instant not only the date of her arrival (May 1, 1911) but also the name of her hometown (the lyrical Drumshanbo), her age upon her arrival (22), and even her coloring and height (dark and 5'7", the same height as my mother, me, and my daughter).

I'd known my grandmother only as a sweet, lumpy old lady who liked to listen to Lawrence Welk while eating marshmallow peanuts, and who refused to talk about her years working as a nanny and maid in Manhattan. But gazing at her name on the Ellis Island website, her life as a young woman new to this country suddenly seemed vivid to me in a way it never had before. My own daughter was twenty-two at that time and living in France, struggling to make a living and adjust to life in a strange place. Why should my grandmother's life in New York a hundred years before have been radically different?

I decided that day to write a novel whose main character was a young Irish woman newly arrived in New York in the years right before World War I, the watershed between the old world and the modern age. I wanted there to be a more modern character who could interact with the older Bridget, and that's how Billie, who arrives in New York in 1976, the same year I did, was born. And then there had to be a contemporary character dealing with many of the same issues—of love and sex, work and motherhood, independence and family—that the women before her did.

My first thanks go to my brilliant editor, Lauren McKenna, who loved this book from its first incarnation as *The Bridget*, whose insights and vision shaped the novel that became *The Possibility of You*. My trust in Lauren as an editor is complete; she improved every character, every scene, every feeling and story in the book.

Another huge thanks go to my agent, Melissa Flashman, at Trident Media Group, who embraced my novel full-heartedly and believed in it unfailingly through its long labor and delivery. Melissa, thank you for sharing my dream and making it come true.

In 1916, 90 percent of the female servants in New York City were Irish. Irish girls were virtually the only ones who came to this country alone; Jewish and Italian women largely immigrated with their families and did not work as domestics. For these Irish women, working in service was difficult yet offered their best chance at liberation from the strictures of the Catholic Church, patriarchal society, a life tied to the farm and to constant childbearing.

For their help with my research of the character of Bridget—and the other "Bridgets" (the derogatory term for Irish servants) like her—I am grateful to the American Irish Historical Society, Eileen Dowling and Joe Lee at NYU's Glucksman Ireland House, and the New York Historical Society. Thanks also for valuable insights to Professor Mary C. Kelly at Franklin Pierce College, author of *The Shamrock and the Lily: The New York Irish and the Creation of a Transatlantic Identity, 1845-1921*, and to Janet Levine of the Ellis Island Library, who arranged for me to listen to oral histories of Irish immigrants. Details of the white-on-white racism against the Irish along with other immigrant groups came from, among many other sources, Noel Ignatiev's book *How the Irish Became White*.

Middle-class American women, in turn, used the services of their Irish maids and nannies to win their own form of newfound liberation, campaigning for women's suffrage, birth control, and "sex rights." The Heterodoxy Club was a real institution in New York, where a wide-ranging group of the most notable women of the day congregated, including such personages in this book as Margaret Sanger, Emma Goldman, and Beatrice Hinkle, along with artists, writers, and performers like Maude.

Beatrice Hinkle, a medical doctor who was the first female member of the American Psychiatric Association, a cofounder of the psychiatric department at Cornell Medical School, and who first translated Jung into English, in 1916, has largely been forgotten by history. I am grateful to Kathy Rosenberg for leading me to Diane Richardson, the librarian at the DeWitt

Wallace Institute for the History of Psychiatry, hidden in the heart of New York-Presbyterian Hospital, who helped me unearth original journals and documents that gave insight into this remarkable woman who was one of the first psychoanalysts in America. For the history of Jungian analysis in the United States, I also talked to Thomas Kirsch, author of *The Jungians*; Susan Lanzoni, a professor of the history of psychology at Yale; and to the Jung Society.

The year 1916 was an important one in the history of New York and all of America, a watershed year between the end of the old world and the beginning of the new. Symbolically enough, it was the year that the balance tipped in the city and cars first outnumbered horses; New York's single traffic light stood at the intersection of 42nd Street and Fifth Avenue, and was operated by hand. The photo archives at the New York Historical Society and the City University of New York helped pin down the look and feel of the time.

Nineteen-sixteen was the year of the first large-scale polio epidemic in America, in which nine thousand children in the city were stricken by the disease and twenty-five hundred died. No one knew what caused the disease much less how to cure it, prompting fear, superstition, racism, and near pandemonium throughout the city and beyond. I was honored to interview Dr. Naomi Rogers, the Yale medical historian, who wrote the seminal book on the 1916 epidemic, *Dirt and Disease*, to build my descriptions of Floyd's illness and death along with the conditions in the city. Other details on childhood illnesses of the time came from John Zwicky, PhD, the archivist at the Pediatric History Center, and Yale pediatrician Howard Allen Pearson, MD.

The other major historical event of 1916, which figures in the book, is the opening of the first birth control clinic in the United States, in Brooklyn, by Margaret Sanger, and its closing ten days later. The Margaret Sanger Papers Project at NYU helped me with my investigation of this turning point in women's reproductive freedom.

Adoption is a major theme in later sections of the book. Adoption rights activist Claudia Corrigan Sheeley enlightened me on New York adoption laws, which still mandate that original birth certificates be sealed and new ones be issued listing only the adoptive parents' names and offering no clue that an adoption even took place. The only way for an adopted child to link his official birth certificate with his original name and birth date is via the New York City Birth Index, a secret I learned from Joe Collins, a Morristown, NJ, private investigator who specializes in tracing the identity of adoptees.

I would like to thank my friend Leslie Brody, a reporter at the *Record*, who evocatively described the Birth Indexes as having pages "thin as butterfly wings" and who led me to Joe Collins. Other people who provided important insights into the experience of adoption from both the adoptees' and adoptive parents' viewpoints include my friend the wonderful German novelist Annette Mingels, my longtime writing partner Linda Rosenkrantz, my sister-in-law Carol Lensmire Satran, and John Dutton, whom I found via the generous Andy Hoffman.

Katherine Borges, director of the International Society of Genetic Genealogy, generously answered hundreds of ignorant questions from me related to a plot twist that didn't make the final version but was fascinating nonetheless.

I was privileged to write whole drafts of this manuscript

through several residencies at the heavenly Virginia Center for the Creative Arts, the best creative home a writer could wish for. And thank you to the Geraldine R. Dodge Foundation, which underwrote some of that work.

I am enormously grateful to be part of an intelligent, supportive community of writers who read many versions of this book, offered invaluable advice and criticism, and helped me navigate the publishing process. My loving thanks go to Rita DiMatteo, Christina Baker Kline, Alice Elliott Dark, Benilde Little, Laurie Lico Albanese, Louise DeSalvo, Debbie Galant, Martin Beiser, Liza Dawson, Dorothea Benton Frank, Alexa Garbarino, and John Paine. My daughter, Rory Satran, and my husband, Richard Satran, both read this book many times and offered excellent ideas and equally excellent encouragement. My sons, Joe and Owen Satran, always gave me new reasons to keep writing. And Nathaniel Kilcer told me a secret that informed Cait's keeping of her own secret.

A giant thank-you to my old friend the brilliant novelist Geraldine Brooks, who contributed the highest praise and made me believe in this book through its many incarnations.

Writer friends Gretchen Rubin and Peggy Orenstein offered insightful publishing advice, and brilliant longtime magazine editors Judy Coyne, Lesley Jane Seymour, and Deborah Carter provided early and meaningful support for the book.

On the publishing end, I'm hugely grateful to editor-in-chief Jennifer Bergstrom for coming up with my amazing title, so much better than my own 256 ideas. I'm thrilled to be working again with publisher Louise Burke and editor Megan McKeever, both smart and inspired, along with publicity genius Mary McCue and the enthusiastic and supportive Alexandra

Lewis. And I'm grateful to Deborah Schneider for encouraging me to change courses and write a different kind of novel, and for being its longtime champion.

Finally, I'd like to thank the artists whose works inspired me along the winding trail of developing *The Possibility of You*. The angelic singer Maude Maggart introduced me to the early works of Irving Berlin, and since the real Bridget's cousin was his cook, he had to play a role in my story. The visual artist Kara Walker inspired me to revisit old themes in fresh ways. Lauren Redniss's gorgeous book *Century Girl* helped Maude come alive. And the photographs of William F. Cone, at the New Jersey Historical Society, introduced to me by the lovely and generous Lily Hodge, first made the world of a hundred years ago feel vivid and palpable and my own.

Most important, Michael Cunningham's beautiful novel *The Hours* helped me envision the structure that finally enabled this novel to take flight. After writing an *Hours*-informed draft at VCCA, I returned to New York to scout out the location in Little Italy where I wanted Cait to live. At the end of a long day, exhausted, feet hurting, I found myself hunting for the perfect coffee shop to record the day's ideas. When I finally found it, I collapsed into a chair only to look up and find myself staring directly into the handsome face of . . . Michael Cunningham.

So, thank you, Michael Cunningham, for appearing from the heavens that day as if to confirm I had taken the right direction. The cake that Billie bakes—that's for you.

Intention? Motive? Consequence? Meaning? All that we don't know is astonishing. Even more astonishing is what passes for knowing.

—Philip Roth, *The Human Stain*

I am left here alone to recreate My WHOLE HISTORY without benefit of you, my compliment, my enemy, my oppressor, my Love.

—Kara Walker, *Letter from a Black Girl*

THE POSSIBILITY
of YOU

I

Cait, Present

They were in the woods, hundreds of them—police officers and firefighters and volunteers and dogs and finally, after a week of living with the heartrending story, journalists as well—walking hand in hand in hand in a sweep across the leaf-covered ground, the dense canopy of trees overhead turning black against the darkening August sky.

"Okay, that's it!" called the police chief. "This is the end for us."

Everyone froze. Cait felt the dry bony hand of the woman who'd been searching on her right slip away; on her left, Martin held fast. After a moment of stillness, they moved with the rest of the crowd to tighten their circle around the chief.

"We've done all we can in these woods," the chief said. "I thank you for your efforts, but you can go home. I'm turning this case over to the FBI."

Cait looked in alarm at Martin, already shaking her head, appalled. "I can't believe he's giving up."

"He's not giving up," said Martin. "It's just time to try something different. It's dark now, it's . . ."

But she was having trouble listening, the images that had haunted her throughout this increasingly desperate week rising up again: Riley, five but no bigger than a three-year-old, buried beneath the dense carpet of leaves, trapped under a rock, cowering in a cave, mauled by a bear, or caught in a fox trap. She wasn't ready to give up on him. She couldn't believe the rest of them were.

"We've got to keep looking," she told Martin. "That little boy, nobody ever cared about him, and now it's like we don't care, either."

Martin tried to gather her close. His shoulder looked so tempting, strong beneath his dark blue T-shirt, its cloth soft as a pillowcase. She could smell the sweat on him from the long day of searching in the late summer heat, but something else, too: the sweet scent of clothing carefully laundered by a wife.

She pulled away, mortified, swiping at her cheeks. "I'm all right."

"No you're not." His hands, large, gentle, were still on her. "What is it?"

They had found each other across the crowded fire hall the night after the story broke: the little boy, son of a meth addict, foster child of a great-aunt who was descending into Alzheimer's, wandered into the woods and never came out. Cait, visiting her parents in New Jersey for the month of August and going out of her mind with boredom, had volunteered to cover the story for the website where her college friend Sam was editor.

Martin, an editor at the *Times*, had similarly volunteered for the gig, since many of the paper's reporters were off on vacation and his wife was visiting her own parents at the beach with their kids. She'd wanted a break, he'd told Cait, his soft-looking lips twisting into a frown. Which may not have been a bad thing.

They were two of the tallest people in the room, he notably older than she—late forties, she guessed—with dark hair and a heavy five o'clock shadow and myopic brown eyes blinking behind tortoiseshell glasses. She noticed him first, scribbling notes like a cub reporter, earnest and sweating in his white button-down shirt and chinos, gold wedding ring glinting in the bright overhead lights of the country hall.

Then the fire chief said something inadvertently funny and she'd noticed him—noticed Martin—suppressing a smile as he ducked his head and scribbled faster. She must have been staring at him—must have been smiling, too, because he suddenly looked up, caught her eye, and grinned full out.

They were a pair after that, swapping information on the story, comparing theories on what had happened to Riley, gossiping about their fellow reporters, drinking on side-by-side swiveling stools at the Blind Pig every night, then shuffling next door and saying good night beneath the bare bulb that lit the portico of the motel where they both were staying, he in Room 10, she in 11.

"I'm going to keep looking," she told him now, pulling free, really believing she was going to head out herself with her little flashlight into the now-dark woods. "Will you help me?"

"You're not going anywhere," he said, taking hold of her.

She looked down at his hand, big, pale against her tan arm. She'd spent the whole of the two weeks before coming up here

3

at her parents' little lake club, the poky place where they'd been going since she was a kid, baking on the dock while her mom sat reading in an Adirondack chair under the dense pines. Cait never burned and her hair, as dark as Martin's in winter, had bleached the same tawny gold as her skin.

"What if that were your son?" she asked him.

Noah, she remembered. Noah was fourteen, his sister Natalie seventeen, heading to college next year.

"That wouldn't be my son," Martin said quietly.

"What if it was me?" she said, and then she broke down for real, pressing her face against his shoulder now, feeling his arms wrap tightly around her, letting herself go, feeling safe in his embrace—so safe, she managed to think, that it was dangerous.

One of his hands moved through her hair, got tangled, then got deliberately more tangled.

"It's not you," he said into her ear.

"It could be me," she told him, pulling back to look at him.

"What do you mean?"

She took a breath but then decided not to say what she'd been preparing to say. "Nothing," she muttered.

There was Riley in her mind's eye again, lost, alone, scared, damaged. Why did she, who'd never felt anything but safe and adored, feel that could be her?

Maybe because she was prone to wandering into the woods. Maybe because she felt, now, like she was lost.

"What?" he pressed.

She shook her head. "Nothing. We better go file our stories or everybody's going to beat us."

They sat, as usual, facing each other across the long folding table that served as a makeshift desk for the reporters covering the story. They each banged out their last Riley stories on their laptops. She found herself reworking her sentences more than was necessary, going back to her notes again and again in search of a better quote, reining in her pace as surely as if she were riding a horse when she felt herself approaching the final paragraphs. As long as she didn't finish the story, she felt, he might still be out there, waiting to be found and written about the next day.

Martin finished first, packed up his computer, and sat playing with his phone till she was done. Then they set off, as they had every night, walking down the dark highway toward the motel. The only thing that was different was that tonight they held hands, loosely, noncommittally, but without letting go.

"Feeling better?" he asked her.

"A little."

"Want to tell me more?"

She took a deep breath and didn't answer. I want to tell you everything, she thought. I want to know everything. But wasn't the very fact that he was married, however ambivalently, the very reason she'd let herself develop this kind of crush on him? Because she knew there was no danger of actually having him, of getting too close?

The night was darker than usual, the moon that had lit their search and their walks home all week narrowed to a fiery sliver. And there was something else: no lights emanating from the Blind Pig.

"Shit," he said, stopping. "If there was ever a night when I needed a beer."

"I have beer," she said, tentatively. "Well, not beer, actually. Whisky."

He laughed. Stood on the shoulder of the moonlit highway and studied her. It felt nice, tipping her head back to meet his gaze. Nice and even more dangerous than heading into the black woods.

"If you have whisky, I have glasses," he said. "The finest plastic."

"I have water. The finest tap."

"I might even have ice," he said. "Or at least I know where I can get some."

And then there was that moment, the moment she might have said, "God, but I'm so tired," and he might have said, "Maybe we can have lunch sometime," but instead, after they let the silence settle for an extra beat, he leaned toward her and they kissed, his mouth salty with sweat, gritty with dust, hungry against hers.

She'd been traveling light for so long, emotionally as well as literally, giving in to sex only when she was desperate and nonattachment was all but guaranteed, when the man looked as if he could satisfy the body without leaving any imprint on the heart.

But that wasn't Martin. I could love this man, she thought as they half stumbled, half twirled toward the motel, their kisses harder and more insistent with every clumsy step. I could love him but I won't. Or I'll let myself love him tonight and then tomorrow we'll both leave and I'll never see him again. He'll go back to his family and I'll go off to Addis Ababa or to Manila and I'll think of calling him every time I'm in New York but I never will.

They forgot the whisky. She paused only long enough to duck into the bathroom and rummage through the big cosmetics case she'd never bothered to unpack at her parents' place, miraculously finding her old diaphragm in its case. And a twisted tube of jelly last used who knew where or when.

He was waiting for her, stretched out long and lean on top of the sheets, his eyes without the cover of his glasses looking like the most naked thing about him. She lay down beside him, leaving the bedside lamp on. The smell of the woods, of the dead leaves they'd spent the day wading through and the trees that had towered all around them, filled the room and seemed to emanate from his skin. She kissed him lightly, tenderly, without force. The decision had been made and they no longer had to pretend to be swept away by passion.

She'd never had sex with someone as old as he was, and though he looked better to her than the hard-body expats who usually landed in her bed, his skin felt looser on its bones, as if it was beginning to slip away. He looked at her more softly, too, taking his time, turning her away from him and lifting the mass of curly hair so he could kiss the back of her neck.

"I've been dreaming of doing that all week," he told her.

She turned back toward him and kissed him again, more insistently this time. What she'd been dreaming of was climbing on top of him, feeling small against his largeness, vulnerable against his ability to care for her. She wanted something from him beyond his cock, beyond obliteration, something more permanent and harder to define.

It wasn't until the sex was over and she was still again, dozing on top of him, that he spoke.

"I want to be with you," he said.

7

I want to be with you, too, she thought. But no. No.

"You're married."

"The way I feel with you—now but not just now; all week, from that first time you smiled at me—I never feel that way with her."

She moved away from him so that he slipped out of her.

"Married guys always say that."

" 'Married guys always . . .'?"

"You're not the first," she said shortly, standing up, crossing to her suitcase, getting the whisky.

"I didn't think . . ."

"Listen," she said, getting back into bed, switching off the light. "Obviously, there's something special between us. But you're going back to Park Slope, and your wife and kids will come home from the beach, and you'll make up and be together again. And I'll go to New York and get my next round of assignments and head out on the road."

She could already imagine it, all the steps, the way it was every year: a few weeks back at her parents', her mom fighting tears the whole time at the thought of another separation and her dad pretending it was fine, the month in Little Italy at her usual sublet seeing Sam and her other editors, and then the long plane ride, the new city, the next story, the place and people and job unfamiliar and foreign enough that she could forget how foreign she felt herself.

"I want to see you when you're in New York," he said.

She unscrewed the cap on top of the whisky bottle, took a long swallow, passed it to him. "No."

"Why not?"

8

"I'm not a home wrecker."

To her surprise and his credit, he laughed. "And this isn't a 1950s B movie. My home is already in shambles."

"Call me when you're divorced," she said. "If you still want me, if I'm still single, then maybe we can talk."

Tough girl. This was so much easier than the way she'd felt in the woods. So much easier than the way she'd felt kissing him.

"Cait," he said. "I'm serious."

He set down the whisky bottle, turned the light back on, took her in his arms.

"You don't want to be with me. I'm a mess."

Just agree with me, she thought. Everything will be so much simpler that way. And really, she knew for a fact that love didn't change anything. She loved her parents and they loved her, too—she'd always been sure of that—but it wasn't enough to make her want to settle down in their safe suburban town, as her mother might have wished, and be happy going to the mall on Saturday mornings, having dinner together on Sunday nights. She loved her friends, but one rollicking night out every six months was usually enough to sustain her. She even loved the apartment she always sublet in New York, but she'd never had the urge to stay there rather than move through a procession of motel rooms as anonymous and ugly as this one.

"Does that have anything to do with what happened in the woods today?" he asked her.

Did it? She couldn't now access the feeling she'd had out there, her identification with the child, if that had been it, or the urge to rescue him. Had it been merely exhaustion that made her lose control, or the feelings for Martin she'd been struggling to keep under the surface, or something else, something deeper?

"Cait," he said. "Tell me. Talk to me."

She made herself focus on him. His eyes were so steady on her, trusting and trustworthy. She could almost imagine being with him, in the lovely little apartment hidden away in the building behind the building in Little Italy. She imagined him in his glasses, and his soft blue T-shirt and worn jeans, bringing her a sandwich in the captain's bed raised so high off the floor that you needed to climb a step stool to get into it, folding himself into the bed beside her where they would gaze out at the treetops over the cemetery.

This vision seemed so appealing, so palpable, that she thought for a moment she might really be able to tell him what she'd really felt in the woods today. That Riley might have been her. That she'd been adopted, so soon after birth that it couldn't possibly have made any difference and by parents who'd never been anything but wonderful, and yet the fact of her adoption had always made her feel completely lost.

Instead, she rested her head on his shoulder and asked, "Do you think Riley's alive?"

He sighed deeply. "I don't know. I want to think so. But that's not the way these things usually turn out."

"I think he is," she said, the boy's small pale face, animated from the countless pictures she'd seen of him, grew vivid in her mind. "I just . . . I don't know. I think he's out there, looking for something."

Martin made a sound, not a laugh, but a bark of surprise. "What would a five-year-old be looking for?"

She slid down so that her cheek was pressed to his chest, her entire world reduced to the thump-thump of his heart. It was so warm down here, so comfortable, so safe-feeling. She remembered herself at five, at seven, even at twelve, standing on the beach holding a shell against her ear, listening to its whoosh, so distant yet so provocative, the faint wind of a far-away land. She'd dig in the sand, down, down, hoping to find clams, gold, China.

"Treasure," she told Martin. "Adventure. Something all his own."

She listened to his heart and willed her own to match its pace. How long had it been since she'd felt so satisfied to be exactly where she was? Had she ever felt that way? She had no desire to leave him and move across the planet, across the room, even across the bed. All those years she'd been digging, she thought, and it turned out the treasure was not in the woods, hidden in the dirt, and it was not in China. The treasure was right here beside her and, for at least tonight, it belonged only to her.

2

Billie, 1976

Billie thought she had cleared everything out from under the bed—the empty tequila bottles and the yellowed *Bay Guardians* and, God help her, the crusty jockey shorts—when she spied, nestled within the dust forest at its unreachable center, what looked like a metal box.

"Jupe," she called, sitting back and straightening up.

The little rental cottage looked so much better now that they'd stripped away the chaos that had dominated it for most of the nine years she and her father had lived there, ever since her mother died. Its whitewashed plaster walls and French windows looking out on a tangle of trumpet vines were nearly charming; the old maps and childhood finger paintings taped to the walls looked almost like art.

"There's something under here I can't reach."

Jupe was in the kitchen, emptying whatever was left in the cupboards into garbage bags. Now he appeared in the bedroom door, his head nearly grazing its yellow-painted frame.

"Way under there," she said. "It's a box or something. Can you pull it out for me?"

Ever compliant, he dropped to his knees and fished under the bed with his long, long arms. His classmates were always asking him if he was a basketball player—racist, he explained to Billie, because it meant that the only way they could imagine a black guy getting into Cal was on an athletic scholarship.

"Maybe it's because you're tall," she said.

"I'm not that tall. Have you seen the actual basketball players? They're, like, freaks of nature. I'm only six-two, which doesn't come close to cutting it on the basketball court."

Tall enough, though, to make a striking contrast to Billie, who was a foot shorter than Jupe, and fair, and blond. She loved the looks they got as they walked across campus, the towering guy with skin dark as coffee and the name of a god holding hands with the tiny childlike girl named for a blues singer. Race and size aside, they stood out even in that sea of hippie weirdos, Jupe with his short hair and his serious glasses and his prep school wardrobe and Billie with her ballet slippers, thrift store dresses, and long fairy-tale hair. Everyone assumed they were lovers, an assumption that Billie relished.

He was the only one who'd been friendly to her in the poetry class she'd sneaked into—Byron, Shelley, and Keats—and the only person she'd connected with on that supposedly liberal campus, most of the radicals, she'd discovered, being really rich kids from Orange County. If you didn't have ratty hair and torn jeans and go to class stoned every day—if you went to class at all—you were suspect: a narc, Nixonian, bourgeois.

No contradictions were allowed, yet Billie and Jupe embodied nothing but contradictions. Jupiter, son of fifth-generation African-American Brooklyn burghers, had attended private schools and would be heading to medical school after spending a year working and studying for the MCATs while living at home to save money. Yes, he hoped to be a pediatrician; yes, he wanted to help poor kids; but he was further from being a Black Panther than, well, Billie herself.

Billie was the one who'd grown up in mostly black neighborhoods, who'd gone to crappy public schools where the teachers may have pitied the children but never challenged them. She was the child of the single parent, the parent who left her home alone while he went to the bar, who slept through the morning alarm, who collected welfare money he spent on drugs instead of clothes or food.

He was also the parent who introduced her to Dickinson and Whitman, who encouraged her to be proud of her individuality, to make her own way in the world. He may not have had the money to send her to college, or even been willing to fill out the forms for her to get financial aid—"I don't want the feds knowing my business, babe"—but he had encouraged her to simply show up at classes as if she belonged there.

"You have more right to be there than those spoiled assholes," he told her. "You're smarter than any of them."

But did it matter if she was the smartest one in the class if she'd never be able to claim a degree, use it to go to graduate school or find a job? And now that her father had died, now that Jupe had graduated and was heading back to Brooklyn, she didn't even have a home or a friend. All she had were a dozen garbage bags full of junk, her father's ancient books, and an owl-shaped vase containing his ashes.

And, right, whatever was in the box under the bed.

"It's like something that dates from the Gold Rush," said Jupe, dragging the tarnished box out from its dusty hiding place. He held it out to her and she traced the initials engraved on the lid: MMA.

"This must be where he was keeping his millions," she said to Jupe.

Her father had always told her he was secretly rich, a prince, an heir. He'd grown up in a castle, he claimed, and one day he'd take her, the rightful princess, back to claim their throne. Once she got old enough to know better, she realized that the rented shacks, the beaten-down furniture, and the rice-and-bean dinners didn't jibe with a background as royalty.

"Open it," said Jupe.

She held her breath as she pried up the lid, half expecting, despite all sensible reckonings, to find a pile of cash, or at least some diamonds and gold pieces. But instead all that was inside was letters, dozens and dozens of letters, written in purplish ink on thick creamy stationery, the handwriting florid and classic, the kind of letters that people like her father never, to Billie's knowledge, received.

This was odd, but even odder was that all the letters were still sealed within their envelopes and all seemed to be from the same person, the most recent postmarked that January, less than half a year ago. Hands trembling, Billie ripped open the top envelope and read aloud.

"Dearest Johnny, I am thinking of you this New Year and sending all my love to you and your beautiful daughter. She must be quite a young lady now and I'm sure you are as proud of her as I have always been of you. My dearest wish is to see you both though I don't hold out much hope of that any longer. You know I turned 80 so I'm not sure how many years I have left. I would come to California to see you if I believed you would open the door to me, but as things stand, it remains your place to return home if you wish it. I love you now as I have always loved you and I have to believe that, somewhere in your heart, you still love me, too. As ever, Your Mother."

"Mother," Billie said. The hand that held the letter dropped to her lap.

"I thought you said you didn't have any other family."

"I don't. I mean, I didn't think I did. I had this dim idea that my father's parents lived on a ranch in Wyoming, but he always said . . ."

Well, he hadn't said, come to think of it, apart from the high-flown stories about princes and castles. She'd just always assumed, since he never talked about any specific relatives and they never saw any and he'd never even hinted that he'd been anywhere in his life outside California, that there was no family. He was so much older than Billie was, forty when she was born, it didn't seem odd that his parents might be dead. But now here was a mother, at least, very much alive, at least as of four months ago.

"But this is great," Jupe said. "You should get in touch with her."

Get in touch, as in talk to her? This was moving too quickly. And wait: Why should Billie think this was great?

"My father never mentioned her. He never even read her letters. There must have been something wrong, something awful. . . ."

"She doesn't sound awful," Jupe pointed out. "And your father, I'm sure he had his good points, but you said it yourself, Billie: he was eccentric."

Jupiter was the only boy she'd ever brought home to meet her dad, the only friend she'd invited home in as long as she could remember. He'd worn a jacket and tie, absurdly, and brought a cake, which got covered with ants while sitting on the kitchen counter waiting to be eaten.

She was ashamed of herself remembering this now, how her real aim in inviting Jupe home was to impress her father that she had a black friend. To even make her father believe Jupe might be her boyfriend. And embarrassed, too, at the memory of how superior her father had acted, the big liberal, the common man, discoursing on Malcolm X and Angela Davis as if he were the professor and Jupe his lowly student, assuming, based on the color of his skin, that Jupe even cared.

"There must be a reason he never introduced me to her."

Jupe took her small, pale hand in his. "Do you think your father always had your best interests at heart?" he asked gently. "He left you here alone now, Billie. You've got to make your own decisions."

She felt tears well up and blinked against them. Ever since she'd found her father sitting up dead in his bed, an empty bottle of pills and a nearly empty bottle of bourbon by his side, *Raise High the Roof Beam, Carpenters* open on his lap and a pencil clutched in his already-stiff hand, she'd tried to be more angry at him than sad. Tried to be relieved that she no longer had to take care of him and could now concentrate on looking after herself.

But the sadness was there, sadness for her father and her mother, too, dead also of an overdose, even if Billie succeeded once again, once again and again and again, in tamping it down.

"At least call her," Jupe said. "I'll help you find the number. She lives in . . ."

He picked up one of the envelopes, examined the return address, then let out a low whistle.

"Wow, Manhattan, East Sixty-fourth Street," he said. "Pretty fancy."

Billie blinked again, but there were no tears this time. "Really?"

"I'll say. This is probably right off Fifth Avenue."

Fifth Avenue was only a vague concept. Billie had never been to New York, had never been farther east than Tahoe.

"This could be great for you, Billie," Jupe urged. "You could drive out with me. Discover your roots."

He said that last word with a wry twist of his mouth. And then he grinned, his big, perfect-toothed, irresistible grin. Jupe had his demons, she knew, but he could also make her believe, as he believed, in the possibility of unambivalent happiness.

"You have this big, perfect, loving family, Jupe, and so you think that's what I'm going to find, too. But what if it's not like that?"

"Well," he said. "You'll still have me."

"We would see each other there?" she asked, her heart rising.

He looped his arms around her and drew her close, his chest broad and hard beneath the damp of his shirt.

"Of course we would," he said, from somewhere far above her.

Her heart quickened and she dared to imagine that in New York, a new place, a new time, everything that she'd wanted to happen in California would finally happen. Early on, explaining why he'd shied back from her kisses, he'd told her he was gay, or maybe not gay, bisexual, or maybe just confused. He didn't look or act anything like any gay man she'd ever seen, not like the flamboyant queens in the Castro or like the butch boys in their leather jackets and combat boots, which made it hard to believe that, deep down, he didn't want her as much as she wanted him. Hugging him, walking home late at night with their arms around each other, lying in bed reading, legs entwined, she felt something more and suspected that he did, too.

In a month or a year, in a new city, who knew what could happen? It was like today, starting in trash and ashes. And ending in a discovery that opened the door to a different life.

3

Bridget, 1916

Early on a June morning, the heat already rising with the sun red and low in the sky, there was a soft knock on her bedroom door. Bridget opened it just a crack to keep from disturbing Floyd, asleep in the nursery beyond. She was still in her nightgown, her auburn hair winding in a long braid around her neck to cover one breast.

It was George, the Apfelmanns' driver, freshly shaven, his collar fragrant with the cookie smell of the hot iron he must have wielded himself, twirling his boater in his hand and beaming down at her. His hair was dark and thick, his heavily lashed eyes changed from blue to green, depending on the light, and his front teeth were endearingly crooked.

Did she want to go to Coney Island? he asked. She and the young master. It was sure to be a scorcher, and with everyone else gone, there was no point in them staying in the house, in the city, on their own.

She hesitated. Maude Apfelmann was in Long Island with Mr. Berlin all weekend for a grand house party; Mr. Berlin had sent a car expressly to transport her trunk—an entire trunkful of clothes for just three days! Mr. Apfelmann had sailed two weeks ago for London to try to convince the Brits they should eat his Apple Candy, and would be gone weeks more. Alone with the boy for the weekend, Bridget wasn't supposed to take Floyd anywhere without explicit permission, not even to the park. Between the horses and the cars, Maude said, if you didn't get trampled, you'd get run down.

"Mrs. Apfelmann wouldn't like it," Bridget said.

"So we won't tell her," said George.

Her heart skipped a beat. Dare she? While Maude might forbid the outing, mightn't she approve of Bridget taking control, pleasing herself, being a bit bolder? "You're in America now, you must become a modern woman!" Maude had commanded, her childlike hand pounding an imaginary lectern. Bridget had overheard Maude and her suffragist friends from the Heterodoxy Club talking excitedly at luncheons Maude hosted in the capacious gray living room, with its tall arched windows and white grand piano and walls featuring pictures of the half-naked Maude in her Ziegfeld spangles and feathers. Down with the pope, to hell with the patriarchy, we women, all women, must live as well and as fully as men!

Behind her in his crib, Floyd stirred, then clambered up on his sturdy legs.

"Mama!" he crowed.

Bridget rushed over to him, embarrassed at what George might think.

"Not Mama, sweetheart, it's Bea," she said. "Would you like to go to the beach, darling? With George, to the place where they have rides and big waves?"

With that, it was settled. As the open car hurtled south on Broadway, Bridget kept one hand clapped to her hat and the other arm wrapped tightly around Floyd. It was a glorious day, the warm air bathing the early-morning streets. They swerved onto the Brooklyn Bridge and the horizon opened. Both banks of the river were lined to the north and south with docks and huge cargo ships and factory buildings, the blue of the sky all the brighter, since there was no smoke issuing on Sunday from the tall chimneys. She could feel Floyd simultaneously relax against her and begin to pulse with delight. He jabbed one tiny finger into the air again and again, pointing at the clouds, the gulls, the soaring cables of the bridge. A majestic ship passed beneath them, its sails as stiff and bleached and billowing as a nun's summer veil.

This was the first time since she'd arrived in New York in March that Bridget had seen the harbor or the rivers. On the few occasions when she'd wandered far enough west or east to the grim streets near First Avenue or the darkness of Ninth Avenue beneath the El, any view of the water had been blocked by factories or rail yards. The only sign that there was even a river beyond the borders of the city were the glimpses she'd gotten of the giant stacks of the ships themselves, fat black cigars standing upright, belching smoke into the air.

"Faster! Faster!" commanded Floyd, though as the car left the bridge into downtown Brooklyn, George had no choice but to slow down to navigate the tangle of trolleys crisscrossing the avenues on their maze of tracks.

After the trolleys came the trees: trees and grass and wooden houses, so much sky and greenery Bridget could almost imagine she was back in Ireland, riding in the carriage to the market. With no mechanical distractions, Floyd settled back down against her and soon, without even seeing his face, she knew he was asleep. Over the child's blond head, George smiled at her and she smiled back and then they held each other's eyes, as they had at her bedroom door when she said yes.

When they parked on Surf Avenue, Floyd woke up and George hoisted the boy onto his shoulders.

"What shall we do first?" asked George. "Take a trip to the Orient and see the elephants? Or maybe go to Niagara Falls. We could ride the Scenic Railway. Or try the Loop de Loop. What do you say, big fella?"

"All!" caroled Floyd to the sky.

"All, says the prince! Then all he shall have."

They started in the Oriental Village, where they saw Egyptians hammering brass and Arabs weaving rugs, acrobats juggling fiery clubs and dancers with bare midriffs twirling so fast, they made Bridget dizzy. She rode with Floyd on a velvet throne atop a camel, bumpy as a carriage on a rocky lane, and tasted a tiny, sugary cup of Turkish coffee.

Then they took Floyd to the Village of the Midgets, where everything—the houses, the shops, the people, even the animals—was tiny. Floyd delighted in the miniature farms and little bakeshop, the scaled-down houses and the small theater, continually looking up at Bridget and George as if he were checking whether they might have gotten smaller, too.

They ate lunch standing up at the brand-new Nathan's, where a crowd jostled three deep to try the new low-priced hot dogs. George drank three beers in quick succession, offering Bridget a taste. Though milder than Irish beer, she didn't like it any better. Then they toured the Alligator Farm, treated Floyd to three rides on the carousel, and took A Trip to Niagara, in which they rode a train along a suspension bridge above a replica of the falls, George's arm finding its way around Bridget's shoulders.

Walking along the boardwalk with George beside her, Floyd again held high on his shoulders, Bridget felt that she could hardly register the ocean before her, the half-naked people on the beach, the rumble of the elevated trains, even the elephants and the dancers and the jugglers on the boardwalk, the sounds of the organ pipes and the air guns, the warm sweat smell of the hot dogs or the yeastiness of the beer, so distracted was she by George himself.

It was as if heat emanated out from the muscle of his arm through the starch of his shirtsleeve, through the linen of his jacket, directly into her breast, her stomach, lifting everything and setting it alight. The skin of her face prickled; even her hair felt as if it were animated. Floyd fairly danced on George's shoulders, bouncing and crowing, his little arms punching at the gulls far above. Bridget gazed up at him, laying a hand on the silky plumpness of his bare leg, but more to ground herself, to touch something that was touching George, than to hold him still. George seemed happy enough to shoulder the child, whose gyrations gave evidence to everything Bridget was working so hard to hide.

❧

By the middle of the afternoon, the sun that had felt so benign in the morning had scorched the tip of Bridget's nose and the curve of her upper lip. Floyd was growing cranky, his neck flushed with heat rash above his starchy sailor collar.

"What if we cool off the young master down near the water?" asked George.

"He'll get dirty," said Bridget, looking at the long stretch of sand pockmarked with people.

"It's clean dirt," George said gently. "If he gets sand on his knees, we have a whole ocean full of water to wash it off."

At first Bridget tried to pick her way across the beach with her white shoes and stockings on, but she soon realized this would never do. George turned his back and shielded her from view with his outstretched jacket as she rolled down her stockings, pulling them off and tucking them into her shoes. The sand was nearly intolerably hot against the soles of her feet, which had not been bare out of doors since last summer when she walked through the meadow at home.

"I better carry Floyd," she said.

She'd never worn a bathing costume and had never been able to imagine wanting to reveal herself that way, but now she longed to be one of the women in the skimpy black outfits, the skirts above their knees, their arms and shoulders bare to the sun. Some held parasols or kept their straw hats clamped firmly to their heads, but the younger women were hatless, their faces tilted toward the light as if to receive a blessing.

One girl—an Irish girl, Bridget thought, with her orange hair and her freckled fair skin—abruptly opened her eyes and scrambled to her feet and raced her beau to the water, splashing into the foam of the waves. Bridget caught her breath at the sight of it. To submerge herself, to sink into the sea up to her thighs, her stomach, her chest, to feel the powerful waves break over her . . . Despite the heat of Floyd pressed against her, she shivered.

Very lightly, George touched her elbow, which seemed to make Floyd squirm in her arms.

"Down," the child demanded.

"No, darling," she said, gripping him more tightly.

"You'll turn him into a sissy." George pointed to a group of small children who looked to be two or three, Floyd's age, a couple even younger, splashing in a puddle left by the tide near the shore. Some wore shorts, some only diapers; others were naked, covered in wet sand, looking like savages. Ecstatic savages.

"Come: we'll take off his fancy clothes and keep them out of harm's way. And we'll watch him to make sure nothing happens."

She hesitated another moment and then thought, I am being ridiculous. As soon as she set Floyd down where the sand was damp and cool, he scampered away to join the children in the puddle. Bridget stood back and watched him fondly, stomping in the pool, splashing sand onto his legs, swishing his hands in the water and then running in mad circles, soon leading the pack. She was so caught up in Floyd that she didn't feel George taking her hand until he squeezed it tightly.

"See? The young master is having fun," he said.

She blushed, distracted by how strong George's hand felt around hers.

"You're as good with him as if he were your own," George said.

"He *is* my own, in a way," she said quietly. Wasn't she the one, after all, who woke up with him at night, who bathed him in the morning, who cooked his cereal and taught him his prayers and kissed away his tears?

"If he was your own," George said, "he'd be even handsomer, and smarter, and better behaved."

"Ah, go on, now," she said, embarrassed but pleased.

"You would be a wonderful mother," George insisted. "Do you want that? Someday, I mean. To have children of your own?"

Bridget didn't answer. She'd left Ireland swearing that she would never marry, had no desire to be a mother. She'd told Maude so when she was hired, believed full-heartedly that she'd rather love and nurture another woman's child than take on the burden of her own.

Burden—that's what it had seemed like back home, watching women, her own mother, her sister, her friends from the lane, bear child after child, only to see them die, or to die themselves. How could marriage to the men she knew back there, with the smell of pig on their shoes and black under their fingernails, be preferable to your own clean room, white sheets unsullied, a peaceful bed?

And yet, with George—a Kilkenny man, no less—all her ideas had gotten swirled around. She looked at him now, trying to think of how to answer, and instead asked, "What about you? Do you want a family?"

"I'd always thought I'd go west," he said. "Ride horses, own a ranch, you know, like the cowboys. But now . . ."

And then he leaned in and kissed her, his upper lip notching perfectly into the space where her own mouth had parted in surprise.

She heard the cannon-like boom of the huge wave rather than saw it, and then felt its coldness rush across the tender tops of her feet. It flooded the puddle where Floyd had been playing, knocking down several children. Bridget saw from the corner of her eye one baby, stunned onto its back, sucked with the undertow toward the ocean, but she couldn't worry about him, she was already rushing toward Floyd, lunging to catch him but watching him tumble face-first into the churning surf.

George was right beside her but she was faster, plunging her arms into the water and scooping the drenched child to her breast. George tried to lift Floyd from her but she held fast, not caring about the water and sand soaking into her dress, rocking back and forth until Floyd began howling because she wouldn't set him down.

"That's all right, now," said George, trying to embrace them both. "It's just the tide coming in. We'll move back here a bit."

"We have to go," she said. "We shouldn't have come."

"What are you talking about?"

"I have a bad feeling. We have to go back."

She was already walking away from the ocean, using her stocking to brush the sand from the screaming boy's pink skin, focused only on getting him dressed and home.

"Luna Park . . ." George said weakly. "I was hoping to show the lad the lights. And there's a new attraction, Aerial Night Attack. . . ."

She stopped shaking the sand from Floyd's sock and looked hard at George.

How could she have let herself get carried away by her feelings? The child was her responsibility, and she had all but turned it over to this man who had no sense of responsibility at all.

"That sounds wholly unsuitable for a child."

"It's not a *real* attack," George said, his brow knotted, his handsome face laid over with anguish. "It's just a play. . . ."

Kneeling on the sand, she wrestled the boy into his underwear, then his shorts.

"I thank you for this day, George. But now please take us home."

She stood near the crib in the darkened room as Floyd, bathed now and wearing fresh pajamas, the clothes he'd worn to the beach already rinsed in the sink and hung to dry in Bridget's own room, settled down to sleep.

"Good night, dear," she said softly.

"Night night, Mama," said the child.

This time she didn't correct him and let the word linger in the sweet air of the nursery. And wasn't she his mother, or at least as good as?

There was a sound from far below in the house, the front door slamming, light footsteps, Maude's footsteps, hurrying up the stairs. The higher Maude climbed, the more the pressure rose in Bridget's chest. Bridget tiptoed across the nursery and out into the hallway, her finger already held to her lips.

Maude, her thick, pale hair a nimbus around her beautiful face, in shadow now but glistening, Bridget could see, with the exercise of climbing the stairs and perhaps excitement left over from the weekend in the country, stood on the landing, her eyes bright, her sequined chiffon dress slightly askew.

"Asleep already?" Maude whispered, disappointment and relief mingling in her voice.

Bridget nodded.

"Anything special to report?"

Bridget shook her head no.

"All right, then, dear Bridget," Maude said, startling Bridget by pecking her on the cheek. "I'm off again for the evening. I don't know what I'd do without you, and I hope I shall never find out."

4

Cait, Present

Cait sat in the apartment she always sublet in New York in September, utterly still, clutching the plastic stick. It seemed as if the noises from the city outside—even the sounds of the birds in the trees of the neighboring church-yard, the flashes of sunlight through the windblown branches, the rhythm of Cait's own breath—had all stopped, and every particle of reality was trained on her discovery that she was pregnant.

She gazed out the window, at the vista of un-city-like green. Although the apartment was in the center of downtown Manhattan, south of Houston Street, in the heart of Little Italy, it seemed so quiet and removed she might be in Vermont, or Tuscany, or at their lake in the woods in New Jersey. The squat brick building where she lived was as hidden as the lake was: you had to pass through the hallway of the building in front and then out through a cement courtyard to get to it, hidden within a ring of taller buildings, further sheltered from the street by the walled graveyard of the old church next door. Beyond the leafy churchyard, on village-like Mott Street, people walked small dogs, unloaded trucks, hosed off sidewalks, their days proceeding unaltered.

It had happened with Martin, of course, from that one night when they were covering the story in New Hampshire, the story she was putting the finishing touches on now. She'd written it as a news story for the website where her friend Sam was an editor, and then had gotten an assignment from *Vanity Fair* to do it as a longer piece, "The Invisible Boy," about Riley's life figuratively and now literally out of sight of the world. Born at home, raised in a meth lab, palmed off on a not-quite-all-there great-aunt, Riley might never have been discovered missing if the aunt hadn't uncharacteristically called the police. It was still possible, after all, to live without anyone knowing, or caring. No one had ever paid any attention to Riley until he disappeared, which he had done so thoroughly, it sometimes seemed as if he'd never really existed.

Thinking about Riley when she was writing her story had, of course, made Cait meditate on Martin. He'd called her, emailed her after they'd parted, until she'd had to tell him flat out that she didn't want to see him again. She wasn't interested in having a relationship with a married man, and she wasn't interested in a newly unattached man, either, and in fact she wasn't interested in any man at all. He should recommit to his marriage, or if he couldn't do that, he should get out and figure out what he wanted from life; he shouldn't leave his wife for her, no matter what, and if he did leave his wife, he'd have to get himself together before he could manage being in a new relationship. She said this as if she knew a lot about being in relationships, not as if she'd read it in some women's magazine picked up in an airport.

No matter what he decided, she was heading off on the road again, to do a story on orphans in Addis Ababa for Sam's website. Yes, it had been wonderful for her, too. Who knew: maybe they'd connect sometime in the future, when everything had changed.

Well, now everything had changed.

Or had it?

Thinking about Riley, about Martin, was what got her thinking she might be pregnant in the first place. She hadn't been so alarmed about missing her period, had just vaguely been aware she was a little late. She remembered having it in the plane on the way home at the beginning of August; what a pain that had been, changing soaked-through tampons swaying in the cramped airplane bathroom. So she should have gotten it again by Labor Day, she calculated. It was the third week in September now. More than a month since she'd slept with Martin.

She'd been crampy (her period coming), and tired (the heat), and queasy (her period again, or maybe the heat). Round, popping out of her bra, having trouble zipping the Prada dress she reserved for such occasions as expense-account lunches with magazine editors and interviews with prime ministers. She'd vaguely considered losing weight, but rationalized that after a month in Africa it would no longer be an issue.

But it would be now.

She could go to Planned Parenthood, right down the street,

where she often went for her Pap smear and annual checkup, and take care of it. Have an abortion, or not even that: swallow a pill, have a slightly-heavier-than-usual period, pretend the pregnancy had never existed. Just like Riley. No, not like Riley. Riley was a child, a person, and this was ... not a child. A potential child. But not a living, breathing, thinking, laughing, crying child like Riley or the thousands of others she'd seen in Africa or Southeast Asia or Eastern Europe that she could adopt if she wanted a child, just as her parents had adopted her.

Oh, God, there it was again, the feeling she'd had in the woods when they'd called off the search for Riley, the feeling she'd begun to think was as much a phantom as the little boy himself, the desperation and sadness and panic that it was she who was missing, she who was lost and must be found.

This was a feeling she'd managed to hold at bay until now, resolutely shutting it off when she was eight and fifteen and twenty-seven and the sense of floating unmoored in an infinite darkness had risen up and threatened to claim her. Other adoptees she'd met over the years had described it: the feeling of belonging to no one and nothing, of being unwanted, neither alive nor dead but disappeared, like Riley. She'd always claimed she didn't feel it, but the truth, she realized now, was that she hadn't allowed herself to feel it. But it had been there forever, waiting, and now, with Riley turning the doorknob, it had flown loose.

The treetops outside the apartment's three big windows were still green but darker now, rustling in the wind. It was still hot outside, muggy, but cold air was coming: fall pushing its way in.

Someone was pregnant with her once, just as she was

pregnant now. This was something she tried, had always tried, not to think about. She'd always claimed, to herself as to everyone else, that she didn't want to know anything about the woman who'd given birth to her. She gave me away, she always said, if anyone was insensitive enough to press her on the issue. Why should I be interested in her?

But she was interested, she felt now, suddenly, intensely; more than thirty years' worth of interested. Who was my biological mother? Was she young or older, rich or poor, alone or in a relationship? Was she in love with my father? Was she raped? Was she a drug addict, incompetent, beyond caring, the way Riley's mother had been? Did she want me at all? And if she didn't want me, why didn't she have an abortion? There may not have been RU-486 in the seventies, but abortion was legal and safe and if anything more available and acceptable than it was now.

And so why give your baby away at birth rather than end your pregnancy? Catholic? Ignorant? An early pro-lifer? Or, like Cait, in the grip of something infinitely more complicated?

Virtually the only thing Cait knew was that she'd been born in New York, and that had never seemed like a clue before, probably because she'd never tried to solve the mystery. Her birth certificate, like that of all children adopted under New York's closed system, listed Vern and Sally as her parents—not her adoptive parents but her parents, period. If they had not chosen to tell Cait that she was adopted, there would have been no official evidence of the fact.

But they had told her, of course, had told her from the beginning, as was the fashion in the 1970s, when most adoptions were still closed but talking about them was not. They'd had a book called *Why Was I Adopted?* But Cait didn't see herself in the cartoon drawing of the girl on the cover, with her straight dark hair and big smiley face, with her older brother and grinning cat. When she preferred *Sleeping Beauty* or *The Berenstain Bears* for her bedtime reading, Sally and Vern seemed relieved, and the adoption book sifted to the bottom of the pile.

Cait never talked to her friends about being adopted, and it wasn't until fourth grade that anyone noted how different she looked from her parents. By eleven she'd grown taller than her tiny, round mom, Cait's hair wildly curly to Vern's thick straight thatch and Sally's fine pale waves, her eyes green to their blue. And then there was Cait's tawny skin, bronze even in winter. Are you Latina? people asked her now when she traveled. Middle Eastern? Biracial?

But back on the Immaculate Conception playground, the tough new girl Patty McPartland had a different word for what Cait was: jigaboo.

"What's that?" Cait asked, feeling herself flush, knowing it was bad even if she didn't know what it was.

They were standing in a knot of girls at the far edge of the playground, by the jungle gym, out of hearing of the nuns.

"It means you've got black skin," said Patty. "And kinky hair."

"My skin isn't black," said Cait, afraid she might start crying.

"It *is* darker," said her friend Mary Beth, holding her own freckled arm next to Cait's.

Cait gazed down as if seeing her arm and Mary Beth's for the first time. Yes, her skin was golden brown, the color of the honey made from the bees her father kept out by the blackberry bushes, but Anthony Gambizzi got tanner than she did: she'd seen him at the lake. And her only hair that might be called kinky were the blondish curls around her face, too short to be caught in the French braid her mother plaited wet every Sunday night as they watched *America's Funniest Home Videos*.

Cait realized then what Patty was talking about. "I am not a Negro," she said, stomping away from the girls.

That night, freshly aware of how much paler her mother's milky skin was than her own, Cait asked Sally why Patty had said that. Was it, could it be, true?

Sally gathered her in close, maybe the last time Cait could remember letting her mother hold her as if she were still a little girl.

"You're white, just like us," Sally assured her. "I'm Irish and German and Polish and your dad is English, Scottish, Russian, Italian—all kinds of things. And you're all kinds of things, too. But we're all white."

Cait wanted to be reassured, but she was old enough at that point to know something about biology and genetics.

"The lady you got me from," she persisted. This was how, the few times she'd spoken about it, she referred to the stranger who'd given birth to her. "Was she white?"

"Yes, dear!" Sally had cried, half-exasperated, half-laughing. "Now, no more of this nonsense or I'm going to call Sister Miriam and have that Patty McPartland punished."

It was not that event alone that made Cait more aware of all the ways she was different from Vern and Sally—not just in how she looked but in her tastes and talents, at her very core. As she became a teenager, a woman, she grew less like her mother, not more. Sally was ever sweet, ever patient, satisfied to spend her whole life in their little New Jersey town tending her hydrangeas and baking cupcakes and working as a part-time nurse's aide only because she had failed for so long to have a baby. Cait, on the other hand, loved to read, hated gardening, couldn't wait to explore the world, lived in horror of settling down in the suburbs and becoming a full-time mom. Any kind of mom.

Was her biological mother an adventurer like she was? she wondered now. She'd always assumed—because she'd effortlessly excelled at both school and sports, winning a crew scholarship to Stanford, while neither Vern nor Sally had gone to college—that a good measure of her native intelligence and athleticism must be due to genetics. Her image of her biological mother morphed in her mind from a nebulous ghost to a tall, tan woman wielding a lacrosse stick. No, galloping down a beach on a horse. No . . . this was ridiculous.

But who was her birth mother? As decisively as she didn't want to know for all those years, Cait now did want to know, desperately wanted to know. Felt she had to know so she could make the right decision—the decision that would leave her with some amount of peace—about what to do about her own pregnancy.

At another time, in a different situation, she might have been able to get the pills, do what needed to be done with some heaviness of heart, but without feeling truly torn. She would have been able to think of it as becoming unpregnant in the same way she'd become pregnant, like putting a splint on a cracked ankle.

But this time, for all kinds of reasons she could identify— her powerful feelings for Martin, her fascination with Riley— along with all kinds of reasons she couldn't, was different. This time she couldn't write off what was growing inside her as a mistake, something she could fix and move easily beyond.

Becoming pregnant, deciding whether to have a child, seemed like the central issue of her life. An issue she had to resolve, now and not tomorrow, once and for all.

She picked up her cell phone and dialed.

"Sam," she said.

Lanky blond California girl Samantha Rogers, her longtime editor, Stanford classmate, the closest thing she had in New York to a classic girlfriend.

"I'm not going to be able to do that Africa story after all."

"What's going on?"

"Something's come up. I think I'm going to spend a couple months in New York."

"Wow," Sam said. "Is that moss growing under your feet?"

"Maybe," Cait said. "We're getting old."

"Oh, come on. You know thirty-five is the new thirty."

"Seriously. I'd love to do something else for you, though."

"Like what?"

This was one of the big things that Cait appreciated about Sam: that even though they were friends, Sam's primary focus was business. Sam went through men with the same regularity she went through her black suede pumps or white shirts. Why should she make any of them permanent when there was always another, fresher model on the horizon?

"I'm not sure. I was thinking about trying to find my birth mother. Maybe there's something there."

Sam whistled. "Like what?"

"I don't know yet. I'm not sure what I'm going to find or if I even want to write it. I'll think of some other ideas, too."

"Okay. Let's get together soon, okay? We'll come up with something then."

It took only a quick call to her landlady, Jane, who'd moved to the Berkshires with her much younger boyfriend, to arrange to stay in the apartment through the end of the year. Jane only sublet to and through people she knew, anyway, and so was happy to have a trusted tenant in place for several months. She was an old Lower East Side hippie, relying on these under-the-table sublets to pay her bills but wanting the situation to be personal and trusting. She left now-valuable art by her old friends—a Peter Hujar photograph of an angelic-looking blond girl in a white dress, bouncing a ball; a Kiki Smith print of a nude woman in a fetal curl—hanging on the walls, and Cait would open a Charles and Di coronation tin to find a gold necklace or a roll of twenties.

Cait breathed, trying to get used to the feeling that she was here now, that time was opening up in front of her. Her work, her living arrangements, changed, changed, just like that. Her life transformed in ways that yesterday were unimaginable.

Or was it? Was this a new direction, or a detour that would circle her back to the road she'd been on before?

She was sitting cross-legged on the high captain's bed and leaned forward, feeling the stretch in her thighs, her breasts nearly touching the rough woven bedspread, her thumb playing over the buttons of her phone. She was thinking about him before she even let herself consider what she was thinking; she dialed, like jumping off a high dive, before she could have second thoughts.

"Martin Lebowitz," came his deep voice.

Life changed again, just like that.

"Martin, it's Cait."

There was silence. She caught her breath.

"Cait Trippel."

"I know who you are, Cait." He sounded pained and she wished she could undo the call, hang up and move forward as if it had ever happened. But, as with the pregnancy, she knew that wasn't possible.

"I'm just calling to say hello."

"What are you doing? Where are you?"

"I'm still in New York. My plans have changed and I'm going to be staying here for a few months."

"Oh, Cait . . ."

He sounded even more disappointed.

"I'm sorry," she said. "I shouldn't have called."

"No, you should have, of course you should have, it's just that . . ."

"You changed your mind about me."

"The last time we talked, Cait, you told me I should recommit to my marriage, remember?"

"Right, right, and I meant that."

"You said I needed to decide whether I was in or I was out."

"I know I did."

"And you were right. So I'm trying . . . I mean, that's what I've been doing. I've been making an effort. I mean, not like it's some awful job or anything, but I've been reading these make-your-marriage-better books . . ." He laughed. "It's stupid, I know."

"It's not stupid, Martin." She meant that. In fact, she was more drawn to him now almost than she'd ever been before. Typical, she thought. Now that you think you can't have him, it's safe to want him.

"I'm happy for you," she told him. "Making things work

43

with your wife—it's the right thing to do. That wasn't why I was calling."

"Oh, okay, great," he said. A beat. "Why were you calling?"

"Oh, just to say hello. To let you know I would be in town. In case we, like, bumped into each other in the subway, so you wouldn't think I was a big fat liar when I told you I was going to be halfway around the world."

"I would never think that," he said seriously.

You are a fool, she thought.

"Okay," she said. "I'll see you in the subway."

"Cait," he said, lowering his voice. "I do want to see you. Can we get together for coffee or something? A drink?"

"I don't think that's a good idea, Martin, if you're trying to make your marriage work. Do you?"

There was a long silence.

"I'd like to be friends," he said finally.

"I don't know if that's possible."

"Don't you trust me?"

"No," she said.

There was a long silence, but she could sense him there on the other end of the phone, as if they were lying in the dark together, not touching, eyes closed.

"Well, what about this?" he said finally. "Come for dinner. To my place—*our* place. Meet Lynn. My family. I'll invite some other people from the paper. We'll make it lunch, a proper British Sunday lunch. Lynn loves that."

Cait was about to tell him he was crazy, that there was no way she was going to his house for a meal to meet his wife and his kids, that the whole idea was outrageous, when she realized: Of course I'm going to go. How could I refuse this opportunity?

She told him a Sunday lunch sounded lovely and he promised to get back to her with a date and she hung up, part intrigued, part appalled. That was definitely something to look forward to.

There was only one more call she needed to make, and that was to her parents. She knew how excited her mother was going to be to hear she'd be staying in town through the holidays, and her father, too, though he might have a harder time showing it. And she also knew if she was ever going to find her birth mother, they were where she had to start.

She dialed all the way to the last number before she stopped and turned off the phone. She didn't have to call them. It would be so much easier to say what she had to say if she went out to New Jersey and said it face-to-face.

5

Billie, 1976

Billie sat in Jupe's idling car on Sixty-fourth Street, staring up at the tall, imposing limestone house. The door was painted a black as shiny as coal and was flanked by two Christmas tree–shaped boxwoods in white stone planters. Unlike the other houses on the block, there was no front stoop; the front door was on the same level as the sidewalk.

"It's so big," Billie said.

"I didn't know there were private houses like this in Manhattan anymore," said Jupe.

"I don't feel good about this."

"They're expecting you. It's going to be fine. More than fine."

She shook her head. They'd been driving for seven days and all she wished was that the trip were longer.

"Come up to the door with me," she said, tugging on Jupe's sleeve, crisp even in this heat.

He laughed softly. "Sweetie, it's not going to help anybody for you to show up at the door with a black man."

"Well, then, wait here for me," she said. "Just in case."

"I'll sit here till somebody answers the door and I know you're all right. If you need me, you have my parents' number and the directions to their place. You can do this, Billie."

She looked at him for a long moment as if she needed to memorize his face. Then she leaned over and kissed him quickly on the lips, not caring whether or not he thought that was crossing some line in their friendship. Without saying good-bye, she grabbed her backpack and the owl vase that held her father's ashes and hopped out of the car.

Although it was only the beginning of June, it felt steamy in New York in a way that it rarely did in Northern California. Muggy. The pavement was hot beneath the thin rubber soles of her Chinese Mary Janes. She could feel the sweat forming where her backpack pressed against her T-shirt, where she cradled the owl vase against her chest. She pressed the doorbell and cast a glance back at Jupe, who waved to her from the car.

"Yes?"

A tall woman with steel-colored hair and silver-rimmed glasses stood peering out at her. She wore a plum-colored silk dress; a rope of ivory pearls lay over her imposing bosom. On her feet were black leather oxfords with curvy heels and wide, ribbon-like laces; Billie flashed on the shoes worn by the nuns the one year her father had sent her to Catholic School.

"I'm Billie," she said, barely able to hear her own voice over the pounding in her ears of her heart.

Behind her, she heard Jupe's old Audi accelerate and drive away with a nearly inaudible toot of his horn.

"Johnny's daughter," Billie added.

The old woman studied her and then pulled her into a wordless embrace, her powdery scent filling Billie's nose. The owl vase cut into Billie's ribs and the pearls bit into her cheekbone though the woman's breasts were as soft as a pillow.

"Grandma?" said Billie, the word uncertain on her lips, her voice muffled by the woman's flesh.

"I . . . Grandma . . ." The woman released Billie and broke into a loud laugh, showing teeth as yellow as her pearls. "No, child, I'm not your grandmother. I'm Bridget, her . . . companion. Your father surely mentioned me to you?"

"My father . . . no. He didn't tell me much."

It had seemed too complicated to explain everything during their single awkward telephone call. All Billie had said was that she was sorry to report that her father had died, that she'd found the letters, that she was coming to New York and would like to meet her grandmother.

"Oh, you poor thing. I imagine you've had a rough time of it. Such a shock, such a shock to hear about your father. Of course, we were devastated. Come in, darling, off the street."

Inside, the house was dim and cool and hushed, as if it existed in a different time and place from the hot, bustling city outside. Bridget led Billie back along the hallway with its black and white marble checkerboard floor. At the end of the hall, Billie took in flashes of an enormous old-fashioned kitchen, lined with tall white cabinets with interiors painted the turquoise of a tropical sea and stacked with enough white dishes to feed a school.

But instead of going toward the kitchen, Bridget started to climb the grand staircase that curved upward, its pale pink walls like the interior of an enormous shell. Bridget moved slowly, taking the steps one at a time, and Billie hung back, trying not to stare at the broad back of her skirt, at the support hose thick as bandages that stopped below the knee, or the flash of pale cottage-cheese thigh above.

The polished wooden banister felt smooth as satin beneath her hand. On the second floor, there was a heavily curtained dining room with a lace-covered table, set with a dizzying array of crystal and silver implements, and a pale gray living room with a high ceiling and tall windows letting in arches of sunlight that spilled across the blond wood floor. Over the white-manteled fireplace hung a larger-than-life-size oil portrait of a delicate blond woman.

Billie stopped in the hallway, transfixed.

"Who is that?" she asked Bridget.

But for the poof of fox fur and the long pink gown, the woman in the portrait could have been Billie's mother. Could have been Billie herself.

"Why, that's Maude, of course. That's your grandmother."

"She's so . . ." Billie was searching for the right word. Familiar? Beautiful? "Glamorous," she said finally.

"She was a famous actress in her day," Bridget said. "A wonderful singer, the toast of New York. But you probably know all that."

"Who are you talking to?" came a voice from above. "Did I hear someone at the door, Bridget?"

"Yes, Maude," said Bridget, winking at Billie. "I have a surprise for you."

"Surprise? I don't like surprises! What's going on down there, Bridget? Who's that with you?"

Bridget put her fingers to her lips in a warning for Billie to be quiet.

"We're coming up, Maude!" she called.

Billie felt herself grow nervous again as they mounted another flight of the curving stairs, her heart skipping in her chest, sweat trickling down her body. She wished she'd made Jupe stop somewhere so she could shower, change. Her long hair was tangled, frizzy, hot against her neck. At least she might have twisted it up, changed out of the purple T-shirt and Indian-print skirt she'd been wearing since Ohio.

Through an open door she saw what looked like a gentleman's room from another era: heavy dark wood furniture, a wall of bookcases, a linen counterpane on the bed, and a silver grooming set arrayed on the top of the dresser.

"That's Mr. Apfelmann's room, where I sleep now," Bridget said. "I've moved down, since it's just been the two of us and it's gotten harder to climb the stairs."

She opened the door across the hallway and said, "Here we are, Maude."

All Billie saw at first was a wash of purple. Then she realized she was looking at not one room but three that opened jewel-box-like, one after the other. The first and smallest room had dark purple walls and was furnished with a gilt writing desk and a pair of delicate chairs covered in a bright magenta silk. Then came the bedroom, painted a vibrant lavender, with its canopy bed covered in a tapestry woven with purples and pinks and reds and golds and greens, like an ancient garden, always in full bloom. And at the far end of the suite was a room painted the pale lilac of the underside of a flower petal, in the middle of which sat a taffeta chaise of brilliant fuchsia, a silk and ermine throw folded neatly at its foot.

The tiny woman leaning against the lavender satin pillows on the bed blended in so perfectly with her surroundings that it took a moment for Billie to focus on her. She was wearing purple, too, a darker lavender silk robe with a matching ribbon tying back her long, still blond hair. She seemed young and old at the same time: her face looked smooth, but her neck and her hands, which rested on the lavender satin coverlet, were as wrinkled as Bridget's.

"This is Billie," Bridget said. "Johnny's daughter, come all the way from California to see us."

In this most unlikely of places, with this odd old woman, Billie felt a sense of connection that she hadn't felt—well, that she'd never felt, in truth, with her distant hippie father in their run-down, sorry house. The sense of peace here, the order, the beauty, made her feel calm and safe. And looking at Maude was like looking at herself in the distant future, a self she might actually want to become.

"Who?" Maude said.

"Johnny's daughter," Bridget said more loudly. "Your grand-daughter, Maude."

"Come closer," said Maude, narrowing her eyes.

Billie set down the owl vase and shrugged off her backpack and moved hesitantly across the dark purple carpet, cushiony as the moss deep in Muir Woods. Although an air condi-tioner blasted from a shaded window at the farthest reaches of the suite, the air grew warmer, became even humid, as Billie approached her grandmother. Though Maude was under the covers and still dressed in nightclothes, she was wearing, Billie saw, lipstick and eyeliner. On her cheeks were two bright pink circles, like the painted cheeks of an antique doll.

"Closer," said Maude.

Billie lowered her head, close enough to see grains of sugar caught at the edges of Maude's lipstick.

"You are positively . . ." Maude hesitated a long time. And then she finally uttered, "Breathtaking!"

"I told you!" Bridget crowed.

"I'm just so surprised!" said Maude, shaking herself, suddenly all business. "I never expected . . . Stand back a bit there. You have my exact coloring! Turn around for me now. What a nice figure you have."

"She's petite as you were at that age," said Bridget.

"I'm still petite," snapped Maude. "I still have every item of clothing I've ever worn, and it all still fits me. Bridget, bring me that Balenciaga, the one I wore to Peggy Guggenheim's ball in, when was it, '52."

"Not now, Maude," said Bridget, still patient but with a sterner edge to her voice. "We're talking about Billie."

"Billie?" Maude said. "That's your name? What kind of a name is that?"

"My father named me after Billie Holiday."

It was the first time Billie had spoken.

"Huh," Maude said. "If Johnny wanted to name his daughter after someone, he could have named her after me."

She set her lipsticked mouth in a pout for a moment before she spoke again.

"So, what are you doing here, child?" Maude asked.

"I found your letters," Billie said simply. "I wanted to meet you, to see for myself."

"What is she talking about?" Maude said in an irritated tone to Bridget.

"Yes, dear," said Bridget. "What is it you wanted to see for yourself?"

"I wanted to see you," said Billie. "I wanted to see where my father came from and I wanted to find out why he'd kept his family, my family, hidden all these years."

Making this speech, Billie wished she were still holding the owl vase, for protection.

Maude pressed her lips in a thin, angry line. "Your father was a very troubled boy."

"He was devastated by his father's death, when he was just a wee boy, don't you know," Bridget broke in. "Poor Mr. Apfelmann collapsed in Central Park right in front of the child's eyes. And then that school never gave him any support. . . ."

"Stop making excuses for him," Maude snapped. "You've always done that, and who did it help? Nobody. Johnny was an overly sensitive child who went on to become a juvenile delinquent and then an alcoholic and a drug user. He turned his back on his mother and his home and his legacy. And now he's gone and made his only child an orphan."

"Oh, Maude," Bridget said. "The child traveled all the way here to meet us for the very first time. Why would you say such things? You drove Johnny away; are you trying to drive Billie away, too?"

"*I* drove Johnny . . ."

"It's all right," said Billie, on the verge of tears. "I don't have to be here."

Maude sat up straighter in the bed and patted her hair, lifting her little pink chin in the lavender-tinted air.

"Of *course* I don't want to drive her away," Maude said. "You know that, don't you, Billie? I would *never* do such a thing. I am sorry if I said hurtful things about your father, but we were very hurt by him, Bridget and I, weren't we, Bea? And you have to admit, dear, that dying like he did, that must have been hurtful for you, too."

Billie bowed her head, less to signify agreement than to keep them from seeing how awful she felt.

"And look at us," Maude said. "We might be frightful old ladies, but we're not monsters. This is no *gulag* he grew up in, is it, now?"

Billie could only shake her head no.

"No," Maude said decisively. "Your father was raised as a prince, and he grew up in a castle, and he chose to walk away from it, for reasons that only he understood. And now he's not here to enlighten us."

The prince, the castle—all the old stories passed again through Billie's mind. So he'd been telling the truth after all.

"Johnny must have wanted Billie to meet us when she came of age," said Bridget, "or else why would he have left our address for her to find?"

This idea, that her father might have intended this meeting, lifted Billie's heart immensely. It made her feel almost as if he were in the room with them right now, some other, better version of him.

"So my father . . . grew up here?" she asked.

"Certainly he did," Bridget said. "Until he finished college and went into the service."

"Why don't you take Billie to see the rest of the house?" Maude cut in. "She can stay in Johnny's room."

"Oh, I don't know . . ." Billie began, though her protest was feeble. While she hadn't exactly planned on staying here, she didn't really have the money to stay in a hotel and wasn't sure she'd be welcome or comfortable at Jupe's parents' house, either. What little they'd owned in California had been sold or junked and the lease torn up; the truth was, she had nowhere else to go.

"Of course you're staying," said Bridget. "This is your home. We are your family. You are welcome to stay here for, well, for as long as you like. Forever."

6

Bridget, 1916

Floyd began sniffling two days after the trip to the beach. It was just a cold, Bridget thought: a little summer cold. No need to reveal the outing to Coney Island, the chill the child must have caught from the frigid water, the open car. He'd soon enough be better, and there was no reason to alarm Maude.

But by Saturday afternoon he seemed not better but worse, coughing and tired, sleeping an hour longer than usual during his nap and still waking up cranky. It wasn't like the boy to be so out of sorts, even if he wasn't feeling well. Maude ought to know the child was ill before she left for the evening.

Though Floyd didn't feel feverish, his head hung limp against Bridget's shoulder as she carried him downstairs, and he dropped his bunny twice. With the child in her arms, Bridget walked into the master bedroom without knocking.

She was shocked to see Maude—at least, she thought it was Maude—standing in the middle of the room, holding her arms above her head and swiveling her hips as she danced laughing in a circle. A red kerchief covered her blond hair and the skin on her face was blacked over with some kind of grease, so she resembled a Negro woman. A Negro woman with blue eyes and pale pink hands.

Floyd let out a cry of fright and nestled even more closely into Bridget's shoulder.

"Oh, darling, don't be afraid, it's only Mummy!" Maude cried, fluttering closer to them.

"I told you no one would recognize you," came a low voice from deep in the room.

It was only then that Bridget saw the doctor, Dr. Elliot, who'd come to treat Mr. Apfelmann's indigestion, reclining on the fuchsia chaise in Maude's dressing room. Instead of his white coat, he was wearing a satin costume trimmed in gold, a crown perched on his lap.

"We're going to the Heterodoxy Club's summer costume party! Emma Goldman and Charlotte Perkins Gilman and just everyone who's anyone is going to be there. Oh, Bridget, isn't it a doodah?"

With Mr. Apfelmann still in England on Apple Candy business, Maude's social life had escalated to the point that she was out every night. Soon enough, she told Bridget, she'd be shut up at home again with her much older husband, who preferred his easy chair and a volume of poetry to Maude's theatrical parties. There were whispers among the other servants about Maude meeting other men when she went out in the evenings and on weekends, but Bridget had never seen any evidence of that until now.

"I'm sorry to intrude, ma'am," Bridget said, unable to look Maude in her ridiculous face. "It's Floyd. His cold seems worse since he woke from his nap."

"Oh, poor darling," said Maude, her grin collapsing as she reached for her son.

"Let me see the child," said Dr. Elliot, standing and moving toward them. "Come, lay him here on the bed."

As Bridget tried to set Floyd down on the violet silk spread, he cried out as if in pain, screaming more loudly as the doctor tilted his head back to look in his nose, as he palpitated his neck and pried open the boy's mouth to peer into his throat.

"For goodness' sake, Nanny, can't you make your charge behave?" Dr. Elliot said.

Bridget looked toward Maude, who said, "The boy doesn't feel well, Jim. It's not Bridget's fault."

"It's unusual for him to complain like this," Bridget said, relaxing on Maude's support. "It's what made me think it might be something serious."

"I didn't ask you for a diagnosis," the doctor snapped. "This is a case of *matricus interruptus*—or, in layman's terms, a little boy who's trying his best to make sure his mother doesn't go out for the evening."

Maude laughed.

"A small cold is all. Nothing to be concerned about. Indulging his complaints will only make things worse."

"But I think there's something more than that wrong with the child—"

The doctor cut Bridget off without looking at her. "There's nothing wrong with him that a little discipline and competent care wouldn't cure. Really, Maude. Any ignorant Irish servant who challenged my authority like this in my own household would find herself on the boat back to Cork before she could say a Hail Mary."

"Oh, Jim, you're such a Neanderthal," said Maude, taking the doctor's arm and winking at Bridget. "Bridget is much more competent at child care than I am, I'm afraid. Why don't we leave her to do her job and you can do yours, which tonight is keeping me entertained."

Back in the nursery, Bridget had to struggle against tears, but told herself that perhaps they were right. Perhaps she'd been spoiling Floyd; maybe he was simply trying to manipulate his mother, whom he saw so seldom. But when she tried setting Floyd on the floor with his toys and busied herself tidying the playroom, feeling the doctor's advice at least deserved the benefit of the doubt, she turned to find the child lying on the rug, curled on his side.

"Oh, sweetheart," she said, rushing to him. "You really are sick. That awful doctor was wrong, wasn't he?"

She gathered the boy up and set him on her bed, fluffing pillows behind his back so he'd be more comfortable. But still he didn't want to sit up, moaning and holding his neck in an odd way.

Again, she brought her lips to his forehead. He looked so miserable, she kept expecting to feel his skin hot beneath her mouth. But he was only a little warm, not burning up.

That was good, wasn't it? If he were really ill with something serious, he'd be more feverish, wouldn't he?

There was a soft rap at her door. It was the parlormaid Nora, dressed to go out and carrying a tapestry bag. Lingering behind her in the hallway were Maggie and Ruthie, the other maids.

"We're going to stay with Ruthie's sister in Bronxville," Nora said. "Mrs. Apfelmann gave us the whole day off tomorrow. I assume you're stuck here?"

"Floyd is under the weather."

Nora pecked into the room without real interest.

"Where's her ladyship?"

"Gone out," Bridget said shortly. She knew what Nora would say, how her lip would curl, if Bridget revealed anything about the doctor having been there or about Maude's outrageous costume.

"Too bad," said Nora. "Can I get you anything?"

"Will you sit with him while I make him a little milky tea?"

"Oh," said Nora. "We're already rushing for the train."

When Bridget heard the front door slam after them, she got into bed with Floyd and pulled the covers close, opening his favorite book of Grimm's fairy tales.

"Once upon a time in a land far, far away . . ." she began to read, but then she saw that his eyes were closed. If he wasn't going to look at the pictures, there was no point in telling a story from the book.

"Would you like Bridget to tell you a story from the farm when she was a little girl?"

Floyd nodded, ever so slightly.

"Well, on the farm where we lived, there was an enormous

tree, with leaves that were gold instead of green, and a trunk and roots so big that inside them lived a whole city of fairies."

Floyd's eyes popped open. She smiled at him.

"It's true! Dozens of fairies, hundreds of them! Only you couldn't see them, of course, because fairies are so quick, and so smart. So, one day, my brother Patrick and I decided we were going to build a little house for the fairies, a house that was so beautiful it would lure them out of the tree and inside its walls, and then we'd slam the door shut and catch them. At least one of them, anyway."

Floyd was watching her steadily now.

"So Patrick and I worked for days on this house, nailing the walls together and decorating it with leaves and flowers. We even made little chairs and little beds for the fairies. And then we set the house right in the roots of the trees, where no cows could get at it, no wind and no rain, on a night when the moon was full."

Floyd nodded, as if concurring with their tactics. Telling it now to him, Bridget could remember how thoroughly she had believed in fairies herself, imagining as she placed each violet blossom in the house how comfortable the tiny being would find it, how warm each leaf would keep each fairy who slumbered beneath it.

"Well, we tried to stay up late to watch the fairies march into the house, but we grew too tired, and finally we went to our own beds to sleep. As soon as we woke up in the morning, we rushed out to the tree, and what do you think we found?"

"What?" Floyd breathed.

"The house was gone!" Bridget said, aware suddenly of what

a disappointing ending this was. "The fairies had taken it away!" she said, trying to salvage the story but realizing this wasn't really helping. "They liked it so much they carried it inside their tree and it was never seen again."

Floyd looked like he was on the brink of tears.

"Until my brother's birthday," she said, "when ten fairies carried the house, covered with flowers, right into our bedroom and played with us there all day long!"

Floyd managed a laugh, though on any other day, Bridget knew, he would have been leaping out of bed, insisting Bridget build a fairy house with him, even pulling her outside to the park to gather sticks and flowers and hunt for the fairies' hiding places.

"That's a love," Bridget said, giving him a kiss. "Now it's time for sleep, darling. Just for tonight, you can fall asleep here in the bed with Bridget."

That special treat persuaded him, and he shut his eyes and dropped nearly instantly to sleep, making a noise that was almost like crying.

She wasn't aware that she had nodded off, still fully dressed, until she awoke to the sound of thunder, lightning flashing in the sky outside her window. Floyd, thank goodness, continued snoring softly beside her. She got up and lifted the little boy to carry him to his own bed.

Immediately he awoke, crying out as if in pain.

"There, there," she soothed. "It's just time for bed."

"Ow! Ow!"

He *was* in pain, his left hand clapped to his neck. But as she set him back down on her bed, she noticed something more alarming: The child's right arm hung limply at his side.

"Floyd. Floyd! Lift your arm for Bridget, darling."

But he didn't seem to be able to move his arm.

She scooped up the moaning child and rushed downstairs, hoping that while she had been dozing Maude had come home. She even wished the doctor were there. But though it was past midnight, Maude's bedroom was empty; the whole house was empty. Then Bridget thought of George, whom she hadn't seen at all since their outing to Coney Island. Maude had kept him busy since her return, going to parties and shopping and out to lunch and to the theater. Customarily, when Maude went out in the evening, George drove her; but perhaps, given the delicacy of her arrangement with Dr. Elliot, they had taken the doctor's own car.

Wrapping a raincoat around her and Floyd, she ran out through the kitchen door barefoot over the wet flagstones to the garage. The garage was dark but the car was there. She pounded on the door that led to the men's quarters, struggling to shelter Floyd's warm, immobile body from the driving rain. At last George appeared, blinking in the dark, pulling up his suspenders over his undershirt.

"It's Floyd," she told him. "He's ill. Will you take me to the hospital?"

He drove fast, dodging around trotting horses and racing a streetcar through an intersection, not even slowing down at the cross streets, screeching to a halt in front of what Bridget saw was the Hospital for Ruptured and Crippled Children. Ruptured. She held Floyd tightly, his breathing loud and labored, his eyes shining up at her.

"That's a love," she crooned. "Everything's going to be all right now. Everything's all right."

George helped them out of the backseat, sheltering them with the umbrella until they were in the lobby, where a nurse in a starched wimple sat at the front desk.

"We need a doctor right away," said George.

"What seems to be the trouble?" asked the nurse.

"We don't know what the fucking trouble is!" George exploded. "We just need a doctor, for Christ's sake."

"You can't—"

Bridget was afraid that the nurse was about to turn them away, back into the night, with Floyd only getting sicker and George angrier. But instead of waiting for that to happen, George grabbed Floyd from Bridget's arms and started running, banging through the double doors, plunging into the depths of the hospital, Bridget taking off after him.

In contrast to the brightness of the lobby, the hallways seemed hushed and unpopulated. Each time they encountered a nurse, George demanded to know where they could find a doctor, and finally they came face-to-face with a man wearing rimless glasses, a surgical mask hanging on his chest.

"Can you help us?" George asked. "My child is ill."

"You'll have to go to the emergency center."

"This *is* an emergency!" George shouted, Floyd limp in his arms, shaking with George's rage. "This is an emergency right here!"

Bridget caught her breath, afraid this doctor, too, would turn them away; but after studying the child for a moment, he said, "All right. Follow me."

Everything happened quickly after that. The doctor found

an empty examination room, called a nurse to help, who took Floyd from George and laid him on the examination table.

"It's all right, darling," Bridget said, reaching out to touch the child's forehead. "There's the best little boy."

She didn't know whether he heard her, he was so weak, seeming to sleep or perhaps slip from consciousness, both of his arms and his right leg, too, now unmoving, his neck at a painful angle, his breath so shallow it seemed barely to enter his mouth when it left again.

And then the doctor sent her and George out to the waiting room.

"You have to find Maude," Bridget whispered. "Go now. I'll be fine here on my own."

She stood against the wall, waiting for the exam-room door to open, for Floyd's voice, for George to return. It was hours before the nurse appeared. The nurse shook her head, just once, just slightly, but enough so that Bridget knew the news was not good.

The doctor had done a lumbar puncture. It would be some time before they had a conclusive analysis. But he was almost sure that what they were dealing with here—that's how he put it, "what we are dealing with here"—was infantile paralysis.

"Polio," he told Bridget. "Removing the spinal fluid should relieve some pressure and help calm the child. Now our only hope is to try and remove the toxins from the system. We'll do some bloodletting and also introduce a disinfectant solution."

"Disinfectant?" gasped Bridget. "But won't that harm the little one?"

The doctor sighed loudly. "Let me explain this to you. If the child lives in an environment of filth, it stands to reason that the filth will invade his body. And the only way to combat that is to purge and cleanse his blood and his organs the way you might a dirty floor teeming with flies." His lip curled. "Well, not, perhaps, the way you might."

"See here, Doctor," Bridget said heatedly. "That child lives in a perfectly clean and lovely home. He had never even been outside the house until a month ago, never so much as got a speck of dirt on his little finger or a spot of mud on his knee. So you can't say he's ill because he lives in fi-fi-fi- . . ."

She was so overwhelmed the word would not come out.

"Do you live in Brooklyn, madam?" the doctor demanded.

"We live just off Fifth Avenue, in the Sixties," said Bridget proudly.

The doctor blinked. "And is your husband Italian?"

"I don't even have . . ." She stopped herself. "None of us are Italian."

The doctor shook his head. "This doesn't add up."

"Where is he?" she whispered.

The doctor gestured toward a curtain and abruptly walked away.

Floyd's skin was as pale as marble, his eyes closed and his body broken looking. As soon as she saw him, Bridget gave in to the impulse she'd been fighting all evening and sank to her knees, closing her eyes, collapsing around him.

"Sweetheart," she said. "Sweetheart, it's your Bea."

Beneath the lids, his eyes moved, but they didn't open.

"That's my boy," she said, kissing his cheeks, his forehead, his lips. His breath was so shallow it was barely there. "That's my brave boy, my good boy."

He's still alive, she thought. He's alive right this minute.

And then, in the space of a breath, he wasn't. He didn't look any different than he had, but some animating spirit—his soul, Father Gervase and the nuns would have called it—was gone.

There were sounds from the hallway: two men fighting, it seemed, and then a woman's voice, louder than the others. George, Bridget heard, and the doctor. And Maude.

"Do you know who I am?" Maude was saying. "I am Mrs. Jacob Apfelmann. My husband is a close personal friend of Mayor Mitchel's. Get the mayor on the phone. Get the president, President Wilson, on the phone! The king! My husband is right at this moment with King George himself!"

"Maude." Bridget stepped out of the exam room, Floyd's body in her arms.

She felt as if she were at once frozen and on fire, as if she simultaneously wanted to die and felt nothing else could ever hurt her again. The worst thing that could happen had happened. The one thing she was never supposed to let happen had happened. And no matter how many times she replayed the steps in her head, she couldn't reanimate the small pale boy who lay limp in her useless arms.

"Oh, God," Maude said, clapping her hand over her mouth. Her face was streaked with remnants of the black makeup, which looked as if it had been washed off by the rain. Her golden hair was hanging down in clumps, her dress streaked with mud.

Maude took Floyd from Bridget and began shaking the boy.

"Wake up," Maude said. "Floyd, wake up, Mama's here."

Floyd's head flopped back, his arms loose at his sides.

"Floyd, Floyd, do you hear me? You have to wake up right now!"

"Maude," said Bridget, horrified, moving to stop her. "Maude, he's gone."

"He just has to listen to me," insisted Maude. "Indulgence encourages disobedience, Bridget. Floyd, you must do as I say."

Bridget put her arms around Maude. Around them both.

"Stop," she crooned. "Stop now. The boy is gone, Maude."

"No, no."

"Stop now." Bridget started rocking. "Stop."

Maude bowed her head and began sobbing, first quietly and then more and more noisily. That was heartrending enough, but soon Maude was punctuating her sobs with screams, which seemed to begin as exhalations but rose until they rang out like true cries to the heavens.

Bridget held tight, no longer trying or wanting to quiet Maude. There was something thrilling as well as terrifying about Maude's shrieks, like music from some otherworldly place.

The doctors came, the nurses came, the police came, all rushing to join the circle around Maude and Bridget and the dead child, but no one was willing to come any closer. George left and returned with Mr. Berlin, who had already cabled Mr. Apfelmann in London. Finally Mr. Berlin reached in and touched Maude's shoulder, breaking the barrier, and then someone moved to wrench Floyd's body from Maude's arms. Still Maude kept shrieking and shrieking, and Bridget thought it was the most terrible sound she'd ever heard.

Until Maude stopped, and everything went silent, and then Bridget knew: this was worse.

7

Cait, Present

Cait stepped off the bus at the bottom of her parents' street and started trudging uphill, feeling as always as if she were walking back into her past. There was the McKennas' split-level, where she used to babysit for their five kids, and there was the Rizzos' sleek brick ranch, where she made friends every summer with their two-years-younger daughter so she could swim in their pool, and there was the Ralstons' center-hall Colonial, still painted white with maroon trim, where her best friend, Nancy, had lived from first through fourth grade.

The Ralstons had moved away decades ago, and most of the houses on the block had been sold and filled with new families Cait had never met, with new children drawing in chalk on the sidewalks and riding their bikes down the hill and swimming in the Rizzos' old pool. Cait's parents were among the few holdouts who continued paying the town's high property taxes long past the time they could justify the expense by having children in the schools.

"I like living in a place where there are children on the block," Cait's mother, Sally, explained. "Where would we go? Our friends are here. And your father has his yard."

Cait's childhood home, pale green with cream trim and the bright red roof that Sally had chosen in a giddy moment of suburban rebellion, was in sight now, the leaves on the Japanese maple out front just starting to tip crimson. Cait's heart rose, as always, in anticipation of hugging her parents and sinking into the feather-stuffed blue couch where she'd watched countless episodes of *The Simpsons* and eating a slice of the fresh-baked cake that inevitably waited on the kitchen counter. And at the same time it sank, knowing how trapped she always felt under her parents' constant gaze, how the anxiety level rose in the house if she left to so much as fetch a carton of milk. Going for a walk was a betrayal: "Why don't you go for a walk out back with Daddy?" her mother would counter. "You can pick some blackberries." To gain any true sense of freedom, she had to go halfway around the world.

If her parents had known she was coming, they would have been sitting on the wicker chairs on the front porch, watching for her to walk up the street. But Cait hadn't called first, so she found the porch empty, the front door shut and locked, the TV sounding faintly from inside.

She rang the bell and saw the curtain move on the dining-room window and then heard her mother hurrying across the oak floor to fling open the dark-green door.

"Why, Cait!" her mother cried, blinking up at her. "What a wonderful surprise!"

Cait bent down to hug her mother, so small and round; it was like hugging a teddy bear. Although Cait still thought of her mother's hair as light brown, it had faded almost entirely to white, soft and sparse as the fuzz on a dandelion. She was conscious—of course she was conscious—of the fact that her parents were in their late seventies now, but it still surprised her anew each time she saw them to find that they were old. After an hour or two she'd forget again, and their flesh-and-blood, gray-haired, stoop-shouldered, wrinkly skinned selves would soften into the ageless personages they'd always seemed to her: not young, not old, just her parents. But for this moment, she embraced her mother gingerly, as if afraid she might break the fragile bones, or squeeze the life right out of that faltering heart.

"Vern!" her mother cried. "Look who's here!"

But then her mother shot her a quick look, excitement fading to concern.

"What is it, dear?" Sally asked. "Nothing's wrong, is it?"

"No, no." Cait rushed to assure her, but was instantly stabbed with guilt. Because being pregnant—that was something wrong, wasn't it? Certainly, in the absence of a marriage, it would be in the eyes of her parents. And in the context of Cait's own life it was, too. And then there was the matter of why she was actually there. Surely, asking about her biological mother wasn't something that her parents would consider right.

Her father, tall, still strong looking, his hair gray but thick on top of his head, hobbled out from the shadows of the living room, yellow-plaid short-sleeved shirt gapping where his belly strained against the buttons.

"Hello, sweetheart," he said, awkwardly patting her arm.

Her father was easier to deal with than her mother: less engaged, maybe, more restrained, but so much simpler to be around. He'd retired from the fire department years before but still worked, as the manager of an electronics store. Though they could have easily survived on his pension, he said he liked to keep his hand in. Liked to keep busy. When he and Cait were both home, they could sit silently but companionably for hours, reading the paper or watching a game, not speaking, though Cait was pleasantly aware of his company, while Sally bustled around, picking up newspapers and glasses and making coffee and chatting and not being annoying, exactly, but as intrusive and distracting as a fly.

"We just finished eating," her mother said.

It was 6:15, still light as afternoon.

"But I can fix you a plate," her mother continued. "We have a leg and a thigh left. I'm sorry I don't have any breast, but when you're not here, Dad and I figure we can each go ahead and take one for ourselves."

"That's okay," Cait assured her mother. The only time she'd felt anything like queasy, for reasons she now understood, was when she'd been in the vicinity of chicken: passing the chicken rotisserie place on Delancey, coming upon the packets of pale beige cutlets in the Whole Foods refrigerator case. Even *thinking* about chicken now made her uneasy. "I've already eaten. I'd love to just sit out back while it's still light."

It *was* beautiful out there, her favorite part of the house, more immutable and less evocative than the rooms inside: the apple tree she used to climb spreading its thick branches to shelter the entire patio; her father's tomato vines—bare of fruit but still staked up—in the garden, crowded against browning hydrangeas and thick purple asters; the bees asleep in their plywood hives. The lawn was still summer green, the thick wall of rhododendrons shielding their yard from the others that surrounded it. Settling into the cushions of the old wrought-iron chairs, Cait could hear the cries of the neighborhood children. A dog barked; the first firefly appeared.

"So I thought I'd stay in New York for a little while," Cait said. "Till Thanksgiving, at least. Maybe through the holidays."

Sally clapped her hands. "Oh, dear, that would be so wonderful. What a treat to have you home for Christmas." Then she stopped. "That doesn't mean there's anything wrong with your work, does it?"

"No," Cait assured her. "Everything's great. I just . . . well, I just decided that instead of writing about that orphanage in Ethiopia, I wanted to do a different story."

"Oh, really?" her mother said. "What story is that, dear?"

Cait felt guilty; this was almost too easy. But she would do the story on her adoption search; she could do the story, depending on what she found out. Depending on how much she wanted to expose herself. Which, if history was any indication, was not very much at all. Journalism had always provided an effective cover for her real self, her real feelings and real life. At least until she broke down that day in the woods.

Cait sucked in a deep breath. "I've decided to look for my birth mother," she said, trying to tame the quaver in her voice. "I thought I'd write about that."

Her father, predictably enough, didn't comment, though

there was something in the way he cleared his throat, some steeliness in his gaze toward the darkening beehives, that told her he'd heard. Sally, too, was unnaturally focused on the back of the yard, though she was already blinking fast against tears.

"I suppose I always knew this day would come," Sally said finally. "Though I thought, after so much time, that you might have decided that was something you didn't want to bother with."

"Bother with"—that was vintage Sally. Sally wouldn't come out and say she didn't want Cait to look for her birth mother, but she'd use some subtle turn of phrase to send the message just the same. Is this why I've never looked before now? Cait wondered. Because I knew it would hurt Sally?

"It's nothing against you, Mom," Cait said, putting her hand over Sally's, cool in the evening air, the skin soft with age, bones close to the surface. "It's just something I have to do."

But that wasn't quite accurate, now, was it? Because it wasn't simply something that Cait suddenly needed out of the blue to do. It was something she felt compelled to do because of her own pregnancy. And her own pregnancy was not something she intended to confess to her mother and father, not now.

"I understand," said Sally, slipping her hand away and folding her arms across her chest. "Oprah did a show on this last year."

"That's right," said Cait. She wasn't familiar with the Oprah episode, but she knew that her mother felt that if Oprah supported it, then it must be good. "So then you get it. I need to start by talking to you guys, because I just don't really know where else to start. I remember you told me the story . . ."

She'd been hearing the story for as long as she could

remember, used to ask her parents to tell it again and again. "Mommy couldn't grow a baby in her own tummy" was the way they explained it to her when she was little, and so they'd prayed and prayed, asking Jesus to send them a very special baby, and then one day the phone rang and their prayers were answered. There was a little girl who had just been born who was waiting for them to be her mommy and daddy. And so they got in the car, drove across the bridge into New York City, and went to the hospital where they picked up Caitlin Sara Trippel, the most beautiful baby who had ever been born.

"Which hospital?" she asked now.

"What?" Sally said, rubbing her arms.

"Which hospital was it where you picked me up?"

It had never occurred to Cait to ask even this basic question before, which seemed to her to be a stunning omission. Had she always been that devoid of curiosity, that afraid to hear the facts?

"I don't remember. It was on the East Side, I know that, because I remember your father drove down the FDR Drive, not the West Side Highway. We had a terrible time parking."

"Uptown?" Cait asked, trying to be patient. After all, she'd made it through the past thirty-something years without knowing this detail. What did it matter if she had to wait another five minutes?

"I don't know," her mother said. "Not *uptown* uptown. But not downtown, either."

They sat silently for a moment.

"Are you cold?" Sally asked. "Do you want to go in?"

It was fully dark in the yard. The children had all disappeared. Only the fireflies remained to keep them company.

"Not really," Cait said. "I just want to try and see what you remember. Before we get distracted. Do you remember what hospital it was, Daddy?"

"I don't know," he said. "One of those big ones."

"Could it have been New York Hospital?" Cait asked.

"It could have been," Vern said. "That must have been it. New York Hospital."

"I remember you said you got me through an agency. The Catholic something."

Sally traded a look with Vern and said, "The Catholic . . . oh, I don't know, dear. It was so long ago."

"Catholic Social Services Agency," Vern said, slapping his hands on his thighs and standing up. "I for one am freezing. I'm going inside."

"Oh, Daddy, let's just finish this, okay?"

"We'll finish inside. Your mother is not supposed to get a chill. Sally?"

Sally stood up and so did Cait, her attention shifted now.

" 'Not supposed to'? What does that mean?"

"Oh, it's nothing," Sally said.

"Your mother's been having some problems," Vern said. "With her health."

"Problems?" Cait said, following them into the house. "What kind of problems?"

"It's just a little pain," her mother said.

"It's her heart," Vern said. "They're doing tests."

"What are you talking about?" They were in the kitchen now. Vern flipped the switch and the light blazed on overhead. Cait could see that her mother looked embarrassed, suddenly smaller and frailer than when Cait had arrived. Cait took her mother by the shoulders. "Mom, what's going on?"

"They don't know," her mother said. "It's probably nothing."

"It's not nothing," her father said. "She hasn't been feeling well for a while, Cait. She didn't want to worry you, right before you left again. But now that you're going to be around"— he shrugged—"there's no point in hiding it from you."

"I wish you wouldn't hide anything from me," Cait said. "No matter where I am."

"Can we not fight?" Sally said.

"We're not fighting," said Vern. "I just wish we could put this adoption stuff aside so we don't upset your mother right now."

"Of course," Cait said, feeling ashamed at having pushed things but frustrated at not having learned more. "I didn't mean to worry you or make it your problem. I just thought if I had the name of the adoption agency, you said it was the Catholic Social something . . ."

"Catholic Social Services Agency," said her father. "It was a closed adoption, Cait. That's the way they did it in those days. We didn't know anything about her, and she didn't know anything about us, and that's the way everybody wanted it."

"That's the way she . . ." Cait said. "You mean you knew . . ."

"Can you leave it alone now?" her father said, more heated than she'd seen him in recent memory. "We're glad you're going to be around here more, dear, especially right now. But for your mother's sake, I can't have you opening this whole can of worms."

8

Billie, 1976

I thought I'd go out," Billie said.

She was standing in the doorway of her grandmother's bedroom. Maude, in yet another lavender bed jacket that matched the room, with a fresh satin ribbon in her hair, set down the *New York Post* she'd been reading through a gold-handled magnifying glass.

"Out?" Maude said. "Why ever would you want to go out?"

Billie bit back a giggle. She'd already learned that Maude did not have much of a sense of humor about herself.

"This is New York," Billie said. "I've been here almost a week, and I haven't even seen anything."

"What's there to see?" Maude said impatiently. "Dog doo in the streets and Negroes knifing each other."

"I don't think that's all there is, Maude."

Maude did not want to be called Grandma, Grandmother,

Nana, or any of the other alternatives Bridget came up with. Billie tried Mrs. Apfelmann, but that did not sit well, either. Maude suggested Miss Montgomery, but when Bridget scoffed at that—"Really, Maude! You should be ashamed of yourself!"—they'd settled on Maude.

"Well, where are you going, exactly? I can't have my granddaughter just running around the streets."

This was such a new experience for Billie, the thing she'd always dreamed of: living in a big, clean house with nice food and people who cared about her making sure she was all right. She couldn't remember her father ever asking where she was going, not even when she was five or six, leaving the house in the morning before he was awake and not coming home until all the other kids had been called in for dinner. Ironic that, now that she was nineteen and truly able to look out for herself, someone finally wanted to know where she was going.

"I just want to go for a walk," Billie told her. "See the sights: the Empire State Building, the Statue of Liberty."

And other places she'd read about: the coffeehouses of Greenwich Village; the White Horse Tavern, where Dylan Thomas had drunk himself to death; Chinatown; and the art galleries of SoHo.

And Jupe. She wanted to see Jupe.

"It's not safe for you to be out there alone. Bridget will go with you."

"No!" Billie yelped.

Nothing against Bridget, who was so sweet. For all Maude's fussing over her now, it was Bridget who'd put fresh sheets on Billie's father's childhood bed, Bridget who'd cooked her dinners and washed her clothes, setting up the old ironing board in the kitchen and, over Billie's protests, starching the collars on her Salvation Army blouses into stiff points. But seeing the sights of New York with an old lady in tow wasn't what Billie had in mind.

"I'll be perfectly fine by myself," Billie said. "Besides, I have a friend here I'll probably get together with. So you don't have to worry, because I'll be with him."

" 'Him'?"

Maude arched her eyebrows and shot Billie a meaningful look.

It's not like that, Billie wanted to say. He's gay, or sort of gay, anyway. Plus, he's not one of those Negroes you're so worried about. But she figured none of that would be reassuring.

"He's just a friend," she told Maude. "He's the guy I drove out with from California."

"Just a friend, eh? There's no such thing as men friends. There are only men you want to sleep with but, for whatever reason, don't."

"Things have changed, Gran—" Odd that, given Maude's prohibition of the name, Billie kept having the impulse to call her Grandma. "Maude," she concluded.

"Oh, do you think your generation invented sex?" Maude said. "Let me tell you, we had plenty of sex in my day. *Loads* of sex! And not just after we were married, either. It was *more* exciting back then, the glances, the flirtation, the buildup until *wham! bam!*—"

"No, I don't think we invented sex," Billie said, cutting her off before it could get any more graphic. "I just mean, in terms of relationships between men and women, there's a whole range of new possibilities now."

"New possibilities, hmmmmph," said Maude. "I've had a lot more experience with these matters than you have. There's nothing wrong with a little fooling around, but if you want a man to take you seriously, you act like a lady and you bring him here to meet me and Bridget, do you hear?"

Billie would love to show Jupe her grandmother's house. He'd be dazzled by the art, she knew, which included everything from cubist Matisse through Méret Oppenheim's fur teacup to one of Andy Warhol's soup cans: chicken noodle. He'd be as fascinated as she was by her father's old bedroom, by the boyhood artifacts, from a baseball signed by Babe Ruth to an 1895 silver dollar preserved as if Johnny would be coming home from school at any moment. And she'd like to introduce Jupe to her grandmother and to Bridget, too, to get his opinion on these curious creatures who were suddenly playing the kind of familial role that he seemed to think would be so good for her.

Yet, she couldn't imagine Maude's reaction if she brought a black friend home—a black *male* friend—or Bridget's, either. And as happy as she was to discover a home and a family, she needed to lay down some ground rules or this arrangement was never going to last.

"It's not . . . I don't know, the 1950s anymore, Maude," Billie said. "And I'm not a little girl. Don't get me wrong, I like being here, but you can't hold me prisoner."

"Prisoner!" Maude exclaimed. "Whoever heard of such a thing? I'm just trying to impart some of the, well, *guidance* you obviously didn't get from your father. That dress, for instance."

Billie looked down. She was wearing a thrift store favorite: a 1950s housedress printed with planets and stars, wrapped over a pair of loose white pants she'd made from a $1 remnant of sari silk.

"I love this outfit," Billie said.

"Of course you do," said Maude, swinging her legs off the side of the bed and standing up, which seemed almost as miraculous as when Clara got up from her wheelchair and started to walk toward *Heidi*. "But this is the Upper East Side of Manhattan, and you are an Apfelmann. If you are going to insist on traipsing out in the street, I am going to insist that you do so in better clothes."

Billie was surprised by how agile her grandmother was, her shoulders erect, her step smooth. She brushed past Billie and opened the closet, pulling a chain to bathe the vast space in a pink glow. It was nearly as big as a shop in there, the yards of racks hung with hundreds of items arranged by color and style.

"Let's see," said Maude. "You'll need a day outfit, nothing too fussy . . ."

She walked her fingers down a line of dresses and pulled out a white linen middy dress complete with navy sailor collar and red tie, holding it up for Billie's inspection.

When Billie didn't respond, Maude said, "You're right. Too antique."

She dropped the dress to the floor and riffled through the racks again, finally pulling out a Jackie Kennedy–esque navy pique shift.

"What do you think?" Maude said. "This would be lovely on your figure."

Billie shook her head in horror. "I'm nineteen," she said. "Not fifty."

85

"True," said Maude, letting the Jackie dress fall atop the other one. "See, you do have my sense of style along with my figure. Why don't you come in and see if you find anything you like?"

The closet carried a whiff of age layered over with expensive perfume. As her fingers moved through the clothes, Billie realized that this was a trove more lush and varied than anything she'd ever encountered in a vintage-clothing or thrift store. The fabrics were thick and creamy under her hands, silks and polished cottons, faille and dense linen. It was like a museum of fashion in there, containing everything Maude had worn over the past sixty years.

"Do you have so many clothes because you were on the stage?" Billie asked.

Maude frowned. "What do you know about my being on the stage?"

"Bridget said you were in the theater. That you were a famous singer."

"I wore stage clothes—costumes!—in that life, which is long dead and gone," Maude said firmly. "These clothes are from my real life."

Billie's fingers lighted on a chiffon flapper dress, bright flowers splashed across a black background, a handkerchief skirt wafting over a slim black underslip.

"Oh!" cried Maude. "I wore that on the Île-de-France! Your father was with me. We cruised the Mediterranean. I remember dancing on the deck in that dress, the way the skirt moved in the sea breeze . . ."

"How old was my father?" Billie asked.

"He would have been . . . oh, nine or ten at the time. It was not that long after Mr. Apfelmann died. I remember he sat down below reading a book the whole time. I could not coax him up on deck to so much as play a game of shuffleboard."

The book Billie could picture, but the rest of it—her father aboard a luxury ship, even in this house, as a boy—was beyond her imagination.

"That's so sad," Billie said.

Maude seemed for a moment to be far away, lost in the same vision Billie was of the young Johnny hiding in his cabin, but then Maude shook her head briskly as if to dispel the dream. "It was a long time ago," she said. "Now, try this dress on. I can't wait to see how it looks on you."

Billie expected her grandmother to retreat while she changed, but Maude just stood there with her arms crossed, a faint smile on her face. Billie turned her back and slipped out of her old clothes, self-conscious that she wasn't wearing a bra, and then let Maude's dress, light as a cobweb, slip down over her head and settle with a whisper onto her body. She turned back to face her grandmother.

"It fits you perfectly!" Maude said, actually clapping her hands together in a flutter of applause. "Now sit down and let me fix your hair."

"Oh, I don't think . . ." said Billie, reaching up to lift her heavy blond curls from her neck.

"No argument!" said Maude. "Sit down. Oh, such fun."

Billie settled onto the ruffled stool in front of the large oval mirror, flanked by two smaller white-framed replicas, as Maude stood behind her and began brushing her hair. Maude's face looked more animated, happier, than it had since Billie arrived.

"In the twenties, of course, we all bobbed our hair," Maude

said, pulling the brush energetically through Billie's waves, her cheeks dimpling as she worked. "That was not my best look, I can tell you, which I'm sure you can understand. I preferred my hair long, like yours, but I never let it get all wild and fuzzy like this."

A memory floated up of sitting on the bed in the apartment in Santa Rosa or the trailer in Mendocino or maybe even the cottage in Oakland while Billie's mother tried to brush the tangles out of her long hair. Her mother's hands were not strong, like Maude's, and she moved the brush through Billie's hair as if she were petting a kitten: fondly but absently, without purpose. At some point her mother set down the brush and wandered away and Billie kept sitting there, waiting, the hair on one side of her head smooth, on the other side in an impossible tangle.

Where had her mother gone? That she didn't know. She only remembered the light, aimless feel of the brush, the pleasure of being the focus of her mother's attention, the long empty wait, the realization that her mother wasn't coming back.

"You and I, we have natural beauty," said Maude, pulling Billie's hair back and twisting it into a rope, "but that doesn't mean we can't take steps to make it even better."

Now her grandmother coiled Billie's hair up the back of her head, twisting it until it was curled up on top in a thick bun.

"There," Maude said, meeting Billie's eyes in the mirror. "What do you think?"

"I think I look . . ." Billie said, staring in the mirror and searching for the right word, ". . . like a grown-up."

Maude laughed. "You *are* a grown-up!" Maude cried. She reached for the bobby pins that were piled in a silver jar on the dressing table's mirrored surface and began sticking them into the back of Billie's new coiffure. "Why, when I was nineteen, I was already married. I already had Floyd!"

"Who's Floyd?" Billie asked.

A shadow blotted the smile from Maude's face. "My first son," she said. She maneuvered a final two pins into the hairdo. "There," she said, stepping back to get a better look at her work. "That looks lovely. Bridget! Oh, Bridget! Come up here and look at our girl!"

From two flights below, Billie heard an answering call and the first of Bridget's heavy steps on the stairs.

"So my father had a brother?" Billie persisted. "I have an uncle?"

"We'll talk about all that another time," said Maude impatiently. "For now, quick, I want to put a little makeup on you before Bridget gets here."

"I never wear makeup," Billie said, covering her face with her hands.

"Just a little bit," said Maude, already moving in again, selecting a lipstick from the vast number that stood at attention on the vanity. "Come on, now, dear. So Bridget can get the full effect."

Billie sat reluctantly but obediently back as Bridget's footsteps grew closer.

"Now, don't let her feed you too much," Maude said softly as she drew the sweet-scented lipstick across Billie's lips. "I can smell that she's been baking you cinnamon buns, apple pies. You'll get fat like her if you eat those things, and we don't want that, do we?"

Billie couldn't help laughing, though she loved Bridget's cooking.

"You don't need blush, just a little mascara," said Maude.

She finished applying the mascara and spritzed perfume onto Billie's neck just as Bridget stepped through the doorway.

"Bridget, look at our girl, how lovely she is!" Maude exclaimed. "Who does she remind you of, Bridget?"

"You, Maude."

"Me, fifty years ago!" said Maude, with a tone of satisfaction.

"Longer," said Bridget, smiling. "When first we met."

"Phoo," said Maude, suddenly turning businesslike and hurrying back to her bed and climbing under the covers. "That was before the war, when we wore those horrid long dresses. It should have been against the law to keep beautiful legs like mine and Billie's here covered up."

"That's right, Maude," said Bridget, shooting Billie an amused glance.

"Billie wants to go out," said Maude. "Do you think we should let her, Bridget?"

"Well," said Bridget. "Now that you've gotten her all dolled up, it would seem a shame not to. It's a beautiful day outside."

"Bridget, run and get the camera so we can take a picture of Billie in this outfit. Oh, wait!" cried Maude. "We forgot shoes!"

She hopped out of bed again, lithe as a girl, and hurried over to the closet, where she searched through one of the several hanging fabric shoe bags until she found a pair of gold high heels with T-straps.

"I don't think I could walk in those," Billie said doubtfully.

"Oh, pooh, I'll teach you."

Maude watched, arms crossed, as Billie tried to get into the shoes. But she couldn't even set down her heel: the shoes were at least two sizes too small.

Maude frowned. "I can't understand it. We're the same exact size in every other thing."

Billie shrugged, relieved she wouldn't have to try to walk in the torturous high heels. "I guess it's because I've always worn flip-flops or gone barefoot."

Maude shook her head. "I'll never understand what your father could have been thinking."

"Leave the child be, Maude. Now, hold still for the picture." Bridget held up the camera, a large old-fashioned affair with a flashbulb that popped, making lights swim before Billie's eyes. "You look lovely. Have a good time."

"Don't go far," said Maude. "If you walk toward the park and then turn left on Fifth Avenue, Bergdorf's is only four blocks away. You can do a little shopping and then right next door is the Plaza, where you can have tea."

"Be back for supper," said Bridget. "I'm making chicken."

"Give her some money," said Maude. "In case she needs anything."

"Call us if you get lost," said Bridget, slipping a twenty-dollar bill from her pocket and pressing it into Billie's hands. "I'll write down our phone number and address, just in case."

"I know the phone number and address," Billie said with a reassuring smile. "Don't worry. I'll be fine."

Out on the hot street, the dress danced around Billie's bare legs the way she imagined it had around Maude's on the deck of the ship. Maude's perfume filled her nose with flowers, blocking out the smell of dogs and exhaust.

She felt pretty, almost as if she belonged in the neighborhood.

People hurried by—so many people: men with short gray hair and gray suits, ladies as starchy as Pat Nixon, dark-skinned women in white uniforms pushing big old-fashioned baby carriages, mothers and children hand in hand.

I'm a rich girl, she thought, but then immediately felt ashamed at puffing herself up with such a notion, not even true, not even something she wanted. But still, she would allow herself: I live here. I live on this beautiful street. I'm wearing a dress that was worn on the Mediterranean Sea.

At the end of the block was a wall of green: Central Park, which Jupe had pointed out to her right before they'd turned onto Sixty-fourth Street and she'd seen her grandmother's house for the first time. As Maude had instructed, she turned left onto Fifth Avenue, strolling past large stone apartment buildings with elaborately uniformed doormen guarding their brightly polished doors. Where the canopies of a few of those buildings met the curb, limousines—real limousines!—idled. In New York, it seemed, everyone was rich.

She wished Jupe could see her. She imagined his eyes lighting up in admiration. He'd tell her how beautiful she looked, how sophisticated. She imagined his hand on her arm, his head bending close. He wouldn't be able to help kissing her, wanting her, falling in love with her.

She'd thought when she left the house that she would try to call him—she never had any privacy to make the call at Maude's house, and the one time she'd managed to dial Jupe's number, a woman had answered and she'd slammed down the phone—but the only pay phone she passed was missing its receiver, and besides, all the money she had was the twenty-dollar bill Bridget had given her, the sole item in her little black silk bag.

At the corner of the park, horse-drawn carriages were lined up, bowers of bright plastic flowers festooning their dark canopies and the street beneath them littered with huge piles of steaming shit. Billie sprinted across the intersection and walked across a plaza, enjoying the light spray from an enormous fountain, glad she was wearing her comfortable pink sneakers and not high heels.

She spotted Bergdorf's and worked her way toward its doors, energized by the crowds of people—tourists with cameras, and people who looked like they worked in offices, and some teenagers and hippies, too—that swirled all around her. She pushed through the store's heavy revolving doors only to stop dead in the cool hush of its interior. Seemingly dozens of clerks and guards turned to stare at her, the only customer in the place.

Someone bumped into her from behind and propelled her forward. Now she saw that there were other shoppers, women in formal dresses and suits, one silently inspecting a broad-brimmed black straw hat, another a sparkling atomizer of perfume. A gray-suited man held the leash of a miniature pug, both man and dog with their noses cocked up at an identical angle. Billie inched forward, still feeling the gaze of the guards, afraid someone might rush up and ask to help her. The sneakers that had felt like a blessing moments before now seemed to mark her as a pretender.

To turn and leave immediately seemed even more suspicious, so she made her way as quickly as she could across the floor, searching for another exit sign. Finally she found one and spilled through another revolving door, grateful to be back on the loud, hot street.

Just across the way was the Plaza. Her throat was parched, and the idea of tea, which had seemed slightly ludicrous when her grandmother had suggested it, now sounded appealing. She climbed the red-carpeted steps of the hotel and pushed through yet another revolving door.

It was brighter and busier inside the hotel than it had been in the store. The most gigantic bouquet Billie had ever seen, big as a tree and all white, stood on a table at the entrance to what looked like an elegant tearoom. Slowly, Billie approached.

"I would like to have some tea," she managed to say to the man guarding the entrance, who was holding a menu like a shield.

"Reservation?"

"N-no," Billie stammered.

He glanced at a book open on a pedestal.

"I'm afraid we have nothing available," he said.

Behind him, Billie could see dozens of empty tables.

"What about one of those tables?" she asked.

"Reserved," he snapped, and then without another word turned away.

It didn't matter. This wasn't her kind of place anyway, any more than the store had been. These were relics of another era, her grandmother's era. Outside again, she recrossed the street, circled around the line of horses, and turned into the park, where the formal feel of the posh streets devolved into a rush of children roller-skating, old people reading newspapers or feeding pigeons, kids her age lounging on benches or on the grass, dressed in tie-dyed T-shirts and Mexican peasant blouses, army shorts and elephant sandals. One girl lay with her head in a boy's lap, holding a joint with her pinky crooked and blowing smoke rings.

As Billie tripped past, the girl turned languidly in her direction and Billie smiled. She imagined herself saying hi, opened her mouth, and believed she was actually going to do it, but the girl blinked once, slowly, and turned away.

A thin man with skin as shiny and dark as a coffee bean, wearing a dirty white undershirt and a gold medallion as big as a cookie, stepped into Billie's path.

"Loose joints, loose joints," he muttered.

Billie jerked away from him, only to nearly stumble into an old woman pushing a grocery cart, wearing a huge woolen sweater littered with dried leaves and twigs.

Billie spun around, her heart hammering, suddenly feeling the thin silk of the dress clinging moistly to her between the shoulder blades, under the arms. She looked above the trees of the park toward the upper reaches of the buildings along its boundaries, trying to gauge how she could escape.

"Hey, princess," the old woman, tailing her, said in a surprisingly energetic voice. "Spare some change?"

Billie was about to say no, she didn't have any change, the way she habitually did to the panhandlers in Union Square in San Francisco. Then she remembered Maude's $20.

"Here," she said, fishing the bill out of the purse and pressing it into the woman's soot-covered hands, recoiling from the sight of the woman's long fingernails, curving like the stairway in her grandmother's house.

She walked away as quickly as she could, her throat dry,

pretending she knew where she was going. After what felt like far too long, she burst with relief onto Fifth Avenue again and the familiarity of the stone buildings, the soldier-like doormen with their gold-fringed epaulettes. After heading a block in the wrong direction, Billie spun around and hurried back to Sixty-fourth Street, where the street grew quiet and the crowds thinned out and where there was a place that was suddenly starting to feel more like home.

9

Bridget, 1916

On the morning of July thirteenth, Bridget didn't wake up as usual. It was the hottest morning yet of a heat wave that had gripped the city for days. Though she'd thrown the windows open against city regulations, no air was moving through them. In her stifling room near the top of the house, she hadn't been able to fall asleep until dawn, the crickets still sounding outside. Exhausted, she slept on as the sun rose in the sky and didn't wake until she heard an insistent buzzing at the front door, followed by an even more relentless pounding.

The air in the house was hot and thick, and Bridget felt as if she were moving through steam. Even the thin lawn dressing gown felt too heavy against her skin as she made her way to the door, the rest of the house still tomb quiet.

Standing in the front courtyard, grasping a piece of yellow cardboard in one hand and a rock in the other, was the florid-faced Mrs. Cushman, one of Maude's suffragist friends. Mrs. Cushman seemed astonished to see Bridget, to see anyone, answer the door—which made no sense, given all her pounding and buzzing. Then the woman took in Bridget's nightclothes, the messy nest of her hair, and hopped backward, nearly tripping over her own feet.

"Are you ill?" Mrs. Cushman asked.

"What? No . . . I . . ."

She's afraid I've got infantile paralysis, Bridget realized. She's afraid I got the disease from Floyd and now I'm going to give it to her. Smoothing her nightdress, Bridget tried to think of a palatable explanation for how she looked, but then she decided Mrs. Cushman didn't deserve one.

"No, I'm well, thank you," Bridget assured her. "We're all perfectly healthy. Please come in. I know Miss Montgomery will be happy you're here."

Bridget opened the door wider but, instead of entering, Mrs. Cushman took a further step back. There was a rumble of far-off thunder and they both looked toward the sky, which Bridget saw only now was dark as soot and threatening rain.

"Oh, no," Mrs. Cushman said hurriedly. "This isn't a social call. I'm volunteering with the health department—most of us in the Heterodoxy Club are—to educate people about infantile paralysis, and when they said your house might have to carry a placard . . ."

"Placard?"

Mrs. Cushman held up the yellow piece of paper.

"I don't know if you're able to read this," the lady said. "It's an awful lot of technical language. It's just basically a warning, for anyone who might be thinking of visiting with a babe in arms. . . ."

But that wasn't all it was, Bridget could see at a glance, fighting back her anger that this person who advocated for the rights of women and the disenfranchised could be so dismissive of Bridget's own rights. Bridget quickly took in the message on the sign, making sure not to show that she fully understood.

INFANTILE PARALYSIS, it read in big black letters. Underneath that, in parentheses, it said "Poliomyelitis" and then, "All persons not occupants of these premises are advised of the presence of Infantile Paralysis in it and are advised not to enter. The person having Infantile Paralysis must not leave the apartment until the removal of this notice by an employee of the Department of Health. By order of the BOARD of HEALTH."

The city was in the grip of a mania. Barely three weeks since Floyd had fallen ill, no one guessing what was wrong with him until too late, and now all of New York was on high alert against what the newspapers called "the baby-killing disease." Every day the death toll climbed: 30 to 50 to 75 to 100 to 150. Everyone with enough money spirited their children away to the country and the rest were shut up inside their suffocating apartments.

Holiday festivals were canceled and children were banned from movie theaters. In the park, the goat carts had disappeared and no toy boats floated in the pool. And at the playground, Bridget saw with a shock that they'd emptied all the sand from the sandboxes and covered the concrete with oil to keep down the dirt, the dirt that bred the germs.

The Italians brought it is what they said, though the Negroes were immune. Kissing was dangerous, the newspapers reported. Cats were thought to spread the disease, and dogs, too, with thousands of animals turned out into the streets by fearful families, to be caught and exterminated by city officials. There were cat-catching contests, with boys whose families needed money more than they needed the boys rounding up cats and turning them into the police for a bounty of ten cents a head. There were fly-catching contests, too, with flies blamed for picking up the disease from infected children, open garbage cans, and dead animals and spreading it on their feet and wings.

Close your windows! the health department ads commanded. Cover your garbage! Clean your house! Kill all flies!

"But why do we need to have this placard on our door?" Bridget, genuinely confused, asked Mrs. Cushman, "The child is dead and buried. There is no one sick here."

"The nursery," Mrs. Cushman said. "It still contains the germs."

"They've taken all his things. Taken them and burned them."

She thought with a pang of guilt of the stuffed rabbit and the fairy-tale book that she'd stolen from the room and secreted under her bed before the Health Department arrived.

"Has his room been disinfected?" Mrs. Cushman asked. "Have the floors been repainted? The wallpaper stripped off and replaced?"

"Uh . . . n-no . . ." Bridget stammered.

"Then you're not officially cleared," the lady said. "I volunteered to come here myself, for poor Maude's sake, hoping to inspect the house and deem it satisfactory and so avoid the placard. But finding the windows open and coming upon you in such a slovenly state in the middle of the day . . . though perhaps that's an Irish trait, something to do with an overly emotional expression of mourning."

A gust of wind shot down the street, bending the saplings toward the pavement and sending a garbage can clattering into the gutter. Then there was a sound from above in the house and, afraid Maude was up and would hear them, Bridget quickly stepped outside into the courtyard, softly pulling the door shut behind her. Another blast of wind, the strongest yet, blew Bridget's gown tight against her body and whipped the loose strands of her auburn hair across her face. A neighbor, hurrying home, glanced anxiously her way and then increased his pace.

"Mrs. Cushman," Bridget said in a low voice, hoping that Maude would not hear them and come down to investigate. "Can't you just leave us be? We've lost our only child, and Miss Montgomery and Mr. Apfelmann are having a very difficult time. . . ."

Mrs. Cushman drew herself up taller, ignoring the raindrops pelting the loose pink skin of her cheeks.

"I am here on official business," she said. "It is the welfare of your entire block—no, of the children of the entire city—that I'm safeguarding. I can't give special favors to anyone, and I'm sure that's an ethical stance with which Miss Montgomery would agree."

Bridget saw herself screaming, saw herself pushing Mrs. Cushman, imagined the lady toppling backward, lying in a heap on the sidewalk as Bridget, satisfied, walked back into the house and slammed the door.

Instead, Bridget held out her hand. "I'll hang the placard, ma'am. I know where the chauffeur stores the tools, and I'll hammer it up straightaway."

"I am under orders to see myself that it's done properly," Mrs. Cushman said.

But the rain was driving down hard now, the wind so strong it felt as if it might blow them all the way down to Madison Avenue.

"Come in, then, please," said Bridget. "Come in and wait out of the rain. Miss Montgomery is just inside and you can visit with her while I fetch the hammer."

Mrs. Cushman hopped from one foot to the other, casting anxious glances at the sky.

"All right, then," she said finally, thrusting the placard toward Bridget. "I'll leave this with you. But see that you hang it directly."

"Of course, ma'am," Bridget said, suppressing a smile.

Bridget waited while the woman hurried toward Fifth Avenue. Moment by moment it grew cooler and cooler until it felt like weeks rather than minutes had passed and summer had turned back into spring. Standing like this, her face lifted to the rain, her hair whipped by the wind, felt like childhood to her. Like happiness.

She stayed as she was until Mrs. Cushman had completely disappeared and all that was visible at the end of the block was the windblown tangle of the park. Then she lifted the placard into the wind and let it sail, like a kite freed from its earth-bound string, high, high into the wet, black sky.

Later that evening, after the storm broke with a riot of thunder and lightning, leaving the city drenched but ultimately as hot and muggy as before, the doorbell rang again and there on the landing was George.

She hadn't seen him since right after Floyd died, when Maude fired him along with everyone else in the house except Bridget, finding reasons to blame each of them for Floyd's death: Nora and Ruthie for letting flies and dirt into the house, Sarita for importing Italian germs to the kitchen. George she'd accused of not driving fast enough to the hospital, of not searching hard enough to find her, of drinking when he should have been saving Floyd. When Bridget tried to tell Maude that if it weren't for George, Floyd would have died even more quickly, and more painfully, George said it was all right, he knew Maude wasn't in her right mind, he was sick of wearing a monkey suit anyway.

And now here he stood, dressed in a starched white uniform and worrying a white hat with a shiny black brim in both his hands. He peered behind her into the house, seemed to be trying to look up the stairs.

"I thought you'd gone away," she blurted.

He smiled, turning the hat again. "How could I go away," he said, "when you're still here?"

She bowed her head and smiled, stepping back into the hallway and opening the door wider to let him in.

"But we have to be quiet," she said. "They're resting upstairs."

She could feel his eyes hot on her back as she led him into the kitchen and filled the kettle and lit the stove and shook leaves into the teapot. He kept standing, leaning against the table, watching her. He told her he'd gotten a job driving the disinfectant truck, one of the ones that plied the streets every night sweeping up the garbage and spraying down the pavement to keep away the flies and the germs.

"I thought you were through with driving," she said.

"It's different doing it for the kids, to keep them from getting sick."

She nodded without looking at him, trying to focus on the tea. Her heart had levitated in her chest and had taken to fluttering rather than carrying on its reliable beat. Her arms, her hands, her cheeks, the back of her throat, they were all vibrating.

"You know I don't blame you for that," she said, turning to face him. "For what happened to Floyd."

"I know," he said, casting his eyes toward the ceiling. "How is her ladyship doing?"

Bridget shook her head quickly, handing him his cup of tea. "Not well."

He took the tea but, instead of drinking it, set the cup on the table and reached for Bridget.

"And how are you doing?" he asked tenderly, brushing a strand of hair back from her brow. "You're thin. You look tired."

"It's hard to sleep in this heat," she said, looking away. "I lie there, thinking. . . ."

"I couldn't stop thinking about you," he said, "wondering how you were, how you were faring on your own here, whether you were thinking of me."

"I thought you'd gone west." Now she stared directly at him, feeling as if she were on fire, as if she might burst into flame.

"I was going to. I wanted to! But I couldn't leave you here all alone."

He moved his face toward hers and she thought of that day on the beach, the feel of his lips fitting perfectly against her own, and it seemed as if her mouth was swelling up to meet his. But before they could kiss, Maude's voice came floating down the stairs.

"Bridget? Bridget, is that someone here about Floyd?"

Bridget pulled away and went out into the hallway and started up the stairs, her face flushed, terrified Maude would come downstairs and fly into a fury at finding George there. Maude hovered on the second-floor landing, dressed only in a sheer white nightgown, the dark blurs of her nipples and triangle of hair down below showing through.

"It's all right, Maude," Bridget said, taking her hands, alarmed at how lost Maude seemed. "It's no one."

Maude looked around wildly. "I heard something. I think it was Floyd."

"Floyd's passed away," Bridget said gently, starting to lead Maude toward the stairway. "You know that, Maude."

Maude hung back. "That's not true," she said, her voice rising. "You're supposed to be taking care of him. What have you done with him?"

Bridget's heart lurched. This had happened again and again, Maude roaming the house at all hours, searching, calling for Floyd. Not believing he was dead. Ranting that he must have been kidnapped, was lost in the park, was hiding under a bed.

But this was the first time she'd turned her suspicions on Bridget, seeming to guess at the fear and guilt that ran like a sewer beneath the quiet drudgery and grief of Bridget's long days.

The sense that Bridget herself carried deep inside that she was supposed to have been taking care of Floyd. That it was her fault that he had died.

"Let's go back to bed now," Bridget said to Maude, feeling even guiltier when Maude meekly allowed herself to be led. "You'll have a lovely rest, and then we'll talk about Floyd."

"I'll see Floyd?" Maude asked, her voice rising like a child's. Her hands, despite the heat, were freezing.

"We'll sleep first," said Bridget. "Come with me now. There's a good girl."

When she had settled Maude back in bed and slipped her one of the sleeping tablets left by the doctor—when she'd whispered to Mr. Apfelmann, who sat reading as usual in his room, to listen in case Maude cried out again—she finally made her way back downstairs, nearly forgetting that George was there.

"What was that?" George said, standing stock-still in the same place she'd left him.

"One of Maude's terrors," Bridget said sadly.

"I'm worried about you," George said. "You shouldn't be shut up here on your own with them. You should have some help, some relief. You should get away. . . ."

"I can't leave them now," she said. "They need me too much."

"I need you, too," George said, moving again to put his arms around her.

"They don't have anyone but me," Bridget said, shrinking from him.

"*They* don't have anyone!" said George. "Who do *we* have but each other?"

Bridget pulled free and said, "I have them."

10

Cait, Present

It was the date of her Sunday lunch at Martin's; not actual lunch, Martin warned, but a big afternoon meal more akin to dinner, the way it was done back in North London, where Lynn grew up.

"I can't wait to see you," he said.

She was nervous, riding the F train to the Ninth Street stop in Brooklyn, picking her way along the wet sidewalk, peering at the addresses on the three-story brick houses and brownstones. To try and calm down, she stopped on a quiet corner and called her parents, telling herself maybe she was just worried about her mother's health. Though Sally kept claiming that she was fine, and had several times refused Cait's offer to accompany her to the doctor, Cait hung up as anxious as ever. She had dressed and undressed and redressed for this lunch three times, afraid to look like she was trying too hard and then to look like she wasn't trying at all and then realizing she was restricted to the few items of clothing that still fit her. It wasn't that being pregnant had made her fat, exactly, but that her boyishly lean body had acquired the curves of Scarlett Johansson. Va-va-voom.

Luckily the weather had turned chilly, so that she could hide the gaps in the front of her good white shirt with an oversize cardigan that also covered the unsnapped waistband of her favorite jeans. She definitely should not have worn the boots with heels, but she couldn't help it. She was willing to accept that Martin had gone back to his wife, she was not looking to lure him away, she was certainly not even feeling sexy; but at the same time, she was not dead, damn it. Pregnant, but not at all dead.

And, jeesh, there he was, straight ahead, the vision of him unfolding himself from the top step of his brownstone so startling that she nearly slipped and fell on the sidewalk. It had rained all night, the sky dark and stormy all morning, and then suddenly, as Martin stood up and beamed at her, the clouds broke and the sun lit the street like klieg lights switching on to illuminate a movie set. Cue the married man. Cue the pregnant girlfriend. And . . . *action*.

"Hey," she said.

"Hey." He was grinning, maybe more widely than she herself was. "I wanted to be sure you'd find me."

That was an odd way to put it. "Find you?"

He opened his mouth to respond, but then the front door opened and a woman stepped out: small all over, a straight brown pageboy going to gray, bright red lipstick against yellow teeth. "Martin," she said. "I thought you were going to peel those potatoes."

"I was waiting for Cait," he said. "Lynn, this is Cait, the journalist I told you about, the one I met in New Hampshire on the Riley story. Cait, this is Lynn."

Lynn smiled down at her and said, "Oh, hello. Frightful story, that. Martin seemed more affected by it than the usual disaster story."

"It was . . ." Cait searched for the right word. ". . . shattering."

Cait held out the bright pink roses she'd brought, their scent strong and sweet as air freshener, thorns wrapped in thick paper.

"Oh, lovely," Lynn said, taking them. And then, turning away and laying her free hand on Martin's shoulder: "Martin? Once you get Cait settled, I could use a hand in the kitchen, all right?"

Inside, the place looked like a real house rather than an apartment, more her parents' house than her own tiny sublet. Martin led her on a tour: the yellow-painted front hall, the sepia photograph of his grandparents, newly arrived from Russia; the Tuscan vase bought on a family trip to San Gimignano; a set of jewel-colored glass dessert plates—did Cait remember those?— he bought at a yard sale in New Hampshire last summer. But the homelier artifacts of their family life interested Cait more: a basket piled with a jumble of different-sized and different-gendered shoes, the plaid cat bed, and the blue-and-white dog bowl—evidence of the reality of Martin's life apart from her.

"Let me introduce you around," said Martin, steering her into the living room, warm and fragrant with the smell of a wood fire.

There were two couples there, an older man with white hair and black-rimmed eyeglasses whose name was John and his round-faced, smiling wife, Rosalie, who lived downstairs in the garden apartment; and two women, both named Jen, whom Cait quickly figured out were a lesbian couple, colleagues of Martin's from the *Times*, one an editor in the business section, the other a writer in Style.

Martin offered to get Cait a drink, which she refused on the excuse that it was so early in the day, and then when he retreated to the kitchen to help Lynn, Cait busied herself with small talk: Where do you live and what do you do and what is that like?

Why did I come here? was the question that was looping through Cait's mind, though of course she knew why: to get a look at the wife, the house, the kids, the life, to make it more real and so to help herself forget Martin, or the possibility of him.

If I have this baby, she thought, he will never know his father. Or her father.

As Cait did not know her own father.

This was a new notion, the idea of the father. It had always been easy enough to posit a biological mother, the one who had definitely been there, who had decided to give birth to Cait and then had decided to give Cait away.

But a father, a man with an actual life, a voice, a family, a body so much more substantial than a sperm—this was something she had never seriously considered until now. That not only was she missing one parent, she was missing two.

"Shrimp?"

It was Lynn, gripping a silver tray piled with big pink

shrimp. Cait was suddenly starving, a normal state these days, and gratefully helped herself to two of the shrimp and a cocktail napkin.

Lynn flashed a smile and moved on. Does she know? Cait wondered. No, she couldn't possibly know. What kind of woman would knowingly invite her husband's lover for Sunday lunch?

"Are you sure I can't get you a drink?" Martin said, coming up behind her. "Whisky, maybe?"

Though his veiled reference to their night together made her squirm, she smiled at him. "I'm good with club soda."

"So, Cait," he said. "How are you?"

"I'm great. Fine."

"Are you working on the Riley story?"

"I finished that one. Now I'm doing something else."

"Oh, really? What?"

Rosalie had joined them now and was politely listening to their conversation.

Cait took a deep breath, addressing Rosalie along with Martin. "It's kind of a personal story and a how-to. I'm adopted, you see, and I've decided to look for my birth mother."

"Wow," said Martin. "You didn't mention that when we met."

We got distracted, Cait thought. We got distracted by our urgent need to fuck each other's brains out.

She nodded at Rosalie, struggling to keep a placid look on her face. "I was adopted at birth and I've never tried to find my birth mother until now."

"Do you know anything about her?" Rosalie asked, peering up at Cait. "Was she Hispanic, maybe? Middle Eastern?"

"I don't know anything at all," Cait told her. "My parents—I mean, my adoptive parents—don't seem to know much, either. So I'm not sure where to start."

"You know, I think Jen did a story about this," Martin said, reaching out to tap the taller, fairer half of the lesbian couple. "Jenny K. Didn't you do a story last year about a kid who'd been adopted?"

Jenny looked distant for a moment, and then her eyes lit up. "That's right. That kid in Long Island who it turned out lived around the corner from his birth mother. She was his history teacher!"

"No," Rosalie said.

"Yeah, it was pretty amazing. Neither of them had any idea."

"How did they figure it out?" Cait asked, thinking of her own neighbors, her own high school teachers, none of whom she could imagine as a genetic relative.

"The kid had some kind of rare disease—nothing life-threatening, but hard to treat—and he had all these genetic tests done, which made him curious about his background. His parents helped him, hired a detective to track the birth mother down."

"Couldn't the adoption agency put them in touch?" Cait asked.

She'd been trying, and failing, to find the Catholic Social Services Agency her father had mentioned, and had also tried every other agency she could find with "Catholic" in the title, striking out every time.

"If it's a closed adoption, as most of them were before the last decade, all the records would be sealed and the agency wouldn't give you any information. In fact, the original birth certificate is basically impossible to get, even if you petition the court. If a birth mother doesn't want to be found, it's really difficult to find her."

Cait's heart sank. She'd been assuming all along that the biggest roadblock was her own desire to connect. Once she wanted to find her birth mother, she always figured, she could, especially given her reporting skills. It had never occurred to her that it might not be possible.

"So, who was this detective your people hired?" Cait asked.

"He was someone who specializes in this," Jen said. "Really great guy. I could try and dig out his contact information."

"I'd be grateful," Cait said.

"You can give it to me and I'll pass it on to Cait," Martin said, touching Cait's hand, an electric shock from which Cait recoiled.

Jen grinned at him and then at Cait. "Of course. Awesome."

She knows, Cait thought suddenly. He's told her about me.

The room shifted as Cait realized that she was being checked out at least as thoroughly as she was checking out Lynn.

Lynn appeared from the kitchen, a fresh coat of bright lipstick on her mouth and a martini glass edged in red in her hand. For the first time since figuring out she was pregnant, Cait craved a drink. It would make all this feeling—this jealousy, this competitiveness, this self-consciousness, this yearning—so much more bearable. The old Cait, the nonpregnant Cait, would have gotten sloshed as quickly and efficiently as possible, guzzling single malt or gin, hold the vermouth and I'll have that olive for dinner. But as relieved as she would have felt to sink into oblivion, Cait was glad her circumstances forced her to be here now. To feel what she was really feeling.

And what she was feeling was that she wished that she'd never told Martin she didn't want to see him again. Had never urged him to make things work with his wife. Their mutual biology was obviously insisting on bonding them. Why couldn't Cait be as smart as her own eggs?

"So, Cait," said Lynn, "I hear you're a globe-trotting journalist." She had that British way of wrapping words in irony, so that "globe-trotting journalist" sounded like "pretentious phony."

"Well, something like that."

"Heading off somewhere again soon?" Lynn narrowed her eyes.

Does she suspect? Cait wondered. But no. Lynn was just being curious. Or pretending to be curious. A good hostess.

"I'm staying in New York for the moment. What about you, Lynn? What do you do?"

"Totally boring," Lynn said. From the pocket of her full skirt, she took a plastic facsimile of a cigarette and stuck it in her mouth, sucking. "Psychotherapist. I sit around all day and listen to people's problems."

Would I dislike her so much, Cait wondered, if I didn't hate her? It definitely cheered her up to believe she would.

"But you get to spend August at the beach," Cait said.

The French doors leading out to the garden banged open and in stomped an overgrown-looking boy with a mop of dark hair and a hangdog look, wearing very muddy sneakers.

"Noah, close the door, it's freezing in here! Honestly." Lynn hurried over to attend to her son and Cait watched them, trying not to look like she was watching them. Lynn took the boy's dirty shoes and then directed him toward the kitchen, probably to wash up. He looked so much like his father, the same brand of handsome.

Is that what Cait had to look forward to? A lifetime of gazing into a miniature facsimile of Martin's face?

"Hey, Cait."

It was him again. That voice.

"I want to introduce you to my daughter."

Cait spun around to find herself face-to-face with a girl nearly her own height, with the broad shoulders and strong handshake of an athlete. Field hockey and lacrosse, she remembered Martin telling her.

"Natalie," Cait said. "You're a sports star, your dad says. And a scholar, too."

Natalie laughed delightedly but did not seem surprised. "Oh, Dad. Always bragging on me."

Cait asked Natalie where she wanted to go to college, and the girl began rattling away, Martin beaming appreciatively at her side, comparing the advantages of NYU, which was so cool but too close to home, with Middlebury: she worried whether the town was too small. . . .

"Natalie wants to be a writer," Martin cut in.

"But not like what dad does. Creative writing. Like for TV."

The girl's teeth were so white and even, Cait noticed, her laugh rich and unself-conscious. She seemed to have taken the best of her father—his thick chestnut hair and his height, his facility with words—and yet emerged fully herself, the kind of wholesome, intelligent, strong, and all-around lovely girl that any mother would be thrilled to call her own.

Cait nodded as Natalie continued to debate the merits of various colleges, but she was caught up in wondering whether

her own daughter, if this baby was a girl, if she had this baby at all, would be as lovely as Natalie. Imagining the invisible constellation of cells as a strong, smart, engaged, gorgeous young woman made Cait feel absolutely that she must have this child. Not only that she must have it but that she wanted to have it, and that she wanted to have it with Martin, that she wanted all of this: the man, the marriage, the house, the children, the life.

And then she saw Martin looking at his daughter, smiling, laying a hand on her shoulder, so much love on his face, reminding Cait of . . . no, not of the way he had looked at her when they were together in New Hampshire, but of her own father, how proud he'd always been, how much adoration she'd always felt, looking at him looking back at her.

"Nat!" It was Lynn, calling from the kitchen. "Can you give me a hand?"

Natalie vanished, leaving Cait alone with Martin, the air all at once dense between them, as if the heat they'd experienced in New Hampshire had suddenly been flipped back on. Something that made him different, better than most other men, Cait thought, was his ability to focus completely on a woman, as if there was nowhere he'd rather be than with her, and nothing he'd rather be talking about, including himself.

He brought the beer bottle he was holding to his lips and that's when Cait noticed that his hand, his entire arm, was trembling. He was nervous, she realized. He was standing here in his own living room, surrounded by his family and friends and all his possessions, and he was a lot more nervous than she was.

He took a sip of his beer and lowered his head toward her. "I miss you so much," he said, his voice too soft for anyone else to hear.

It was all she could do to keep from flinging her arms around him, or was it slapping him, or was it kissing him, or was it running out the door screaming? Or maybe she only wanted to tell him that she missed him, too.

But then John moved in to ask Cait where she lived, and Noah tossed a basketball over the guests' heads to his father, and Lynn appeared in the archway to the dining room, calling them all in to lunch. Cait floated toward the dining room, thinking only of where she was going to sit, hoping it wouldn't be next to Lynn. Then she stopped cold in the archway.

She didn't know how she hadn't picked out the smell before. Maybe the roses she'd brought, sending out their perfume now from the blue vase in the center of a table, had masked it. But there on their plates, one on each of the scallop-edged ironstone plates, sat a . . . well, not a chicken, but some small bird—quail, maybe, or Cornish hen—grilled to perfection and emitting the subtle scent that had come to make Cait violently ill.

Just sit down, she told herself. You've come this far, you've made it through everything else, you can get through the eating of . . . not a chicken! It probably tastes nothing *like* chicken!

But the instant she took another step, she knew it was no good. Her heart began racing, cold sweat springing up under her arms, her breakfast bagel and grapefruit and even the club soda she'd just swallowed already rising in her throat.

"I'm sorry," she blurted, swerving back into the living room and banging out the French doors onto the deck. She'd just managed to stumble down the wooden steps and a few feet across the soggy grass when she hurled straight down into the golden leaves and dried bluish flowers of a hydrangea bush. Its few bare stalks stabbed threateningly at her eyes as she bent over again and again until her throat was scorched and she felt that everything inside her had been emptied out. Everything but the one thing she might have wished to be emptied.

She straightened and drew in a deep breath, and that was when she saw them: all the guests and the entire family gathered on the deck, as if for a snapshot.

"Are you okay?" Martin finally ventured, taking a step toward her.

I'm fine, she thought of saying. I'm just pregnant, with your child, who will certainly be as beautiful and intelligent and lovely as the children who are here today. Come away with me and be my love and let's raise it together.

But how could she ask him to leave this place, to which he was as rooted as the dog bowl, as the portrait of the ancestors? How could she ask him to leave these people, who already loved him as much as she might ever hope to?

"Just a bug," she called. "I'm so sorry, but could you call me a taxi?"

11

Billie, 1976

On the day before July fourth, Billie sat on the train rumbling across the Manhattan Bridge, dressed in a pink-flowered sundress of her grandmother's from the 1950s, her pink Chuck Taylor high-tops on her feet. Her grandmother had been horrified by her footwear choice but had not liked the glitter-embedded rubber fisherman sandals, Billie's only other option, any better.

"Let me buy you some nice stilettos," she'd moaned. "Men like the look of legs in high heels."

"Jupe is not my boyfriend, remember?" Billie said, smiling.

"That doesn't mean you shouldn't look your best. Perhaps there will be other fellows at this party."

Billie highly doubted that. She was heading to Jupe's parents' house in Bedford-Stuyvesant for a family barbecue. She'd finally connected with him by phone and he'd invited her out for the holiday festivities, the first time he'd had off from his new job and his prep course for the MCATs.

"You don't want strange men in the street whistling at me, do you?" Billie teased.

Maude's first objection to Billie's going to the party was that she feared Billie would be molested by all the sailors in town from the Tall Ships. When Billie countered that she thought her conservative grandmother was a supporter of the military, Maude responded darkly that it was not the *American* sailors that concerned her.

"They're from all sorts of places," Maude said. "France. Turkey. Albania."

Billie had finally enlisted Bridget's support for the venture and Maude had reluctantly given permission.

"But I want you home before dark," Maude said.

"No," Billie said firmly. "I'm nineteen, not nine. My father never gave me a curfew."

"And I should follow his example? It's not a safe night to be traveling by yourself."

"Then I'll ask Jupe to take me home. Or if it's too late, I'll just stay over at his place. Don't worry. Please."

The windows of the graffiti-covered subway car were open to the hot breeze, the river far below thick with the ships that had converged on the city for the bicentennial celebration. Once the train reached the other side of the river, it dipped underground again. When she got out of the train, Jupe was standing on the other side of the turnstile, waiting for her. She nearly yelped for joy, throwing herself into his arms, kissing him just below the ear and hanging on to his arm as they trooped up the stairs and through the unfamiliar streets of Bedford-Stuyvesant.

All she'd seen of New York so far was the posh neighborhood where her grandmother lived; here the sidewalks were cracked and littered with broken glass, there was no green apart from a few weedy trees struggling up from the pavement, and the only shops were cut-rate bodegas and check-cashing storefronts with bulletproof windows.

Billie clung even more tightly to Jupe as they passed a knot of boys huddled together on the stoop of a building that looked abandoned. The boys suddenly stood and moved apart; there was a flash of light and then a deafening boom as a firecracker exploded at Billie's feet. Billie screamed and jumped so high she nearly knocked Jupe over.

"Are you kids fucking crazy?" he screamed in a voice that was angry, aggressive, as opposed to the cultured, gentle tones she'd always heard him use. "Get the fuck out of here before you kill somebody."

"Make me, you fucking Oreo," one of the kids said.

"Faggot," said another.

Jupe quickened his step, clutching Billie. She could feel her heart pounding and she almost wished she were back safe on Sixty-fourth Street.

"All my grandmother's fears come true," said Billie, laughing nervously.

They turned a corner onto a quieter street, with trees and real houses interspersed with brick buildings. She started to relax. Jupe's arm was still around her and it felt good, like a band of happiness bracing her body.

"Say, I didn't think of this," he said, "but I should have invited you to bring your grandmother."

Billie laughed uneasily, trying to imagine it: Maude in one of her ancient Chanel suits, sitting in the back of a town car, gliding up to Jupe's house. The consternation on her face when she absorbed the fact that every single person in Jupe's neighborhood was black.

"That's okay. I'm nervous enough as it is."

In the warm, sunny Saturday afternoon, there were people congregating on every stoop, it seemed, sitting on folding chairs on the sidewalk, leaning out of windows, and Jupe seemed to know them all, calling out hellos, introducing her as they walked. He had a story connected, seemingly, with every building, every fence, every tree. His parents' big purple house, he told her, was less than a mile from where his ancestors, the freed slaves Jupiter and Phoebe Masterson, a baker and a midwife, settled in the 1850s. Mastersons, he said, didn't like to stray far.

Jupe's mother, Marie, was a big woman, her breasts jutting out like the prow of a ship. Her hair was gray, elaborately curled and pinned, though her face was unlined, her skin much lighter than Jupe's. She led Billie on a tour through the house, pointing out the Masterson family artifacts that seemed to be everywhere. Furniture, quilts, silver, samplers—all these things had been carefully handed down, polished and preserved, but used, too, and displayed. The family still had the original Jupiter's recipe for boiled corn bread with dried blackberries (*Place the corn in the mortar and pound to meal or flour*) and Phoebe's herbal remedies for everything from premature labor to sore nipples. The family Bible resided on a lace-draped table in the living room, inscribed with the names of every known member of the Masterson family, including birth, marriage, and death dates.

"All the names are in there," Jupe's mother said. "Everybody in the family, from as far back as anybody can remember."

Marie indicated that Billie should sit on an orange velvet settee and then perched beside her, gently setting the open Bible on Billie's lap.

"See here," Marie said, running her finger, the color of a manila envelope, down the list of names inscribed in fading ink. "There's the first Jupiter, he's way back, we're just guessing about his years. And here's the original Cato, which is a name we still use every generation, at least once. Cicero, Kizzie, Mahala, Nettie, Eleazar—they sure had some names in those days."

Billie nodded, afraid if she breathed too hard she might turn the ancient paper to dust.

"Here's our boy," Marie said, jumping her finger to the bottom of the page, where Jupe's name was inscribed with his birth date, April 6, 1954. Marie leveled a look at Billie. "And when he gets married, his wife's name and his children's names will go right here after his."

Billie glanced up at Jupe, who winked at her.

"Where are your people from, Billie?" Marie asked.

"I grew up in California," Billie said, "though my father was originally from New York."

"Billie's staying on the Upper East Side, in the house where her father grew up," said Jupe. "I told you that, Mama."

"I forget things these days."

"She forgets *nothing*," Jupe said, smiling.

"Tell me something, dear," said Marie. "Are you one of those college girls, or do you want to have a family?"

"Oh," said Billie, shooting another look at Jupe, not sure of the right way to answer. "Both, I guess."

"I don't know about you young women," Marie said, shaking her head. "Thinking you can have it all. Have *nothing*, seems to me, running out to work all day, then coming home to take care of a man and a house and babies."

"Mom, things have changed," Jupe said. "Men change diapers nowadays."

"Mmmmph. They change one little old diaper and brag about it for the next twenty years. I'll remind you of that when your poor wife is running up and down the stairs and you're lounging back, watching TV."

So they didn't know. As far as Jupe's mother was concerned, he was just an ordinary guy who was going to get married and have babies.

Jupe's brother, Cato, appeared, looking like a younger, shorter, more muscular version of Jupe. And then his dad, nodding a hello to Billie but more concerned with getting Cato to read a column in the *Daily News* about that night's Mets game. A timer went off in the kitchen and Jupe's mother jumped up, scooping the Bible from Billie's lap. Then the doorbell rang and Jupe's older sister Coralie and her husband and two small children bustled in, carrying six-packs of beer and an old-fashioned picnic basket.

The whole family and a raft of guests—Marie's aunt had joined them, and a couple of cousins and their children, and an elderly neighbor for good measure—repaired to the backyard, cemented over and all but filled with two long picnic tables.

The patio was circled with a garden thick with climbing red roses and tomato plants and shaded by an enormous tree that arched over from a neighboring yard.

"It's the tree that grows in Brooklyn," Jupe said, gesturing upward toward the feathery leaves. "Acanthus."

The shade helped cut the heat, still dense in this valley surrounded by chain-link fences and houses and taller buildings and a patchwork of yards that ranged from verdant gardens to concrete dumps. Dogs barked, music—Motown, jazz, salsa—blared, and every once in a while a firecracker went off, followed by shrieks and laughter.

Billie sat still and quiet in the swirl of noise and activity and people, nibbling a chicken leg, sipping at a warm beer, content to watch and listen. Though she had grown up in neighborhoods and gone to schools that were always more black and Asian and Hispanic than they were white, here she was conscious of being different. Her grandmother's house was more foreign to her than this lively city yard, so why did she feel more at home on Sixty-fourth Street? Was it because the house on Sixty-fourth Street *was* her home, a place that was bred in her bone, if not until recently in her experience? If she hadn't grown up with money or surrounded by fine things, there had always been a certain gentility about her father and all the sorry places they lived—her father's watercolors and drawings taped to the walls, books filched from the library piled on shelves, worn Oriental rugs covering splintered wood floors—that she realized now had its antecedents in the grand mansion on Sixty-fourth Street.

Jupe sat beside her on the picnic bench, his arm across her back and his fingers gripping her waist, his thigh pressing against hers. Several of the people there seemed to assume that she was his girlfriend. Despite her protests to her grandmother, she *did* feel like his girlfriend—at least, as much a girlfriend as he had.

Could somebody change? she wondered. Could Jupe get married, have babies, inherit the house and the life that his parents had nurtured and hoped to hand down? Could she become a pampered princess, indulged, fussed over, comfortable with plenty?

Well, why not? Those possibilities seemed more vivid in this moment than her sneaking into classes at Berkeley, than Jupe slinking off for a waterfront blow job. That was the shadow life, as murky and distant as some gaslit past, while this—the loving families, the bright day, the feel of his hand just below her ribs—was real.

And who knew what else could become real? That she should be here, in New York, with these people, had been so unimaginable a few months before that it exploded her sense of what might happen in her future, of what and who she might become. The only thing that was fixed was her sense of adventure; the only thing she believed for certain was that she could be and do whatever she wanted.

The afternoon dimmed and softened into evening, everyone lingering in the yard, torches lit to ward off the mosquitoes and to keep the night at bay. Coffee was passed, along with sweet home-brewed wine and store-bought cherry pie and dripping hunks of watermelon. The music grew louder, the talk and the laughter softer. The children, restless, played beneath the picnic table. Billie could hear them giggling down there, feel them brushing against her legs, and wished she could join them, cozy in their makeshift house as the conversation of the grown-ups buzzed far above, meaningless as the twittering of birds.

Finally, Jupe's father got to his feet and yawned elaborately, which seemed to be a cue for everyone else to stand, too. He ambled into the house, followed by Jupe's brother; Billie and Jupe helped Marie clear the table. Inside, the game was turned on, the lights were turned off; fans whirred in all the windows. Some people found seats on the sofa or stretched out on the floor, while others said their good-byes.

"Should I go?" Billie whispered to Jupe.

"Stay," he said, rubbing her back. "Why don't you just stay?"

They slipped away up the dark wooden staircase and down a hallway that seemed to have as many doors leading from it as in a hotel, all the same gleaming caramel-colored wood with shiny black doorknobs. Jupe's room was the very last one at the end of the hall, messy, clothes and books and magazines strewn across the green-carpeted floor, the bed—high carved oak headboard set into the curve of a bay window—unmade.

Jupe turned on a Victorian-style lamp with a round pink shade and flipped off the overhead light but left the fan turning lazily from the ceiling fixture, sweeping shadows across the walls. He climbed onto the bed, held out his hand. Laughing, she got into bed beside him, snuggling into his arms.

"It's amazing," she said. "The whole big family you have behind you."

"You have a family behind you now, too," he pointed out.

She snorted. "One old lady who doesn't know what to make of me is not the same thing."

He frowned. "Just 'cause I have a big family," he told her, "does not mean that I don't also feel alone in the world."

"Oh, come on," she said. "Why would you feel alone in the world?"

"You met my family," he said. "Do you think I'm like them? Do you think that any one of them understands anything about me?"

"So, they don't know—"

He cut her off. "They suspect. They've probably suspected since I was three and loved to dress up in my mother's clothes. They just hope that maybe I've grown out of it."

"Your mom was talking about writing your wife's name and your children's names in the family Bible."

"Well, I'd like to have children one day," Jupe said. "I hope that comes to pass."

"With a woman?" Billie said playfully.

"Of course with a woman, how else? You know I've always been with girls as well as guys."

She knew it theoretically, but she'd never seen Jupe with another girl, or with a guy, either; it had always been just the two of them wrapped up in each other, and whatever he did with other people, he did apart from her, never talking about it beyond making vague allusions. She was supposed to be cool about it, Billie knew. Bisexuality, threesomes, casual couplings between strangers sleeping beside each other on the floor after a party—that was all supposed to be cool.

The trouble was, she didn't always feel cool.

"My grandmother thinks I'm your girlfriend," she said. "Even though I told her I wasn't."

"Well, you *are* my girlfriend," he said.

"I am?"

"Of course."

In the dim room, his eyes were so dark they looked black, so deep and soft that she felt like she could fall right into them and keep on falling. She loved him, she thought. She'd loved her father but he was dead; she was growing to love her grandmother and Bridget. But right now, the only person on earth she truly loved was Jupe.

"I love you," he said, as if he'd been reading her mind.

She caught her breath. "You do?"

He nodded solemnly. They kissed lightly and then again, a real kiss this time, lips moving more hungrily, licking, biting.

They separated, breathing hard, surprised by their passion.

"I love you, too," she said.

They undressed slowly and got into bed. It was steamy in the room, no air moving through the open window, though the fan sent a breeze over their slick skin. She'd been with boys before but never with anybody she cared about, anybody she loved. She licked his neck, his nipples, the crease of his thigh, tasting salt. He was hard and his penis jumped at the touch of her tongue.

When she sat on top of him and guided him inside her, there was a moment of hesitation, as if he was changing his mind, or his body was changing it for him. They looked at each other for a long moment in the dark room, two friends again, silently communicating the way they might have at any other more ordinary moment.

Do you really want to? she felt as if she were asking.

I'm not sure, she felt him say. This changes things.

I want things to change, she telegraphed back.

Then she closed her eyes, not wanting to read his answer on his face, and after a few seconds of hesitation in which she was sure she was losing him completely, she felt him grow excited again, as excited as she was, gripping her hips as she began moving again and crying out in unison with her.

She fell asleep and when she awoke, the house was quiet, the only sound the *click click click* of the fan circulating overhead. She was lying on top of the sheet, her head hot and sticky against his shoulder. She really had to go to the bathroom, but she didn't want to wake him and she didn't dare get up and try to find it in the dark.

As quietly as she could, she rolled away from him and gazed out the window at the city night, haze illuminated by street-light. They had said "I love you," her first time. What did it mean? Were they together now in a different way than they'd been before? Would he be with her and stop being with men? Did she need him to stop, and if she did, would he be able to?

She'd always hoped, with her father, that he'd stop drinking, stop taking drugs, smoking, lying around doing nothing. When he didn't, she'd thought it was some failure on her part—that he hadn't loved her enough to stop.

But now, she thought, maybe he had loved her enough, and he still couldn't stop. Or maybe he could stop, and he just didn't want to.

12

Bridget, 1916

When the fall came and the weather grew cool and the epidemic passed but still Maude did not get better, it was George who suggested that Bridget appeal for help to Maude's friends in the Heterodoxy Club.

"I used to drive her down to the Village every other Saturday noontime," he told Bridget. "They'd meet above a sweetshop, a whole gaggle of suffragists and artists and lady doctors. They were supposed to be her friends."

He was so concerned with finding a solution to Maude's problems, Bridget suspected, because he knew that Bridget would not feel free until Maude's health improved. Bridget and George had been seeing each other regularly, less often than George would have liked, but as often as Bridget could manage.

"None of those Heterodoxy ladies have come to see her," said Bridget doubtfully.

In fact, the only member of the Heterodoxy Club who'd come to the house was Mrs. Cushman on her mission of condemnation—not an experience that added to Bridget's confidence in the club.

"A lot of these ladies go away for the summer. The club doesn't even meet in August," George said. "But now that they're back in session and the danger is past, maybe one of them would be able to help. Maude always said they were smart ladies."

Finally, Bridget agreed it was worth a try. She had never been to the Village before. It was so confusing, the streets all in a jumble with names instead of numbers, and she was happy to have George's help navigating the way to the address of the club, which turned out to belong to a two-story wooden building on a corner. "Oasis of Washington Square," trumpeted the awning. "Candy, Cigars, Coca-Cola." Above, on a board nailed right to the clapboard, was a hand-painted sign, black on white, that read: "Garret Coffee House." Bridget patted George's arm good-bye and passed through a double doorway lit from above by a round white light like a moon. She climbed the worn wooden staircase, the indigo paint of the treads worn through at the center to wood splintery and pale as skin.

The room was packed with women but was otherwise spare as a country pub, with narrow rough tables and chairs lined up along the walls, bare lightbulbs dangling on black cords from the raftered and whitewashed ceiling, and plain linoleum covering the floor. Pressed tin rose halfway up the walls in a kind of imitation wainscoting, and the only decorations were beer signs that urged, "Drink Me."

Emma Goldman, who Bridget recognized from a party at the Apfelmanns, stood at the lectern at the front of the room. She was as plain as a charwoman, with her gray-threaded hair pulled back into a tight bun and wire-framed glasses perched on her unpowdered nose. She was talking, Bridget heard with a blush, about birth control. Birth control was essential, Miss Goldman said, if women were to be freed from the tyranny of marriage.

"Marriage is a vicious institution," she thundered, "which makes women into sex slaves just as capitalism makes men into wage slaves."

Bridget was mortified yet at the same time felt a tingle of excitement. George had started showing up at the door every night, touching her, holding her, kissing her. The feel of his lips on her neck, his breath on her skin, made her want nothing but more. And she wanted him to overpower her, too, in a way. The idea of slavery, of being forced to open herself to him, was appealing because she did want to, but felt unable to choose it.

"Are there any questions?" Miss Goldman asked. "Any topics for further discussion?"

Hands bathed in sweat, heart pounding so hard she was sure everyone in the room could hear it, Bridget stepped forward and said, "Miss Goldman, excuse me, please, but I have a request on behalf of one of your absent members."

Emma Goldman squinted through her thick glasses at Bridget. "Yes?"

"It's Maude Montgomery, Maude Apfelmann, Mrs. Apfelmann. As most of you know, her small son Floyd died early last summer at the start of the infantile paralysis epidemic."

Thinking of Floyd made Bridget feel braver, more right about what she was saying. She heard her own voice grow steady and stronger. All the women in the room had turned their pale thoughtful faces toward her and were listening with as much attention as they had paid to Miss Goldman.

A hand shot up from the crowd. Bridget saw with horror that it was the awful Mrs. Cushman.

"Aren't you the person I encountered at the Apfelmann's house when I was making rounds for the sanitation brigade?" she demanded. "Aren't you Maude's *Bridget*?"

Bridget turned her face as if slapped at the sound of the derogatory term for an Irish servant. She wouldn't have expected it from someone in this supposedly enlightened club, not even from Mrs. Cushman. I'm here to help Maude, Bridget reminded herself. And I'm not going to let that old biddy stop me.

"Mrs. Apfelmann doesn't know I'm here, but she's having a very difficult time," she continued, looking everywhere but at Mrs. Cushman. "I need your help—I mean, she needs your help—getting back on her feet. I know there are lady doctors in your group, or maybe just a friend, someone who can advise her, who perhaps has been through something similar...."

The women began buzzing, talking to one another. For a moment Bridget had the awful idea that they were only gossiping, that just as none of them had ever visited Maude, no one would offer to help. Then up from the crowd stood a small, slim woman, as lovely as Maude herself, with a thick coil of coppery hair almost the same shade as Bridget's own.

"I am Margaret Sanger," she said. "I was out of the country when Maude's son died, but I lost a child myself last year and I know what kind of pain poor Maude is feeling. I'd be happy to visit and see what I can do."

Another woman stood up, too, her wren gray dress as plain as Bridget's, her bark-brown hair parted in the center and pulled tight at the nape, her hazel eyes behind her rimless glasses lively and unnaturally large, as if they took in more light than other people's.

"I am Beatrice Hinkle," she said. "I'm a psychoanalyst, recently returned from working in Vienna with Dr. Freud and Dr. Jung. Perhaps I can be of some assistance to Mrs. Apfelmann."

A few of the other ladies stood then, too, offering food or flowers or simply a visit. When Mrs. Cushman finally struggled to her feet and tried to raise a concern about the possible lingering contagion in the Apfelmann house, Bridget was happy to find that everyone ignored her.

Bridget was worried about telling Maude about Dr. Hinkle's visit, fearing she would refuse to meet with the doctor, or that she would see it as a betrayal that Bridget had appealed to the Heterodoxy Club for help. But Maude greeted the news that one of the lady doctors from Heterodoxy was coming to see her with great excitement and no curiosity beyond what she should wear.

"You say this doctor has been living in Europe?" Maude asked Bridget. "Then she must be very fashionable."

"I think she's rather more serious than fashionable," said Bridget.

"And she's a medical doctor?"

"She's a psycho—" The exact term the doctor had used escaped Bridget. But Mrs. Sanger, who'd visited a few days before, had explained it in a more down-to-earth way. "She is a doctor," Bridget said, remembering Mrs. Sanger's words, "but instead of mending a broken leg or sewing up a wound, she repairs broken hearts."

"Ah," sighed Maude. "Well, that sounds like a very useful occupation. Now, what do you think I should wear?"

It was the first time that Maude had changed out of her nightgown since Floyd died. Bridget helped her wind her pale hair up on top of her head and do up the buttons that ran down the back of her black silk day dress overlaid with a navy cutwork panel, a nod to the cooler weather. Then Maude sat on the magenta silk chair in the antechamber of her bedroom suite, awaiting the doctor. When Dr. Hinkle arrived and Maude extended her hand to shake the doctor's, Bridget noticed it was shaking.

"Would you like some tea?" Maude asked. "Bridget has made some trifle."

"Oh, no," said Doctor Hinkle. "Although we'll talk, we mustn't consider this a social occasion. I'm not here to be entertained, but to open and heal your soul."

"My!" said Maude. "All right, then. What do we do first?"

"We sit. Actually, I sit, and you lie down. That is how

Professor Jung conducted his sessions, and therefore how I do my own."

"I should lie . . . on the bed?"

"No, not on the bed."

"Perhaps on the chaise?"

She gestured toward the beautiful fuchsia taffeta chaise in the inner chamber.

"Ah," said Dr. Hinkle, "that's ideal."

"Bridget, could you perhaps bring in one of the gilt chairs for the doctor, and one for yourself?"

"Oh, no," Doctor Hinkle said hurriedly. "No offense, Miss . . . Early, is it? But analysis is something that is conducted in strictest privacy, only between the doctor and the patient."

Maude's small damp hand closed over Bridget's wrist. "Bridget is my closest confidante," explained Maude.

"I'm sorry," Dr. Hinkle said gently. "But the analysis can only be effective if it takes place behind closed doors."

"That's out of the question," Maude said, clutching at Bridget more tightly. "Bridget told me you fix broken hearts, but the truth is, both of our hearts are broken, and for the same reason. We both need your treatment."

"That may be," said the doctor, "but then, I'd need to treat you individually. You may share the same grief, but no matter how close you are, in the end you don't share the same heart."

Tears hovered in Maude's eyes and she moved even closer to Bridget.

"It's all right, Maude," Bridget said, giving Maude a reassuring hug but then pulling away. "You take your turn with the doctor now and I'll be right outside in case you need me."

⌁

"She tells the doctor her dreams," Bridget explained to George.

It was a beautiful Sunday afternoon in October and they were strolling through Central Park, the weather crisp and the trees gone all red and gold. Now that the disinfectant trucks no longer patrolled the streets, George was working days, digging the tunnel under the East River for the new subway line between Manhattan and Brooklyn. He hated going underground, he said: it reminded him of his father descending into the mines. But he liked the other fellows and the job paid enough for him to rent an apartment uptown, above an old stable behind a building his friend Nick managed, and to support a wife, a statement to which Bridget never responded.

"Her *dreams?*" George whooped. "And what good is that supposed to do?"

"She says the doctor analyzes them and that helps her discover the source of all her problems."

"The source of all her problems is that her little boy died," George said heatedly. "I could have told her that in two minutes, for free."

George was prone to outbursts like this. He'd go along calmly and patiently and then suddenly seem to explode with some truth that seemed to have been lying coiled in wait within him. Bridget had to manage him, she felt, to keep him from exploding too precipitously, but at the same time she found it thrilling that he had this potential within him, like a powerful horse that might if touched wrong gallop out of control.

"It's more complicated than that, the doctor says," she said gingerly. "There are all sorts of things involved: symbols and memories and troubles that started with her parents and grandparents."

There was more, too, about a man with a white beard in one of Maude's dreams being an archetypical father and a forest representing sexuality and women being in psychic bondage to men; but judging from the skeptical look on George's face, Bridget decided it might be better not to expand the discussion.

They had followed a path through a copse of birches that suddenly opened onto the field that hosted the goat-cart rides. Bridget had been here last spring with Floyd. It was the same scene now as then: three young boys in dirty livery sitting in the drivers' seats of the carts as three other boys collected the nickel fee from the wealthy young children and their nurse-maids or parents waiting for a ride.

They might have been her brothers, these boys. They were Irish, she could tell, with their freckled faces and their sun-burned noses and their long-lashed blue eyes, all too thin, maybe seven or eight or nine years old, only one of the boys, the one who looked to be in charge, approaching adolescence.

The last time she'd been here, in the spring, Floyd had clamored for a ride, and Bridget, hesitating at first because she knew it was the kind of thing that would horrify Maude, had finally relented. When it was Floyd's turn, he'd scrambled up into the cart, bouncing with excitement; but when Bridget tried to follow him, the small boy who was collecting the money stopped her.

"Children only," he said in a reedy voice. "The goats, they's too w-w-w-wee."

She'd started at the sound of this word she hadn't heard any-one use since she'd landed in New York.

The child had held out his hand. "That's five . . . five . . . five . . ." he said, searching for the word, ". . . a nickel!"

Reaching into her bag, on impulse she'd drawn out a silver dollar from the expense money Maude doled out generously and unthinkingly. Leaning down, she'd slipped the coin into the boy's hand.

"That's for you to keep," she'd whispered.

The boy had looked stunned and then, the instant that the cart with Floyd in it lurched away, he dashed over to the biggest boy and turned over the dollar. It was only then that Maude saw the man who'd been lingering at the edge of the bushes. Skinny and pale, wearing rough clothes that looked straight from the old country, he walked quickly across the grass, met halfway by the older boy, who readily handed over Maude's coin.

The man was there now in his stand in the bushes. Bridget nudged George.

"See that Fagan over there," she said, jutting her chin. "He takes all the money the boys get for the rides."

"Crusty bastard," said George. "He probably beats them and buggers them for good measure."

A shiver ran through Bridget and she hugged George's arm more tightly.

"I went after him one day when I was here with Floyd," she told George.

She'd run across the grass yelling at his back until finally, determined to draw his attention, she'd screamed, "*Paddy*."

That got him. Slowly he turned around to face her, a sneer on his face.

"What are you on about?" he said.

"Why are you taking money from those children?" she demanded, before she could lose her nerve. "They're the ones doing all the work."

"I bet he was sorry he'd tangled with you," George laughed, patting her hand. "Mama hen."

But the truth was the man had not been intimidated at all.

"They're my carts and my goats, ain't they? And my kids." He'd snickered at his own joke.

"I gave a dollar to the boy," she said. "Not to you."

"Mind your own business, you uppity bitch," he spat. "You're no better than me."

She wanted to tell George this now, to goad him into going after the man and giving him the beating he undoubtedly deserved. But at the same time she worried it might make George see her the way she believed the man did: as a servant, an immigrant in a plain blue dress, a woman so soft she'd waste a dollar on a strange boy.

But instead of saying anything, she turned away from the goat carts and the field, away from the memory, and back toward the birches. In the dapple of afternoon sunlight coming through the golden leaves, George suddenly stopped, turned to face her, moved his hands up to her hair.

"Darling," he said. "I want you. I want to marry you, Bridget."

He wrapped his arms around her and pulled her into a kiss, long and warm and deep, the world outside his lips and his body fading to a distant fog. He held her so tightly she felt that nothing could ever harm her, and at the same time she felt him hard against her hip, the reality of what he wanted from her made flesh. This was not some pig farmer with a sloppy mouth and a dirty bed, looking for a woman to cook his meals and bear his farmhands. George was a lover, smelling of soap and musk this Sunday afternoon, a man intent on giving her a different life from any she had imagined possible.

But what exactly would this life entail? She imagined more kisses, more ardent embraces, the rapture of a romantic world made for two. But there were other eventualities that went along with that vision that seemed less desirable. She wasn't thinking of the first lovely baby but of the fourth in five years. The work of washing and cleaning and cooking that was more difficult than anything she'd undertaken at Maude's. The reality of life without money or comforts, which she knew all too well from the farm where she'd grown up.

But surely there were other possibilities, too, possibilities she could not now name, or else why would anyone get married? And while life at Maude's could be peaceful and comfortable, a future in service had its dark side as well: loneliness, isolation, the knowledge that whatever attachment you formed to anyone in that life, adult or child, was really a poorer kind of love.

"I think I'll be able to broach this with Maude soon," Bridget told George. "She's sleeping better and she said I can hire some other girls to help with the housework, leaving me to supervise, to be more of a companion."

He pulled away, the stallion rearing onto his hind legs. "Damn Maude!" he cried. "Did you hear what I said? I want to marry you, Bridget! What's your answer now? Is it yes or is it no?"

"It's yes," she breathed, hardly believing it herself. "But I need a little more time. . . ."

"I've waited and waited," he exploded. "Are you just trying

to let me down easy? Because if you don't want me, tell me straight out and I'll go. I'll do what I was planning to do before I met you."

She worked to gather him back into her arms, to calm him, to keep him contained just a little while longer.

"Don't go," she said. "I'll tell her about us and I'll be with you. I promise. Very soon."

13

Cait, Present

The day after the party at his house in Brooklyn, Martin called.

"I wanted to make sure you were all right," he said.

"I'm fine."

"I have that information for you."

"Information?"

"The contact information for the detective. The adoption guy."

"Oh, yes, right. Of course."

His name was Frank Maguire, Martin told her, and he lived out in Jersey. Took off every couple of months to work with orphans in Guatemala, so she might not be able to reach him right away. But he was supposed to be the best in the business.

"I'll call him this afternoon," she said. "Thanks. And thank you for yesterday. That was . . ."

She was about to say "fun," but then she realized that even if she was hiding the fact of her pregnancy from Martin, she wasn't that big a liar. But she was saved from having to come up with a substitute adjective by Martin.

"A disaster," he said. "I don't know what I was thinking. I guess I just wanted to see you so badly, I told myself it would be okay to have you there. And then it was completely ridiculous, introducing you to my kids and to Lynn, which made me feel like a total jerk to everybody."

"Yeah," she admitted. "I figured I couldn't pass up my one chance to see them, to see where you lived, but then I felt badly about being there, too. Your kids are so sweet."

"My kids are lovely," he said. "There are other things I'm not so happy about."

She didn't say anything, figuring it was up to him to volunteer what exactly those things were.

"Lynn and I had a big fight last night," he said.

"Oh," she said. "I'm sorry."

"I told her, Cait."

For a moment Cait thought she hadn't heard him right. She kept waiting for the words to reconfigure in her mind in some other, more plausible, way, but finally she said, "Wait. You *what?*"

"I told her about us. I didn't plan it. I wasn't going to. But then I just did."

"Jesus, Martin."

It had rained in the middle of the night, washing many of the dying leaves off the trees in the churchyard next door. Staring out the window, waiting for Martin to say more, Cait noticed that the church's slate roof and the gravestones and the still-bright grass were all plastered with wet brown and gold leaves, while the light in the apartment had suddenly grown brighter.

"I just . . . When I saw you again, I realized my feelings were as strong as ever," Martin said. "I felt like, whatever happens with you, it was wrong to hide that from my wife."

Cait drew in her breath. "I thought you said you were trying to make things better."

"I thought I was," said Martin. "But I realized I was only telling myself that because I thought I couldn't have you."

"What makes you think you can have me now?"

"I don't," said Martin. "I mean, I know nothing is a given. But seeing you . . ." He let out a moan. "Come on, Cait, don't lie to me now of all times. I felt it from you, too, when I saw you yesterday. At least, I thought I did. That you missed me. That you still wanted me, too."

Cait was silent for as long as she could stand it, not wanting to rush to say something she wasn't sure she meant, and at the same time trying to decide how much truth to tell him.

"I . . . do feel something for you, Martin. Something special. But I don't want to be responsible for breaking up your family. That's no way to start a relationship."

He groaned. "Things weren't good long before you, Cait. Lynn and I, we haven't really been happy since—well, if I'm really honest about it, since Noah was born. A long time. I just told myself that there wasn't anything better for me out there."

"How do you know there is now?" Cait asked.

She knew it sounded provocative, but she had her own doubts: that she could be better for him, that she could be good for anyone. More than fifteen years as an adult woman and she had never been in a relationship that lasted longer than six months. Never lived with someone in an actual house, never negotiated the mundane details like dinner and laundry, never mind child care. She had a lot of doubts about herself.

"I don't know," Martin said simply. "But I think what we have is something worth taking a risk on."

"We don't really have anything, Martin," she said, "except a crush on each other and one night of great sex."

And this baby, maybe, she thought.

To her surprise, he laughed. "Well, that's more than I have with Lynn."

"Come on, you have two beautiful children together. A home, money, years of history. Those aren't things you throw away for a girl you had a little fling with."

"I don't think what we had, what we have, is a fling, Cait," he said, heat rising in his voice. "Really, enlighten me if I'm deluded about this, but I feel something more than that for you. And I'm well aware what I'm walking away from; don't you think that's what kept me here all these years? I love my kids. I love my stupid fucking backyard. But I know they're not enough to make me happy, because I didn't feel happy for years until I met you."

They were both quiet then for a long while. She was through arguing with him; ready, excited to see what was next.

"So, what happens now?" she asked, suddenly wishing he were there with her, that she could put her arms around him and tell him her own life-changing news. *Their* own life-changing news. Soon, she told herself. But not yet.

"I moved out to the carriage house, where Lynn has her office," he said. "I'll sleep on the couch tonight and then her clients will sit there tomorrow and expect her to make their lives better."

"When am I going to see you?" she asked.

"As soon as possible. Tonight?"

She was about to agree, but then, flipping to the calendar on her phone, she saw that tonight was her drinks meeting with Sam.

"I'm busy tonight. I'm seeing my editor."

She could reschedule Sam, she knew, but she didn't really want to.

"Right now?" he said.

"Martin . . ."

"Okay, okay, tomorrow—no, *shit*, Nat has a game. And then Wednesday Noah does. We haven't said anything to them yet and I just feel right now I want to be there for them as much as I can." His voice broke on the last few words of the sentence.

She said nothing, waiting for him to recover himself.

"Thursday," he said finally. "But I don't know if I can wait till Thursday."

"You can wait. Let's take things slowly." Which he obviously needed even more than she did.

"Cait," he said, and paused.

She was afraid then that he was going to say "I love you" and spoil everything. But then he just said, "I'll see you Thursday," and they hung up, leaving her in a world that had spun when she wasn't watching to a dizzyingly new place, yet again.

Cait and her old college friend and now editor Sam were in a groovy—Sam's word—cocktail lounge upstairs through an unmarked door on Houston Street, made out to look like a soigné lounge in old Saigon, or maybe Shanghai, or at least like some hipster Disney version of one of those places. The only light beamed from candles inside small filigreed tin lanterns on the tables; the waitresses, slim and graceful as dancers, wore tight cheongsams. The drinks had names like the Gin-Gin Mule and the Kill Devil; Cait's mistake was ordering club soda.

"Are you sick?" Sam asked, unwinding her bluish-green mohair scarf from her neck, shrugging off her red suede jacket. She was slim and boyish-looking, with dark brows and close-cropped blond hair, the kind of woman other women found attractive but men often mistook for a lesbian.

"Not exactly."

"Getting your period?"

"Definitely not."

"Oh, Jesus," said Sam, her intense hazel eyes boring into Cait's. "You're knocked up."

Cait was glad the place was so dark, Sam couldn't possibly read her face very well. They were as close as two women who didn't have close girlfriends could be: college roommates who'd traveled together and worked together and indulged in a confessional girls' night out a few times a year.

"Why would you say that?" Cait asked, trying to sound casual. But if she managed to hide her true feelings from people she interviewed and from her parents and even from Martin, she couldn't hide them from Sam.

"It's so obvious!" said Sam, leaning in to get a closer look. "Look at your boobs! And I don't think I've ever been with you when you haven't ordered a drink. What's going on here?"

"Nothing's going on," said Cait, ashamed of her own priggishness. "It just happened is all."

"It just *happened*?" Sam seemed shocked. "Are you actually thinking of *having* it?"

"I'm not sure yet," said Cait. "Maybe."

"We saw each other two weeks ago. You didn't give any indication that settling down and being a mom was even vaguely in your scope. What changed?"

Cait felt all her defenses on red alert. This was the real reason, she realized, that she didn't want to tell Sam. She knew, of course, that Sam would disapprove, and she wasn't prepared to do battle over her decision. She hadn't even made a decision, and the longer she kept the whole matter hidden from anybody who might feel they had a right to offer an opinion, the more time she'd reserve to figure it out for herself.

And yet, she couldn't let herself get too upset, given that Sam was only saying what Cait might have said to a contemporary who found herself in the same dilemma Cait was in now.

"Who's the guy?" asked Sam, leaning back in the banquette.

"Just somebody I met. On a story—a journalist." Cait hesitated. "He's married. But it looks like he and his wife are splitting."

"God, does it get any worse?!"

"I know," said Cait. "The truth is, I know it's crazy. I should have just scheduled the abortion the minute I found out I was pregnant. But I can't bring myself to do that. Not yet, anyway. You can say all these things in theory, about choice and life and whatever, but when it's you having the abortion, it's not so easy."

"I've had two abortions and I wouldn't call either of them easy," Sam said. She drained her glass. "But I never doubted they were the right decision. I don't for one minute wish I'd had those babies or think my life would be better or even think I could have given those . . . children decent lives, with no father and a mother who was either working all the time or on welfare."

"Oh, come on," Cait said. "Your parents would have helped you."

Cait had spent one Thanksgiving at Sam's parents' ranch outside Santa Barbara. There was an antique Karmann Ghia in the driveway, a real Picasso on the thick plaster walls, too many horses to name. Even now, Sam was wearing jeans that were artfully rather than accidentally torn—jeans that most people couldn't afford on Sam's Web editor's salary.

"What makes you think I would have wanted their help?" Sam said. "Or that they would even have accepted a child? My first abortion, they were thrilled I'd gotten rid of it."

Cait had always known about Sam's first abortion, which happened when Sam was still in high school. Her mom had arranged everything, held her hand through the procedure, made her milk shakes and watched *My So-Called Life* with her back at home.

"And the second one?"

"The second one was just last year. The guy was somebody I wasn't involved with, I'd used birth control but it didn't work, I felt sad but I didn't feel guilty. I hadn't been sloppy and I didn't want a child."

Cait thought it was almost like hearing herself describe her own situation, if she had been a different person "I can understand why you had the abortion," Cait murmured, squeezing her friend's wrist. "I really can."

"Come on, Cait, tell me the truth: Do you really want to go through with this pregnancy? I know it's wrenching, but the whole thing could be over and you could just pick up where you left off."

"I don't think that would be possible for me," Cait said, recognizing this truth for the first time. She might decide not to have this baby. But she wouldn't be able to repack her wish to find her biological mother or to deny her urge to be a mother herself, to experience the bond from birth with someone who shared her DNA. "Everything's different for me now."

"But it's not, really. The baby, whatever: that's just a fantasy. You have to put yourself first, Cait. What's best for *you*, apart from what's best for this baby?"

"I can't answer that," Cait said quietly, steadily. "It's almost like I *am* this baby." She shook her head, made herself laugh a little. "I know that doesn't make sense. But it has to do with the adoption thing . . . my own adoption. It's brought up this wish in me—no, more than that, this *drive*—to find my own mother, to find out why she had me."

"Wow," Sam said. "That's huge."

"It *is* huge. And I want to love and care for a child in a way that my biological mother didn't care for me. I mean, I know Sally, my mother, did that. But now I want to be the mother. I want to be the one doing the loving, in the way that my birth mother didn't love me."

"But isn't that kind of an argument for adopting one of those kids in Kazakhstan, who are already born and need love and care?"

"Well, who's to say I won't adopt one of those children also? More than one."

"So, what, now you're going to be the Angelina Jolie of journalism? There are a lot of babies in the world, Cait. And new chances to get pregnant just about any month."

"You don't know that," Cait said, crossing her arms over her belly. "We're heading into our late thirties now, Sam. What if this is my one chance? What if this baby is destined to win the Nobel Prize or, I don't know, become president?"

Sam gazed at her for a moment, her hazel eyes somber, and then burst out laughing. "Oh, give me a fucking break," she said. "What if *you're* destined to win the Nobel Prize and having a baby fucks up your brilliant career? Having a kid would definitely change your work."

"It already has. I want to do this story I mentioned to you on the phone, about looking for my birth mother."

"Right. Sounds intriguing. What have you been able to find out?"

"Nothing yet. But I'm in touch with a detective and I'm going with him to the New York Public Library on Thursday to try and find my real name."

Sam looked shaken, her beautiful brows knitting together. "Your real name? What does that mean?"

"Apparently this is how you start, trying to match the number on the birth certificate you're issued when you're adopted with the number in the New York City Birth Index, which corresponds to your original birth certificate and which lists your original name and your birth mother's last name."

"Can't you just get your original birth certificate? Apply through the Freedom of Information Act or something like that?"

Cait shook her head firmly. She'd already explored all this, grilled the detective, trolled online adoption forums, and talked to people who ran adoption agencies. Under the laws governing closed adoptions, which had been on the books since the 1930s, there was virtually no way for anyone, including the adopted person, to get the original birth records unsealed.

"The laws were put on the books by a governor who was an adoptive parent himself and who believed, as most people did at that time, that it was all about nurture. So if you adopted a child at birth, you were as good as his only parent, and who he became would be totally up to you, to your love and care and attention."

"And genetics don't have anything to do with it."

"That's right," said Cait. "Or that's what they believed then."

"So, what do you think of that?"

Cait laughed. "It's bullshit, obviously. As much as I love my parents, there are ways I've always felt different from them—apart from the way I look, I mean. Why am I comfortable talking to anybody about anything, while they shy away from the most trivial confrontation? Why do I love to travel when they think crossing the bridge into the city is a huge deal?"

"Though surely nurture counts for something, too; otherwise, why raise a baby at all?" Sam said. "Just throw it out in a field and figure it's going to grow up to be whoever it's going to be, whether you make any effort or not."

The image of the baby in the field made Cait think about Riley, out in the woods by himself. Was there any way to save a boy like Riley, who had started out with so little? If Cait were to raise him—say, find him and adopt him and teach him and love him as much as . . . well, as much as Sally had always loved her—would he grow up to be smart and strong and confident and happy? Or was it already too late, too late even before he disappeared?

And Cait, with her thick hair and her golden skin, her bravery and her wit: to whom did she owe gratitude for those strengths? To Sally and Vern, for rocking her in the middle of the night and cheering at every school play and crew meet and helping her with her college applications and telling her, every day for every year of her life, that they loved her more than they loved themselves?

Or those thick-haired, golden-skinned, brave, and quick-witted strangers who had, by accident or design, in ecstasy or in tears, created her and brought her into the world?

Would she ever know them, she wondered, and if she did, would it help untangle this mystery of who she was and who she might be? Of who her child might be, too, another generation conjured from a mysterious recipe mixing not sperm and egg so much as effort and air?

Amazing to think she had to decide this minute, or one minute soon, whether she wanted this child, knowing nothing about him or her. What you really had to decide was whether you wanted to have the child no matter what or who it would turn out to be. Or at least, as perhaps Riley's mother had, that you didn't want to not have it.

Having an abortion meant you had to make something happen rather than just let it happen. There were more than a million abortions in the United States each year, Cait knew from her research, nearly a quarter of all pregnancies. But 40 percent of pregnancies were unplanned. If you could simply wish a pregnancy away, how many more women would do so? Would Cait?

She did believe in the right to abortion—would never wish to return America to the days before *Roe v. Wade*. Adoption had seemed like a reasonable recourse back then. Girls were sent away, they gave up their babies, then they pretended it had never happened. Or they pretended to pretend.

"The other piece of thinking behind the old adoption legislation is that birth mothers needed guaranteed protection," Cait told Sam. "The fiction was that they could hide the fact that they'd ever had a baby, put the experience out of their hearts and minds, and go on with their lives without fear that the adoptive parents or the child would ever hunt them down."

"Like you're doing," Sam said.

"Thanks, bitch."

"I know," Sam said, playing with the little umbrella that was rattling sadly in her now-drained glass. "But in terms of the story, I guess you have to wait to see how this plays out— whether you can track her down, whether she wants to meet you, and what you find if you do get together with her."

"You're right," said Cait. "I'll keep you posted. But it's not going to drag on. I have a deadline."

"What's the deadline?"

"First week in November." Cait had visited Planned Parenthood; she'd checked. "Last opportunity for me to have an early abortion, if I decide to go that way."

Sam reached across the table and squeezed Cait's hand. "Good luck," she said. "Whatever you decide. I'm here if you want to talk about it."

14

Billie, 1976

My grandmother said that if I was sleeping with you," Billie shouted into Jupe's ear, "I had to bring you home for dinner so she could meet you."

They were sitting on a bench on the deck of the Staten Island Ferry, speeding across the harbor, the wind whipping her hair up toward the sky. Straight ahead was the Statue of Liberty, which she still hadn't visited, looking more majestic than it did in pictures. Jupe's arm was around her and she sat relaxed against him, relishing the warm solidity of his body against her back compared with the frenzy of sea spray on her face and chest and bare arms.

Jupe laughed. "I can't believe she said that. What did you tell her?"

"I told her you'd come." Billie leaned forward and swiveled

her head to look at him, wanting to gauge the reaction on his face. "I hope that's okay."

Jupe frowned and didn't meet her gaze. But he said, "Of course that's okay. I'm really curious to meet her."

Then he seemed to relax and laughed again. "She sounds so far-out. The sleeping together stuff—that's outrageous."

"Bridget of course rushed to tell her that we weren't sleeping together, that we were just friends. But Maude said that she was old, not stupid. And that I should formally invite you over." Billie hesitated a beat. "So consider this a formal invitation."

"All right," said Jupe. "When?"

"I thought we could have a little party for Bridget's birthday, which is next week. Maude said she'd hire a caterer so Bridget wouldn't have to do anything, but I said I wanted to cook. I've never cooked for them and I haven't cooked for you, either, in a long time."

Not since the dinner she'd made for him and her father, in fact, which seemed like it had happened a lifetime ago rather than earlier that year. Jupe was the person in Billie's life who'd known her the longest now. He was the only one who'd met her father as an adult, who'd seen her home in Oakland, which made her feel more deeply connected to him than she felt to Maude or Bridget.

She was nervous about the dinner, wanted Jupe and her grandmother to like each other, wanted her grandmother to approve and welcome Jupe into—well, into the family. Bridget's opinion was less crucial. Billie felt a frisson of worry every time she tried to imagine the look on her grandmother's face when Maude saw that Jupe was black—at this point, it seemed too late to introduce the fact before they met—but she tried to push that away. Maude would see what a wonderful person Jupe was, how intelligent and kind, and how important he was to Billie. Compared to that, how could her grandmother care about the color of his skin?

On the evening of the dinner, Jupe arrived at the house on Sixty-fourth Street wearing the same suit he'd worn to meet her father, khaki poplin, with a blue oxford cloth shirt and a navy and yellow striped tie and brown wing tips. His hair was freshly cut, tight to his head. He gripped a bouquet of dark red roses that looked as if they'd been cut from his mother's garden, and in the other hand held a bottle of Bordeaux. Billie broke into a smile and kissed him, his upper lip salty with sweat.

"You didn't have to dress up," she told him.

"Yes I did."

She led him up the stairs to the living room, where Maude and Bridget were waiting. The gray silk drapes had been pulled back just enough to let a breeze move through the open windows and cool the majestic space. But the paintings on the walls were still in shadow and so was Maude, her yellow hair smoothed back into a chignon, diamonds the size of chickpeas twinkling in her ears, a soft pink dress showing off her complexion.

If Maude was thrown by the fact that Jupe was black, she wasn't showing it. Billie introduced them, and Maude extended a small pale hand to shake his, smiling coolly.

Bridget, dressed in a light blue silk dress with a moonstone broach at the bodice, struggled to her feet. Billie registered the look of surprise on Bridget's face as she greeted Jupe.

"For you, ma'am," Jupe said, holding out the roses. "Happy birthday."

"Oh, Billie," Bridget fluttered, "would you put these in that silver vase that's on the dining room sideboard? They would look so lovely on the table."

Billie retreated to take care of the flowers and open Jupe's wine so it could breathe, and when she returned, Maude was saying to Jupe, "I'm afraid we live quite in the past here. You'll have to forgive our old-fashioned ways."

"Not at all," Jupe said.

Billie perched nervously on a chair between Jupe and Bridget.

"So, Jupe!" Bridget said brightly. "Billie never told us that you were a Negro!"

Billie groaned and flopped back in her chair.

"She didn't?" said Jupe, turning a frozen smile to Billie. "That's interesting. Maybe she didn't notice."

"Well, we don't notice, either," Maude said, patting Jupe's hand. "As an actress and a singer, I've always had many, many black—is that the word you prefer now?—friends. I knew Josephine Baker, Harry Belafonte. Why, Sammy Davis once entertained my guests in this very room."

"And we've had many very nice black ladies working here," Bridget said, eagerly picking up the theme. "Mary, who's helping us tonight, and Thelma, who used to do the cooking, and, oh, more than I can mention, though they were not all nice, I can tell you that, just like all the whites aren't nice."

Billie had been mortified when Mary showed up to help that afternoon, all dressed in her black-and-white maid's uniform. What would Jupe think about being waited on not just by a maid but a black maid? But Billie had been afraid that making Mary leave would cause even more trouble than letting her stay.

Jupe, Billie was relieved to see now, seemed more amused than perturbed.

"Have you ever had a *white* cleaning lady?" Billie asked.

"Oh, not for years and years," said Bridget. "I think my cousin Kitty's girl, Sally, was the last one, and she didn't last long. White girls think that kind of work is beneath them now. Of course, when I first came to this country, all the cleaners and maids and cooks and nannies were Irish. They used to call us green niggers."

Billie covered her face with her hands and moaned.

"Really?" said Jupe. "I never knew that."

"They also called us The Bridgets. Some of the girls I met on the boat told me I should change my name to something more American: Bertha or Beatrice."

"And I told her that Bridget was a *lovely* name and she shouldn't give it up because of some narrow-minded prejudices," Maude broke in. "I told her, 'Even if you decide to call yourself Bea, *I* will always call you Bridget.'"

Maude looked around the darkening room, seeming pleased with herself, as if she'd established her bona fides as a tolerant person. Billie knew Maude hated both the liberal mayor Ed Koch and the presidential candidate Jimmy Carter, but she hated Ford and Nixon, too. Maude supported the arts, Billie learned from mail and papers she found lying around, giving substantial sums to small theater companies and large museums alike, but she was withering on the subject of welfare.

Billie's father had been the radical, the anarchist, but he'd always told Billie they were better than everyone else, and even when Jupe had visited, he hadn't roused himself to offer him a drink, to prepare a meal, to talk beyond his Black Power rant before retreating to his Kafka. Whereas Maude was actually trying.

Billie stood up. "I'm going to check on dinner," she said, leaving the room before Maude could stop her.

Downstairs in the kitchen, Mary had taken the lamb out of the oven and was spooning the roast potatoes into a bowl.

"Thank you, Mary," Billie said, wishing again that she could send Mary home. "I'll help you bring everything upstairs."

"Oh, no, Miss Billie," Mary said now. "Mrs. Apfelmann, she wouldn't like that. You just go upstairs and get everybody into the dining room and leave everything else to me."

"All right," Billie said reluctantly. "And please, Mary, call me Billie. Miss Billie makes me awfully uncomfortable."

Billie tried to make Bridget, as the birthday girl, sit at the head of the table, but she refused and Maude stiffly took her customary place, Jupe rushing to pull out her chair. Billie poured the wine, despite disapproving glances from Maude, feeling as if she'd need more fortification to get through the dinner. They were all silent as Mary entered the room bearing the enormous ironstone platter piled high with fragrant slices of lamb, holding the plate steady in her skinny arms as they each helped themselves. She arrived separately with the potatoes, then the peas, until she finally pulled the double doors closed to leave them alone.

Everyone exclaimed favorably over the food, though Billie worried that the lamb was too rare, the potatoes overdone, the peas cold. She was grateful, though, that the racial inquiry from the living room seemed to have died down. Jupe remarked that Matisse was one of his favorite artists, better than Picasso in his opinion, which won Maude's agreement. Maude asked Jupe about his studies at Berkeley, what he intended to do in the future, where he might want to go to medical school.

"Of course, it all depends where I get in," he said, "but I might like to go back to the West Coast, to UC San Francisco."

Billie felt a shock run through her.

"I thought your first choice was NYU."

She'd started thinking she might apply to NYU herself, or maybe the New School. She felt certain that Maude would pay her tuition and had already begun imagining with pleasure how wonderful it would feel to be a bona fide student, entitled to ask questions in class and receive grades for her work, while living in a place where she had space and leisure to read all the required books, to luxuriate over the writing of a paper. And maybe at some point she'd move out of her grandmother's house and into a real dorm, or even an apartment with Jupe and some other people. Or just with Jupe. She hadn't remembered him saying before that he was thinking of going back to the West Coast.

"UCSF has one of the best neonatal care units," he said to Maude. "I've been working in a pediatric clinic since I've been back here, and so many of the kids we see were premature, low-birth-weight babies. I want to specialize in early-infant care."

"That sounds like an excellent idea," said Maude. "And the weather is so much better in California than it is here."

"I've never been to California," said Bridget. "I always hoped we'd visit Johnny there, but it wasn't meant to be."

"*Hoped* to visit Johnny?" said Maude. "We didn't hope to visit Johnny."

"*I* hoped," said Bridget, addressing Jupe directly. "I never stopped hoping."

"You are a dreamer, Bridget," said Maude, "while I am more of a pragmatist. It comes, I suppose, from having been on my own from a young age. I joined the Ziegfeld Follies when I was just sixteen years old, you know."

"Wow," said Jupe. "That is young."

"There were girls in the Follies even younger: thirteen, fourteen. Mr. Ziegfeld didn't want to know. But I couldn't have been happier: dancing, singing—that was my life. What would I have done in Carbondale, Pennsylvania? Taken care of my sick mother and a bunch of brats? No, thank you, sir. It was the stage for me."

"Maude was the most celebrated singer of her day," Bridget said. "Her best friend and accompanist was none other than Mr. Irving Berlin."

"I'd love to hear you sing," said Jupe. "Maybe after dinner . . ."

"Oh, no," said Maude. "I gave that up long ago. Mr. Apfelmann didn't like the idea of his wife performing."

"When did you and Mr. Apfelmann get married?" asked Jupe.

"I met Mr. Apfelmann in 1912, a year after I arrived in New York. I was already the star of the show. Mr. Apfelmann sat in the front row every night for the entire run. We married in 1913. He had to give half his business—he founded Apple Candy, you know, I'm sure you've heard of it; we make the very best candied apples and regular caramels, too—to his first wife and grown-up children, who never talked to him again. But he said I was worth it."

"I imagine you were quite a beauty," said Jupe. "I mean, you still are. I can see where Billie gets her good looks."

"Yes, the resemblance is uncanny," said Maude. "Don't you agree, Bridget?"

"I certainly do," said Bridget. "Billie looks almost exactly like Maude did when I first met her."

"And when was that?" asked Jupe.

"Nineteen sixteen. I arrived on St. Patrick's Day. It was snowing, I remember."

"I felt so bad for you that Easter," said Maude. "Newly arrived in New York and too cold and rainy for a proper Easter Parade."

"It was Nora and them that wanted to show off their new hats and clothes," said Bridget. "I didn't care about any of that."

"Well, perhaps you should have," said Maude. "You've got to take care of yourself, wear nice clothes, put on some makeup, do something with your hair. That's what I keep telling Billie here. She's a beautiful girl but she's not making the most of her assets."

"These days girls consider their minds to be more important assets than their looks," Billie said gently. "That has more to do with what I want out of life."

"Of course it does," said Bridget.

The double doors opened and Mary entered the room to clear the plates. They were all quiet while the maid moved around the room, the only sound their murmured thank-yous.

Billie hoped that she could slip out to work on the cake, but as soon as Mary left the room, Maude took up the conversation where they'd left off.

"What things do you want out of life, Billie?" Maude asked. "We never get to have a serious conversation like this."

"I want to get an education—I mean, a proper one. I want to help children, too: girls like me who've lost a parent or whose families are poor."

"Your family isn't poor," said Maude.

"But I was poor growing up," said Billie. "I never knew there was even any possibility of money. I still feel poor."

"But you're not poor anymore," said Bridget, laying a hand on her arm. "Isn't that right, Maude?"

"Yes, yes, of course," said Maude. "I did write your father out of my will years ago, but it's a simple enough job to put Billie back in."

"Wrote Johnny out of your will?" exclaimed Bridget. "You never told me that."

"I don't tell you everything, Bridget," Maude said placidly.

"Well, I don't tell you everything, either," said Bridget, tears springing to her eyes. "Write Johnny out of your will—I can't imagine such a thing."

"He didn't see fit to communicate with us for thirty years. Thirty years! He didn't care to know whether we were dead or alive. Why should I have left him any money? Why, dear Bridget, tell me that?"

"Because you promised," said Bridget stonily. "Because he was your son, and no matter what he did, nothing would ever change that."

Maude shook her head, lifted her chin. "You don't have to

get all emotional about it," she said. "We have a guest here, dear Billie's friend, and of course now that we have Billie everything has changed. Billie, you can rest assured that when I leave this earth, all I own will be yours. And I will give you whatever you want in the meantime. You must go to college, to Europe; you must have every advantage in life that I can provide. Now no more talk about money."

Maude turned to Jupe and asked whether he'd read anything interesting lately, and the air lightened as after a brief thunderstorm. Billie slipped out of the room and ran downstairs to put together her cake. In the kitchen, the oven was off, the air had cooled, all the dishes were washed and dried, the dish towel folded in a neat square over the lip of the big cast-iron sink. Mary was gone.

Was all this really hers? And what did that mean? It was thrilling to think of her college being paid for, of not having to work to buy books, or to buy all her clothes at the Salvation Army. But inheriting this place, and having whatever she wanted, as Maude had said, in the meantime—that was not something she'd conceived of before, and even now not something she felt she understood, the possibilities of having so much.

She felt like a character in a fairy tale, complete with a fairy godmother wielding a magic wand. What was supposed to happen next? She would marry the prince and live happily ever after. And yet, somehow she had the unsettled feeling that she was not that close to a happy ending.

The three cake layers sat already cool on a rack; the frosting, whipped white and fluffy as a cloud, waited in a bowl. Billie whispered a silent thanks to Mary for the help. She was a little drunk, she realized, and exhausted, more from the tension of introducing Jupe to Bridget and Maude than from any work she'd done. Using a spatula, she carefully transferred the first of the cake layers to a white scalloped stand she'd selected earlier that afternoon, slathering the top with frosting and then piling another layer atop that, adding more frosting, crowning the whole thing with the third layer.

But when she stood back to admire her work, she discovered that instead of balancing the layers, she'd cemented all the flatter sides together, so that the entire cake listed to one side. And when she tried to lift the top layer to turn it, she found the frosting had hardened and she succeeded only in cracking off a half-moon-shaped handful. She scooped up a knife full of frosting and dragged it across the top of the cake, but the butter cream was so gooey that it lifted dark crumbs from the surface of the cake and blended them into itself, like a powerful wave churning up sand.

She'd bought a tube of pink frosting at the gourmet shop, with a special tip designed for writing. She'd imagined fashioning delicate roses, writing an elaborate message in flawless script. But instead the letters oozed out fat and indistinguishable, veering off the edge of the cake. "Hopp Birthda Bridg," it seemed to say.

Well, she thought, it wasn't perfect, but it would have to be good enough. She carried the cake up the winding stairs and into the darkened dining room, where she lit the tall white candles she'd bought, eight in all, one for every decade of Bridget's life. They all sang, off-key but lustily, and Bridget succeeded in blowing out every candle but one. No one seemed to notice the place where the cake had broken, and once it was cut, the lopsidedness didn't matter. It tasted delicious; everyone said so, even Maude.

There was a moment then, sitting around the table with the candles glowing, everyone's faces illuminated by candlelight and relaxed, smiling, when Billie thought that maybe everything bad that had happened—her mother's death, her father's, feeling so lost for so long—was all so she could end up here, like this, in her grandmother's house, which surely she would never have known even existed if her father were still alive, with this man she loved but would never otherwise have fallen in love with. Maybe it really was all for the best.

When the meal was over, Maude bade them all good night and went up to bed. Billie said that she would finish cleaning up and insisted Bridget go to bed, too. Jupe helped Billie carry the plates and the leftover cake downstairs and they stood together near the sink, she washing, he carefully drying each plate and putting it away.

"I hope you didn't mind those things Bridget said," Billie said, embarrassed. Bridget was so much more awkward, even after all these years, than Billie's sophisticated grandmother. "I'm sure she didn't mean any harm."

"That's all right. She's just of a different generation. She was really sweet."

"I'm so glad you feel that way," Billie said. "It's ironic, because the one I was worried about was my grandmother, but I thought she was really nice."

"You did?" asked Jupe.

"You didn't?" Billie stood with the soapy plate suspended in her hand, water dripping down the underside of her forearm and off her elbow.

"I don't know. With her I felt something, a little edge. I actually think she's kind of racist."

"Really? You think Bridget was nice but my *grandmother* was racist? I didn't get that at all. I thought Maude really liked you."

"Hmmm," said Jupe. "Maybe I'm just being sensitive."

They kissed good night at the front door, a sweet kiss without heat. On the way upstairs, Billie noticed that Maude's bedroom door was cracked open.

"Billie?" her grandmother called from over the hum of the air conditioner.

Maude was sitting up in bed with a *Town & Country* open on her lap, her hair down, makeup off.

"Jupe is a very nice young man," her grandmother said. "Very bright. Very cultured."

"Thank you," said Billie, relief washing over her. "I'm glad you thought so. I told him I thought you liked him."

"Of course, he's very young," said Maude. "He's got a long road ahead of him with medical school."

"I know," said Billie. "But he's so smart. I have complete confidence in him."

"And you," said Maude. "You're very young, too. There's so much yet of the world for you to see. So many things to do."

"That's true," said Billie, wondering where her grandmother was going with this.

"You and Jupe," said her grandmother. "You wouldn't say the two of you are . . . serious, would you?"

"Serious? We're not planning on getting married, if that's what you mean."

"That's good," said Maude. "He's a nice boy, but I have something very different in mind for you. Now, run along to bed. You did a beautiful job with the dinner and the cake and you must be exhausted."

15

Bridget, 1916

Bridget fixed a special breakfast tray for Maude with all of the favorites she had begun enjoying once again—pink grapefruit, strong coffee with hot milk, burnt toast with butter and strawberry jam—and carried it herself up to Maude's bedroom, trying to keep her hands from quaking.

"You look well this morning, Maude," Bridget said, setting down the tray and clasping her hands behind her back so Maude couldn't see how nervous she was.

Maude was sitting up in bed wearing a violet silk bed jacket that matched the sheets, her blond hair curled prettily around her shoulders. Just tell her, Bridget thought, trying to turn her focus away from the room and toward George, toward how happy they'd be together. Just say the words.

"Maude, I'm giving my notice," Bridget said, distressed to

hear how much her voice was trembling. "I'm going to marry George McLean."

Maude took a bite of her toast. "Why ever would you want to do that?" she said mildly.

Bridget was struck momentarily speechless. "I love him, Maude," she finally managed. "And he loves me."

"Oh, pooh, love," Maude said, letting her toast drop to her plate. "And so you're going to live on a chauffeur's salary instead of in this nice warm house with me?"

"He's not a chauffeur anymore," said Bridget, aware how weak this argument sounded. "He works for the city. And you're doing so much better now, Maude."

"I'm better," said Maude, "but it's you I'm concerned about. You've traveled so far, dear Bridget, in the figurative as well as the literal sense. You left your home in the old country and have made your way into the new world. You've become a modern woman, my dear, with all the independence and strength that is your right to claim. Why would you choose to go back to that ignorant life you left behind, shackled to a man and having his babies?"

"I only want what most women want," Bridget said. "A home and family I can call my own, people to love who will love me back."

"But I love you!" Maude cried. "And George McLean, that big buck, just wants to get into your knickers."

"Maude!" said Bridget. But she was scandalized only at hearing the words spoken aloud. Underneath, she worried that it was true.

"And, well, what's wrong with that?" Maude said, lifting the second triangle of toast and licking the butter off its warm brown top. "You should want it, too! Sex needs to be separated from marriage and babies and duty and all the rest of the things that keep women imprisoned. That's something, if you're going to be a modern woman, that you need to learn."

Maude was holding her delicate buttery fingers stiffly out in front of her. Bridget moved to hand her a napkin.

"You know you can have everything, don't you?" Maude said then. "You can keep your handsome chauffeur happy, and then come home and sleep in your nice, clean, peaceful room here. I'll even give you a nice Christmas bonus and raise, so you can take your time and save your money. Your money, mind you. I'm just thinking of a solution that would be best for *you*, dear Bridget, even if it means that both George and I have to sacrifice a little bit for your benefit."

Bridget was blushing so furiously, she felt like her face might burst into flame. "What's that, Maude?"

"Our friend Mrs. Sanger is opening a new clinic in Brooklyn so all women can have access to contraceptive devices."

"But isn't that . . . against the law?" Bridget stammered. She read the newspaper, had it all to herself, now that Mr. Apfelmann preferred staying in his room with his Carl Sandburg. She knew that the Comstock laws forbade the distribution of contraception. Even publishing information about it was forbidden.

Plus, to the Church, using birth control was a mortal sin, as black a mark as abandoning your baby or killing yourself. But Bridget didn't believe in the Church, had left mindless devotion to its rules behind when she left Ireland, was not even sure she had any faith in God, since Floyd had died. And so the Church's laws shouldn't matter to her, should they?

"Wealthy women get Dutch caps from private doctors and the law looks the other way," said Maude. "It's only poor women who are condemned to having babies practically every time they have relations. Mrs. Sanger wants to change all that. She can help you. I'll speak to her on your behalf and set up an appointment."

Bridget was surprised to find a queue the day she went to Mrs. Sanger's family-planning clinic. She walked right by the place initially, not guessing why all the women, many of them with children, were there. They were poor women, she saw, most of them poorer than she was, with their cracked shoes and their cheap scarves, with their children with the runny noses and their unintelligible languages. There were no other Irish there, from what she could see, no other servants, no one like her.

But she had a special appointment, arranged by Mrs. Sanger herself. Instead of waiting in line, she went straight to the door. A hand pulled her inside and she was ushered immediately to a closet-like examining room, a dark cloth pinned over its high window, and instructed to undress from the waist down.

She was nervous, sitting there holding the rough cotton sheet over her bare bottom, her striped blouse buttoned neatly at her throat but her skirt folded across the back of a chair, her stockings balled up inside her shoes, her step-ins hidden beneath the skirt. At home, with her brothers, she'd dressed before she removed her nightgown, and put on her nightgown before she undressed, and had never seen herself naked until she'd moved to Maude's, where there was a private bathroom with a mirror—and even then she hadn't deliberately looked, and had certainly never examined herself between the legs, never mind been examined there by someone else.

When she told George about Maude's idea—that Bridget should come here and get a contraceptive device so that they could be together now, and then later, when they'd had time to save a little money and fix up their home, they could marry and think about starting a family—he took her in his arms and kissed her, until she was afraid she wouldn't be able to hold him off until she had a chance to visit the clinic. They would . . . do that, she promised him. The minute she returned.

The door of the examining room opened and in walked Mrs. Sanger herself. Bridget was struck again by how pretty and slight she was, with her gorgeous hair the burnished red of the leaves in Central Park. She seemed more like an actress or a singer, someone like Mrs. Apfelmann herself, than a crusader like the stern-faced Emma Goldman or a medical person like Dr. Hinkle.

"Now," Mrs. Sanger said, her voice so gentle Bridget felt herself relax, "before we do the exam, let's first go through the basics of the female reproductive system."

Bridget listened eagerly to Mrs. Sanger's lecture, nodding as if she understood perfectly. Growing up on a farm in a house full of boys, she wasn't totally ignorant: she knew the basic mechanics of the penis, for instance, while some of the Irish girls in town didn't seem to be aware that it even existed, much less how it might find its way to making a baby.

But the timing of the release of the egg in the monthly cycle, the means by which the sperm could be kept from meeting the egg, the precautions that must be taken with each act of intercourse—this was news. Restricting the sexual act to those days immediately after and immediately before one's menstrual cycle would go some distance to preventing pregnancy, Mrs. Sanger said. But to be safe, one should always use a contraceptive device.

Suddenly there was a bang loud enough to make both of them jump. For a moment, it seemed as if it were just one of those city sounds, and Mrs. Sanger picked up what Bridget assumed to be one of the birth control devices, looking like a cross section of a boy's rubber ball, opening her mouth as if to speak.

But then there was another noise, louder this time, followed by a shriek and a pounding at the door of the examining room. Frowning, Mrs. Sanger opened the door and in the waiting room Bridget got a flash of the blue uniform of a policeman.

It all happened so fast. Mrs. Sanger vanished, Bridget scrambled to pull on her skirt, abandoning her step-ins and her garter belt and stockings on the floor, carrying her shoes in her hands. It was pandemonium in the waiting room, with policemen grabbing files and equipment, Mrs. Sanger and several nurses in the clutches of the police, women scattering in every direction. Bridget was afraid that she would be arrested, too, but she managed to slip by two of the cops who reached for her. Then she ran down the sidewalk, gravel and broken glass biting into the soles of her feet, her blood staining the flagstones.

It wasn't until the subway station was in sight that she stopped to put on her shoes and her breathing slowed and she allowed herself to believe that she'd escaped. The whole time she'd been running, she'd imagined the police right at her heels, felt the phantom fingers stretching toward her backbone. No one even looked her way. She was safe.

But poor Mrs. Sanger wasn't safe. Or a lot of the other women who'd been in the clinic. And was she really safe herself?

She might have escaped the police, but she still had to face George and Maude. They were both going to be so disappointed when they heard what had happened today. She couldn't bear either George's impatience or Maude's disapproval. And the truth was she wanted the birth control perhaps more urgently than either of them. For her, it was the only way to keep George close and to build something for herself, too, to buy both a little more love and a little more time, to create a life that was different and better than any she could now envision.

But then, who had to know what happened today? she wondered, walking to the platform, swaying in the train as it rumbled high across the darkening river. They would read about the closing of the clinic in the paper, but that might have happened five minutes after she walked out the door, contraceptive device all safe in her purse. If using birth control was a sin, she wondered, where was the sin in not using it? If, rather than lying about using contraception, she simply did not use it, was that wrong? All she had to do was follow Mrs. Sanger's directions and the instructions in the pamphlet to have relations only at those times of the month when it was safe. Then George would be happy, Maude would be happy, and everyone would get, in the largest sense of the term, what they most desired.

She didn't expect to like it so much, what they did in their bed in George's makeshift apartment; had always heard of it (what little she heard at all) spoken of as an unpleasant business, like going to the toilet, a duty to be borne. The first time, trying to remember what Mrs. Sanger had said about safe times and the basics of preventing pregnancy even without a device, it may have been like that: furtive, painful, blind while it was happening and oozing afterward like a blister worn raw.

But then, as the days and nights went on, she felt her nervousness and her shame fall away. She began to let him see her, and run his lips all the way down her naked body, to put his fingers inside her, even (once) to let him press his huge thing to her lips. She'd been horrified by the dank sweaty smell of it and the tickly hair and aroused at the same time, that he might force it between her lips. Shocked at her desire to taste it.

Involuntarily, she cried out and, misinterpreting, he'd pulled away instantly and positioned himself instead between her legs. She'd been disappointed but open and wet and had bucked against him that time, startling both of them by how completely she'd lost control, crying out so loudly and rhythmically—"Aaah! Aaah! Aaah!"—that he'd wedged the fleshy edge of his hand between her teeth and she'd first sucked it, then bitten down on it, hard, to will herself to be quiet.

"What was that?" he'd whispered afterward as they lay, throats parched, in the dark room, moonlight illuminating the ceiling.

She didn't know. "I love you," was the only explanation she could offer.

After he fell asleep, she made herself get up and dress quietly and slip away, hurrying through the dark streets one block over and one block down to take the El back to Sixty-fourth Street, turning her own key in the lock long after all the servants had gone to sleep and, if she was lucky, sliding unnoticed past Maude's room and up another flight to her virginal bed.

But sometimes Maude was up and called out to her, or awoke in the middle of the night and wanted to talk. That was Bridget's main duty these days: talking to Maude. It wasn't even Floyd primarily that Maude wanted to talk about; sometimes the topic was Bridget herself.

"Your color is high," Maude said the morning after the night she'd cried out. Frost edged the windowpanes and the smell of cinnamon filled the house.

"It's turned cold," Bridget said, hoping that would serve as an explanation.

"I don't think it's cold but *heat* that's putting the bloom in your cheeks," said Maude, propped in her bed, a pink silk bed jacket tied with a pink velvet ribbon at her throat, her golden hair half tamed into a braid that hung over one shoulder.

Instead of answering, Bridget busied herself arranging magnolia leaves, stiff as George's shirt collars, in a vase, taking care to alternate the shiny green and burnished matte undersides as Maude had instructed. Thanksgiving and Christmas were coming, and though no preparations had been made in the house for their celebration, the standing holiday deliveries—the magnolia leaves and the boxwood swags, the fruitcakes and the stationery hand-edged in red ink bright as blood—had started pouring in.

"I'm sure it's fabulous," Maude said.

"What?" Bridget asked, pretending ignorance.

"Your George!" Maude said, grinning. "Come, now. You owe me some entertainment, after I made it all possible."

Bridget was tempted to tell her right then the truth of what had happened. Maude of course knew about the clinic being shut down—it was in the papers every day, with Mrs. Sanger and her sister Ethel Byrne set to go to trial right after the New Year—but Bridget had let Maude believe her own assumption: that Bridget was lucky to be one of the last to avail herself of the clinic's services.

"I don't know if what I'd say would be very entertaining," Bridget said. Talking about the intimate details of her life with George to anyone, even Maude, would be a betrayal of him, she felt. And yet, part of her longed to ask Maude whether it was normal, the way she cried out, her hunger to do things she could not in her conscious mind even allow herself to think about.

"Bridget, put down those damned leaves and come sit here by me on the bed," said Maude.

When Bridget had settled on the satin coverlet, and let her eyes rest on Maude's, Maude took her hands and squeezed them.

"Now, Bridget," said Maude, "I hope that whatever's happening with George, that you're getting some pleasure out of the act, too."

Bridget swallowed hard and managed to nod, wondering if she'd call what she felt pleasure.

"Women are every bit as capable as men of experiencing sexual pleasure," Maude continued. "And despite what the men themselves may tell you, it doesn't have anything to do with having some big thing pounded into you. Women have a pleasure center near the opening of the vagina, and the stimulation of that is what brings them to orgasm. Have you had an orgasm yet, Bridget?"

It was all Bridget could do to keep sitting on the bed. "I don't know," she whispered.

"You don't know! Well, it feels like a sneeze—oh, but much better than that, like a sneeze that builds and builds until you can't stop it and it rushes right out of you. You can practice touching yourself. . . ."

"Oh, I don't think so," Bridget said, pulling her hands away and hopping off the bed.

Maude laughed. "Maybe *you* should be the one consulting Dr. Hinkle. She may look like the primmest little thing you ever saw, but Dr. Hinkle just *loves* to talk about sex. She says that my feeling of liking a larger man and an older man is connected to something that might have happened with my father, something improper, back when I was growing up. That house was so dirty—did I ever tell you that?—and small, so cramped, and he'd come home, I'd be asleep, I don't really remember, but that feeling of something pressing down . . ."

Maude was breathing rapidly, as if something were squeezing her lungs now, not speaking for so long that Bridget finally sat back down on the bed and took Maude's hand, cold as the glass in the window.

"It's all connected, isn't it?" Maude said, fixing her blue eyes on Bridget as if asking for her confirmation of this idea. "That's what Dr. Hinkle says: that all these thoughts and feelings and events are connected and that we're all connected, too, that my dreams and fantasies are connected to your dreams and fantasies, but I don't know if it's true. Did you ever feel swallowed up by George as he presses down, in a way that was both good and frightening?"

Bridget thought of George's penis, the crack at its tip salty against her lips.

"What Dr. Hinkle says is that whatever really happened

with my father is connected to my marrying Mr. Apfelmann," Maude went on. "Maybe that's why I haven't been able to bear to let him touch me for so long, since Floyd died."

"Oh, Maude," Bridget said, thinking that another baby would be a better solution to all of Maude's problems than any psychiatrist or anything Bridget herself could do. "It would be so wonderful if you and Mr. Apfelmann could be closer again and you could have another baby. Just think, a little girl . . ."

But Maude shook her head no. "Did you know that we had a white marriage?" Maude said. "Sexless, I mean. That's why I saw other men. Sex is always so much more exciting anyway when you're not married. It's that illicit feeling, that naughtiness. See, Bridget, I've done you and George both a huge favor to insist you get started with your romantic life right away. Once you get married, you'll never again know bliss like this."

Could that be true? Bridget hoped not. As wonderful as it was in bed with George now, she anticipated it getting even better once they made it legal. She would no longer feel the guilt and shame that sometimes gripped her now, imagined how much more delicious the experience would be if she felt entitled to relish it.

"If you're smart, Bridget, you'll never get married," Maude said, frightening Bridget by gripping her shoulder. "In this state you have to prove adultery to get divorced, and if you can't do that, you're stuck with him forever. No, Bridget, take my advice and go on as you are with your marvelous sex life and your nice home here with me, the one who loves you best!"

16

Cait, Present

Frank, the detective, was a big man in a cheap suit; improbably, Cait liked him immediately. He had a deadpan face and sandy hair thick for someone his age, messier than seemed consistent with his white shirt and tan polyester tie. In the lobby of the New York Public Library, where they met, he enclosed her hand in both of his, well padded and warm.

She followed him down a hallway with a marble floor the color of sand, so highly polished it shimmered. She felt as if she were wading in the clear Caribbean Sea. Frank, lumbering ahead, reminded her of her father, Vern, she realized, also tall and soft, fond of huge bowls of vanilla ice cream, the spoon clutched in a hand so large it could birth a calf.

Ex-cop, Cait figured, as Frank held open the Genealogy Room door, peppered with nail heads like a passageway in a castle. She felt as if she were stepping into a different century. The room had red tile floors and long oak tables and wagon-wheel light fixtures hanging from thick black chains and carried a scent of old paper and leather bindings.

There were double-height stacks, the upper ones on a cat-walk, and tall arched windows that looked out on the trees in Bryant Park.

"We're looking for the New York City Birth Index," Frank told her. "There's one for each year. You have your birth certificate with you, right?"

Cait's birth certificate, like that of every child adopted in New York since the 1930s, listed her adoptive parents, Vern and Sally, and noted the date and time and city of her birth, but mentioned nothing about adoption.

"See that number?" Frank said, pointing to the upper right corner of the document. "We're looking for an entry with a number that matches those last five digits. It might take a while. But when we find the matching number, we've found your original name."

The indexes were kept behind a locked metal grate, two for each year. She expected them to be large ledgers full of spidery handwriting on onionskin paper, like something from Hogwarts, so she was disappointed to find they were regular typeset bound volumes with hard white covers, organized alphabetically by last name. And further disappointed when she saw that though each child's first and last name, birth date, and birth county were listed, only the first five letters of the mother's last name were recorded.

"How will we find my birth mother using this?" she asked.

"I'm not sure yet," he said, passing her the M–Z volume for 1977 and setting the A–L on one of the long tables, opening it to the first page. "That depends on what we find here."

He ran his index finger, thick as a cigar, down the column listing the birth certificate numbers, looking for a match.

"So I just go page by page?" she asked, panic rising in her chest. This could take days. Weeks. And days had already passed since she managed to contact Frank, weeks since the fetus began taking shape.

Frank leveled a look at her, his blue eyes weary although it was morning. "Until this state decides to unseal adoption records," he said, "there's no other way to do it."

She began scanning, learning after just a few pages that she had to stop imagining people attached to the names and focus only on the numbers. They worked in silence for what felt like a long time. Frank had a calm about him, a steadiness, that she found soothing. There was a sense that he was in this with her for as long as it took, assuming she could bear to stay in it herself. Every page she turned, she thought: this will be it. And every page she was disappointed.

Finally she looked up and sighed deeply.

"Why am I doing this?" she asked.

She meant the question rhetorically, but Frank, she could see, was a literal guy.

"My typical client has always felt that she doesn't fit in anywhere," he said, frowning. "Even if she didn't know she was adopted, she says she didn't feel like she belonged in her family. She's looking for a sense of identity, of belonging."

" 'She'?"

"It's usually a she. I'd say ninety percent of my clients are women."

His finger was hovering. She could tell he wanted to go back to searching.

"Why is that?" she pressed.

"A lot of women feel compelled to look for their birth mothers when they have a child of their own, or they're thinking about it, wondering how a woman could do such a thing—give up her baby."

As if on cue, someone at the other end of the table surreptitiously unwrapped a chocolate bar. The scent hit Cait strong and fast; her stomach lurched into her throat.

"Excuse me," she said, hopping up and hurrying away, carrying the book with her. She thought she'd have to leave the room completely but, breathing deeply, she managed to regain her composure. It was ironic that only chocolate, her longtime favorite, and chicken, which she'd never before known even had a smell, should inspire this reaction.

When she sat back down across from Frank, he was staring at her, not the page.

"When are you due?" he asked. "Spring? Early summer?"

"How did you know?"

"I'm a detective. Remember?"

"I don't know if I'm going to have this baby," she said. "That's why I'm doing this. I have to know first who my birth mother was, why she did this, who I really am, before I can decide whether I'm going to become a mother."

Frank looked hard at her.

"How long do we have?" he asked.

"Six weeks."

Instantly, he went back to scanning the numbers.

When she found it, it was like people describe winning the lottery: she had to check and recheck the numbers to make sure her eyes weren't fooling her. The birth date matched hers. The baby in the records whose details matched Cait's was named MASTERSON, BRIDGET. All that existed of her mother's identity was a fragment of a last name, or perhaps the entire thing: APFEL.

Bridget Masterson. Could this really be Cait, before Vern and Sally transformed her into Caitlin Sara Trippel? It must be. Wordlessly, she squeezed Frank's shoulder and pointed to the page.

"I found her," Cait said, breathless with excitement.

"No," Frank told her, shaking his head, his sad-looking face seemingly incapable of breaking into a smile. "You just found a place to start looking."

"Bridget Masterson," she told Martin later in the restaurant where they met, a dark place with candles on the tables and uncomfortable chairs on a side street in Nolita near her apartment. "Do you think I seem like a Bridget?"

He studied her. "Definitely. More than like a Caitlin."

"I always hated my name," said Cait. "When I was a little girl my parents called me Katie, spelled the usual way with a *K*, which made it more confusing. As soon as I was old enough to insist on it, I started making everyone call me Cait."

"Like Cate Blanchett," he said.

She screwed up her mouth. "Not quite. But the fact I was given a different last name on my birth certificate from my mother's may mean that my birth parents were married, Frank said, or at least that they had some kind of relationship."

"That's interesting. Though if they were married, why would they give their baby up for adoption?"

"True. Frank said that would be unusual. But not unheard-of. My father might have died, they might have split up. They might have just been really poor—I don't know."

"So where do you go from here?"

Cait let out a deep sigh. "It's hard to know where to go. I tried Googling Bridget Masterson and there are dozens of them, all over the country and overseas, too, at all different time periods. There was a creepy entry about a Bridget Masterson who died of a botched abortion in Chicago in 1925. The father of her baby then committed suicide by gassing himself."

Caught up in the events of the day at the library, Cait hadn't stopped to think about how this story would sound to Martin. But now she saw he had a strange look on his face.

"That is creepy," he said. "But what does it have to do with you?"

"Nothing," she rushed to assure him. But she felt as if something had been spilled from her bag and now lay exposed on the table between them, and that she might not be able to keep pretending that it wasn't there.

"What about you?" she asked him. "How is everything going?"

"All right," he said. "Surprisingly all right. Lynn is apparently in touch with some old boyfriend of hers."

Cait was surprised. "Already?"

Martin nodded, his thick hair falling over his eyes. "She seemed to take a lot of pleasure in telling me she'd never completely stopped being in touch with him, that she'd always fantasized about getting back together with him, that they'd been sending little messages to each other on Facebook and by text, for Christ's sake. Like a couple of fucking teenagers."

"You sound upset." So upset that Cait couldn't help wondering again whether Martin really wanted to leave his wife and family. Whether he really wanted her.

"I'm not upset that she did it. I'm relieved, as a matter of fact. But it makes me feel like a sap for trying again when all I wanted was to be with you."

"I wasn't exactly giving you a choice about that," Cait said.

"True."

"If I'd gotten on the plane for Africa and never called you, you'd still be happily married."

"If you hadn't called me, I'd still be unhappily married and I might never have found out the truth about her, about me, about anything," Martin said. He reached across the table and took Cait's hands. "I don't want us to be like that. If we're going to be together—hell, even if we just end up being together for a little while—I want you to promise that you'll always tell me the absolute total truth and I'll do the same with you."

Cait sat there gazing into his steady, trusting eyes, feeling the pressure of his hands around hers.

"I'm pregnant," she said.

They kept sitting there, staring at each other for a long moment, as if nothing at all had been said.

"It's yours," she said finally.

He burst into nervous laughter. "I assumed." Then his face collapsed just as quickly back into seriousness.

"I'm terrified," he confessed.

"Me, too. I don't know whether I want to have it."

She felt the pressure of his hands falter against hers, though he didn't look away, and he didn't let go.

"I don't know whether I want to have it, either," he said. "Jesus, Cait, I already have two kids that I feel like I'm putting through hell. I'm freaked-out about paying for Natalie's college, about trying to keep Noah from becoming a total pothead, and now to start all over with a new baby . . ."

He shook his head and finally broke their gaze, looking so shattered she felt certain, for one instant, that she couldn't have this baby, or at least she couldn't have it with him.

"I have a lot of doubts, too," she said. "I mean, I'm going to be able to keep working, but I'm definitely going to have to give up the career I've spent all these years building. You and I, we barely know each other, never mind being prepared to become parents. And I don't even know who the fuck I am or how I got here. How can I bring a kid into that?"

She expected him to say something—to protest, maybe—and when he didn't, she was at first disconcerted. Wasn't he going to tell her that everything would be okay? But he was looking straight at her again, and that steady silence suddenly felt preferable to an argument. She could say what she really felt and he would listen without rushing in to talk her out of it. He hadn't let go of her hands.

"I wish I could just jump into this with you with both feet," he said. "I'm crazy about you, Cait. I wish we were both, I don't know, twenty-eight and starting out, ready to do the whole house, kids, marriage thing together."

His thumbs were moving over the tops of her hands. His

knees were warm against hers. Her heart seemed to have grown so that it felt like it was filling her chest.

"But you're terrified."

"I'm terrified of waking up again with a baby in the middle of the night. I'm terrified of the fevers that make you frantic that they're going to die and of bolting after them into traffic and of all the fucking endless deadly back-to-school nights. I'm terrified of braces and pimples and the age when they tell you they hate you. I'm terrified of having to pay college tuition when I'm seventy."

"Wow," she said. "That was pretty cogent."

"What are you terrified of?" he asked her.

She hadn't thought of it that way before. She had to consider for a long moment. And then, when she knew the answer, she found herself reluctant to say it. Honesty, she reminded herself.

"I'm terrified I won't be able to love it," she said.

He sat there holding her hands, listening, steady as he'd been before.

"Because you know, this Ms. Apfel, she had me, and she couldn't love me," Cait said, surprised at the emotion that flooded her voice.

"You don't know that," he told her, squeezing her hands. "She might have loved you very much and just not been able to take care of you."

She shook her head. "It feels like she had me, and didn't want me, and gave me away. Her own flesh and blood."

The tears came for real then, and she pulled her hands away and worked at wiping them from her eyes, sniffling hard to keep from breaking down at the table. Martin reached over and lightly rubbed her arm.

"So you see," she said to him, when she was back in control, "I can't have this baby, not knowing. I can't have it, assuming I'll love it or want it. Because the possibility that I won't is very real for me."

He didn't say anything, simply nodded, which was the best possible response.

She drew in a full supply of breath. "So, do you hate me now?" she asked. "Do you want to see what I decide about having the baby before you decide whether you want to be with me? Because I'll understand if you do."

He turned his head to the side and looked at her strangely. "Of course not," he said. "Why would you think that? I want you, with or without the baby."

"And you're not going to pressure me—to have it, to not have it, whatever."

"It's your decision, Cait. I hope you'll talk about it with me. And I hope you'll let me talk about it with you. But ultimately it's you I care about."

"Are you saying you don't care about the baby?"

He laughed softly, shook his head, looked down at the table, took her hands again. "I'm saying I care about you," he said. "I love you. I want you. I want to work this out with you, whatever it takes. That might be hard for you to believe right now. But I'm going to make you believe it."

17

Billie, 1976

Billie went downtown to the Planned Parenthood on Bleecker Street to get an IUD. She and Jupe were sleeping together regularly enough now that she had to get a reliable form of birth control. She'd had pills from the Women's Health Collective in Berkeley, but she'd exhausted her supply; and besides, they made her feel sick. There was no question that Jupe would wear condoms; nobody did. All Billie knew about birth control she'd learned by reading *Our Bodies, Ourselves* while standing up in Cody's Books on Telegraph Avenue. Based on what knowledge she'd gained from that, she figured an IUD was her best option.

The feeling at Planned Parenthood was very different from the feeling at the Women's Health Collective. Instead of macramé plant holders shielding the windows, there were bars. Rather than worn couches with crocheted pillows in the waiting room, there were plastic chairs. The waiting room was crowded with women of all ages; when they finally called Billie's name, she was shown into an exam room and handed a paper gown and a jar in which to pee, as opposed to a cup of peppermint tea.

A real doctor with a stethoscope and white coat entered the room, holding a clipboard. She was young, with long blond hair and long red fingernails; she looked like Dr. Barbie. Billie had never been to the doctor. Her father hadn't believed in doctors. When she'd gotten sick, he had brewed herbal teas or crushed baby aspirin in brandy, feeding it to her with a teaspoon. It was better for her immune system, he had claimed, to let the germs run their course.

The paper on the table crinkled under Billie as the doctor asked her in an accent like Archie Bunker's at what age she'd first gotten her period, when her last period had started, how long she'd been sexually active, whether she'd ever had any pelvic infections or venereal diseases. Billie said she was there for an IUD and the doctor told her to lie back on the table and put her feet in the stirrups. Relax, the doctor said, sitting on a stool between her legs, gently pushing her knees apart.

They hadn't done this at the Women's Health Collective; they had just given her the pills. The women there had worn T-shirts and jeans, had sat across from her in chairs and talked—not quite like friends or like mothers or teachers but like emissaries from an enlightened world of womanhood. She had to be on birth control pills, they'd told her then, even though she wasn't having regular sex. It would maximize her freedom.

This hurt, the prodding and the poking. The doctor put something cold in her vagina, swiveled it so that it spread her wide open, drew the spotlight closer so that it beamed up into her. Then the doctor stood and, with the fingers of one hand up inside her, pressed on her abdomen with the other hand, staring thoughtfully at the wall.

"When did you say you had your last period?" the doctor asked.

Billie tried to remember. She was sure she'd had at least one period since she'd been at her grandmother's house, but seemed to recall that it had been a weirdly short one, though that sometimes happened since she'd been taking the Pill. She definitely hadn't had it during the drive cross-country. And before that—it was all a blur of her father's death, cleaning out the house . . .

"I'm not exactly sure," she admitted.

"All right," said the doctor. "Get dressed and wait outside."

"Is the IUD in?"

The doctor studied her as if trying to decide what to say. "Not yet," she said finally. "Wait outside. We'll call you back in."

Billie waited. And waited. And waited. She wished she'd brought a book; Bridget had recently given her Carl Sandburg from Mr. Apfelmann's vast collection, a poet she remembered her father reading. She'd always been able to shut out whatever reality swirled around her and sink into a book she loved, but here all there was to do was stare at the other women while pretending not to.

Finally she was called back in—not to the same room but to the doctor's tiny office.

"I assume," said the doctor, not quite meeting Billie's eye, "that you're unaware of this."

Billie found it hard to focus on what the doctor was saying, whatever it was she was saying, because of her thick New York accent: *yawr unawah a dis?*

"Of what?" she finally managed.

"You're pregnant," the doctor said flatly. "Ten or eleven weeks, it looks like. If you want to terminate, you've got to decide now."

Billie was flabbergasted. "But that's impossible," she said. "I've been on the Pill."

"What pill? Do you know the brand name, the dosage? Have you been taking them every day?"

She didn't know what pill. And she had taken them every day—almost every day . . . except a few times when she forgot. But she always made up for it. Until she ran out.

"Are you sure?" she asked the doctor.

"I felt it," the doctor said flatly. "That's why I made you wait, so I could run the urine test. One hundred percent positive." She lifted a pencil, tapped the point on her datebook. "So, what do you want to do?"

Whaddayawannado?

"I . . . I don't know," said Billie, still trying to process the information.

"You've got to decide. Twelve weeks is soon. It gets a lot harder after that."

"I have to decide right now?"

The doctor hesitated. "Not right this minute," she relented. "But tonight, tomorrow. Don't wait, or it's gonna be too late for the early procedure."

Billie wandered out into the summer street, dazed. She walked without direction until she found a phone booth, but it swallowed her dime without giving her a dial tone. On she walked, through Little Italy and into Chinatown, stopping at every phone she passed, finding one after the other broken or malfunctioning until she was out of change.

She went down into the subway and rode it across the bridge. The day was as hot and sunny as it had been on July fourth weekend, but there were few boats in the river now. She was in shock, like after her father died, but this was different because she felt, oddly, not totally bad. She was aware of her arm curling protectively around her oh-so-slightly rounded stomach, of an undercurrent of pleasure at being alone yet not feeling alone, the way she felt when she was lying on her father's childhood bed reading a book while hearing Bridget working in the kitchen three floors down.

Walking through the streets of Bed-Stuy without Jupe was a more jarring experience. No one spoke to her and the looks she got were not friendly. "Hey, baby," one guy called, making kissing noises. She passed a group of boys walking home from school. One of them reached out and grabbed her breast.

She ran. By the time she got to Jupe's house, she was drenched in sweat and breathing hard. Marie came to the door and looked at her, puzzled.

"Jupe's at work," Marie said.

"Oh."

She knew that, but in her panic to reach him, to talk to him, she'd forgotten.

Marie's face softened. "Come in, sweetheart," she said. "Have an iced tea."

Billie wanted to tell her. Sitting in the kitchen, sipping the cold tea, feeling the ice against her upper lip, tasting the strong bite of lemon, she felt as if she were sitting in the kitchen on

Sixty-fourth Street with Bridget. If she had been, she would have told Bridget. Why had she come here instead of gone home? Marie was kind, like Bridget. And Marie, Billie felt somehow, would be excited about the baby, would allow Billie to feel excited rather than simply overwhelmed and scared.

But she was afraid at the same time that Jupe wouldn't want her to tell his mother. That she needed to tell Jupe first, and leave the rest of the telling up to him.

"Maybe I should go out to Jupe's clinic," she said to Marie.

Marie looked doubtful. "You don't want to be taking the train to that neighborhood," she said. "He'll be off soon. You just wait here for him."

"Is he definitely coming home after work?"

Because he didn't always, she knew. Sometimes he went somewhere else, somewhere he didn't talk about with her.

Marie shrugged. "Should," she said. "You just wait and see."

When Jupe finally walked in, Billie was sitting in the living room, watching the evening news with his mother. His brother had come home earlier and was upstairs listening to music, thumping through the floor. His father was out in the yard, making a fire in the grill for hamburgers.

"Hey," Jupe said, his eyes wide with surprise.

He was wearing a yellow sport shirt with short sleeves, unbuttoned at the neck, and neat khaki pants.

"Hey," Billie said, wanting to rush off with him but not wanting to seem impolite to Marie, as if she hadn't really wanted to sit there with her, watching television. She had wanted to, could have curled up on the couch with her head in Marie's lap, watching television for the rest of her life. But now she felt the urgency to tell Jupe the news bubbling back up.

"Billie here came all the way out to Brooklyn to see you," Marie said, giving Jupe that raised-eyebrow-over-the-glasses look.

"Great," Jupe said unenthusiastically. "What's going on?"

He moved to sit down and join them in front of the TV, but Billie jumped up and said, "Just something I really want to talk to you about. Can we go for a walk or something?"

She saw Jupe and his mother trade a private look, but Jupe said, "Sure, okay. Don't hold dinner, Mama."

They went out in the late summer evening. There were more older people on the street now, lawn chairs on the sidewalks, boom boxes turned down low. She and Jupe didn't speak until they'd turned the corner off his block, as if the street were an extension of his living room.

"I went to Planned Parenthood today," she told him. "They said I was pregnant."

He stopped and stared at her. "You told me you were on the Pill."

"I *was* on the Pill. But I guess I must have forgotten to take them for a day or two, and then when I tried to make up I got it wrong or something. Oh, Jupe. I'm sorry."

She didn't know why she was apologizing to him, except that he seemed so angry. She started crying then, suddenly feeling as if she'd been holding the tears in all afternoon, and after a moment's hesitation he took her in his arms. Her head was pressed against his chest and she felt her tears soaking his crisp yellow shirt.

Finally, when she was quieter, he gently pulled away.

"You know you can't have this baby, don't you?" he said, bending his head down to compel her to look him in the eye.

"Yes," she said. "No. Why do you say it like that, that I can't have this baby?"

"Because you can't," he said. "You're not prepared. *I'm* not prepared. There's no way I want to do this, Billie."

It wasn't that she'd been so sure she wanted to have it. But his negative reaction was forcing her into the opposing corner.

"You said you wanted to have children," she said. "You said you loved me."

"I do want to have children," he said. "Someday. Maybe. Definitely not now."

"But now is when it's happening."

"It doesn't have to happen, Billie. This is something you have control of. *We* have control of. Abortion is legal. It's easier to get one in New York than anywhere else; people come from all over the country to get one here. It doesn't have to be a big deal."

"It's a big deal for me!" she said. "I just lost my father, my mother's dead . . . Maybe I want to have this baby."

Did she? Did she really want to have a baby? It was not something she would have gone out and pursued deliberately. But now that it was here, was she really going to get rid of it? Maybe she couldn't imagine being on her own with a baby, but what about living in her grandmother's huge house, backed by her grandmother's vast amount of money? Or in Jupe's house, for that matter, with his loving family to help.

"Billie, you can't possibly mean that," said Jupe. "You want to go to college, travel, all those things your grandmother was talking about the other night. You're nineteen years old, for Christ's sake. You can't be a mother."

"Why can't I? My mother was nineteen when she had me.

Maude was not much older than that when she had my father, and she'd already had one child."

"Yeah, but look what happened to them! Jesus! Your mother obviously couldn't handle it. And whatever Maude did to your father, he turned out all fucked up."

Billie felt as if he had slapped her. "My mother didn't get addicted to drugs because she had me," she said. "She had problems even before that. And Maude—I'm not like her, either. I'm much more loving, more together. I've been taking care of myself for years and I know I could take care of a baby. I think I could be a good mother."

"Oh, Billie." Jupe shook his head, tears pooling in his dark eyes. He reached out and gripped her arms. "I think you could be a good mother, too. But later. When you've had a chance to do things in your own life. When you're with somebody who wants to have a baby with you."

She stood very still. "You don't want to have a baby with me?"

He looked agonized. He did not let go. "Oh, God, Billie, I don't know, I can't say never, but no, not now, not for a long time. And I . . . Billie, you know that I'm not just with you."

"You're not just . . ." she repeated dumbly.

"I'm not just with you, Billie! I go out at night, without you, to clubs, down to the Village. I meet guys; I have sex with guys, Billie. I meet them in bathrooms, out on the docks, I go there . . ."

She wrenched away from him, holding her hands over her ears. "I don't want to hear about it!" she cried. "I don't want to know about it!"

He grabbed for her arm but she pulled free of him and hopped back.

"You've got to listen, Billie!" he was screaming. "You've got to know! I thought you understood! I can't be just with you. I don't know if I can ever get married. I don't know if I can ever have children. I don't know if I can do that, Billie. I just know I can't stop what I'm doing now."

"No," she said, crying full-out now. "No."

"Hey," he said, exhaling, his body collapsing. "I'm sorry. I didn't mean to hurt you."

He tried to put his arms around her, but again she stepped away. She was afraid that if she let him get closer, she would begin again to believe only what she wanted to believe: that with her, he could become the man she'd known from the beginning that he wasn't.

"I want to be there for you, Billie," he said, continuing to reach out for her. "I want to help you. I'll pay for it; I'll go there with you when you get it done."

"No!" she screamed. "No, I don't need that."

"Come on, Billie. I love you. I care about you. I don't want to leave you alone."

"But you don't want to be with me," she said. "You can't be with me. You don't want to have this baby."

He hung his head. "No," he said at last.

"Then I don't want you," she said, whipping around before she could change her mind and running away.

18

Bridget, 1916

A few weeks after her visit to Mrs. Sanger's clinic, Bridget was relieved to wake up to find her underwear, her white gown, the white bedsheets—even the mattress pad—stained red bright as roses. Thank God. Feeling the blood course out of her onto the rag she'd lodged between her legs, feeling the tug and the cramping that usually accompanied her heavy first day, pulling the sheets off the bed, rinsing them over and over in cold water, scrubbing them with bleach until her knuckles bled, too, all she felt was glad, vindicated.

But now, Christmas Eve, her period had failed to come for long enough that she had to face the truth.

She'd been punished. She'd been punished for Floyd's death and punished, too, for trying to get the contraception. Punished for lying to George and to Maude; punished for having sex with George out of wedlock. Punished for loving it.

George whistled as he bustled around the drafty living room of the carriage house, sawing first the bottom and then the top off a Christmas tree he'd found on the street so it would fit beneath their low ceilings, nailing the tree directly onto the rough wooden floor so it would stand up. Laughing, he draped Bridget's stockings and silk pants on its branches, calling for Bridget to admire his new brand of decoration.

"Stop it, now," she said, snatching the finery from the tree, snaring one stocking in the process. "These are my only extra pair."

"Ah, don't be cross," he said, putting his arms around her, sliding one hand down below her waist. "Maybe Santy Claus will buy you some lovely new things."

"I hope there's no money wasted on silliness like that," she said, batting him away. "Anything extra should be going straight in the bank."

Maude had given Bridget a month's salary as a Christmas present, all wrapped up in a white envelope with a red satin ribbon. Maude clapped her hands when Bridget opened it, then gathered her in a huge embrace.

"I hope you'll buy yourself a gorgeous dress with it!" Maude said. "Or a big posh hat, something extravagant, something that makes you feel beautiful and pampered. You deserve that, my darling."

Bridget had brought the envelope to the carriage house and hidden it in the bottom of a canister of flour, somewhere George would never look. She should tell him, she knew, but it wasn't as if she were really going to buy a hat with it, or anything that wasn't for both of them and their baby.

What if he didn't want the baby? What if he didn't want

her? She imagined him getting drunk after she told him, slamming out the door and not coming back.

Just let us have Christmas, she thought, as if she had any bargaining power left with God. As if there were a God. Leaving George in the living room with the tree, she busied herself with cooking his favorite meal: a roast chicken and the browned potatoes he loved and dressing and gravy and even a cranberry relish.

When the meal was ready, she found him sitting in the darkened living room, snoring lightly, the newspaper open on his chest, a nearly empty glass of whisky on the table beside him. She lit the candles, laid the plates, carried the steaming dishes and platter into the living room, before she woke him.

"Oh," he said when she touched his shoulder. "Oh, this is lovely."

She was quiet, thinking of the clock: they would get to midnight, they would get to morning, they would get through their exchange of small presents and through dinner with their friend Nick and his wife, Concetta, and their family, and then she would tell him.

"This is the first happy Christmas of my life," he said.

She looked at him in surprise. "Really?"

He nodded. "Growing up, there was nothing, just Da drunk and Ma weeping."

They had not had much at her house, either, but there had not been weeping.

"And then on my own all those years . . ."

He shook his head, put down his fork, dug into his pocket, pulled out a small velvet box.

"Here, darling," he said. "This is for you."

It was a ring: not gold, not diamond, but beautiful nonetheless, aquamarine—the color, he said, of her eyes. She was so moved, she didn't bother to point out that her eyes were hazel, not blue, and certainly not aquamarine.

Just get to midnight, she thought, just get to morning; but before she finished the litany she was in tears.

"What is it?" he said, alarm contorting his handsome face. "Do you not like the ring?"

She tried to shake her head to reassure him but could not even manage to do that convincingly.

"Bridget, what on earth is the matter? Are you going to leave me, is that it? Is that why you've been so snappish and silent all day?"

"Oh, God, no," she said. Though part of her thought, as much as she was afraid of him getting up and walking out on her, if she had that option, that's exactly what she might do. Walk out on the baby, on him, on the uncertain future that certainly lay ahead.

"Tell me," he said, kneeling beside her. "Is there someone else? Or is it Maude, that viper, trying to come between us . . . ?"

"No! No, it's not any of those things, George. Oh, God, it's that . . . I'm going to have a baby, George. I'm expecting. I mean . . . we are. . . ."

He went silent and white, his face frozen.

"I thought you said . . ."

"These contraceptive methods are not always effective." Though she felt almost worse about continuing the pretense than she did about its result.

And then he folded in toward her.

"But that's wonderful!" he cried, embracing her, trying to kiss her. "Oh, darling!"

"No!" she said. "No. Oh, George. We can't afford this. We need to put away money, and, well, get a proper apartment. And..."

Talking as if there were still a choice to be made.

"I don't care about any of that!" he said. "I just want you. You and the little one."

"I want you, too, George, but I also want ... I wanted ... so much more. I came all this way ... we both did ... for something better than how we were raised, and now to go back to that ..."

He was looking at her strangely. "Don't you love me, Bridget? Because I love you. I love you and I want to marry you."

She did love him. Despite all her fears, all her reluctance, she did. But was that enough?

It would have to be, that was all. She wrapped her arms around his neck, kissed him half on his ear, half on his jaw. Now she'd told him the truth, at least all of it that mattered, and there was nothing more to say.

She went back to Sixty-fourth Street as planned on New Year's Eve, intending to tell Maude only that she was marrying George and to give her notice—no need to mention the baby at this point and make her news more devastating than it had to be—and was aghast to find the house in an uproar. Maids rushed through the halls, balancing flower arrangements so tall they nearly brushed the ceiling. Ice sculptures, pyramids of champagne glasses, and overflowing platters of food were being ferried into the house, up and down the stairs.

Bridget stood in the front hallway, stunned silent by the preparations, when Maude appeared, flushed with excitement.

"Oh, Bridget! At last you're here! Hurry, now, you must get dressed."

"Maude, I don't understand. What's going on?"

"We're having a party!" Maude exclaimed. "Our annual New Year's Eve party. You know I wasn't planning to have it this year, after Floyd, but then everyone I saw at all the holiday parties said I simply must. Even Dr. Hinkle encouraged me. She advised me to step back into the river of life."

"Well," Bridget said, not wanting her doubt to be evidenced by her voice, "if the doctor said . . ."

It had been such a good sign, they all thought, when Maude had started venturing out of the house for a few holiday events, then a Broadway opening of Mr. Berlin's, and Heterodoxy's emergency meeting to support Mrs. Sanger's poor sister, Ethel Byrne, on a hunger strike after the closing of the birth control clinic. But this party . . . wasn't it going too far?

"Where's Mr. Apfelmann?"

"Oh, that old party pooper, he's in his room and says he's not going to come down. So you must be my escort, Bridget, or I yours, it doesn't matter. I'm just so glad that you're back home."

Home. But this wasn't home. Not anymore.

"Maude, I have to talk to you."

"Not now!" Maude said. "Oh, can't you see how much there is to be done? I don't expect you to serve, of course, but I need you to direct the girls, make sure they put something under the vases so they don't mark the tables. And the ashtrays have to be placed away from the paintings, so the smoke doesn't mar anything. These new girls, they don't know the kinds of things that you know, Bridget."

For a moment Bridget wavered. Maybe her news could wait until tomorrow. Tonight she could help Maude get through this party, and then tell her tomorrow, when she was more relaxed, in a better mood . . .

But no. This was a party, after all, not a funeral, not an illness. Maude hadn't asked Bridget's opinion on whether she should have it. Maude had just assumed that Bridget would do whatever Maude told her to do.

"Maude, I'm leaving," Bridget blurted.

"What? But you can't leave. The party is starting in two hours. . . ."

"I'm leaving for good, Maude. I'm leaving tonight."

Maude stared at her uncomprehendingly. Her hair was already done for the party, parted in the middle and smoothed back into a golden figure eight at the nape of her neck. Her lips opened and two pink patches appeared on her cheeks.

"I thought we discussed this," Maude said finally. "I thought we agreed."

Bridget was already shaking her head no. "I want to marry George, Maude. I don't want to wait. I want to marry him now."

"But that's ridiculous," Maude said. "Why would you chain yourself to that drunken imbecile?"

Bridget felt her breath catch in her throat at Maude's harsh words. "That's not right, to call him that, Maude. He's always been a friend to you, has waited all these long months now for your sake...."

"For *my* sake, ha! For the sake of his own hard rod, more like! And now that he's got you where he wants you, what will you do when he gets tired of playing house and leaves you, dear Bridget? What will you do then?"

The maids had vanished from sight, Bridget noticed, and the footsteps had gone quiet. But Bridget was sure they were listening.

"It's not like that, Maude," she said. "Maude, I wasn't planning to tell you this yet, but the fact is I'm having a baby. I'm expecting."

Maude looked at her, eyes wide and wild, for a long minute in which Bridget felt anything could happen. Maude might swing at her, she thought, might scream, might fall to the floor sobbing. Might throw her arms around her, kiss her, exult in congratulations.

Instead, Maude's face went blank. "I don't understand," she said in a flat voice. "You said you went to Mrs. Sanger's clinic."

Bridget felt her cheeks flame, somehow feeling more caught out in her lie by the confrontation than by the fact of her pregnancy. "I went," she stuttered. "But the police came before I could get . . . I mean, I didn't . . ." She took a deep breath. "I had to leave before I could get the device. I was afraid to tell you. Or George."

Maude's face showed no reaction to that news. "So you didn't get the device, and then you lied about it, and then you . . . I don't understand. Were you *trying* to become pregnant? Did you want to show me up? Is that it, Bridget?"

"No," Bridget rushed to assure her. "Show you up? No, Maude. I did talk to Mrs. Sanger, and she gave me all the information on ways to avoid that, and I had a pamphlet—"

"A pamphlet," Maude sneered.

"Yes, a pamphlet! I tried to do what it said, but I guess I counted wrong or made other some kind of mistake, and it didn't work, and now I'm with child."

Maude let out a breath, seemed to be thinking. "So you didn't intend to get pregnant?"

"No."

"You don't want to be?"

"No. Not now, anyway."

Here Maude finally startled Bridget by reaching out and grasping her arms, Maude's face softening.

"But, dear Bridget," Maude said gently, "you don't have to go through with this. There are ways to stop pregnancies from going any further . . . safe ways . . ."

Bridget pulled back. "You mean abortion?"

The newspapers were full of horror stories about abortions, about women dying and abortionists being arrested, about the millions of babies killed amid outcries for stronger enforcement of laws that made abortion a crime not only for the practitioner but for the woman herself.

"It's not the end of the world," Maude continued in a soft voice. "With a private doctor and a clean surgery and some lovely gas, it doesn't have to be any more bothersome than a heavy period. Women I know—the *nicest* women, Bridget—have done it, some of them several times. Why I—"

"No, Maude," Bridget said, shaking her head, backing away.

"I may not have intended this to happen, but now that it has, I don't want to get rid of it. I love George, Maude. And I'm going to love my baby."

Now it was Maude's turn to look as if she were waiting for Bridget to say that she was only joking. When she seemed to realize that Bridget was serious, her mouth set in a hard line.

"It isn't right," Maude said. "People like you having babies they don't even want, when people like me, who have everything in the world to love a baby and to give a baby, can't have them."

"I wish you could have a baby, too, Maude...." Bridget began.

"No you don't," said Maude, her mouth turning ugly. "I had a baby, and you killed him. You killed Floyd. I should call the police on you. You shouldn't be allowed to have children, to be anywhere near children. You're an ignorant Bridget who's never going to rise from the mud, and your brat is going to be as ugly and stupid as you are. Go on, go on, get out of my house, get out, get out...."

In an instant Bridget was out the door, up the sidewalk, running back toward George. She could still hear the ring of Maude's awful words reverberating through the air, piercing even in the silence.

19

Cait, Present

Cait tried all the tools at her disposal, artfully Googling every combination of "Apfel" and "Masterson" she could think of, throwing "Bridget" and "Trippel" into the mix, poring over the genealogy sites, even going to the New York Department of Records to see if there was anything she could find there—some record of a marriage between an Apfel and a Masterson—but coming away empty-handed. So much information so accessible, yet not the piece she needed to find.

"Apfel" was an unusual name, which helped narrow things down somewhat—but that meant a couple thousand results on the genealogy search engines as opposed to literally millions for Masterson. Plus, "Apfel" might be her birth mother's last name or those might be only its first five letters, widening the range of possibilities to "Apfelberg," "Apfelby," "Apfelfeld," "Apfelman," or any one of dozens of other variations.

In one way, all the Apfel people were easier to pin down than the Mastersons. The Apfels mostly came from Germany and Austria, mostly in the late nineteenth and early twentieth centuries, and mostly settled in New York and the upper Midwest, near Chicago and in Wisconsin. Although some seemed to be Christian and some Jewish, virtually all were white.

The Mastersons, on the other hand, were a vast sprawling group that had been in the United States for centuries, lived equally in the South and the North, the East and the West, in cities and the country. Mastersons had fought in the Revolutionary War and the Civil War, they were members of Cherokee tribal councils and the NAACP, along with Ivy League clubs. Being a Masterson, Cait thought, did not define her so much as it exploded the range of possibilities of who she might be and where she'd come from.

In the New York directory listings, there were an unwieldy number of Apfels and variants and an impossible number of Mastersons. She checked with adoption registry services to see if any birth mother was searching for a baby with her birth date named Bridget Masterson or even Apfel, but came up blank.

She was lost, more lost than she'd felt before she started this search, when she was an honorary Trippel and otherwise only purely herself, a tribe of one. Every answer seemed to yield dozens of new questions, every discovery hundreds of new paths to explore.

Among the most disturbing of the new possibilities was that Vern and Sally had lied to her or at least covered up the truth. Frank confirmed that there had never been anything called the Catholic Social Services Agency. Though her father might just have been mistaken about the name, there were other clues that there were parts of Cait's history that they were hiding. The fact that her birth mother had named her, Frank said, was an indication she had some attachment to Cait and may not have—or at least may not have intended to—give up her baby right away.

She'd heard Vern and Sally's story of getting her so many times that she'd always taken the repeated details—the call that a baby girl had been born, the drive across the bridge, the handover in the hospital—as gospel. If that story was not true, how had they come to be her parents? And if they'd lied about that, what else might they have lied about?

Cait had not wanted to upset her mother—had been avoiding the subject of her search and adoption, hoping she'd discover all she needed to know without having to involve them again. But now she realized she had to go back, had to find out whether the names "Apfel" or "Masterson" rang any bells, had to try once again to get the real story.

She didn't want to talk to them at home again; they were too comfortable there, she felt, too easily defended. And she couldn't have them to her tiny apartment. A nice restaurant in New York? She imagined Vern in his only suit, Sally with her hair freshly curled, wearing her Macy's best, and rejected that idea: they'd never relax enough to discuss anything more controversial than the dessert list. A boat ride? Too public. The beach? Too cold. It was late October already, the leaves fallen from the trees.

At last she suggested they drive out to the little lake club in New Jersey where they'd been members ever since Cait could remember. She'd played on the half-moon of a sand beach as a toddler, learned to swim and sail in the lake's protected waters, gotten her first kiss and smoked her first joint with her friends there as teenagers. She looked forward to sinking back into its unchanging landscape—the log clubhouse, the red-painted wooden floats, the rows of Adirondack chairs beneath the pines—each summer when she visited her parents.

She'd never been there in the fall before, but it was a beautiful day, the place utterly deserted. She'd collected the fixings for a picnic from her favorite gourmet shops in New York—smoked salmon from Russ & Daughters and marinated vegetables from Eataly, apples from the Union Square farmers' market and cupcakes from Magnolia Bakery—and had even rented a Zipcar to transport it along with her parents to the lake. She wanted to be the hostess this time, not the child.

They spread a blanket on their favorite dock, the one that during the summer was always occupied, and she laid out the food. Her parents sat in their beach chairs, Cait at their feet, the breeze fresh on her face, a few fleecy clouds skittering across the bright fall sky. While the sun felt warm on her skin, the water was choppy and looked cold, closer to ice than to a warm bath.

"Are you all right, Mom?" Cait asked. "Do you want a blanket for your shoulders?"

"I'm fine," Sally said. "Dad and I don't come out here nearly enough since you're gone."

"Do you ever think of not rejoining?"

"Oh, no," her mother said. "We know how much you like it when you come in the summer. And Dad still likes to fish."

Martin liked to fish, too; Cait could imagine bringing him here, him fishing with her dad. She'd never brought someone home, someone serious—the very idea had always horrified her—but with Martin, she was actually looking forward to it. She might have told her parents about him now, but it felt like he was several places back in line behind other, more urgent, even more delicate revelations.

"So, how are you feeling, Mom?" she asked. "You said those first tests turned out okay?"

"Oh, yes," said her mother. "Everything is fine."

"That is not strictly true, Sara," said her father. He called Sally Sara when he wanted her to know he meant business. He turned to Cait. "The doctors said your mother has an atrial fibrillation that could be disturbed at any time."

"I'm sorry, Mom, but I'm confused. Are you supposed to do anything special to take care of it? What does that mean, 'disturbed'? Do you need to watch what you eat, avoid exercise, or what? Or is it just stress they're worried about?"

"Yes, stress," her mother said. "I'm supposed to avoid stress."

"You say that like it's some ordinary reason you're supposed to avoid stress," Vern said darkly, "but in your mother's case, Cait, stress could trigger a heart attack that because of her condition could be fatal."

Cait could feel her own heart beating faster at the idea that her mother could fall seriously ill. At the idea that her mother could die. Here I've spent all this time searching for the mother who gave me away, she thought, when I should be spending every minute I can with the mother who raised me.

Like that, her plan to ask her parents more about her birth mother evaporated. It wasn't worth it. They'd told her all they could. She didn't want to upset them for the sake of extracting another kernel of information that would probably prove useless. Whatever her failure to track down her birth mother meant to her decision about having this baby, she'd have to live with that. She and Martin.

A little blue butterfly flitted by, seeming by the millisecond to change its mind about which way it was going. It zigzagged over the water and then along the shoreline, dipping down toward the grass, then up into the trees, without apparent design. It's just following whatever feels best, Cait thought. It doesn't have any sense of winter coming, of avoiding the snake in the brush, the bird swooping down from above. And why anticipate potential disaster, when you might train your energy on seeking a brighter patch of sunlight, a sweeter bloom?

"I was wondering," her mother said, "whether you'd made any progress in finding your birth mother."

Cait thought at first that she might not have heard Sally right, but then Vern said, "See, that's the exact kind of thing you shouldn't be thinking about."

Her father looked annoyed, but her mother was studiously ignoring him, looking at Cait with open curiosity, blinking her placid blue eyes.

"It's okay, Mom," Cait said. "We don't have to talk about that."

"But I want to talk about it," Sally insisted. "Have you found her? Is that why you don't want to tell me anything?"

"No, I just don't want to upset you. It doesn't really matter."

Her mother's eyes filled with tears. "Of course it matters," she said. "I feel more upset by the idea that you don't feel like you can talk to me than I would be by anything you might tell me."

Cait glanced toward her father, who heaved a frustration-laden sigh and turned his gaze to the bare trees on the far shore.

"I've been working on finding her, but with no luck," Cait said reluctantly to her mother. "I did find some names I thought of asking you about. 'Apfel': Does that mean anything to you? I think that's her last name, or at least part of it. And 'Masterson.' 'Bridget Masterson.' That seems to be the name she gave me when I was born."

There was silence on the dock then. Neither of her parents said anything. A fat bee buzzed lazily by; another gust of wind buffeted her face.

"I never heard 'Masterson,'" Sally said. "Did you, Vern?"

"No," her father said, staring at the water, a grim look on his face.

"And 'Apfel'—I'm not sure about that one, either. What do you think, Vern?"

"You know what I think," he said.

"Now, Bridget," Sally said. "I had a second cousin named Bridget."

"You did?" For the first time there was some glimmer of some connection, however tenuous.

"She was my mother's first cousin, older than my mother, came over here from Ireland years before my mother did," said Sally. "Do you remember Bridget, Vern?"

"You had a cousin named Bridget, I saw a movie with Brigitte Bardot; I just don't know what any of that has to do with anything!" Vern burst out. "I already told you everything I think is important, Caitlin. Your mother and I wanted you, we tried to love you the best we could, and I'm sorry if that's not good enough for you."

Cait could only remember three or four times in her entire life that her father had burst into anger like this, and now she was even more stunned to see that he was working hard to blink back tears. To hide his eyes, he bent low and began gathering the picnic things.

"Dad, I'm sorry," Cait said, appalled, moving to try to embrace him. "I know you love me. I don't want to hurt you, I really don't."

"Then why do you need this, Caitlin? If you were a teenager, some messed-up kid, I could understand it, maybe. But why now, after all these years, when you're a grown woman, with a full life of your own?"

The world froze, the unchanged vista of her childhood feeling like a photograph that they were all trapped inside. She could apologize again, tell them it didn't matter, pack the issue back away somewhere deep, deeper than the place she'd kept it hidden all these years.

But was that possible? Even if she never found her birth mother, which now seemed likely; even if she decided not to have this baby—even if she left Martin and once again kissed her parents good-bye and went back on the road—it would not be as that same person, traveling fast with a bag that weighed nothing. Now she felt herself surrounded by so much emotion, so many questions, that she felt as if she might never be free again.

She took a deep breath. "I have to tell you something," she said. "There's a reason I'm doing this now—an important reason. I'm pregnant."

She watched the news sink in for a moment. Her father looked shaken but her mother, she saw, had tears swimming in her eyes.

"Pregnant," her mother said, with feeling. "A baby. Oh, Cait, that's so wonderful."

Her mother moved to hug her and Cait wanted to be hugged, but she couldn't let her news stop there, with congratulations. Her unfolding relationship with Martin, the care they took to always try to tell each other the truth, was making it hard to hold anything back.

"I'm sorry," she said. "It was an accident. And I don't know whether I can go through with having it. That's why I have to find out why my birth mother, whoever she was, had me. That's why I've been on this mission, asking all these questions. I just feel like I have to know."

"Oh, sweetheart," her mother said. "I'm so sorry. But how can you think like that, that you might not go through with—"

"I hope you know we're here to support you," her father said, "no matter what you decide."

"Thanks, Dad," Cait said, laying her hand on his, large and warm from the afternoon sun.

"But we hope you decide to have it!" said Sally. "You have to know how I feel about that—how much I would love a baby."

"I know, Mom," Cait said, taking her mother's hand. "But as much as I want to have a baby for you, I need to know first that I can do it for myself. I hope you understand."

She found herself starting to cry like a little girl. Ashamed, she pressed her eyes to her knees, wrapped her arms around her legs, and gave herself over to the sobbing she knew she wasn't going to be able to stop.

First she felt her mother's arms around her, light, hesitant, and then stronger. And then she was in the shadow of her father's body, enveloped by his massive embrace. How many years, decades, had it been since she'd lost all control and been comforted by her parents like this? She knew it had happened, yet it had been so long ago, when she was so young, that she could not remember it. The same way she couldn't remember crying and being held by that other woman, that unfindable stranger, her other mother.

20

Billie, 1976

illie took to her bed and didn't get out. She kept hoping, on some level, that Jupe would call or show up at
the door, tell her he was sorry, he didn't mean it, he
really did want to have a baby with her, and then . . .

And then what? They'd get married and live happily ever
after? In some ways, when she imagined him saying that, she
felt herself shrinking from the whole idea, not wanting to have
the baby, going through with the abortion, even pulling back
from her relationship with him. They could be friends, the way
they'd started out, and someday she'd find somebody else to
love for real.

Or maybe she couldn't love. Maybe she was unlovable. Her
own mother hadn't loved her—at least, not as much as she'd
loved heroin. And her father, he hadn't found it worthwhile to

stay alive for her, either. What made her think that she could love a child, or that a child could love her back?

But she'd always sworn she'd be better than them, always *had* been better than them. If they couldn't love her enough, then she'd love herself more. She'd learn to cook, figure out her own homework, get herself to school, earn her own spending money. And one day, she'd always thought, she would be the kind of mother she'd always wanted, the kind of mother she'd never had.

Not like Maude. Maude acted like she thought she was a good parent. But she wasn't one—at least, she wasn't the kind of parent that Billie wanted to be. No wonder her father was screwed-up, with a mother like that: cold, self-involved.

It was Bridget who struggled up the three flights to bring Billie food, water, a warm washcloth, and clean underwear. Billie tried to pretend she didn't care about eating, but she liked it that Bridget made the effort and also was embarrassed that Bridget had to work so hard on her behalf.

"I don't feel like eating," she told Bridget. "You don't have to cook anything for me."

Scrambled eggs, oatmeal, chicken soup, raisin toast, and big milky bowls of tea had all been presented.

Bridget felt Billie's forehead with the back of her cool, bony hand, then pressed her lips there, a warmth that beamed directly into Billie's brain.

"You're not feverish," Bridget said, pulling back, looking confused.

"It's just a stomach bug," Billie said. "It's not a big deal."

Finally, when Billie had been in bed for five days, Maude

came up the stairs, her step lighter and more energetic than Bridget's. It was the first time Maude had been up to the room where Billie slept, her father's old room.

Maude stopped in the doorway and looked around with wide eyes as if she'd forgotten it was there: the boy's blue walls and ancient leather baseball mitt, the ball signed by Babe Ruth and the silver-framed picture of Johnny on the pony. She didn't step into the room but instead gripped the doorframe.

"What's going on?" she asked.

Bridget, who had huffed up the stairs behind her, started, "The child hasn't been feeling—"

"I want Billie to tell me," Maude said.

Billie struggled to prop herself up. After all those days in bed, she really did feel weak.

"I'm sick," she began, putting a little croak in her voice.

"If you're sick, go to the doctor," Maude snapped. "If you're not sick enough to go to the doctor, take a pill. Otherwise, a strong young girl like you has no reason to be in bed."

Maude started to turn away and Billie blurted, "I'm pregnant."

There'd been the illusion, under the cushion of Bridget's indulgence, that if Billie didn't confess the truth, it might turn out not to be real. But Maude's hard gaze, her direct voice, the chill of her very presence, were like a police searchlight from which it was useless to try and hide.

Billie heard, from the depths of the hallway, Bridget's gasp. Maude turned slowly back to face her.

"What did you say?"

Was there time to take it back? Pretend she hadn't said it?

"I'm pregnant."

There was a long silence and then Maude said, "Is it that Jupe's?"

"Of course it's Jupe's," said Billie. "Who do I know besides Jupe?"

"I don't know. I don't know who else you're seeing or what you're doing when you leave here. Bridget might think she's covering up for you, like she used to cover up for your father, but you're not fooling me."

Billie looked helplessly at Bridget.

"Have you talked with your young man about it?" Bridget asked quietly.

Billie nodded.

"And what did he say?"

Billie burst into tears. "He said he doesn't want it. He said I should get an abortion."

"Quite right," Maude said. "Very sensible."

She continued to hover in the hallway, not moving into the room, but not retreating downstairs, either.

"Maude," said Bridget, shock and horror in her voice. "How can you say that?"

"Oh, Bridget, don't be so backward," said Maude. "It's 1976: abortion is legal in this country. It's as simple these days as having a tooth out. Simpler."

"But it's not a tooth," Bridget said. "This is Billie's child we're talking about, Maude. Your great-grandchild."

"It's not a child." Maude lifted her chin. "It's not a child until it can live and breathe on its own. Right now it's just a . . . a peanut."

Bridget ignored that. "How are you feeling, Billie dear?" she asked gently.

"All right," Billie said, shifting in the bed.

"Bridget means how do you feel about having this baby?" Maude said. "You can't possibly want to keep it."

It was Jupe all over again.

"Why not?" Billie said.

"Why not is because you're still a child yourself. Why not is because you have your whole life ahead of you and you don't need a baby weighing you down. This Jupe, he isn't going to marry you or help you take care of a baby; he already told you that. How do you intend to support yourself? How are you going to take care of a child?"

"Maude!" Bridget said, scandal in her voice. "Billie is our responsibility now. And so is her child. Anything she needs, anything her child needs, we can provide."

"That is up to me," said Maude.

"That is *not* up to you," said Bridget. "That is Billie's *right* as Johnny's child and your grandchild. And someday in the not-too-distant future, all your money and everything you own will be rightfully hers. You told her so yourself."

"I'm not dead yet, as much as you may wish it so," said Maude tartly. "Billie, I hope you will come to your senses and decide to terminate this ridiculous pregnancy."

"I don't know how you can say this, Maude," said Bridget. "When I think of how desperately some people long for a child. My cousin's girl, Sally. You yourself, Maude—"

Maude cut Bridget off. "I will send you to my private physician, Dr. Finkelstein on Park Avenue, who will arrange everything," she said. "You will be yourself again within a day and you can put this whole unfortunate episode behind you."

After a moment of silence, Bridget began speaking again in a quiet voice. "And if you decide to have this baby, Billie, as I sincerely hope you will do," she said, "we will stand behind you and help you in any way: with a home, with money, with caring for the child, with everything you need."

The next day Billie climbed out of bed and started walking. She needed to get away from the house, away from the devil and angel—but which was which?—of Maude and Bridget perched on her shoulders, urging their opposite viewpoints. The air was fresh and cool for the first time since she'd arrived in the city, the sky bright, like it was back home in Northern California. Immune to Maude's warnings or Bridget's concern, she left the house early every morning and each day explored the city. She walked across Central Park, down to the Ferry Landing, up through Spanish Harlem. She spent an entire afternoon sitting in the incense-scented coolness of St. John the Divine, feeling as if she were inside a spectacular vault. She toured the Fulton Fish Market, which made her feel like she was in San Francisco, and finally rode the boat to the Statue of Liberty, walking up the spiraling stairs all the way to the top.

One day she walked by the Planned Parenthood on Bleecker Street, the place where she'd found out she was pregnant what felt like months rather than a few weeks before, and considered going in. I could do it this afternoon, she thought. Put myself under the care of Dr. Barbie and be home, empty inside, by dinner. Her grandmother would be happy then, would approve of her and love her again. On impulse, she walked into the crowded waiting room, approached the receptionist, added her name to the list, and sat down.

She sat there for a few minutes and hopped up and went to the desk again. "How long do you think the wait will be?" she asked.

The receptionist looked without interest at the list. "Hard to say. Maybe forty-five minutes."

"Do you think you'll get to me before lunch?"

"Maybe. If not you'll be the first in when we get back at one."

"I'm going to wait outside."

She went back onto the street, thinking that she would walk around the block, maybe see if she could find a place to get a bagel. She was hungry all the time; that was one symptom of the pregnancy. She constantly had to use the bathroom. And when she got back at night to her grandmother's house, she fell into bed and slept a blessed dreamless sleep for ten, eleven, twelve hours.

Before she was able to find a coffee shop, her need to pee drove her into a bookstore. There were new books in the front, around the cash register, and a vast storehouse of used books, smelling like the stacks at Berkeley, stretching an entire city block into the back of the store. A shaggy-haired salesman directed her to the tiny washroom in the store's farthest corner, and then she made her way back toward the front of the store, wishing she had time to explore its shelves. But she had to hurry back to Planned Parenthood if she wasn't going to lose her place in line.

Then, on a table in the front of the store, she saw it: *Our*

Bodies, Ourselves, reminding her of Cody's and how she used to love reading there, standing up, moving from book to book, sometimes finally flopping down on the cool cement floor in the back of the store and letting herself get lost in a novel. But as she moved to flip open *Our Bodies, Ourselves* to the section on abortion, or maybe on having a baby, or maybe both, another book caught her eye. It was called *A Child Is Born* by Lennart Nilsson, and on the cover was a close-up photograph of a fetus.

She had a dim memory of having glimpsed these photos before, one or two of them, in a magazine, or reproduced somewhere, but she'd never seen them in a book, in sequence: the cells dividing, the arms budding, the eyes emerging from the head. She found the picture closest to where her own pregnancy was, nearly twelve weeks. It looked like something less than a baby. But it was not, as Maude had called it, a peanut.

She went back out in the street, feeling as if she had acquired a new and highly fragile possession that she now had to transport safely and continually. Instead of turning south toward Planned Parenthood, she began walking back north. Her feelings about being pregnant were clear, she realized; they just weren't simple. She did not want to have a baby. She did not want to be a mother, not now, maybe not ever. But what was inside her was a living human being. She had to respect that, even if her grandmother didn't. What became of it after it was born, whether she would be able to take care of it herself or take care of it with Bridget and Maude's help or find some other solution, would reveal itself over time. But, for now, she'd made a decision and she felt light, free, compelled to do nothing more difficult than wait.

༄

When she got home, Bridget was in the kitchen, cooking dinner. The smell of onions frying in butter filled the front hall, intoxicating and delicious. Billie's stomach growled. She went into the kitchen and sat down at the pine table. Bridget stood over the stove with a wooden spoon in her hand, moving the sizzling onions around the ancient black pan.

"Hi," Billie said.

Bridget looked at her and smiled. "Hello, my dear."

"I've decided," Billie said.

Bridget waited, her eyebrows raised.

"I'm going to have it."

"Oh, sweetheart." Bridget came over to her, spoon raised, and enfolded her in a loose butter-scented embrace. "I'm so happy."

"I'm scared," Billie said.

"Everyone feels like that."

"Did Maude? When she was pregnant with my father, I mean."

"Every woman does. Having a baby is exciting, of course, but it's also terrifying, how your body changes, what childbirth will be like, whether the baby will be okay, how you will be as a mother."

The onions sizzled on the stove behind Bridget, who was smiling widely. Billie couldn't bear to point out that while she'd decided to have the baby, that didn't necessarily mean that she was going to raise the baby.

"Why didn't you have children, Bridget?" Billie asked. "I mean, children of your own."

"Well, your father and Floyd, too, they were like my own."

"But didn't you ever want to leave here? Get married and have a family?"

"I was married, once."

"You were? I didn't know that! What happened to him?"

"He died," Bridget said. "In the First World War."

"Oh, that's terrible. I'm so sorry."

"It was a long time ago," Bridget said, returning her attention to the onions. "But you can't imagine how much it cheers me now to have a fresh young life in the house, and a baby on the way. And Maude, too, though she may not be able to show it."

At the mention of Maude, Billie's heart seized up. She was also going to have to tell Maude about her decision, but Maude was not going to be as happy about it as Bridget was.

"Do you think my grandmother's going to be really mad about me having this baby?"

"Oh, don't pay attention to her," said Bridget. "She's all bark and no bite. In the end, she'll come around."

But Maude did not come around. As the months wore on, as Billie's stomach swelled, Bridget became more attentive, more loving, and Maude grew more distant, barely speaking to Billie, acting as if she were an unwelcome boarder in the house. Billie tried not to care, but she did, dreadfully. While Maude's coldness wasn't enough to propel her back to the abortion clinic, it made her wish she weren't pregnant, made her feel that having a baby was causing her to lose her grandmother.

Billie felt so hurt by Maude's silence and disinterest that she began to wonder whether she even wanted Maude to care about her again. Why try to win the attention of this nasty, disapproving, frigid person—this person who'd driven her only living son away, who'd alienated him for his entire life—when she could get so much more from Bridget, who was warm and supportive, nurturing and compassionate? Who cared about money when you could have love?

When she was at home, Billie spent all her time with Bridget, sitting in the kitchen, watching the small television propped on Mr. Apfelmann's massive dresser in Bridget's room. She didn't need to talk to Bridget or share any big emotional moments in order to feel sustained; watching *Mary Tyler Moore* or *All in the Family*, she loved to let herself rest against Bridget's soft arm, to close her eyes and doze.

The weather grew frigid, colder than anything Billie had ever felt, the sidewalks icy. She ordered tall lace-up boots from L.L.Bean, excavated an enormous raccoon coat from the attic that Bridget said had belonged to Mr. Apfelmann in the early twenties. She ventured to the movies, to museums, to coffee shops in the Village, hungrily watching the other young people. Sometimes, at NYU, she'd slip into the back of a big lecture hall, just like she'd done in Berkeley. She'd pretend she was a student, one of them, that they were her friends.

But she wasn't one of them, the skinny girls with the low-slung jeans, the shaggy-haired boys with the mustaches and aviator glasses. They'd look at her belly and, appalled, quickly turn away. It might have been a goiter she was carrying, or a machine gun. She'd walk through a crowd of her contemporaries and a path would clear.

She missed Jupe, but she'd sworn she wasn't going to call him, she wasn't going to write him, and he never called or wrote to her. Sometimes she got a tingling sensation walking around a corner downtown or sitting in a coffee shop, sensing that he was nearby, that he would appear, that they would kiss awkwardly, talk, reconnect, be together again. But that never happened.

At night, when she tried to go to bed, the baby seemed to wake up, tossing and turning inside her so energetically that it was impossible to fall asleep. It became uncomfortable even to sit still and read or watch television. The only thing that seemed to calm the baby down was loud music and dancing.

Billie tried dancing around her room, but Maude yelled for her to stop the noise and so she began going out in the evenings, by herself, downtown to clubs like Max's Kansas City and CBGB. She didn't love punk music—too frenetic and chaotic compared with the Pete Seeger and Grateful Dead tunes she'd been raised on—but the baby seemed to love it. She didn't mind being alone in the clubs: it was dark inside, and hot, and too loud to talk to anyone even if you had someone to talk to. She had a beer and a cigarette—Maude's Dr. Finkelstein said drinking and smoking were okay, in moderation—and moved in time to the new band onstage, the Ramones. Even in that dense crowd, people left a space around her.

The only person who ever approached her was a tall, skinny girl with dark messy hair that Billie caught staring at her. The girl leaned down and shouted something in Billie's ear.

"What?" said Billie.

"I asked if I could touch your stomach."

Billie looked to see if she was joking. The girl had a playful look on her face, but a sincere one, too. She kept staring directly into Billie's eyes, waiting.

"All right," Billie said.

Carefully, the girl placed her hands on Billie's abdomen as if she were taking hold of a basketball and stood there, waiting. The baby obliged with a kick and then seemed to flip over.

"Wow," the girl said, grinning at Billie, her eyes lighting up.

Billie smiled. It was the first time anyone besides Bridget had touched her in months. She could have stood there like that all night.

The girl removed her hands. Again she leaned in close and shouted into Billie's ear. "I remember that," she said. "I had a baby, too."

Billie drew back in surprise. The girl looked barely older than she was and was so thin, almost like a boy. She didn't look like anybody's mother.

"You did?"

The girl nodded solemnly and then said, her voice so close it might have been right inside Billie's brain, "I gave him up. I put him up for adoption."

The girl kept standing there, her breath in Billie's ear.

"I wanted him to have nice parents, regular people," the girl said finally. "Not like me."

She drew away and flashed a grin at Billie, then turned and disappeared into the crowd.

There was so much more that Billie wanted to ask her: How did you find the people? Did you pick them because you wished they were your parents? Did you see your baby, hold him? Do you miss him? Are you glad you gave him away? Do you ever want him back?

But the girl had vanished. A boy with a metal bar through the middle of his nose and a safety pin in his eyebrow, his blond hair shaved short, stuck out his tongue and kissed another boy in a red plaid cap and leather pants. Somebody snorted coke off a long, curling pinkie nail; a small-breasted girl in patent leather pants began jumping, jumping in time to the music.

Billie was alone again, standing there wondering whether she should head out into the night and trudge back uptown, when she saw the girl who'd given away her baby climb onto the stage and grab the microphone. Billie watched, astonished, as the girl started singing.

She had a vision then of her own future: that there would come a day, not too long from now, when this baby would no longer be inside her, part of her. When, whether she kept the baby or like the girl gave it away, she would be thin again, free to walk across a room, jump onto a stage, sing, be once again herself alone. Imagining this, her heart lifted up with something like hope.

Of her future as a mother, she was still uncertain. And the future of the child inside her was something that seemed even more difficult to divine. But she understood—maybe for the first time since learning she was pregnant—that no matter what, she'd still have a future as herself.

"Who is that?" she yelled into the ear of a boy standing next to her, gesturing toward the stage.

"The singer?" he said. "That's Patti Smith."

21

⤳

Bridget, 1917

Before dawn on the eighth of August, much earlier than Bridget's rough calculations, the pains began. They were more like waves of tightness at first, like an unseen hand squeezing her abdomen with force enough to push the baby into the world. Too excited to sleep, she got up and moved around the carriage house, tidying everything that was already tidy. The cradle borrowed from Nick's wife, Concetta, the young Italian mother who'd become her friend, was beside her bed, the linens washed and ready, the tiny sweaters and caps she'd knitted and gowns she'd sewn stacked neatly within.

Everything was ready and waiting except what she most wanted: George. They'd gotten married in January, but then in April, the same week the United States entered the war, he was laid off from his job in the tunnel, and the only one he could find instead was driving for the kind of fat cat he despised. In

July, he lost that job and ended up in a bar, and then another bar, and another, finally finding himself in Times Square, where he encountered Uncle Sam on stilts. Uncle Sam on stilts was so funny, George couldn't help but go into the recruiting station; and once inside, it seemed the only thing to do was join up.

That's how he explained it to Bridget, anyway, when he finally found his way home the next morning.

"What are you talking about?" she said. "What about me? What about the baby?"

"This way at least I can provide for you. You'll have a check every month."

"I don't want a check! I want you!"

"Don't you think it's my duty to fight," he said, "now that America is in the war?"

"You said this was a British war. You said you'd never fight alongside the bloody Brits."

He had said that—had even privately rooted for the Germans, though he hated them, too.

"You're not coming back," she said.

He laughed aloud. "Of course I'm coming back. Now, not another word."

They made love that weekend, enough for it to last him until the war ended, he said. He held her while she cried, and kissed her tears, and tried to calm her fears. On Sunday night he sat in the bathtub, the water cool against the summer heat, smoking a cigar and sipping a beer, joking and teasing her until she smiled.

And then, the morning he was supposed to leave, he seemed to falter.

"We should go back to Ireland," he said. "I'll fight with the

Brotherhood. You can stay with one of my sisters, in Kilkenny town. You'll have the baby there. And I'll go back to see you, when I can."

"No," she said. "I never wanted that life, the wife and mother alone at home in Ireland. You stay here with me."

"I can't do that."

And then he was gone, leaving her on her own to cope with the baby who seemed now intent on pushing its way into the world.

By the middle of the morning, what she felt had turned to real pain, so intense she was forced to hang on to the furniture while the waves moved through her, after which she felt so exhausted she thought she might sleep. But then another pain was upon her. In the kitchen, leaning on the sink, her water broke, spilling across the linoleum as if the bathtub had overflowed. The pains galloped ahead more quickly and insistently then, and the Irish midwife up on 102nd Street she'd planned to call suddenly seemed impossibly far away. With difficulty, she got herself down the rough wooden stairs and across the cobblestone courtyard and into the front building to Nick and Concetta's apartment.

Concetta said she would go for the midwife right away, leaving the children with her mother-in-law; but when she talked to her mother-in-law in Italian, the old lady vigorously shook her head no, arguing with Concetta.

"She says it's too late," Concetta finally told Bridget. "She says she'll deliver the baby herself."

"Oh, no . . ." Bridget began, but then she was hit with a pain so massive, she staggered against the wall.

"She'll go back to the carriage house with you," Concetta

said, seeming more certain now. "Don't worry, she's done this lots of times before."

The grandmother would not let Bridget lie down until it felt as if the baby would drop out right onto the floor. Then she finally pushed Bridget back onto a clean white sheet on the double bed, her gnarled fingers reaching between Bridget's splayed legs, kneading and stretching her most intimate flesh in a way that felt stranger than the labor itself.

And then the horses came, a team of wild horses galloping straight through Bridget's body, wild and unstoppable, and she felt the baby slide out with an explosiveness that was nearly erotic, as stunning as a bolt of lightning bursting from her core.

"*Un figlio!*" cried the grandmother, and Bridget, uncomprehending, raised her head, taking in the fat purply child with dark hair and head round as a melon, the umbilical cord stretching out like the entrails of an animal, obscuring the child's genitals.

"A girl?" asked Bridget hopefully.

"*Bello. Bellissimo.*"

The grandmother was beaming. She placed the baby on the cloth-draped table and tied its cord with a lace she'd snapped smartly from her own shoe, swaddled it tightly in flannel, and laid it across Bridget's chest.

"*Guarda, che bello. Mangia, mangia.*"

This word Bridget understood. The grandmother reached up and propelled Bridget's nipple into the baby's rosebud of a mouth. Instantly, Bridget felt a cramping down below that she knew meant the afterbirth was coming. With effort, she concentrated on the baby and tried to ignore whatever the grandmother was doing at the end of the bed.

And it did seem so miraculous and wholly absorbing, how complete the baby was, its eyes gazing at her as dark blue and murky as the ocean, its nails tiny shells at the ends of its perfect fingers, five, yes, five she counted. And she thought in its plump cheeks she could make out the crease of a dimple, just like its father's.

"Dear George," she imagined writing. "Our baby is here, healthy and beautiful. She arrived on August 8th and I named her . . ."

She looked at the grandmother, bundling around the bedroom now, cleaning up.

"A girl, right?" she asked, trying to remember the Italian word for it. "*Una bambina?*"

The grandmother looked confused, then burst out laughing. "No, no *bambina. Bambino, bambino!*"

With expert fingers, Concetta's mother-in-law untucked the swaddling flannel.

"Boy!" the grandmother cried, gesturing extravagantly to the unmistakable evidence. "*Grazie a Dio!*"

He was a lovely boy, a baby far superior to any other, Bridget thought with a ripple of guilt. True, she'd loved Floyd, she'd loved her brother Patrick, they'd been wonderful children, too; but George Junior was something extraordinary, healthy and gorgeous and cheerful beyond comparison. He nursed with gusto, pausing only to look in her eyes and chortle; he slept for so many hours straight, she sometimes resorted to waking him simply to assure herself that he was all right; and when he wasn't eating or sleeping, he lay on the bed or on his little blanket on the floor and beamed and laughed, wholly absorbed in kicking his legs or staring at his curled hands.

Oh, he was beautiful, beautiful, and she felt she'd never known a love like this, not even for the child's father. In writing to George about the baby, she almost felt as if she had to tamp down her enthusiasm for fear her husband would become jealous.

True to his promise, George wrote every day, but his letters came in unpredictable waves, so that she sometimes waited for days and days with no word, and then found so many onionskin letters pleated into her mailbox that, when she unlocked its narrow brass door, they scattered like dry leaves onto the vestibule's tile floor. Her news seemed to take even longer to reach him, so that weeks passed before he received word that his son had been born.

Because of his experience driving, they had him piloting ambulance trucks and not crawling through the trenches, a blessing and a curse, he said. Plus, he was fighting alongside all Yanks—no sign at all of anyone from home—which frustrated him. He apologized to her, from this distance, for joining the army so impulsively, and said he wished he were there with her and their child. *I'd find all the adventure I need in your arms.*

He began to seem not quite real to her, like her family back in Ireland or like Floyd or Maude, characters from a story who might never have been flesh. Sometimes she even forgot what he looked like, though when the infant George smiled and dimpled, there was his father in his highest spirits, beaming through the tiny face.

If George's letters were sporadic, the checks were not, arriving without fail on the first of every month, enough money to pay the rent and buy food and to put a bit aside, too. They didn't need much, she and George—when she said the name "George" now, she thought of the baby before her husband—with him still nursing and baby clothes suited to the colder weather lent to her by Concetta, pregnant now with her fifth. The grandmother sent Nick and Concetta's oldest child across the courtyard bearing plates of cloudlike ravioli with garlicky tomato sauce, crisp moons of eggplant, and tangy sausage tender as a chicken breast. In return, Bridget baked apple pies and butter cookies shaped like stars, and hosted one or two or all of Concetta's children to tea parties in the carriage house to give their mother a tiny break. The baby loved being among the crowd of children, squealing with delight as they cavorted around him.

When the letters stopped coming from George, Bridget didn't worry. The holidays were drawing close, after all, making the mail even less reliable. By Christmas, though, she grew concerned. She tried to picture George in a trench over there, or marching across an icy field, thinking of her, imagining they were together for the holiday. She hadn't really expected a present from him, though she'd knitted him a green muffler and socks she hoped weren't too thick. But she'd wished for a word, some message of love for her and the baby.

She could hardly believe that the Christmas before, she had just discovered she was pregnant, that she had still been working for Maude.

The first week in January, when the wind again bit through the inadequate windows, the check from the army did not arrive, and she received no response to her letters of inquiry to the post office and the government. She was forced then to dig in the flour canister for the money that Maude had given her, but the envelope was not there. She was so incredulous, she dumped the entire canister full of flour into a bowl to make sure, but there was no money. There was just enough in savings to pay the rent and the six dollars for gas on account of the cold. There would not be rent money enough for another month.

When February came and she still had not received a letter from George or a check, she left the baby with Concetta and went in search of a jewelry merchant who would buy the aquamarine ring.

He was a Jewish man, not Jewish like Mr. Apfelmann but Jewish with a long beard and ringlets in front of his ears and a black satin beanie on his head. He held a telescope-like lens in one eye and peered at the aquamarine.

"Ten dollars," he said, letting the ring clatter to the thick green glass counter.

"Ten dollars!" she blurted. "But my rent is twelve!"

He shrugged. "That's what I'll pay. Take it or leave it."

After checking with three other gem merchants, all of whom offered her even less, she went back to the original merchant and said she'd take the ten dollars.

The money held tight in his hand, he leaned in closer.

"I'll give you twelve," he muttered, "if you give me a feel."

She strode quickly out of the shop, her face flaming, regretting not that she'd tried to sell the ring but that she'd almost sold it to such a horrible man. Of course, she wouldn't give him or anyone else a feel for two dollars, or for any amount of money; yet, now that he'd introduced the possibility, it kept playing at her mind. That was one way that she or any woman could always get money: become a prostitute, even just an occasional one. No, no, she wouldn't do that, couldn't do that. She walked all the way uptown in the cold, skirting the black-crusted snow that laced the sidewalk, to clear her mind of these terrible images, vowing to find a better way.

The letter was waiting for her when she got home. George had been reported missing. His company had been in battle, with many casualties, but his body had not been found, nor had his whereabouts been determined. His pay was suspended pending an investigation.

Bridget cried that night, holding the puzzled baby on her lap, and then brought the child into bed with her, tucking him in on George's side, against the wall, and sleeping curled around his cushiony warmth. She woke in the morning to find his diaper had soaked through onto her gown, chilling her stomach and filling the bed with a urine-y tang, but how could she be annoyed when he grinned widely the moment she looked at him, pumping his fists and cycling his legs joyously in the frigid bedroom air? How could she worry about what they would do, when all she wanted in this world was exactly what she had: this child, in her arms, alive.

22

Cait, Present

C ait was astonished, the morning after her trip to the lake with her parents, to hear an unannounced knock at her apartment door and look through the peephole to see Sally, her mother, standing in the hallway. Sally was looking toward the floor, but Cait knew every sparse white curl on her head, recognized the powder blue trench coat Sally had worn since Cait was in high school. Cait pulled open the door and blurted, because it was the only thing she could think to say, "What are you doing here?"

"I wanted to talk to you," Sally said. "Alone. And I thought it would be better to do it in person."

Cait stood aside to let her mother into the apartment, but couldn't help peering out into the hallway, so dumbfounded was she that Sally had not only shown up in Little Italy but come here on her own.

"Dad's not with you?" she asked. And then, suddenly alarmed, "Is everything all right?"

"Yes, everything's fine. Your father doesn't know I'm here," Sally said. She reached into her stiff, caramel-colored purse and pulled out a slim silver cell phone. "Modern technology," she said, wagging it. "He thinks I'm at the mall."

Sally looked so awkward, Cait hurried to pull out a kitchen chair for her.

"Do you have any white wine?" Sally asked. "I thought maybe this would be easier if we had some wine. Well, if *I* did."

Cait was about to joke about it being eleven o'clock in the morning, but thought better of it. She remembered seeing a bottle of wine in the back of the refrigerator when she moved in; she fished it out now and set it and a wineglass on the table, rummaging until she found the corkscrew and then working to open the bottle while her mother sat there without talking. As curious as she was, Cait found herself wanting to delay the revelation. The minute she heard it, she sensed, she would never be able to find her way back to the person she was now, the person she'd always been.

She popped the cork from the wine bottle. Poured. Sat down. Waited.

"Those names you asked about yesterday," said Sally. She picked up her wineglass, took a long. swallow. "They were familiar."

Cait felt the skin all over her body prick up. Her heart, her breath, even the blood flowing through her veins—it all seemed to tingle and expand.

"What do you mean?" Cait asked. "What do you know?"

"Caitlin, we didn't get you from a Catholic adoption agency. We got you through a private lawyer."

"What lawyer?"

"This lawyer called us, out of the blue, said he'd heard we were trying to adopt a baby. At the time, I didn't think too hard about it. We'd been to a lot of different agencies and I was beginning to lose hope that I would ever get a baby. I was turning forty, and they didn't let you adopt if you were over forty back then."

Cait could feel her heart beating in her throat. "So the lawyer called you . . ."

"He said there was a baby. A baby girl. She was available, it wasn't definite for adoption, but for fostering. But if we took her—took you—on that condition, then if she did become available for adoption, we would have the first chance."

Sally was staring at the table as she talked, as if these long-ago events were being projected on its shiny surface.

"We went into the city, your father and I. Drove over the bridge, just like we told you. But instead of going to a hospital, we went to a law firm, this tall building, fancy offices, way up on some high floor. I remember how quiet it was, the carpet so thick, glass doors that slid open and closed without a sound, people in dark suits speaking in low voices like they were in a library."

Cait got up, came around the table, crouched down, and put her arms around her mother. Sally looked up, blinking, her face full of wonder and pain.

"And then I saw you," said Sally, "and you were so beautiful, I forgot everything else. The lawyer's secretary was holding you in her arms. You had those big bright eyes, so smart, staring at us like you knew something special was happening, and this long dark hair sticking straight up, and this fat round beautiful face."

Cait's mother clapped her hands over her eyes and started sobbing. Cait, shivering, tried to hold her mother steady but Sally just sat there and shook and shook as if her body had been seized by an earthquake.

When at last she calmed down, she asked Cait, "You understand, don't you? Why we did what we did?"

"I don't know what it is you did, Mom," Cait said quietly.

"We didn't ask any questions. We didn't want to know where you came from, how we got you, anything. All the lawyer told us was that the daughter of one of his clients had this baby and wasn't able to care for it, wanted it to go to a family outside of the city, a nice family, regular-like, homey. A family that would really love a baby.

"And that was us. We would have done anything even before we saw you, but once that secretary laid you in my arms, bam, that was it. I was a goner. I wrapped you up and took you home and from that first day, you were mine. I was praying every day and night to every god I could think of that we were going to get to keep you. When we finally got the call, about eight months later, that you were ours to keep . . . I swear to God, Caitlin, that was the happiest day of my life. I didn't know it was possible to be so happy."

Cait hugged her mother hard this time, wishing she could crawl onto Sally's lap and nestle there the way she had when she was a little girl.

"We went back to the same lawyer's office and signed the papers. We were given your new birth certificate, with our names as your parents. I never knew the name of your birth mother back then, didn't know anything about her, or about your father, either. I didn't want to know. I didn't want them to be real to me. I wanted to pretend that you were ours and ours alone, because that's the way it felt."

Cait moved back to the other chair but was leaning across the table, holding her mother's hand.

"So the names I asked you about the other day . . ."

Sally drew in a breath, took another swallow of wine. "When we got you, the lawyer told us you hadn't been named yet, which seemed odd at the time, because you obviously weren't a newborn, you were at least a month or two old. But again, we took that at face value, and just started calling you the name we'd picked out. Then when you said Bridget, out at the lake, combined with Apfel . . . the bells started ringing. Last night, lying awake in bed, it came to me.

"My cousin Bridget, the one I mentioned to you, worked for a family in Manhattan, a rich family named Apfelmann. I worked there briefly myself, when I was in nursing school. But I didn't really get close to Bridget—she was so much older than me, older than my mother, even—until after we had you, when she called and said she'd retired and asked if she could visit us, for holidays and Sunday dinners and the like.

"It was really wonderful. My mother had died by then, and it was almost like Bridget became a second mother to me, a grandmother for you. She had a special thing for you, Cait, always. She'd be at our house all the time, playing with you, buying you clothes and toys. As far as she was concerned, the sun and the moon rose with you. And you were crazy about her, too. You missed her so much when she died."

"When was that?"

"You must have been about four. We brought you to the funeral, thinking you wouldn't really understand what was going on, and you saw her lying there in the coffin and tried to jump right into it with her. You were so happy when you saw her face, calling out her name, and so angry and confused when we wouldn't let you touch her, when she wouldn't wake up."

Suddenly, Cait had a memory—not really a memory, but some distant foggy picture—of that day. She felt herself lifted high in her father's arms, sensed the crowd of grown-ups all around, saw filtered sunlight and rows of wooden chairs as if in a church. And Bridget, yes, the name and the memory, or more the idea, of an older woman—she imagined gray hair, and roundness—made her feel something like happy.

"But she obviously wasn't my birth mother," Cait said.

"Of course not, but it all makes sense now. From the birth records you found. Your mother, your birth mother, must have been the Apfelmann girl. The one Bridget always talked about. Billie Apfelmann."

Billie Apfelmann. Billie Apfelmann. Cait tried to conjure an image from those syllables, but nothing emerged.

"So, who was she?" Cait asked, hardly daring to breathe. "What do you know about her?"

"Nothing. Almost nothing. I wouldn't have had any reason to pay attention, you see. Bridget would talk about Maude, the grandmother, who she'd worked for for something like sixty years. She'd taken care of Maude's children, but there was some tragic story: one of the boys had died, and the other one had been a black sheep, had gone to California and been estranged from the family. John, I think his name was: Johnny. And he'd had this daughter, Billie, who'd come back from California looking for her grandmother after he died."

"And then she had me," said Cait.

"I don't know this," said Sally. "I'm just guessing. Certainly, Bridget never told us. Bridget always spoke of Billie in very fond terms. She was very young, I think, and had grown up poor, without all the family money. By the time we came to know Bridget, she had gone off somewhere far away, California or Europe, maybe. Bridget would get letters from her occasionally, I think. She'd mention them."

Cait caught her breath. "Did she know where I was? Billie, I mean. Did she know I'd been adopted by you?"

"I have no idea."

"And Bridget, she obviously knew the whole story."

"She must have been closely involved in the whole thing, I realize now, if the baby—if you—were named after her. It must have been she who told the lawyer about us. But she never breathed a word."

"And Masterson?"

"That name I never heard," Sally said, shaking her head decisively.

Again Cait felt as if she had a whole new set of answers, and even more new questions. She shook her head, trying to clear it, trying to focus.

"Do you have any idea where this Billie Apfelmann is now?" she asked her mother, thinking at the same time that it didn't matter, she'd be able to find her; and if not, she'd ask Martin to help, and Frank.

But her mother unsnapped her purse and drew out a slip of paper. "I went on your father's computer before he woke up this morning," she said, pushing the handwritten note to Cait. "There was a B. Apfelmann right on Sixty-fourth Street, the same house where I remember working. It's got to be her."

Instead of taking the paper, Cait gripped her mother's hand. "Oh, Mom," she said. "Thank you for telling me all this. I know it's not easy for you. I didn't mean to upset you by telling you about the pregnancy."

She was relieved her mother hadn't mentioned that. After the lake, she'd driven back from the city, found the number for Planned Parenthood, and then sat with her phone in her hand, planning to call, but not being able to punch in the number.

"You know how much I'd love a grandchild," her mother said. "And I envy you your pregnancy. But I really believe it's your decision."

"I've been so worried about your health, too, Mom."

"Your father's exaggerating that," Sally said. "I told him he has to stop. He's the one who's worried, Cait. He's worried about what will happen if you find her. He's afraid of losing you."

"He's not going to lose me," Cait said. "He'll always be my dad."

"That's what I tried to tell him."

Cait smiled and squeezed her mother's hand.

"I'm glad you're not afraid."

"I *am* afraid," said Sally, "but I'm more afraid that you're never going to be happy unless you find her. If you need to find her to feel complete, Cait, then I'll risk anything, even losing you, to make that happen."

23

Billie, 1977

The baby was late, one week, two weeks, as the daffodils bloomed and the trees in the park came into bud. Billie was huge, had long since outgrown all of Maude's miniature vintage clothing, and was wearing instead her grandfather's ancient long-tailed shirts, his enormous-waisted trousers rolled up into tight cuffs at the ankles. After dinner in the kitchen, she'd lean back in her chair and lift her shirt and she and Bridget would watch the baby dance, elbows and feet poking out knobs in her drum-tight skin.

She had been sure since the beginning that the baby was a boy. It was big and so active, jabbing her in the ribs, doing the cha-cha on her bladder. She imagined him as sturdy, active, a dusky-skinned child chasing a soccer ball. When she could imagine him as a child at all.

Finally, Dr. Finkelstein said they couldn't wait any longer.

He said there was one thing he could try before he induced labor, and without telling her what he was doing, he reached inside her as she lay on the exam table and hooked his finger into her cervix and pulled. It felt like he had gouged out some piece of her flesh. When she howled in pain, he clucked at her.

"All I did was dislodge your mucus plug," he said. "How are you going to stand it when the baby comes out?"

He sent her out of his office to walk around for a few hours, telling her not to come back until she was in active labor.

"Don't come back until the pain is so bad you can't walk or talk," he told her.

Bridget walked arm in arm with her up Park Avenue, tulips blooming red all the way up the center island. When they'd left the house that morning, Bridget had told Maude only that she was going with Billie to a doctor's appointment.

"Isn't my grandmother going to want you back home?" Billie asked.

"She can wait," Bridget said. Her mouth curled into a wry smile and she winked at Billie. "If she gets hungry enough, she can get out of bed and make herself a piece of toast."

When the pains hit full force, Billie dug her fingers into poor Bridget's shoulders and panted, panic rising. She had read Elisabeth Bing, but the breathing exercises were not really helping and labor had just begun.

"I'm scared," she told Bridget.

"I won't let anything bad happen to you," Bridget assured her.

At the hospital, they made Billie change into a dressing gown, shaved her, hooked her up to a monitor, and told her to lie back in the hospital bed.

"I don't want to lie down," she told the nurses. "My book

said I was supposed to sit however I felt comfortable. I'm supposed to let gravity help the baby come out."

"Dr. Finkelstein wants you on the monitor, which means you have to stay in bed," they said. "If you move around too much, it won't record properly."

Dr. Finkelstein showed up after dinner. Billie's contractions had slowed and weakened. At least she was more comfortable.

After a consultation with the nurses, the doctor told Billie, "Your labor is not progressing. We're going to put you on a Pitocin drip. To move your labor along."

"I don't want a Pitocin drip."

"Then you'll need to have a C-section. Would you rather have a C-section?"

Billie looked at Bridget, wild-eyed.

"You've got to listen to the doctor, darling," Bridget said.

"It's going to hurt," Billie said, panicky again. "I read that Pitocin really makes labor a lot worse."

"You've been doing too much reading," the doctor said. "Let's start the Pitocin and see how you tolerate it."

It wasn't so bad at first. They turned on the television and Bridget fell asleep in the gold plastic easy chair beside the bed. The nurses kept coming in, checking whether Billie was dilating, turning up the drip, until the pains took hold and started coming fast. Billie could see each one on the monitor, like a wave beginning to build far out at sea, before she could feel it. And then she tried to breathe and ended up, every time, getting slammed, making it through only because the monitor, a beat ahead, signaled it would soon be over.

Finally, sometime in the middle of the night, a monster pain washed over her and she cried out, waking Bridget.

"Oh!" Bridget said, pulling herself to her feet. "Oh, dear!"

She laid a cool palm on Billie's forehead, squeezed her hand, said she'd be right back, and left the room, returning a moment later with a nurse in tow.

"We just checked her," said the nurse.

"You need to get the doctor. She's in the final stages."

"Dr. F. said we weren't to wake him until she was ready to deliver. This could go on for hours."

"This is not going to go on for hours," Bridget said, with a firmness Billie had never heard in her voice. "Check her again."

Frowning, the nurse reached under Billie's gown and felt around. Just then another pain came, bigger than the last one. Billie could see it on the monitor, growing, growing. She tried to breathe but felt the pain crashing over her and gave herself over to a scream.

The nurse yanked her hand away as if she'd felt fire and bustled out of the room.

"You're doing fine," Bridget said soothingly, taking Billie's hand and holding it to her breast. "It will all be over soon and you'll have your lovely little girl."

"Why do you say that?" Billie said, fear rising in her voice as she spotted a new contraction start to form on the screen. "It's going to be a boy."

"Oh, no, dear," Bridget said, but then the pain hit and Billie didn't hear anything more.

Dr. Finkelstein appeared, looking bleary.

"They tell me you're going to have a baby, sweetheart," he said, forcing a grin.

"My name is Billie," she said through clenched teeth.

"All right, then." The smile was gone as he positioned himself between her knees. "Gloves!"

Everything happened quickly after that. The doctor said they needed to get to the delivery room right away. An orderly and a nurse pushed Billie's bed out into the hallway, the IV rattling along beside her.

"Bridget!" she tried to call. "Bridget!"

She could see Bridget trying to keep up behind them, but they turned into a delivery room, spotlight bright overhead, and the door swung closed.

"I want Bridget!" Billie screamed.

"She can't be allowed in here," said one of the nurses.

Billie was transferred onto the delivery table, a new monitor hooked up. The light was so bright she couldn't see. The doctor was wearing a mask.

"Episiotomy," he said.

"No," Billie tried to say, but they didn't seem to hear.

Another pain started to build.

"Now, push, sweetheart," the doctor said. "Push!"

Billie pushed. She pushed and pushed and pushed. It felt good, in a way. Better than lying there, letting the pain pummel her.

If only Bridget were there to hold her hand, to cheer her on, she felt sure she could push the baby out.

But nothing was happening. On the doctor's instruction, the nurses leaned into her stomach as she pushed, trying to squeeze the baby out with their weight.

Over his mask, the doctor glanced at the monitor.

"The baby's in distress," he said. "I'm going in."

"What?" Billie said. Her throat was raw, her hair and brow dripping with sweat.

"Lie back, dear."

A mask was clapped over her mouth and nose.

"Breathe deeply."

That was the last she knew. When she opened her eyes, she was lying on her side. It seemed like the pain was still there from the waist down: along her abdomen, between her legs. But she could tell the baby was gone.

Bridget was sitting beside her, watching.

"What happened?" Billie asked, her voice a rasp.

"They had to do an emergency cesarean," Bridget told her. "They were afraid they were going to lose the baby. You're in the recovery room now."

She was so tired, a massive headache blooming right between her eyes.

"The baby . . ." she said, panic rising again.

Bridget smiled. "She's in the nursery. She's beautiful."

"She . . ."

"I told you," Bridget said, smiling. "It's a girl."

A girl. A girl like she was.

"Is she . . ." Billie started to ask, but she didn't finish her sentence. She didn't even know what she was going to ask.

"She's fine," Bridget said. "They're cleaning her up. You're to rest. They'll bring her in later."

When they finally brought the baby to her, washed and swaddled and sleeping placidly, her face round, her hair straight and dark, Billie thought they must be mistaken. Could this baby have come from her? It looked nothing like her: so big, so round, so dark. But the baby didn't look like Jupe, either. Her skin was golden, her cheeks a blooming peach, her hair straight. She might have been part Native American or Spanish.

But black? Never.

The infant blinked and looked straight into Billie's eyes, as if considering. Then she opened her rosebud mouth and screamed.

Billie struggled to settle the heavy bawling baby on her shoulder, wincing against the pain of the stitches, trying to pat its back and jiggle it to calm it down, but that only seemed to make it scream louder.

"Nurse!" Billie called, and then more desperately, "Nurse!"

She was afraid she was going to drop the baby, or that it was going to wiggle right out of her arms and hurl itself to the floor. She tried to swing her legs off the bed to steady herself, but that tore at her episiotomy stitches.

"Help!" she screamed, wondering where Bridget had gone.

When the nurse finally arrived, Billie said, "I don't think this is my baby."

The nurse checked the baby's bracelet. "Of course it's your baby. Last name Apfelmann?"

"Masterson," said Billie. "I mean, my name is Apfelmann, but her name is Masterson. But I think they must have switched my baby in the delivery room."

The nurse laughed, but when she saw that Billie was serious, she said, "I'll take her away now so you can get some rest. You've been through a lot."

Billie was tired, but once they'd taken the baby away, she worked her way onto her feet and shuffled down the hall until she found the window that opened onto the nursery. She felt sure that she would recognize her real baby there. He would be small and blond, she thought, or else he would look more like Jupe, with curly dark hair, dark skin, a long, skinny body. And he would be a boy. She saw them put the baby they said was her baby, still crying, into its bassinet. But she didn't see another one she thought might be hers, either.

When she told Bridget that she was afraid the baby wasn't hers, Bridget only laughed.

"But it doesn't look anything like me or Jupe," Billie said.

"No. She looks exactly like your father," Bridget said.

Billie tried to breast-feed but she wasn't making enough milk, and the baby had something the nurses called feeding frenzy, biting and clawing at Billie, frantic for more to eat. When they finally tried a bottle, the baby grew calmer, so Bridget could sit and feed her.

Bridget was able to soothe the child, too, to swing her as she walked around the hospital room, crooning lullabies, talking in a soft voice. The baby would stare into Bridget's eyes as if hypnotized. When Billie would try the same thing, the baby would start screaming again.

"You'll get the hang of it," Bridget assured her. "You'll get more confident and she'll respond to that, you'll see."

But each time they left the baby alone in the room with Billie, the child started crying, and nothing Billie did seemed to quiet her. Now, though she'd come to believe the baby was hers, she thought that the baby sensed how ambivalent she was about being a mother, how incompetent she felt, how essentially unworthy she was to have a child. After the nurses wheeled in the bassinet, where the baby lay swaddled and sleeping, looking like an Indian child in its papoose in an old-fashioned storybook, Billie would draw in a ragged breath and try to summon some confidence in her ability to care for the baby, to hide whatever fears and insecurities she felt; but it seemed that the minute she touched the child, its eyes would shoot open in alarm and it would start bawling.

The simple truth was that the baby hated her.

If Jupe were there, she thought, everything would be better. He would know what to do, how to take care of the baby and to make Billie feel better about everything, too. She wished now that she hadn't been so absolute about what she required from him. She wouldn't mind, she thought, if he wasn't her boyfriend or her husband, if they didn't live together, if he wasn't there with her full-time. She just wished he could see the baby and visit once in a while, the three of them together. She wished he were still her friend.

The afternoon before she and the baby were due to go home, she wrote him a letter.

"Dear Jupe," it said. "I wanted you to know that I did have the baby. It was a little girl, 8 pounds, 5 ounces, with lots of dark hair. She was born on April 12th. I know you said you didn't want to be involved but I thought you should know that she is here and that I would love it if you want to see her or me. I don't expect anything from you but I miss you and love you as a person and I don't want to think I will never see you again. Love, Billie."

She put the letter in a hospital envelope, addressed it to Jupe in Brooklyn, and asked Bridget if she would mail it.

Bridget looked doubtful. "Are you sure, dear?"

"Please," said Billie.

They wouldn't let her leave the hospital without naming

the baby. She'd been planning to name it John and had no idea what to name a girl.

"Maybe you should name it after your mother," Bridget suggested.

Billie shook her head. She didn't want to connect an innocent child to a drug addict who'd overdosed and left her only daughter motherless, who hadn't been much of a mother even when she was alive. "I don't think so."

"Perhaps it would be diplomatic to name her Maude."

Billie shivered. "Never."

Maude had not been to the hospital, had not called or sent a gift.

"Well, I think it's nice to name a child after someone in your family, but you could also name her after someone else who's been important to you," Bridget said, "the way your father named you Billie."

Billie studied Bridget, contemplating the possibilities. "That's a good idea," she said finally. "I think I'll name her Bridget."

"Oh, no, that's a terrible old-fashioned Irish name. What about Margaret? Or Anne."

"No," said Billie, warming to the name Bridget. "I want to name her after you. I wish you were my grandmother."

Bridget seemed to collapse, slumping forward, dropping her head, bringing her hands up over her ears. Billie couldn't tell whether Bridget was about to laugh or cry.

Finally Bridget looked up, pale, anguished.

"I love you, too, child," said Bridget, "but you mustn't say that, about wishing I were your grandmother. Maude would be devastated."

"Devastated? How can you think that? She doesn't care

anything about me. She wishes this baby had never been born."

"She'll be excited when we get home," Bridget promised. "You'll see."

But Maude did not come out of her room when they brought the baby home. Billie walked upstairs, still moving slowly from the pain of the stitches and the C-section, hoping, despite herself, that Bridget was right and Maude would want to see her grandchild. Bridget followed, carrying the baby.

"Maude," Bridget called to the closed door. "We're here."

There was no answer.

Bridget had set up a cradle in Billie's room and moved upstairs herself, to her old bedroom, which still had its single iron bed with a white bedspread, a hooked rug on the wooden floor, and a large round mirror above an Art Deco dressing table that looked as if it must have once been Maude's.

Billie was tired, so tired. The pain from the hospital and the difficulty of feeding and caring for the baby seemed to come crashing down now that they were home, without the help of the staff and the nursery. It wasn't merely that she didn't want to take care of the baby or even that she couldn't; it was more that she felt unable to do *anything*.

She felt pinned to her bed by a great immobility, a great sadness, that couldn't be attributed to any one thing. She wanted there to be a reason, telling herself that she would feel better once the episiotomy healed or her breasts stopped leaking milk, once her belly tightened or she got a full night's sleep. She would gaze at the baby at moments when she was sleeping and feel an unprecedented sense of love and tenderness well up.

She kept waiting for that to seep into all the rest of her life, but it didn't happen.

What was this hopelessness? Was she just not meant to be a mother? Was it something she got from her own mother? She'd never felt so much like her own mother as she did now, memories she'd buried for years flashing through her brain. She kept seeing her mother immobile on the bed, dozing while Billie tried to talk with her, ignoring Billie's pleas for food, for a glass of water, for everything.

She remembered herself, very small, standing by the side of the bed, tugging on her mother's limp hand. She didn't want to be like that to her daughter, and yet the baby Bridget would cry and Billie would hold her and feel utterly powerless and paralyzed. She'd stare at the baby and lose touch with where the baby ended and she herself began. It was as if *she* were the baby, as if her soul—the part of her that was alive, that still needed and wanted—were in the baby, and the young woman who lay on the bed was Billie's mother. If Bridget hadn't been there to feed the baby and rock her to sleep, and to feed Billie and make sure she slept, too, Billie was afraid she might dash the baby to the floor or hunt through the medicine cabinets until she found something to kill the pain, and swallow all of it.

Maybe this was why her mother had started using drugs. Maybe she'd felt like this after Billie was born and taken drugs to feel better. If there were a pipe nearby, Billie would have smoked it—anything that promised to relieve this awful weight.

"I'm afraid," she told Bridget.

"You'll be fine," said Bridget. "You're just tired is all."

But it was the older woman who looked tired.

"Has Jupe called?" Billie asked.

"No, dear, I'm afraid he hasn't."

"Do you think I should call him?"

"He's made his feelings clear, hasn't he, dear?" Bridget said gently. "Calling him now will only make you feel worse."

Billie heard Bridget arguing with Maude.

"Of all the things you've done, this is the worst," she heard Bridget say. "The baby is nearly a month old and you haven't set eyes on her."

There were more raised voices that Billie couldn't make out. Nothing more happened then, but a few days later Billie woke up from a nap to find the baby not in her bassinet and Bridget not in her room. Hearing voices from below, Billie ventured to the head of the stairs. Bridget said something, then the baby squealed, and then Billie heard Maude say, "Oh! She is beautiful. Why didn't you tell me, Bridget?"

Bridget laughed and said something grumbly to Maude, but then they both laughed, so it must have been a joke.

Billie listened for another minute but, unable to make out what they were saying, moved down two stairs, then three more.

And then she could hear clearly: Maude was singing. The legendary voice—the one Maude and Bridget, too, claimed had not been used for sixty years—floated up through the house, sweet and pure. Billie followed the sound, tiptoeing to the bottom of the flight of stairs, into the hall, and to the door of Maude's room. Bridget stood beaming by the side of the bed as Maude held the baby propped on her thighs. The baby, Billie could see from the doorway, was gurgling in appreciation of Maude's beautiful singing.

When Maude's song ended, Billie broke into spontaneous applause. She'd felt abandoned by her grandmother, angry, but hearing the song, seeing Maude finally holding the baby, made her heart thaw. Maybe this is what's been wrong with me, she thought. Maybe I just needed her to love me again. And to love my baby, too.

"Oh, Billie!" Maude cried, looking up, delight on her face. "The baby is just beautiful!" She turned her attention back to baby Bridget. "Aren't you, little darling?" she said, wagging her head. "Aren't you?"

Billie smiled and edged slowly toward the bed.

"Those bright eyes! Are they blue or are they green?" Maude asked. "And that hair! I wonder if she'll turn blond—that's what happened with Floyd—or stay dark like this? And that personality! You're a pistol, aren't you? Aren't you?"

The baby, Billie saw as she neared the bed, seemed mesmerized by Maude, her face alight, eyes wide, riveted by Maude's lilting tone and expressive features.

"So, Billie, I think you must have been hiding something from us," Maude said, giving Billie a coquettish look. "Jupe must not have been the only man in your life."

"What do you mean?" asked Billie.

"Why, the baby is obviously white!" Maude said.

Billie shook her head. "She's fair, or at least she is now. But the pediatrician who came around in the hospital said that often happens, and over time, her skin will probably turn darker, her hair will be curlier. . . ."

"No," Maude said decisively. "That's impossible. This is a white child."

Billie was flabbergasted. "She's half white," she said, "but she is half black, too. There's been nobody else except Jupe."

Maude stared for a long moment at baby Bridget. "Well," she said finally. "Nobody has to know that. Her father is no longer in the picture. She's a gorgeous child, and looks like any other white baby. Better. We just will never tell her or anyone else about his racial background."

Billie was already shaking her head in horror. "I'm not going to do that, Maude," she said. "I'm not going to hide her race from her, or her father's identity. I'm going to tell her the truth."

"The truth, the truth," said Maude, her tone twisting into something much darker. "And what good will knowing the truth do her?"

Billie thought of her father, spinning fairy tales about princesses and castles, never telling her the truth about his own life and his own—their own—family. And her mother, locked in a narcotic dream from which she never awoke. The baby started to cry; Bridget picked her up and pressed her close to her chest.

"It's always better to know the truth," said Billie, feeling more like her true self than she had in months.

"If you really want the truth, I'll give it to you," said Maude, sitting up straight in her bed, fluffing the already-perfect bow under her chin. "But I don't think that's going to be better for anyone."

24

Bridget, 1918

All Bridget needed was a job. She knew she could work, was stronger and more resourceful than ever. Moreover, her child would not be a serious impediment to her working. If she was cleaning he would happily watch, or sit quietly while she cared for older children, or cooked, or sewed.

But though she visited several employment agencies and answered any number of advertisements, as soon as she mentioned a child they all said in that case they weren't interested.

Perhaps some kind of piecework that she could do at home? Leaving the baby with Concetta, who was close to having her own baby, Bridget ventured downtown to see Nora, Maude's former maid, who'd built a thriving clothing business. Nora's shop had newly expanded and a seamstress was now employed, with Nora herself presiding grandly from a white-upholstered gilt chair near the window.

"*Dear* Bridget," Nora said, giving her a hug that did not quite involve touching and gesturing for her to sit down. "You must be *freezing* in those thin clothes."

In fact, Bridget had dressed carefully for this interview, feeling the cold only where her soles had worn nearly through—though two dollars for a new pair of shoes was out of the question, and Bridget was hoping Concetta's husband might fix them for a cut-rate price. When she sat across from Nora, she was careful to keep both feet flat on the floor.

"I'm fine," she protested. "Very well. In fact, I was thinking the other day how you once suggested I should work for you, and I'm ready to take you up on that."

"But what about your place with Maude Montgomery, or is it Apfelmann? I was always confused about that. I've heard that she's become quite the little do-gooder, swaddling sick babies and handing out mufflers to the poor, undoubtedly to atone for her many sins. Is that really true?"

Bridget was shaken by this description. "I haven't worked for Mrs. Apfelmann for some time," Bridget said, taking care to keep her tone cordial. "Perhaps you heard: I married George McLean and had a baby."

"Married George! Well, that *is* a feather in your cap, getting that roustabout to settle down. I'm amazed a he-man like George would let the little lady go out to work."

"George has been overseas, with the army, Nora," Bridget said, feeling her defenses crumble. "I've recently gotten word that he's been reported missing in action." They hadn't said the "in action" part, but she knew what Nora would think if she just said "missing": that George had run away. It's what she thought herself sometimes.

"I need to earn money," Bridget explained. "To support myself and our son."

"But I don't see how you could work in the shop," Nora said, "with your child."

"I thought maybe I could do some sewing at home," Bridget offered.

But Nora was already shaking her head. "I only hire the finest Paris-trained dressmakers. No home sewing types."

Bridget sat in silence for a long moment. Perhaps Nora didn't truly understand? Bridget realized a lot of the fault must be her own, wanting to show everything in the best possible light, even—she had to admit it was true—trying to make Nora jealous, to one-up her by throwing her happiness with George and her baby in Nora's face.

"Nora," she said, lowering her voice, "I really need your help. I'll do anything, work at anything, whatever you say, just to have the chance to earn a bit of money. Please. You're my best hope."

Nora smiled, a quick chilly smile, before getting to her feet. "I'm sorry, Bridget, I might consider you for the apartment, but I have two new colored girls there to do the cleaning and the cooking, and no need of a nanny, thank God."

It took every ounce of strength Bridget had—nearly as much as she'd needed when Floyd died, as much as it had taken to get through George's birth—to stand up and walk out of Nora's shop without descending into tears. She was proud of herself, at least, for managing that.

It took her two days after getting turned down by Nora to work up the nerve to go see Dr. Hinkle and, later the same afternoon, Emma Goldman, but she did not fare much better there. Neither of them knew of any work for her, not with a baby, though Dr. Hinkle said she could offer free psychoanalysis, one day a week, and Miss Goldman thought Bridget might help drum up support for the Irish Rebels, though of course that wasn't a paid position.

Bridget wondered whether Dr. Hinkle or Miss Goldman would tell Maude that she had been to see them. She imagined Maude, concerned, getting in touch, offering her a job, or even some money to tide her over. No, thank you, Bridget would say, holding her head high. I don't need your charity.

But charity, she finally had to admit, was exactly what she did need. The Church offered payments to unwed mothers, and when Bridget told the Catholic Relief Board that she was in fact wed, and by a priest at that, they asked to see her marriage certificate, and the letter from the army, and then sent a lady from the board unannounced to the carriage house to make sure George wasn't hiding there. They wanted to know why baby George had not been baptized and insisted he be so immediately. Then the Catholics finally agreed to give Bridget a stipend, in exchange for her cleaning the church. It was daily work, but she could do it any time when there was no Mass, no confessions, nothing else going on in the church. Though, of course, they said, while she worked she would have to find somewhere else to leave the baby.

By that time, Concetta had had her own baby and said she was very sorry, but she couldn't take care of George while Bridget worked. There were baby farms, Bridget knew, where women left their children while they worked: homes out in the country that boarded four or eight or twelve infants at a time. Some were adequate, Bridget supposed, but she'd read terrible things about others, about children neglected, beaten, even killed. She wasn't going to leave George at one of those places.

Other women left their children, even children as young as George, alone while they worked. They put them in a crib or playpen with a bottle of milk, trusting and praying everything would be all right. Or didn't care if it was not.

Bridget didn't want to do this, either, but maybe if she waited until George was fast asleep, fashioned some kind of netting over the top of the crib so that he couldn't climb out, made sure the bottle she left him was full of the freshest milk, and cleaned the church efficiently but as quickly as possible . . .

The first night she tried it, her heart was in her throat the entire time. She was certain from the moment she locked the carriage house behind her and hurried through the dark streets toward the church—as she waxed the stone floor and wiped the blue folds of the plaster Virgin's gown and swabbed the dust from the edges of the leaded panes of the jewel-toned stained-glass windows—that George had woken up and was crying in panic to find her missing, that the carriage house had burst into flames and he was screaming for her to save him.

But she arrived home at two in the morning to find all quiet and well, the child slumbering peacefully as usual, the milk untouched near his curled hand.

It went on like this for two weeks. She discovered she could have the church spotless in three hours and, counting the walk uptown and back down, leave the baby alone for less than four. He'd be fine for that amount of time, she told herself, reassured by the nights she left without incident.

Then one night she arrived home to hear, in the alleyway that led behind the building to the carriage house, a sound that at first she took for the meowing of a cat in heat. But as she hurried closer to the carriage house, her key already in her hand, she realized the cries were George's.

He was standing in his crib, the netting torn around his head and cutting into his neck, his face bright red and covered with tears. When she rushed to the crib and lifted him out, she felt that he was hot as a lit stove.

She managed to calm him down, rocking, cooing, telling him over and over that Mama was here now and would never leave him again; but even after she ran a cool washcloth over his face and neck, he was still warm and had grown listless. Afraid to think it was something else, Bridget told herself it was just a cold. Or that he was teething. She ran a finger over the child's gums but felt no sharp edges poking through. George tried to suck on her finger and she opened her blouse, thinking it might make him feel better to nurse, but he couldn't latch on, and besides, she feared her milk had dried up. She finally resorted to dipping her finger into a glass of milk and he sucked on that, but listlessly, refusing the cereal and the egg she tried to feed him.

He slept and he woke, so hot in the bed beside her that she could barely stand to keep the blanket over them, though she was even more afraid to leave him uncovered. At dawn she woke to find him sleeping noisily beside her, snoring as loudly as his father had ever done, his fever seemingly broken.

She kissed George's cool forehead and heated water to wash his face, carefully cleaning off the mucus that had caked on his cheeks and clearing the sweat from his hairline. She ran the cloth over his tummy and his bottom, eliciting a low-pitched gurgle, and peered closely at his eyes, which still seemed bleary. No, no, she told herself, he was better, there wasn't a trace of fever now, it had been a twenty-four-hour bug. She fed him the cereal warmed from the night before and dressed him in fresh clothes hanging stiff above the kitchen sink.

She was not going to leave him again. Tonight she'd wait until his bedtime and then carry him with her to the church. Surely he'd fall asleep during the walk; she'd lay him on his blanket to sleep in the church while she worked. The priests in the rectory and the nuns in the convent next door were all asleep when she was there anyway. No one would ever know.

"You'll be a good little boy, won't you?" she said to the child later that night, rubbing her nose against his as they made their way uptown. "You won't make a peep."

When they got to the church she left him, God forgive her, lying behind the altar, gazing in wonder at the life-size gold crucifix, while she washed and waxed the pews, taking special care to scrape the chewing gum from beneath the seats, something Sister Dominic always checked for. Behind the altar, George dozed, but then he awoke with a squeal and she rushed to fetch him, thinking he felt warm again. She set him on the wine-colored velvet cushion of the pew as she scraped and washed and polished. He lay quietly beside her, his half-closed eyes fastened on her.

When he grew restless, she tied him to her body with the blanket and, slung tightly there, lulled by the rhythm of her work, he dropped into a fitful sleep. She swung back and forth, back and forth, polishing the curved wooden crests of the benches, dark and smooth as the banisters that wound up the stairs to the very top of the house on Sixty-fourth Street. Whenever she stopped moving, she could hear George breathing noisily, as if he were forced to suck his air in through a tubful of water.

He slept for a long time, which she imagined was healing him: Please, she prayed as she moved her rag along the burnished wood. Please. Please. Please. But then he woke with a howl, his screams piercing the tomb of the church.

"Shhhhhhhh," she said, holding him tightly and shifting from one leg to the other, patting his back through the rough blanket. His cries seemed to be loud enough to ring out through the streets like a bell.

Afraid that maybe his leg or his arm had gotten twisted painfully inside the makeshift sling or that his diaper was irritating him, she lifted him out of the blanket. Away from the warmth of her own body, in contrast to the chill of the church, it was clear, when she touched his cheek and pressed her lips to his neck, that his fever had risen again, higher than before. Not even her brother Patrick—not even Floyd—had burned as hotly as this.

"Oh, God," Bridget muttered, setting George down on the pew, loosening the ribbon that fastened his sweater, edging her fingers into the folds of his neck, laying them against his temples, trying to draw out his heat into the cool of her hands, feeling her panic rise up.

"There," she said, remembering saying the same thing to Floyd the night he became ill. "There, there."

If she didn't do something this very instant, she was afraid he might burst into flames.

"Oh, God," she said again, aware now that she really was talking to God, here in this place that was supposed to be holy.

"Spare him, God," she said aloud, letting her eyes focus on the crucifix and on the statues of the Virgin. "Let him live and I'll do anything you ask, forever."

She was untying his cotton vest now, peeling it open. She suddenly remembered her mother, once when Patrick was running a fever, holding a cool cloth to the child's forehead, his neck, to the crease at the top of his legs and the pulse point under his arms. She looked around the church frantically, thinking that she could carry George downstairs to the lavatory, where there was a sink, and submerge him completely.

Then suddenly he arched his back and, his face as red as blood, let out a shriek that made even the loudest of his other cries seem like burbles. Gathering him into her arms, Bridget's eyes lit on the font of holy water. She'd splash the smallest bit on his face and his neck. That might calm him and cool him, at least until she could get him down to the sink.

He was quiet, too, startled into a hiccup by the cool water, and she was cooing to him, telling him that he was a good boy, that he would soon be well, that she would make sure he was well, when she heard the heavy thunk of the church's door and saw a figure silhouetted against the darkness outside. Bridget held her breath, hoping that it was another poor soul seeking a few moments' shelter. But then she heard the unmistakable brogue of Sister Dominic.

"We were awoken by a scream," the nun said. "I've come to see what was the matter."

Bridget froze, George lying back against her outstretched

arm, Holy Water glistening on his face, soaking the front of his vest.

"What are you doing?" Sister Dominic yelled, her contorted face coming into view. "Sacrilege!" she cried. "Sacrilege, with the bastard child!"

"He isn't . . ." Bridget began.

"Heathen!" the nun cried, swatting at her. "Whore!"

"No!" Bridget said, curling her body over George's so that the nun's blows landed on her back.

"Get out," said the nun. "Out! Out of the House of God!"

Bridget's first impulse was to bolt for the door, anything to get away as quickly as possible, but then she remembered George's blanket on the pew, her coat neatly folded in the vestibule.

"I just have to—" she began.

"Out, before I have you arrested!" the nun said, raising her arm to strike again.

Sheltering the baby, Bridget whirled around with all her fury and knocked the nun out of the way. As the sister fell to the ground, squawking and flapping like a crow, Bridget ran up the aisle of the church and snatched George's blanket, then dashed back toward the door, managing to grab her coat before the sister was able to scramble to her feet.

Once Bridget had pushed out the front door and made her way down the front path and off the church grounds—once she managed to tug her own coat over her shoulders and wrap George in his blanket, realizing too late that she'd lost his hat somewhere along the way—she began to breathe more easily.

But almost immediately the panic rose up again, stronger than before. That had been her last option: What was she going to do now? With charity exhausted, with no way to earn money, how was she going to care for her child, make him well, buy him food, find a way to live? She could go back to the carriage house, scrape together something to eat for tonight, for tomorrow, but what then? She thought wildly of walking to the river, onto the docks, hurling herself and the child with her into the icy water, where at least they would find peace.

And then she knew: There was one other choice. It was one that had risen up again and again over the past weeks, though she'd kept pushing it away. Now, though, she felt the hand of God on her shoulder, guiding her, protecting her in a way she hadn't believed in since her girlhood. Despite George's whimpers and the heat of his fever against her chest, she felt lighter, knowing what she had to do. She felt almost unconflicted as she moved inexorably back toward Sixty-fourth Street and Maude.

Bridget pressed the bell, the door's glossy blackness blending into the moonless night. It was a new maid who opened the door, the light and warmth of the house shining behind the woman like the sun.

"I've come to see Mrs. Apfelmann," Bridget explained. "I'm Bridget McLean—I mean, Early. I used to work here."

The maid was staring at the blanketed curve of George's body held inside Bridget's coat.

"My son," Bridget said, jiggling him a little, though trying not to wake him. "George Junior."

"Wait here," the maid said, leaving Bridget standing in the vestibule and disappearing up the stairs.

The house seemed to have changed little in the months since Bridget had last been there. To the left there was the small reception parlor, never used in her memory except when unwanted visitors came to call. Down the hall, from the kitchen in the back of the house, Bridget could hear the clatter of dishes.

The maid returned. "Madame said to tell you she's engaged."

Bridget's heart skipped a beat. She had thought Maude might be cold or refuse to help, but not that her old employer would flat-out refuse to see her.

Bridget leaned in. "Please," she said. "My baby is sick. Would you please tell her it's important?"

"Madame said to tell you she's very sorry but we don't have any business with you any longer."

The maid advanced on her, meaning to push her back out into the night.

"Maude!" Bridget called. And as the maid began tugging at her clothes, Bridget screamed even more loudly: "Maude!"

From above, there was the sound of footsteps clattering on the stairs, and then Maude appeared.

"What's the meaning of this?" Maude said. "Mr. Apfelmann can't be upset by this carrying-on."

This was what Bridget had expected, one reason that until now she'd shoved away any thought of coming back. But she had to try this so she'd know in her heart that she had tried everything.

"Maude, please," Bridget said, her voice calm with resolve now, strong. "My baby is ill."

Maude took a step forward, enough for Bridget to see that

although she was even slimmer than before, her hair an even brighter yellow, she looked distinctly older, with some dullness and heaviness about her that hadn't been there a year ago.

"Ill?" Maude said. "What's that to me?"

Bridget loosened George's blanket so Maude could see the child. Maude moved closer still, laying her hand on the baby's feverish face.

"But he's burning up!" Maude cried. "Come upstairs. Come quick."

Bridget felt a rush of gratitude as she followed Maude up the familiar stairway, then up again to Maude's own room, where Maude scooped George from his blanket and laid him on her silk spread, peeling away his clothes damp with sweat and holy water. She commanded Bridget to fetch a wet washcloth and then took it from her hands and ran it down the length of George's body, from just below his ear to his tender underbelly, talking in a soft voice to the child as she worked.

"All right. There's a sweetheart," she cooed. "Maude is taking care of you now."

The baby, calmer and also more alert, stared up at Maude with fever-glistened eyes as if mesmerized, kicking his legs, waving his arms.

"Aren't you a handsome one?" Maude said. "Aren't you a beautiful boy?"

Bridget had never seen Maude care for Floyd like this. Maybe what Nora had said was true and Maude really had changed. As Bridget's misgivings slid away, all the friendship, all the love she'd felt for Maude, came flooding back.

"Maude, I'm sorry I stormed out of here the way I did,"

Bridget said. "I know you were only trying to help. I wish we could be friends again. I miss you and I wish . . . I wish I could come back and work for you again. . . ."

Maude had not turned to look at her but was still staring transfixed at the baby, holding his little hands now, gazing into his eyes, and moving his arms slowly up and down.

"If you came back, would you bring the baby?" Maude finally asked, still not looking at her.

"Yes," Bridget stammered. "I mean, I'd have to. There's no other—"

"That's good, because I'd only want you back if you brought the baby," Maude said.

Finally she turned, still holding on to George's hands and cycling his arms, but staring straight at Bridget, her eyes unblinking.

"He's a good boy," Bridget rushed to say. "I could still work, as hard as before, whatever you want, and take care of him. I promise he won't bother you. . . ."

"Oh, I know he's not going to bother me," Maude said, turning her attention back to the baby. "Are you, sweetheart? Are you? No, you're not. You are going to sit with me and play with me and you are going to be my own little darling boy."

25

Cait, Present

Martin offered to go with Cait to Sixty-fourth Street, but she said no, this was something she had to do alone. When she'd imagined finding her birth mother, she'd never seen herself, somehow, walking uptown to a neighborhood she'd been to dozens of times over the years. The block where Billie Apfelmann lived stretched from the Central Park Zoo at the Fifth Avenue end to the Chanel store guarding its Madison Avenue corner. Not five blocks from midtown, with its skyscrapers and gargantuan stores and hotels, this was still a province of town houses, genteel four- and five-story brownstone and limestone buildings with big iron pots of mums and boxwood flanking their front doors.

Some of these town houses were occupied by apartments or embassies, Cait saw, but many were still single-family homes. Very rich families.

Before she actually started looking for her birth mother, she had envisioned someone poor, without resources, someone like little Riley's mother. Now, though, inspired by this posh setting, Cait imagined a tall dark woman with lacquered hair and a designer suit, someone straitlaced and proper, someone who'd had a baby and then wanted to bury the unseemly secret, to forget Cait had ever existed.

Cait hadn't wanted to call first. If Billie Apfelmann was really her birth mother, Cait didn't want to delay the meeting or give her time to prepare a game face. Cait wanted this Billie's reaction to be raw and unfiltered.

When Cait walked up to the black-painted door of the limestone building at the address her mother had given her, she took the slip of paper out of her pocket and checked the house number twice. Instead of Billie Apfelmann's name on the doorbell, there was a brass plate engraved "The Bridget Early Home for Young Mothers." Bridget, that name again. Cait's finger hesitated above the bell and was still hovering there when the door swung open.

"Hey." A very young, very pregnant girl with curly dark hair and a tattoo of a teardrop on her cheek seemed about to leave the house. "Can I help you?"

"I'm looking for Billie Apfelmann," said Cait.

"Oh," said the girl. "Ma. Okay."

She reached over and rang the bell; Cait could hear it buzzing insistently inside the house.

"You're a little old to be a new inmate," the girl said to Cait. "I'm guessing social worker?"

"What?"

"No worries. I hear her on the stairs."

The girl went on her way, leaving Cait alone in the doorway. She held her breath as she saw the feet in soft flat black boots appear on the carpeted stairs, followed by a slim pair of denim-clad legs, and then a blue sweater on a trim torso. Finally, from the shadows of the hallway Cait was able to make out a small fair woman who at first glance looked barely older than she was. But as the woman moved closer to the door and into the light, Cait could see that there were lines in the corners of her green eyes and gray threaded through her light hair.

The woman held out her hand to shake Cait's. "I'm Billie Apfelmann," she said. "What can I do for you?"

Cait wondered if Sally's guess that this was her mother could possibly be accurate. This woman looked nothing like Cait. Dozens of times over the years she'd passed women of every type everywhere in the world and wondered, Could that be my mother? But she never would have wondered that of this tiny, fair woman.

And yet, Cait found herself feeling hurt, somehow, that Billie didn't recognize her.

"You really don't know who I am?" she said, half smiling down at Billie, who was still holding out her hand.

There was a long moment then as Cait watched in suspense and with some amusement the progress of comprehension move across Billie's face. Confusion, first, and then a question, then the search for recognition, and finally realization.

"Oh, God," Billie said, a sob escaping her throat. She threw her arms around Cait and drew her into a hug that was tighter and more heartfelt than Cait had ever anticipated.

"Come in," she said, pulling Cait over the doorsill. "Come inside."

She took Cait by the hand and wordlessly led her into the house and up the winding staircase. Another pregnant young woman, heading down, squeezed past them.

"Oh, Dulcie!" Billie said excitedly. "This is my daughter. The daughter I gave up for adoption."

Cait winced, surprised to hear their relationship presented so baldly.

Dulcie smiled shyly. "Nice to meet you," she said to Cait.

"I'm Cait," she said, and then, for Billie's benefit: "Caitlin Trippel. That's what—"

"I know," Billie said, continuing up the stairs.

At the top of the stairs was an office that had been converted from a former dining room, judging from the crystal chandelier that hung over the long wooden table. File boxes sat atop a buffet, books filled a glass-fronted china cupboard, and an old black computer dominated the far end of the table.

"What is this place?" Billie asked.

"It's a private home for young women who are pregnant and not sure what to do," Billie said. "They can stay here until they have their babies, and even after, till they have some kind of plan."

"Like *The Girls Who Went Away*," said Cait, citing a recent book on birth mothers and adoption that she'd read and reread during her search.

Billie looked at her sharply. "No, not like that," she said. "We're not coercing anybody to do anything here, and we're certainly not hiding anyone or anything. We're the opposite of that."

Billie led her into a front room that was still furnished like a grand living room, though the silk upholstery was threadbare and the oversize pink and blue Oriental rug had been rolled up at one end, exposing a worn parquet floor. Faded gray silk drapes hung on the windows, and there were darker squares on the pale gray walls where it seemed a gallery's worth of paintings had once hung. The only piece of art remaining was a portrait of a beautiful blond woman above the fireplace.

"Who's that?" Cait asked.

"That's Maude Apfelmann, who owned this house."

"Apfelmann," Cait said. "Your grandmother?" And my great-grandmother, Cait thought, though she wasn't sure she had a right to claim that association. "You look a lot like her."

"I look like my mother," Billie said, sitting in one of the silk chairs that flanked the fireplace and gesturing for Cait to take the one opposite her. Billie was wearing no makeup; her hair, slightly wavy, was unbrushed and cut in a simple pageboy that added to her youthful appearance. And her gaze was so clear and direct and straightforward that Cait couldn't help, despite all her fears and qualms, liking her.

"So, Cait," Billie said. "How did you find me?"

"My mother . . ." Cait stopped and felt herself color. That phrase came so naturally to her lips when referring to Sally, but she didn't want Billie to feel insulted or hurt.

"Your mother told you?" Billie's brow furrowed. "I didn't think she knew who I was."

"She didn't, not really. But I hired a detective and did some digging on my own. I found some names, 'Apfel,' and 'Bridget Masterson,' the name I had at birth. She helped me connect the dots."

"Why now?" Billie asked. "I half expected to hear from you when you turned eighteen or twenty-one. At this point, I'd kind of given up hope that you wanted to find me."

Cait considered confessing her own news but bit it back. Not yet, she told herself. She doesn't deserve that much of me yet.

"You could have looked for me," Cait said.

"But I did," said Billie. "Years ago, as soon as I established this place. I left a letter with my name and contact information for Caitlin Trippel at the adoption registry."

"It never occurred to me that you'd know my name," Cait said. "I searched for someone who was looking for Bridget Masterson or Apfel."

Cait felt so flustered by the knowledge that she might have easily connected with Billie early in her search that she was afraid she was going to break down and start bawling before anything even happened. To keep that from happening, she fished in her bag for her notebook and a pen; taking notes always helped her focus on what was being said rather than her reaction to what was being said. Pretend you're interviewing the duchess of Cambridge, she told herself. A Somali pirate. Get the story and don't break down.

"So you've made teenage pregnancy and adoption a career," Cait said, pen poised.

"It's not just a career, it's a vocation," said Billie. "It's a way for me to use everything I know and all my family's money and this place to help girls who are in the same position I was in."

Same position, Cait wrote.

"And what position was that?" Cait asked.

"I was young," Billie said. "I was confused. My parents were dead. The father, your father, was not involved. I didn't know what to do."

Cait wrote, *Young. No par., boyfr. Confused.*

"So, why didn't you just have an abortion?" Cait asked, tapping her pen on the paper, working to control her voice. "It was legal back then. Why have a baby, only to give it away?"

It was so much easier to think of her infant self as an "it." The same way, she realized, she'd been thinking of her own baby.

"First of all, I didn't know I was going to give you away, as you put it—not for sure," Billie said. Billie seemed maddeningly calmer than Cait felt, was having an easier time maintaining eye contact. "I thought about having an abortion, of course; it was normal back then, more accepted than it is now. I just felt . . . I just felt you were alive. That you deserved to be born. That even if I couldn't give you anything else, I could give you that."

Without willing it, Cait ran her hand across her own stomach. Billie's words sounded dangerously like pro-life rhetoric to her, and there was so much of that she didn't agree with. She didn't think that every unborn life was valuable per se, didn't believe that the fetus had the same rights as its mother, believed maintaining a pregnancy was a woman's choice alone.

And yet, she found herself feeling about her own pregnancy exactly as Billie had felt: that what was inside her was alive, an incipient human being, with its own heart and brain and beauty and the same potential for a fruitful life on earth as she'd had.

Would her own child sit across from her one day, asking why she'd done or not done the things she was doing right now? Would her child really want to know that she'd contemplated having an abortion, that she'd been ambivalent at best about going ahead with the pregnancy, that its—no, *his* or *her*—very existence turned on what was being revealed in this room at this moment? Or did we only want to believe, any of us, that we were longed for, that we were welcomed, that we were loved and cherished, even before we became ourselves?

"Is that enough?" Cait demanded, tears threatening to overtake her voice. "To give birth to a child, without knowing if you can love it?"

"I loved you," Billie said softly.

"Oh, right," Cait said, sniffling, not even trying to control the sarcasm. "If you love something, set it free."

Billie looked as if she'd been slapped and sat there for a long moment, pale and frozen, before shaking her head slightly as if to wake herself up.

"I can understand why you're angry," she said to Cait. "I deserve it. But you don't know the whole story."

"That's right, I don't," said Cait, setting the notebook aside. This wasn't a story, she admitted to herself. This was her life. And she'd hidden from the truth and her feelings about it long enough. "Why don't you tell me?"

"I had postpartum depression," Billie said. "Not that anyone called it that. Nobody talked about it back then. Maude and Bridget—Bridget worked for Maude; I was living here with both of them after you were born—certainly didn't know what was going on, and neither did this horrible old-fashioned doctor that Maude sent me to. I just thought I was going crazy. I could barely motivate myself to drink a glass of water, never mind take care of an infant."

"So you were ill." Cait couldn't believe how giddy she felt at hearing this explanation, which made it neither her own fault nor her mother's that she'd been put up for adoption.

"I was ill," Billie said, nodding, "and maybe if it had been a more enlightened time and I'd been treated for depression, I might have pulled through and been able to be a real mother to you. But that wasn't all, Cait. Maude wanted me to cover up something that I wouldn't lie about, and that led to a series of events that brought all the walls tumbling down."

Cait was lost. "What events? What did she want you to lie about?"

Billie shuddered, as if she were living the moment all over again. "She wanted me to hide the fact that you were black."

Everything went still. In the first instant, what Billie said seemed so ridiculous that Cait automatically rejected it. She wasn't black. Anyone could see she wasn't black. And then, with one small shift in her point of view, so many things fell into place, things she'd wondered about her whole life, even today, on meeting her biological mother for the first time and not understanding why they looked nothing alike.

"I had no idea," Cait said.

Shock spread over Billie's face. "You mean Sally and Vern never told you?"

"I don't think they knew," said Cait. "At least, especially now, when my mother's told me everything, I can't imagine why she'd hide that."

Billie was shaking her head, a faraway look in her eyes. "Bridget didn't tell anyone. That makes perfect sense. She was probably afraid they wouldn't take you if they knew."

Cait's face turned hot. The idea that Billie, this stranger, hadn't wanted her was something she could accept, something she'd come to terms with long ago. But the idea that Vern and Sally wouldn't want her . . .

"I may have had problems with being adopted," Cait said hotly, "but I don't think my parents had any problems with it, with me. They always made me feel like I was the perfect . . ."

"No, no," Billie said. "I'm sorry, I didn't mean that your race, that anything about you, would have made them feel differently about you. Honestly, I always assumed that they knew, that they told you. This is all about Bridget, who was very old-school, about her fears and prejudices."

"And yet, you named me after her."

"She loved you," Billie said. "She loved me, too. You . . . you were everything to her. She didn't care who your father was, what your racial background was. She was going to do everything in her power to make sure you had the best parents and the best upbringing possible."

"Why did she care so much? What was it to her? I mean, why didn't your grandmother, who had all this money, this house . . ."

"Maude was only capable of loving herself," Billie said flatly. "She cared about other people only to the extent that they reflected on her. She loved me at first, because I looked like her, but then when I got pregnant with you—with a black man, no less—that wasn't up to her standards."

"Yet, Bridget loved you unconditionally."

"And you, too," Billie said. "Bridget believed, for a long time—for decades, really—that the best thing for me and for you, too, would be to be raised as part of Maude's family, with that money, that protection. And then when she finally came to terms with the evil that lay at the heart of that, she let me go and brought you to Sally."

Billie had used Sally's name several times during the conversation, but for the first time it struck Cait how odd that was. "How do you know Sally's name?" Cait asked.

"I've always known her name," Billie said. "Almost always. Bridget told me all about Sally and Vern, how wonderful they were, how happy you were with them. It's how she convinced me to sign the adoption papers."

Cait felt her emotions rise now, beyond all her efforts to corral them. "So you've known all along who my parents were," she said, no longer caring what Billie felt when she used the word "parents" to refer to Vern and Sally. "Who I was."

"Not from the very beginning," Billie said. "But from early on, yes."

"Did you know where I was, too?" Cait asked.

Billie gazed straight at her but took a moment before answering. "Yes," she said.

"Then why didn't you come and get me?" Cait blurted.

Cait felt as stunned as Billie seemed by her outburst, rising up from a place that had been shut down and padlocked so long ago that she'd forgotten it existed. She flashed on her childhood fantasy, sometimes thrilling, sometimes terrifying, that her mother—her ghostly real mother—would swoop in and save her: from the bully on the school bus, from the snappish teacher, even from Sally or Vern on the rare stormy day. The fantasy was that her mother was out there somewhere, wanting Cait, loving her, prevented from reaching her by moats and vines and dragons, by evil witches or secret spells. Why else wouldn't she come?

Cait felt Billie's eyes on her.

"I don't think you would have really wanted me to come get you," Billie said.

"Because you were so screwed up?" Cait said, wanting to lash out and also wanting to give voice to her grown-up rationalizations that her so-called birth mother must have been a prostitute, or a drug addict, or a rape victim, or a mental patient, or dead. Or else, why had she given Cait away? Why hadn't she ever come looking for her?

"You play mother to all these girls here, they call you *Ma*, but you didn't think I'd want you to take care of me?" Cait said. "Or maybe it was that *you* didn't want to take care of me. You can love all these strangers, but you couldn't love me."

Now the tears that had been threatening to overtake Cait since the moment she arrived spilled over and ran down her cheeks. Billie jumped up and moved toward her, arms outstretched, but Cait put up her hands to keep her away.

"No," Cait said. "You don't get to do that yet."

Billie sat back down, hands curled in her lap like discarded gloves.

"I loved you," Billie said. "I never stopped loving you."

"But not enough to want me?"

"It's not that simple. I wanted you, but at first I knew I couldn't take care of you."

"Why didn't you just have Bridget help you, or Maude? Or use your grandmother's money to hire someone to take care of me? This place is so big, you never would have even had to see me."

Billie's face twisted in anguish. "Were you so unhappy?" she asked Cait. "Because that's not what I thought. I thought you loved Sally, and Vern, too. I thought you were so much happier with them than you could ever be with me."

This brought Cait up short. She had been happy. She had

loved Vern and Sally. She hadn't ever longed, at least not in any conscious real way, to leave them and live with the shadow mother she'd always known she had.

But that didn't stop her from wishing that Billie had tried to get her back, had done everything to hold her close, had loved her—however much enough was. As much as Sally loved her.

"You were my mother," Cait said to Billie, more accusation than statement of fact.

"I gave birth to you," said Billie, "but by the time I was ready to be your mother, I discovered I wasn't your mother anymore."

"I know Sally's my mother," said Cait, frowning in confusion. "But you're my mother, too."

Billie was smiling slightly, but she was also shaking her head no. "I think I better tell you everything that happened," she said, "so you finally know the whole truth. I hope then you'll understand."

26

Billie, Present

Drinking in her tall, dark, beautiful daughter, like a time-lapse progression of the infant and little girl she'd been, Billie would have been happy not to talk at all and instead just sit there and stare. Cait looked so much like Jupe—same style, different color—that it was almost like sitting across from him after all this time. How proud he would have been of his daughter; how happy, in the end, that Billie had ignored his wishes and had their child.

But the time had finally come, Billie knew, to tell the truth she'd long ago sworn she would deliver. She could never have the kind of relationship she'd always dreamed of with her daughter if she didn't start there.

"Maude thought we should pretend that you were white, pretend your black father had never existed, and when I objected and said I wanted always to tell you the truth, she became very angry," Billie told Cait, the events of that night thirty-five years before rising up as vividly as if they'd happened mere hours ago.

Maude sitting in her bed, in the room just above where Billie and Cait sat now, pale hair streaming over her shoulders, eyes unnaturally bright, face eerily calm. So Billie thought the truth was always best, Maude said. All right, then, she'd tell her the truth, her precious, wonderful, beautiful, horrible truth.

"The truth is I'm not your grandmother," Maude said, her voice a singsong, taunting. "That baby is nothing to me. You see, your father, Johnny, he wasn't really my son. Isn't that the *truth*, Bridget? His *true* mother was Bridget."

"The Bridget you named me after," interrupted Cait, the full connection dawning. "The Bridget who engineered my adoption by Sally and Vern. The same Bridget this place is named after now."

"That's right. The woman who was kind to me, who took care of me when I was pregnant with you, who took care of you after you were born. She was my real grandmother. Your real great-grandmother."

After Maude's revelation, Bridget stood frozen for a moment, the baby still held against her as if for protection.

And then she seemed to melt, addressing Billie alone.

"I didn't know what else to do," Bridget said in a rush. "Your father was an infant, deathly ill. My husband had been killed in the war, I had no money, there was no welfare then, mothers couldn't work. I was afraid my baby was going to die. I went to Maude knowing she was my last resort. She took us in, provided for the baby, let me stay with him always. But she wanted him for her own. She wanted me to give her my baby."

Billie turned, horrified, to Maude. "How could you have done that?"

"How could I have done that?" Maude looked appalled at Billie's accusation. "Why don't you ask your precious Bridget? She's the one who gave away her child."

"You're the one who required it of her!" exclaimed Billie. "What choice did she have?"

"Maude said he'd be raised as a rich boy," Bridget said, her eyes dim, focused on the memory. "He'd have every advantage, all the best health care, the finest schools, and I'd be there through the whole thing taking care of him, as good as his mother, just as I had been with Floyd."

"But he wasn't Floyd, was he?" said Maude. "Floyd was like me, blond, sunny, energetic. And George—that's what Bridget called him, though we quickly changed his name to John—was dark like his father, a quiet child. He was an inward child, brooding, even when he was young."

"If he was those things, you made him like that," said Bridget, "petting him one minute, abandoning him for a month in Europe the next."

"Leaving him in your charge!" Maude said with a harsh laugh. "You were his nanny, his *mother*! You should have been delighted I left you alone with him!"

"But he thought *you* were his mother!" Bridget cried. "I would have been delighted if he was satisfied to be alone with me. But you were the one he wanted!"

"Oh, that wasn't the problem," said Maude, waving a hand

dismissively. "The problem was that you spoiled him, over-indulged him, just as you've spoiled Billie here."

"I was trying to make up for everything he didn't get from you, from anyone, after poor Mr. Apfelmann died!"

"Yes, but nothing was ever enough, was it? Because Johnny had a weakness of the blood, a weakness of the genes. He took after his father, the great George McLean, who was a drunk and who ran away from his wife and his unborn child to join the army. You might have inherited that same weakness for alcohol, Billie, along with Bridget's inability to keep her legs shut. So there's your truth, Billie. You're not a rich girl, a thoroughbred, a descendant of mine. You're just an Irish slut and your baby's a little pickaninny."

Billie had reached out and slapped Maude across the face. Telling it to Cait now, she again felt the sting on her hand and the infinitely sharper sting in her heart at the words: "weakness," "drunk," "pickaninny," "slut." No matter how many thousands of times she'd relived that exchange over the years, the memory still pierced her chest like a knife.

Billie rushed from the room, raced down the stairs, and stood panting in the front hall, dizzy from the revelations, wild to do something, but unsure what. She heard Bridget's step on the stairs, the baby's rising wail.

"Billie, dear, I'm sorry," Bridget pleaded over the baby's cries. "I only did what I thought was best for your father. I felt as if I had nowhere else to turn. And Maude was loving, at first. She was so delighted to have the baby, it really did seem like the best possible solution, I never dreamed everything would go so wrong."

"Oh, Bridget, I'm not angry with you," Billie said. "You did the best you could. It's her I blame. She's the monster."

"No," Bridget said. "She doesn't mean to be. She may not have known how to be a good mother, but she was devastated when your father left. It killed her that she never saw him again, that she never saw you."

"Did my father know the truth?" Billie asked Bridget.

Bridget looked away, then back at Billie. "I never told Maude this, but I told him," she confessed. "He never forgave either of us. That's why he never came back here."

"I don't blame him," Billie said. "I can forgive you, Bridget, but I can't forgive Maude, not after the things she just said. I don't want any part of this house, this family. I'm taking the baby and I'm leaving, now, tonight."

She lifted her infant daughter from Bridget's arms. The child felt so heavy to her, so stiff and foreign, yearning away, turning its head, its cry escalating.

"You can't leave tonight," said Bridget. "Where will you go?"

"I don't know," Billie said, trying to jiggle the baby as she'd seen Bridget do, to calm her, though her efforts seemed to have no effect. The baby seemed to be trying to hurl itself from her arms. "It doesn't matter. I'll sleep in the park if I have to. But I can't spend another night under this cursed roof."

"You can't just rush out into the night like that with an infant. You need formula, diapers, blankets, money." As if she was afraid Billie might bolt out the door, Bridget gathered the baby back. "You might think you can sleep beneath a bush, but you can't do that with a child: she'll freeze to death. For God's sake, Billie, think about it. At least wait till morning."

"You keep the baby here till morning," said Billie impetuously. "I've got to get out of here now. If I stay here another minute, I don't know what I'll do to myself. To her. I've got to find a place to stay, get some money together, figure out what I'm going to do."

"Maude will give you money," Bridget said. "It's your due, your inheritance. Even if she doesn't want to claim your father as her son, she adopted him legally and he is entitled to her estate, and as his only child *you* are entitled to that estate."

"I don't want her money, don't you see, Bridget? My father didn't want it, and I don't want it. All I was ever looking for when I came here was love and support, and you're the only one who gave me that. From her I don't want anything."

"I love you," Bridget said. She rocked the baby, whose cries had slowed to faint mewls, on her shoulder. "And I love the baby. But I can't take care of her, Billie, not full time, not by myself. I wish I could but I'm not strong enough now. And she needs someone who can be there for her as she gets older. She needs you, dear."

"I know," said Billie. "I don't want her to grow up here. I don't want her to know anything about Maude or the Apfelmanns or this horrible legacy. I'm going to make a different life for her—a better life—and then I'll come and take her away from here. Just as soon as I can."

When Billie reached this point in the story, she had to stop, feeling herself getting choked up. It was so surreal, sitting here in the same house across from the adult Cait, remembering the last moment the two of them were here together, so long ago. If she had known it would be thirty-five years before she would be with her daughter again—if she had known that by that time they would be virtual strangers—she never would have been able to go through with what she'd done next.

She'd taken the baby back from Bridget and kissed her, first on one cheek, then the other, the infant's skin soft as a tulip petal against her lips. She'd held the baby tight, smelling the sweet spot at her hairline. For once, the child was quiet, warm, breath steady and pulsing like a heartbeat.

Maybe she could stay after all, Billie had thought. Maybe she could not bear to leave.

She wanted to draw this moment out for Cait now, to make her daughter believe that she hadn't wanted to leave her behind, that she truly intended to return, that she'd been cut up inside. And all that was true, but it was also true that she did not return. It was also true that she gave away her daughter not just for that night, or for a few weeks, but forever. And her pain at the moment she'd stepped away did not really matter for anything compared to the larger truth of her leaving.

Maude called down from above, reigniting Billie's resolve. She nuzzled the baby's neck one more time and passed her back to Bridget. She would go back to California, she thought, find someplace cheap to stay in Oakland, then send for the baby. Or she'd go to Belize, where they could live on the beach. Or she'd apply to college for real, get a scholarship, find enough money to support her child that way.

Maude called out again, more insistently this time.

"I have to go," Billie said in a low voice.

"Here," Bridget said, shifting the baby to one hip, fumbling in the pocket of her sweater. She pressed a soft roll of bills into Billie's hand.

"Thank you," Billie said, kissing the old woman's papery cheek. "Grandma."

Stepping out into the night, she felt stunned to see couples strolling arm in arm in the newly warm spring weather, the streetlights casting pools of golden light, the luxurious town houses standing like fortresses of unchanging comfort when she felt as if she'd been wrenched in half more surely than she had when the baby had been cut from her body. She felt more alone than she had when her father died, when her mother died, more alone than she'd felt when Jupe left her. More alone than she'd felt before she knew that Maude and Bridget even existed, before there was a child on earth who would always be her own.

But she had felt something else, too, something she couldn't bring herself to confess now to Cait. She'd felt light for the first time since she'd discovered she was pregnant, since she'd arrived in New York, maybe even since she'd found her grandmother's letters under the bed: free, happy to be weaving unencumbered among the people on the sidewalk, to feel as if she could sit down without needing to balance the baby on her lap, to roll over to sleep without worrying she'd crush a small body, to wake to her own schedule instead of the child's cries, to think only of her own hunger, her own thirst, her own needs, her own tears. She felt so light she could float away, she thought, somewhere that no one would ever find her.

27

Bridget, 1977

B ridget stood frozen in the front hallway, the baby in her arms, listening to—well, what? Billie had slammed the door behind her with a bang, which had reverberated off the walls, but now that sound was only a memory. All was silent.

She turned stonily and began to mount the curved stairway. She'd never tried to make it up three flights with the baby in her arms, and she was afraid that she might lose her footing. It was difficult to hold the baby and also steady herself on the railing. By the time she got to the third floor, she was breathing heavily and her forehead was beaded with sweat.

The child was fussing now and she changed her diaper and dressed her in a fresh gown, fed her a bottle, and eased her into bed. The whole time she was impatient to get the baby to sleep so she could go downstairs and confront Maude, but she tried not to show that. The poor little thing had lost her mother tonight and she needed to feel that Bridget, at least, was there.

Finally, the baby fell asleep. Bridget waited a few moments, until she was certain that her little namesake was breathing deeply in her bassinet, and then she tiptoed downstairs.

Maude's door was closed, but Bridget pushed it open without knocking. Maude was sitting in bed, an issue of *Town & Country* open on her lap. Bridget couldn't believe she'd been afraid at one time, after they lost Floyd, that Maude would die up here. An atom bomb could go off in Central Park and Maude would still be sitting up here, reading her party pages and rubbing cream into her skin.

"That was horrible, what you did tonight, what you said," Bridget told her.

"I should call the police on that girl," Maude said, flipping a page. "Charge her with assault."

"She's gone," Bridget said. "You drove her away."

"Good," Maude said, flipping pages again, turning her head to look at the pictures in an exaggerated way. "I don't know how the little brat found us in the first place."

Bridget grabbed the magazine out of Maude's hands. "She found us because I tracked Johnny down. I wrote to him all those years. And when Billie found the letters and called, I pretended I was you and invited her to come."

"You pretended . . ." Maude said, her mouth dropping open. Then she threw her head back and laughed. "Well, you have more gumption than I gave you credit for. But you obviously made a huge mistake."

"The only mistake I made, Maude, was coming back here with my son all those years ago. I should have known that, whatever you said, you wouldn't be able to love him. You can only love what you see in the mirror."

"That's not true," Maude said. "I tried to love Johnny. I tried with all my heart. But you wouldn't let me. Always going behind my back, taking him places I didn't want him to go, giving him treats that I forbade, and contradicting my word at every turn."

"You said I would be as good as his mother! You said I would be the one to take care of him! And then you decided you were going to be the kind of involved, hands-on mother you never were with Floyd."

"I lost my only child," Maude said. "I couldn't have another of my own. When I finally got another chance to be a mother, I sure as hell wasn't going to stand back and let the nanny get all the love and the attention. Not when it was the same nanny that had let my first child die."

Even in the context of everything else that had been said tonight, that one cut deep. "You wanted to be such a perfect mother, fine," Bridget said. "Then why did you pull away from Johnny after Mr. Apfelmann died, just when he needed you most?"

Maude shrugged. "Nothing I did seemed to make any difference. I was still alive, taking him to insufferable baseball games, on disgusting pony rides, and still he couldn't stop sniveling about losing his father. I lost patience."

"You can't lose patience with a child!" Bridget cried. "You can't give up, not ever!"

"Oh, I know that was your belief, Bridget. Everything Johnny ever did—failing at school, sneaking off and smoking with the other truants, coming home drunk, losing all my money on the horses—you put your arms around him and told him it wasn't his fault and he'd do better next time."

"And what was your solution? Refusing to speak to him. Refusing to look at him. Refusing to love him if he wasn't exactly what you wanted."

"And what other motivation did he have to change? Children are like dogs, Bridget. If they crave the biscuit, they have to learn to sit up. If you give them everything they want for nothing, then why should they even try?"

"Oh, yes," said Bridget. "Your techniques were very effective. Sailing to Europe for three months, six months at a time. Missing your son's school performances, his graduation, parents' weekends at college, virtually every important event in his life. . . ."

"He needed to learn that if he wanted my attention, he had to earn it. If he had worked at school, gotten decent grades, I would have been proud to visit him at college. But when he did so poorly that the only solution for me was to buy his way into school, then to bribe them not to kick him out, well, then, I don't think he deserved my presence at his little events."

"So I went in your place, Maude. Here's another thing you don't know. That fall you sailed to South America, 1938, right before we lost Johnny forever, I went up to Dartmouth to visit him for parents' weekend."

She'd packed the canvas satchel she'd brought with her from Ireland and ventured north on the train, the first time in her two decades in America that she had ever been out of the state of New York. With her savings she'd bought new clothes for the occasion: a fur collar, a soft gray cloche from Best & Co., kid shoes with fashionably buttoned straps. She watched eagerly from the window of the train to see all these places she'd only viewed on a map—New Haven, Hartford, Springfield—disappointed in the dirty factory towns but entranced by the New England countryside, those endless green hills, the trees turning progressively golder and redder as she sped north, all that land and so few people. She'd never suspected that there was a place so much like Ireland so close to where she'd been.

She was nervous, alighting at the White River Junction station with the real parents, so confidently handing their baggage over to porters and hailing taxis. There were other boys there to meet the train. Not Johnny, though, even though she'd wired her travel plans ahead.

The next morning, she finally found him standing with his friends at the welcoming event. Her heart rose up at the sight of him, so tall and dark and good-looking, his shoulders straining against his navy blue blazer just as his father's, his real father's, had done all those years ago on the boardwalk at Coney Island. From the back, the way his hair curled against his neck, something about the cast of his cheekbone, he looked exactly like George. She had the urge to reach out and touch his sleeve. She wanted to see him turn and smile at her with his father's dimples. But when he finally caught sight of her, he quickly swiveled away.

That evening, there came a knock on her door at the Hanover Inn. When she saw him standing there in the hallway, she didn't know whether to throw her arms around him or to yell at him or to tell him how much he'd hurt her. But he spoke first.

"I'm sorry, Bea," he said, walking into the room, although she had not invited him in. "It's just that . . . I thought the other fellows would make fun of me if I told them my *babysitter* was here."

"You could have said I was a family friend," she said. "Or introduced me by my name."

"But nobody calls a family friend who's so much older Bridget—I mean, by their first name like that," he said. "Everyone would have known you were some kind of . . ." He stopped. "That you weren't an actual relative."

"Is that really so bad?" she asked gently.

"Yes, it's so bad!" he burst out. He started pacing, his hands shoved deep in his pockets, trailing the smell of cigarettes on unwashed clothes. She heard the beat of drums somewhere outside. "I don't mean to hurt your feelings, Bridget, but I'm too old to have a nursemaid. Don't you sometimes think it's time for you to get a different job?"

Bridget stood very still. When Johnny had turned his back on her at the Welcoming Event, when she'd been sitting by herself in the room, she'd felt hurt, sad, but not really angry. Now, though, she felt her temper begin to rise.

"What would you have me do?" she asked.

"I don't know: take care of some little boy who needs to have his hand held. Or perhaps you could retire, go back to Ireland."

"You'd be rid of me," she said. "Just like that."

"Oh, Bea, don't put it that," he said. "I mean, it seems to me you'd be happier and feel more useful taking care of a child who needed it, or putting your feet up in front of a nice cozy fire, instead of chasing around after a grown man. I'm sure mother would give you some kind of severance or pension. She's always up for using money as a solution to life's problems."

She could easily have started crying, but felt it was

important to keep control of herself. If she cried, he would feel sorry and apologize, and try to be nice to her for a little while, but nothing would really change.

"And you think that's what I want?" she asked him. "Money?"

He sighed heavily. "I know you loved me and all that mush," he said, "but let's be honest, Bea. In the end, this is a job for you. You're with us because my mother pays you to be."

That was when she snapped. As divided as she and Maude had been about how best to raise Johnny, they had always agreed that he must never know that Maude and Mr. Apfelmann were not his real parents. He must never be told that he'd been adopted. And especially, it must never be revealed that Bridget was his real mother.

Maude had picked the magazine back up now and resumed studying it, paying special attention to a full-page advertisement for a diamond pendant. Bridget watched her, feeling the bile rise in her throat. All these years she'd hung on, hoping that things would get better. Maude would soften, Johnny would come back, Billie would stay, the bargain Bridget made so many years ago would prove to have been the right one. It had all been for love—she had never wanted to hurt anyone—but now, watching Maude, remembering that night with Johnny, she felt like she wanted to reach out and rip Maude's windpipe from her throat. She wished a shower of blood would fill the room, turning all the endless purple purple purple a bright soaking violent red.

"I told him," Bridget said.

Still gazing at the page, Maude said mildly, "You told who what?"

"I told Johnny. That I was his mother."

Maude looked up, as if in slow motion.

"When did you tell him this?"

"I went to see him at college. He didn't want me there instead of you, said I embarrassed him. He told me I should go work somewhere else, that I only took care of him for the money. I couldn't let him go on like that. I told him I was his mother, the one who'd given birth to him, and that he owed me obedience and respect."

Maude blinked once, as lazily as a lizard, her eyes widening as they locked on Bridget's.

"What did he say?"

"He accused me of selling him to you. He asked whether you'd hired me to have him, whether I'd been paid to be impregnated by Mr. Apfelmann. I tried to tell him it wasn't like that, that I'd been poor, desperate. That I'd always loved him, that *you* loved him. . . ."

"But he didn't believe you," Maude said placidly.

Bridget had guarded this secret so closely for so long, terrified of how Maude would react if she ever found out, that she could scarcely believe now how calmly Maude was taking it.

"No, he said I wasn't his mother, and that you weren't his mother, either. That what we did was evil and he didn't care about either of us. He didn't want to see me again or you, either. He left me standing there and he didn't come back."

He left the room, left the school, left the country. He joined the army, she learned, and fought in the South Pacific, then landed in California, worked in Hollywood, got blacklisted, became a union organizer, met Billie's mother and had Billie and drank and took drugs and lived who knew how. His whole life Bridget wrote to him, one letter after another, all saying the same thing: I love you, I miss you, please come home. But he simply didn't respond.

"Don't worry, dear Bridget, I don't blame you for driving him away," said Maude, still in that same maddeningly even tone. "He was the only one to blame. He was already lost to us, was already beyond our help, long before he left. Whereas you were always devoted, loyal, loving. I'm only sorry that Johnny was ever born."

Of all the things Bridget had heard tonight, that was the most disturbing. "How can you wish Johnny had never been born?" Bridget said. "I remember how much you loved him. How much you wanted him. You were desperate enough not just for any child but for him, for *my* child, that you forced me into that devil's bargain."

"Well, I make mistakes, too, don't I?" Maude said lightly. "We all believed back then that everything was up to nurture— that you could take any baby and with the right supervision and the best education and plenty of money, turn him into anything you wanted. But we know now that genetics had something to do with it, a *lot* to do with it, and Johnny was simply a bad seed who should have been flushed away. The same way his daughter and now that little baby are bad seeds."

Bridget felt as if she might faint. "You're a monster," she said to Maude. "I'm going to do what I should have done long ago and leave you. You'll have no one, ever again. You'll die alone and miserable, which is exactly what you deserve."

"Oh, don't be so melodramatic," said Maude, unconcerned. "The girl is gone now and you can hand the baby over to an adoption agency and we'll stay together, the way we always have."

"No, Maude," said Bridget. "Not now, not ever again. I have money of my own that I've been saving all these years. And I have Billie. *My* granddaughter. And my great-granddaughter, too."

"A lot of good those two will do you," said Maude. "Why don't *you* face the truth for once, Bridget? You need me every bit as much as I need you, and I don't just mean for money."

"But I don't need you," said Bridget, shaking her head, feeling the truth of that at last. "I don't need to take care of you anymore to feel I'm worthwhile. I don't need to make up for Floyd's death. And I don't need to stay here in case Johnny comes back, or Billie. I don't need to be here at all."

There must have been something in her voice, as there was in her heart, of the certainty she felt. As she started to leave the room, Maude called after her, in a more pleading tone than she usually stooped to: "Oh, come on, Bridget. This is silly. You can't go rushing out into the night the way that teenager did."

Bridget stopped. "I don't intend to. I need to make arrangements for the baby, and for Billie, too. When she decides how she's going to care for her child, she needs to be able to find me and the baby."

"How are you going to do that," Maude said, "without me?"

"Oh, I'm not," said Bridget, taking hold of the knob so she could shut the door behind her. "You're going to help me."

28

Cait, Present

W hy didn't you come back for me?" Cait asked Billie.

Outside the tall windows overlooking Sixty-fourth Street, the sky had darkened into evening. There were more footsteps in the hallway and on the stairs now, and cooking smells floating up from below. A timid knock came at the French doors, and Dulcie poked her head into the room. "Aren't you having dinner with us, Ma?"

"Save me something," Billie said. "I'll eat later."

In the shadows of the room, Billie's face was softer, the gray in her hair turned to gold, so that she looked to Cait like the teenager she'd once been. How could Cait not feel sympathetic? Yet, Billie had run away, leaving newborn Cait in the arms of an old woman in a house owned by someone who wished her dead. Worse, Billie had not returned.

"I intended to," Billie said, tucking a foot underneath her and looking away. "I did sleep in the park that first night, but I was freezing and terrified. I realized pretty quickly that I could not stay in New York, not long-term, even with Bridget's help. It was much less expensive then, but still much more expensive than other places, and more dangerous, and I had no way to earn a living."

Billie didn't just leave, she told Cait: she called Bridget and told her she wanted to go to California and asked whether Bridget could take care of the baby until she was settled there. Bridget said that if she were thirty years younger—twenty, even—she would do it in an instant, but she couldn't manage. Billie should come and live with her, she said. She'd get an apartment big enough for both of them, find someone to help with child care, make sure Billie had her privacy.

But Billie balked. She'd been wiggling her foot, staring at the ground, and now she looked straight up at Cait.

"I couldn't hack it," she said. "I'm ashamed of the way I behaved back then, but I think that now at least I owe you complete honesty. I don't know if you ever went through anything like this, getting pregnant when you were young, completely unprepared . . ."

Cait quickly shook her head no. Billie Apfelmann might owe her total honesty, but Cait didn't owe Billie Apfelmann anything. Not yet.

"Well, I see it over and over now, which helps me understand myself better, what I was like then. And even to forgive myself. I guess that's going to take a while longer for you."

Cait nodded. "I'm still working on the understanding part," she said.

Billie nodded curtly. "I get that. What happened was that, as wonderful as Bridget had been to me, I just didn't want to live with an old lady and a baby in some apartment in New York. I'd done the thing Jupe thought was going to be the answer to all my problems, found my so-called family, and then all I wanted to do was get away from them. I wanted to be a kid again. Travel, live with a bunch of other kids by the beach, party, sleep, get stoned, go out with lots of guys." She shrugged. "It sounds horrible, but that's the truth."

Those were all the things Cait wanted to do, and did, when she was nineteen, too. But she didn't leave a baby alone to do them.

"So, what about me?" Cait asked.

Billie drew in a deep shuddering breath. "Bridget had this distant cousin, Sally," she said. "She knew Sally had wanted a baby for a long time, had tried getting pregnant and tried adopting without success. Bridget had this idea that Sally could take care of you while I was getting my shit together, and that way Bridget could keep an eye on you without having the burden of full-time baby care. She asked me if it was okay and I said sure." Billie smiled wryly. "I was thinking of this girl I met in a club one time who'd given up her baby for adoption. She'd made it sound like the right thing to do."

Cait frowned. Hearing this piece of the story, her heart went out to Sally, rather than to Billie or even Bridget. Billie couldn't take care of Cait and didn't want to. Bridget wanted to care for her but couldn't. It was Sally, Sally and Vern, who'd embraced Cait on every level, without even knowing whether she could really be theirs.

"So you'd made up your mind to put me up for adoption?"

Billie shook her head. "Not consciously. I kept telling Bridget, and telling myself, too, that I just needed a little more time and then I was going to come back for you." She straightened up, shivered all over. "But then the bad stuff started happening.

"I started smoking a lot of pot and took off for Mexico with a guy I met on the beach. When I was there I met another guy, a Mexican guy, who turned me on to cocaine. By the time I straggled back across the border, I'd slept with a dozen guys whose last names I didn't know, I'd developed an insistent coke habit, and I was pregnant again.

"That time I had no conflict," she told Cait. "I went to a clinic in L.A. and had an abortion. But I was freaked out. I'd been gone for months. I was afraid I was on my way to becoming my mother: a junkie, incompetent, irresponsible, dead by thirty. I called Bridget in New York and told her that if you were thriving, if your foster parents loved you, I was ready to let you go."

A horn sounded outside; the wind blew a smattering of rain against the elegant windows. When had it started raining? When had Cait's feelings toward Billie changed from anger and yearning to gratitude? The only response she could think of, though she didn't say it, was "Thank you."

"The adoption was all totally legal," Billie said. "There was to be no contact; I had no parental rights of any kind. But I knew who was adopting you, because Bridget told me. She even offered to send me pictures, but I didn't want them. You would never know I had even existed, I told myself. I wanted to forget that you existed, too."

Suddenly, for the first time since they'd started talking, Billie looked as if she were going to cry. She got up and crossed the room, pulling the drapes closed with a swish, switching on a lamp, and crossing to a blond wood Art Deco cabinet that she opened with a small silver key she drew from the front pocket of her jeans.

"I need a drink," she said to Cait. "Would you like one?"

Cait shook her head no.

"You don't drink? That's good."

"I'm pregnant."

Billie drew her head back and studied Cait, a smile playing at her lips. "Really? Wow. That's amazing. I mean, isn't it?"

Cait nodded. "It is."

"When are you due?" Billie asked. She splashed Scotch into a crystal glass, filled it with soda, and crossed back to the chair in front of the fireplace, animated, happy, now that she was back in the present. "I've been talking so much about myself, I don't know anything about you. Are you married? What do you do for a living?"

"I hope we can have the kind of relationship where I'll tell you all that at some point," Cait said, "but right now I need to hear the rest of what happened with you. I mean"—she held her hands up, looked around the room; the ceilings, though grayed with dirt and peeling, still sported gorgeous egg-and-dart molding and must have been fifteen feet tall—"a lot must have happened between you being strung out in L.A., deciding to put me up for adoption, and you coming back here."

Billie drew in a deep breath, took a sip of her drink. "I left the country," she said. "I traveled through Southeast Asia, did a lot more drugs, thought I'd stay overseas forever. It was easier there, traveling around. I felt normal there, not fitting in, being alone, never feeling at home."

Cait found herself nodding in agreement. "I know what you mean," she said. "I've done a lot of traveling myself. It saves you from feeling like a freak for not really belonging anywhere, because you're not supposed to belong."

Billie looked surprised. "Really? I thought I saved you from that, by giving you parents and a normal home."

"My mother would read me these books about adoption, tell me they'd chosen me out of all the little girls in the world, and I believed she loved me, they loved me, completely," Cait said. "And at the same time, I didn't look like them, I didn't think like them, and I couldn't help but wonder: Was there someone else, someone exactly like me, who I belonged to more?"

She'd said more than she wanted to, more than she'd planned. Billie was looking at her with something like tenderness in her eyes.

"I saw you," Billie said.

"What?"

"I saw you. When you were four. When Bridget died."

Cait was so stunned, all she could do was stare.

"I was crossing some border in Asia when the immigration authorities pulled me aside. There was a message from the State Department to contact Maude's lawyers. I hadn't been in touch with her since that night I left and expected never to hear from her again. I hadn't been in contact with Bridget for a long time, either, which I felt badly about, but that was part of wanting to forget. In those days, before cell phones and the Internet, you could go to Thailand or Burma and just vanish until you had to show your passport. It turned out Maude had died something like three months before, and Bridget had asked the lawyers to track me down and bring me back to New York."

"So Maude didn't disown you after all."

"Oh, no," Billie laughed. "She did. In the end, she left all her money, this place, everything to Bridget."

"To Bridget? But I thought Bridget had left her."

"Bridget did leave. The lawyers sent me a first-class ticket and I flew back to New York. It was winter, I remember, and I was dressed in some ridiculous tribal garment, with flip-flops on my feet. But Reagan had been elected by then, Charles and Diana were engaged, the world had changed. A limo collected me at the airport; I remember the driver carrying my filthy backpack with two fingers, like he was taking out a particularly disgusting piece of trash."

The limo took her not to the house on Sixty-fourth Street but to a brick building in Queens, where Bridget was living in a one-bedroom apartment overlooking a street populated mostly by Asians and Dominicans. Bridget spent her days sitting in a chair by the window, taking in the action below or watching the same little TV she'd had in her room at Maude's. On her pine dresser was the owl-shaped vase that held Billie's father's ashes, left behind on Sixty-fourth Street and long forgotten, along with a picture of Billie wearing Maude's flowered chiffon dress when she'd first arrived in New York, the portrait of little Johnny in cowboy gear that had been in his childhood room, and a half dozen photos of a sturdy, somber-looking, dark-haired little girl: Cait.

Billie told Cait she hadn't been able to stop staring at the grainy pictures of the little girl, wearing a red smocked dress, clutching a doll, reaching for the round, smiling, sandy-haired woman who was her adoptive mother.

"I was trying to connect with the feeling that you were

mine," Billie said, "but you'd grown so much, changed so much, and so had I. It didn't seem quite real."

Bridget seemed so old, so frail, compared with how she'd looked when Billie had left. Her hands and legs had twisted in on themselves with arthritis and she had trouble moving around. She wasn't able to travel out to New Jersey on her own to see the baby, renamed Caitlin, any longer, and it was difficult to entertain Sally and Vern and the child in her tiny apartment. Vern still came and got her for holidays. But otherwise she could no longer see the child, who was beautiful and smart as a whip, as often as she would have liked.

Billie asked Bridget if she could visit the little girl. She didn't want anything, she said, she just wanted to see her, to touch her, to make sure she was all right.

Bridget was shaken, nervous. Billie had given her daughter up, Bridget said, signed papers swearing she would not seek any rights. Sally and Vern would never agree to it.

So don't tell them, Billie urged. They don't even know who I am, right? You can just say I'm Maude's granddaughter. Or a friend, or even your aide.

It wasn't right, said Bridget. They might guess. She couldn't lie to Sally and Vern, who were so good, so loving, so over the moon about Caitlin.

And who knew how it was going to make Billie feel? What if she wanted the child back? What if she tried to take the child? Bridget wasn't strong enough to stop her. Billie might swear she'd never do that, but Bridget knew what it was like to be close to a child who was yours yet wasn't yours. She knew how irresistible the pull could be.

They stopped short of having a fight. Billie was so happy

to see Bridget again after all that time, felt—now that she was back in New York—how far she'd come in the years she'd been traveling. She might not have settled down, but she'd grown up. Bridget said she wanted to use Maude's money to help Billie get on her feet, and to get Billie's help, too, in finding a way to use the money and the house to do something good, to make up for all the wrongs that had been committed.

Billie thanked Bridget but said she didn't want anything to do with Maude's money. She left on a subway rather than in the limo, found a cheap apartment in the East Village, got a job as a waitress. She sent Bridget a note with her new address and phone number, and kept telling herself she'd visit again someday soon.

Then one day the phone rang. It was Sally. Billie's breathing stopped, her whole body shut down, but then Sally said that she was sorry to call with bad news, but Bridget Early had passed away. Sally was going through Bridget's address book and calling everyone who might want to know about Bridget. She seemed to be aware that Billie was connected somehow with Maude, that Maude had died some time earlier, but nothing more, nothing about Cait. She gave Billie the time and place of the funeral, in New Jersey, and said a polite good-bye.

Billie was surprised at how hard hit she was by Bridget's death. Maybe it was being off drugs finally, for the first time in years. Maybe it was living back in New York, where the memory of everything that had happened, good and bad, was so much more palpable. But she was filled with regret for not being closer to Bridget in those final years, for not seeing her again when she had the chance. And sadness so keen she couldn't get to sleep at night, haunted by the refrain: never, never, never . . .

Billie went to the funeral in New Jersey dressed in a formal black silk dress and a black hat, with dark glasses to hide her eyes. She wanted to pay her respects to Bridget, but she was also hoping to see her daughter.

At the funeral, there were members of the church Bridget had attended in Queens, along with people she'd worked with through the years at Maude's house: Billie recognized Mary along with several other women who'd cleaned and cooked. There was a smattering of older women who Billie assumed were friends. And at the front of the room, face powdered and soft in an open casket, lay Bridget herself, dressed in the pale blue silk she'd worn at the dinner with Jupe, a bone rosary in her folded hands.

Billie had to bite back a sob and wondered how she was going to get through the service, but then Cait appeared in the room and Billie stopped thinking about anything else. The child was beautiful, prettier and more vibrant than she'd seemed in pictures, a filled-in picture of her infant self. She was dressed in a navy cotton dress, obviously expensive, with a starched white collar. As Billie described the dress, Cait flashed on its real-life version, packed away in tissue in Vern and Sally's attic, waiting along with the rest of Cait's best childhood clothes for the little girl they'd always hoped Cait would one day have.

As Bridget had predicted, Billie felt an almost physical drive to rush up to Cait, take her in her arms, run out the door with her. She could see it happening, felt it play out in her mind over and over until she began to feel like she was going crazy.

Sitting in the back of the room on a hard wooden folding

chair, she watched hungrily as Vern walked up the center aisle with Sally at his side, Cait lifted high in his arms. As they approached the casket, little Cait suddenly cried, "Bea!" and tried to leap from her father's arms, her whole body folding forward toward the dead woman.

Her father gathered her back, whispered in her ear, kissed her, and murmured soothingly. The child began to cry then and Vern turned away from the coffin, heading back down the aisle toward where Billie was sitting. Billie imagined herself standing up, reaching out, taking the sobbing child from this man, being the one to comfort her.

But then she saw that Sally, a plump little wren of a woman, had reached out to touch Bridget's hands over the rosary and then swung around, catching up with Vern and the little girl and lifting her arms.

"Mommy!" Cait called.

Billie half rose in her seat.

The child lunged, but it was toward Sally this time. Sally stopped and gathered her daughter close, hugging her and kissing her face until all the tears were gone. Cait's arms were around her mother's neck, and now she was kissing Sally, too, resting her head on Sally's shoulder, looking straight at Billie for one piercing moment and then slipping her thumb into her mouth and closing her eyes.

That was the end. Billie waited until the couple and the child retreated, and then she left through the back door without speaking to them or seeing them again. She wouldn't try to get her daughter back, her daughter who was no longer her daughter.

Even later, when she learned that Bridget had left her all

her money, along with the house on Sixty-fourth Street, when she might have used that vast fortune to wage a legal battle to regain some rights to the child, she instead did what Bridget might have wanted her to do with the money: used it to help other young women who were pregnant, confused, without help or resources. As much as she would have loved to have her baby back, Cait already had a mother, a mother she loved. And that mother was Sally.

They were sitting in near darkness as Billie finished her story, the only sounds the swish of traffic on the wet city streets outside, the tick of a clock, and then, from somewhere above, the dim sound of a television.

With a start, Cait looked at her watch. She had promised to meet Martin at a nearby restaurant at eight; she was already late.

"I have to go," she said, standing up.

"Oh, no," said Billie, standing, too. "Should I not have told you all that? I don't want to drive you away."

"It's not that," Cait said. "It's just . . . I promised to meet my boyfriend."

Her boyfriend. That was the first time she'd called Martin that. The word sounded right in her mouth.

"Call him," said Billie. "Ask him to pick you up here. I'd love to meet him."

Cait hesitated. "Another time," she said softly.

She couldn't wait to tell Martin everything she'd learned, was already picturing the fascination on his big handsome face, his eagerness to hear all the details. But anticipating Martin's questions reminded her of something from earlier in their conversation, something that had never found its way back in.

"You never told me about my father," she reminded Billie.

"Oh, Jupe," Billie said. "Dear, sweet Jupe. He was a lovely man, really, Cait, a wonderful man. After Bridget died, after I came to the decision I did about you, I got in touch with him. He was in San Francisco, where he'd gone to medical school, doing a residency in the neonatal intensive care unit at the hospital there. He'd never gotten the letter I sent him, it turned out, had no idea you'd been born. I told him all about you, told him the whole story. We became friendly again, talking on the phone from time to time, writing letters. When I decided to open this home, he gave me a lot of advice about the medical end of pregnancy, dealing with nutrition to help elevate birth weight, how to handle premature labor. . . ."

"So he's in San Francisco?" Cait said, her excitement bubbling up. "He's a doctor there?"

Billie reached out and laid a hand on Cait's arm. "He died, Cait. A long time ago, in the early nineties. He was gay. He had AIDS. But I saw him many times in those years, and showed him pictures of you."

"Did he have a family?"

Billie nodded. "The Mastersons. His parents are both alive; you have tons of aunts and uncles and cousins out in Brooklyn. They live in a big purple house in Bed-Stuy. I bet his mom will be delighted to write your name in the family Bible."

Cait threw back her head and laughed. Another detail she couldn't wait to tell Martin. More people in the world to welcome and love her baby.

Her baby. She was sure now, ready—beyond ready: thrilled. She had cried for Riley that day, she realized now, not because she was mourning her own poor, broken, lost self, but because she wanted to gather him into her arms and save him. She wished she had been his mother; no, she wished she were somebody's mother. Not Riley's, not an African orphan's, but the mother of a child who was her very own.

Was that wrong? It made her feel guilty, somehow, and she'd pressed the desire away, buried it for so long, like covering over a tiny body with dead leaves, that she'd forgotten it was there. Having her own baby would hurt Sally somehow, she feared, and it would hurt Billie, and perhaps most of all it might hurt her by reviving that pain she had surely felt, in some elemental place, when she had lost the first person she loved.

She was terrified to rediscover that bond, that love, to risk reliving that loss, and yet felt as if she would never really begin living until she embraced it. All that possibility was waiting for her, in the heart that beat even now deep inside her. In the child that was part Martin and part Billie and part Bridget and part Jupe and, yes, part Sally and part Vern and even part Maude, too, and yet, in a way, that was Cait's alone. Her flesh and blood. Her mind and heart.

She was not Billie, not young, not poor, not scared, not alone. She had a man who loved her, who wanted to be a father to her child. And she had parents who'd shown her how a good parent behaved and who showed her that still.

She'd thought that finding Billie would unlock the secret of who she was, and it had, but not in the way that she'd expected. In meeting Billie she realized that she was who she was because of Sally. It was Sally's love that had created the strong, confident, adventurous person that she'd become. If Cait was ready to embrace her own child now in all its mystery, her future as a mother no matter what that would bring, it was Sally she had to thank.

She'd always thought she had two mothers, the one who'd adopted her and the one who'd given birth to her, the real mother and the shadow mother, though she'd always been confused about which was which. But she had only one mother, she knew now. And that was the mother who'd always loved her, the mother she loved.

EPILOGUE

The baby, fat and squalling, with a shock of dark hair, was born in a rush of water and blood. Martin's hand was gripping hers, they were both crying and laughing, and then, when they'd cut the cord and weighed the baby and cleaned her off, Martin took her from the nurse and laid her in Cait's arms.

"Well," he said, laughing. "I guess this settles the Jupiter question."

Cait had been campaigning, if the baby was a boy, to name him Jupiter, an idea that Martin had resisted. Jupiter might be a cool name in theory, he argued, but Jupiter Lebowitz? It sounded like a joke.

"I don't know," Cait said, gazing at her daughter, teasing her husband. "I think Jupiter could work for a girl. Or maybe Jupette."

She hadn't wanted to know the baby's sex, had claimed she thought it was a boy—even that she hoped it was a boy so she could avoid the whole mother-daughter thing that had so plagued her own life. But of course that was the very reason that she desperately wanted a girl: to relive the relationship and get it right this time.

The baby stared up at her with milky eyes, the dark blue of the night sky. She was so fully formed, with her little eyebrows, her rosebud mouth, her fingernails like tiny seashells. Cait couldn't believe that, ten minutes before, this complete person had been inside her body. Or that, starting now, they'd forever be separate.

"She looks like you," Martin said.

Cait was about to protest that the baby looked like him— isn't that what new mothers always said?—but then just had to nod in agreement. The baby did look like her, nearly exactly. It was like gazing at her own baby pictures.

"Is my mother here?" she asked Martin.

He nodded. "I told them they should go back to our place and get some rest, but Sally wouldn't hear of it. Your father said something about her heart, and she told him that if she was going to have a heart attack, she thought the best thing she could do would be to have it right here in the hospital."

Cait laughed. She and Sally had become so close through the months of her pregnancy. When Martin was working, it was Sally who traveled into the city to go to the doctor with her; when Martin's kids spent the weekend at the apartment he and Cait had rented in Brooklyn Heights, Cait often went to New Jersey, as much to spend time with Vern and Sally as to give Martin and his children a chance to adjust to the new arrangement.

On those weekends with her parents, they shopped for baby furniture and supplies and Sally delighted in reliving Cait's infanthood. She'd kept obsessive scrapbooks that Cait found newly fascinating, filled with hundreds of pictures, notes on when Cait had cut her first tooth and said her first word ("hot"), cards and invitations to Cait's christening and birthday parties.

There were even pictures of her with Bridget, which she peered at for clues to all the secrets that had shaped all those years—that influenced them still. But all she saw was a round, gray-haired, benign-looking old lady holding Cait and beaming like any ordinary granny.

"What about the Mastersons?" she asked Martin. "Did you call them?"

Billie had introduced Cait and Martin to the whole extended Masterson clan. Jupe had never told them about Cait, fearing that his mother would disapprove, Billie said, not of Cait's existence but of the fact that she'd been put up for adoption. Most black women, even young unmarried women, kept their babies and always had. But Marie had been beside herself with joy to discover that the son she thought she'd lost long ago lived on in a child and soon-to-be grandchild. Cait's name was duly inscribed, along with Billie's, in the family Bible, and her daughter's name would soon be written there, too.

"There was some trouble about the hospital not allowing all of them into the waiting room," said Martin, chuckling. "But I think several of the relatives gave up waiting around your fourteenth hour of labor, so now only Marie and maybe Coralie are out there with your parents, along with approximately five dozen balloons."

"And Billie?" asked Cait.

Through her long and difficult labor and delivery, Cait had kept flashing on Billie, how painful it must have been for her to go through that alone. While meeting Billie had ironically propelled Cait closer to Sally, giving birth made her yearn to see Billie more keenly now than she had all these months.

"Billie said she'd come see us after we got home, whenever we were ready," Martin said, smoothing back Cait's hair. "I think she didn't want to step on Sally's toes."

The two women had met, but warily. They did not become the warm friends Cait might have imagined and wished but were merely polite with each other, like a spouse and an ex-lover.

The hospital staff was finishing their work; a nurse approached and reached to take the baby.

"Oh, no," Cait said, swiveling away. Already the baby felt as natural in Cait's arms as if she'd been molded to fit there. "I want to keep her with me. At least for a while longer."

The nurse shrugged, flipped off the overhead lights, left them alone in the now dim and quiet room. For a long moment she and Martin contemplated their child.

"I'm thinking about Riley," Cait said, with a twist of her heart. "I wish we'd found him, but at least something good came of the search."

"Us," said Martin.

"I was thinking of our baby," Cait said, resting her head against his. "But, yes, you're right. Us."

He kissed her forehead. "Maybe we should name her Riley," he suggested.

But Cait immediately shook her head no. "Too sad. I want a name that feels as hopeful as I do."

Cait laid her hand gently on her newborn daughter, her fingers blanketing the child's tiny body, separate and at the same time together forever. She remembered what Billie had said about losing sight of where she ended and the baby began, but Cait felt no such confusion. She was the mother, she knew, and this was her daughter, and what else could she name her but Bridget?

The Possibility of You

Pamela Redmond

INTRODUCTION

I had book clubs in mind when I wrote *The Possibility of You.* Exploring timeless issues that affect women—women of my generation, of my daughter's generation, and of my mother's and grandmother's generations, too—as well as the way things have changed over the decades made conversations and debates come alive in my head. I longed to hear women talking about those issues, having those conversations, out loud.

If you're lucky enough to be a member of an intergenerational book club, this novel would be a perfect pick. Alternately, your book club could invite your mothers or daughters (or both), or friends and relatives of different ages, to the meeting at which you discuss this book.

The seed of the idea for *The Possibility of You* involved both my grandmother and my daughter, who never met. After looking up my grandmother's name on the Ellis Island website and discovering that she'd arrived in 1911, when she was twenty-two years old, I realized she was the same age as my daughter, who had just moved to Paris. Two young women, separated by four generations and nearly a century, both embarking on independent lives in foreign countries and having experiences that, in the end, must have felt very similar.

I suddenly was able to imagine my grandmother as a young woman in a way I never could before. While the reality of her individual life in New York was unknowable—she wouldn't talk about it, and there was little written about the lives of Irish maids and nannies beyond the most offensive stereotypes—I was able to research the era and create a Bridget who might well have been her.

I, myself, moved to New York in 1976, and while there was no Maude or Bridget in my life, no Jupiter, and no baby, either, I did spend a week at a friend's grandmother's apartment on the Upper East Side that felt a lot like the house on Sixty-fourth Street, and I went through a pregnancy scare that left an indelible mark on me.

Of course, young women today have so many more choices, so much more information than my grandmother or mother or I even had when I was in my twenties. And yet, the feelings surrounding those choices, the difficulty of those decisions, has remained much the same.

Topics & Questions for Discussion

1. Why does Cait's unexpected pregnancy inspire her to search for her birth mother? How does the fact of her own adoption influence her feelings about being pregnant and the possibility of having a child?

2. Motherhood is a central theme in the story. Of the characters that are mothers, whom did you find to be the most empathetic? How about the least? What does it take to make someone a mother—is it a genetic bond? or an emotional one?—and why?

3. How does Cait's life—emotionally, socially, and economically—compare to Billie's when she was faced with an unplanned pregnancy more than thirty years earlier? Given Billie's situation, was her decision to leave her daughter and seek a new life for herself understandable? Why or why not?

4. Describe Bridget's relationship with Maude, both before and after Floyd's death. Why do you think Bridget remains with Maude for so many years? How would you define their relationship in one word?

5. The scene in which Cait finally meets Billie is the only one told from both characters' perspectives. How does having each of their viewpoints enhance the story? During their conversation, what does Cait come to realize about her past and her future? What is her opinion of Billie?

6. In what ways does Cait's search for her birth mother give her a new understanding about Vern and Sally, her adoptive parents? How does her relationship with Sally, in particular, change over the course of the story?

7. From physical appearances and sexual preferences to upbringings and ambitions, Billie and Jupe appear to embody "nothing but contradictions" (p. 15). What accounts for their close friendship? How does Billie so misjudge their relationship?

8. How does the issue of race play out in the novel? Discuss the scene on pages 163–173 when Jupe joins Billie, Bridget, and Maude for dinner. Afterward, Jupe disagrees with Billie that Bridget is the more racist of the two older women—and that Maude, in fact, was not being "really nice" throughout the evening as Billie believed (p. 173). Whose perception of the situation is more accurate? How so?

9. Discuss the historical aspects of the story, including the suffragist movement and the Heterodoxy Club, birth control restrictions, divorce laws, the attitude toward Irish

immigrants, and the polio epidemic. What, if anything, did you learn that surprised you?

10. *The Possibility of You* spans nearly a hundred years. What were the most dramatic changes from generation to generation in terms of choices and opportunities for women, including those related to marriage and motherhood? What things have remained essentially the same?

A Conversation with Pamela Redmond

There are two epigraphs in the book, one from Philip Roth's *The Human Stain* and the other from Kara Walker's *Letter from a Black Girl*. What was it about these two passages that resonated with you?

The Philip Roth quote speaks to how unknowable our family histories, the lives of our mothers and grandmothers, are to us from the present. Cait goes looking for the truth about her parentage, and the reader finds out much more about her history and the foundations of her life than she can ever know. We all have that curiosity about a past that can never be fully revealed to us, and we're all shaped by experiences that we may never discover.

I saw an exhibition of Kara Walker's art, which I love, early in the process of writing this book. Besides being inspired by how she rewrites African-American and women's history, I thought the feeling in the quote of two people wrapped up in a hate-love relationship, the way Maude and Bridget in particular are, especially resonated with this book.

What inspired the idea to have a character who searches for her birth mother? Is adoption a subject in which you were previously interested or one you have personal experience with?

Originally, this book was only about Billie and Bridget, and there was no contemporary story, so when I decided to add a present-day character, I needed to give her a compelling reason to dig into the past and that's how I came up with the adoption story. Then, the more I read about the struggles of adopted adults searching for their identities, the more interesting the subject of adoption became.

While I am not an adoptive or birth parent and was not adopted myself, I've had several close friends and family members who've had personal experiences with adoption. I have heard their stories and seen their struggles on every side of this issue for years. Even in a happy adoption, as Cait's was, there are struggles.

Can you share with us the significance of the title *The Possibility of You* and how it relates to the story?

"The Possibility of You" connects with all the relationships in the book, from Bridget's search for the possibilities for her future beyond being a servant, to Billie's quest for Jupe's love and for a family, to Cait's curiosity about her birth mother. The babies of these women exist primarily as possibilities. And, of course, most centrally, to the women in the story as well as to all of us, there is the possibility of who you can become as a person and what you can make of your life.

There is a lot of fascinating information in the novel, from statistics (Frank's clients searching for birth parents are 90 percent female) to historical snapshots (the mania that gripped the city during the polio epidemic of 1916). What sort of research did you do for the novel? How long did it take you to write it?

I worked on this novel for more than five years and did a tremendous amount of research. I knew from my grandmother's marriage certificate that she'd gotten pregnant before she was married, a secret that provided the kernel of the book's drama across the generations. Early on, I visited the American Irish Historical Society on Fifth Avenue, whose gorgeous town house provided the model for the house on Sixty-fourth Street. I also went to the Ellis Island Library and listened to oral histories of Irish servants who came to New York in the years before World War I. At the New York Historical Society, I discovered a 1916 street atlas that showed something called the Hospital for the Ruptured and Crippled, which led me to the polio epidemic. I interviewed a Yale medical history professor, Dr. Naomi Rogers, who's an expert on the 1916 epidemic, along with an adoption detective, genetic specialists, adopted adults and adoptive parents, and experts on Irish immigration and the early birth control movement.

You're the author of several baby-naming books, including *Beyond Ava and Aiden: The Enlightened Guide to Naming Your Baby*. Do you use these resources when selecting character names? Along with Bridget, do any of the character names in *The Possibility of You* have special significance or meaning?

My first working title for this book was *The Bridget*. Bridget was my grandmother's real name and she changed it to Bertha or Bea; I never knew why until I discovered that "the Bridget" was a derogatory term for an Irish maid. Naming characters is different from naming babies in that you're not starting with a clean slate; when you choose a name, you have some sense of who you want this person to be. I kept changing Billie's name from Billie to Lily and back again, but once she firmly became Billie, she got a lot tougher than she'd been as Lily.

Reading about real-life figures like Margaret Sanger and Emma Goldman, with their actions put into historical context, is pretty powerful. Which women's rights advocate do you find particularly inspiring? What more can you tell us about psychoanalyst Beatrice Hinkle?

Beatrice Hinkle was fascinating and has been largely forgotten. She was one of the first women psychoanalysts in the United States, she translated Jung into English, and she was an extremely prominent and influential woman of her day. But I was able to find out only little about her until I gained access to a secret library in New York-Presbyterian Hospital, where they have her papers: astounding. But while Hinkle is amazing to me, Margaret Sanger is the women's rights advocate I find most inspiring. She went against the law and conventions to help poor women gain the right to birth control that wealthy women enjoyed via private doctors.

A memorable moment in the novel takes places when Billie is in a nightclub and speaks with a woman who had given up her own baby for adoption. That woman turns out to be Patti Smith. How did you discover this fact, and why did you work it into the story? Are you a fan of Patti Smith's music?

I am a huge Patti Smith fan—her rendition of Bob Dylan's "Changing of the Guard" is my absolute favorite song—and I was inspired to add this very late in revisions after reading her wonderful book, *Just Kids*. She wrote so honestly and movingly about giving up her child for adoption that I could imagine this scene very well taking place. It feels very real and vivid to me.

The Possibility of You spans three generations. What insights did writing this book give you into how things have changed for women over the last century? Were there any important issues you specifically wanted to address, such as post-partum depression or access to birth control?

Definitely access to birth control is huge, but beyond that, as a woman who came of reproductive age at the time Billie did, I really wanted to write about how relatively naive and idealistic and also repressed people were about sex and pregnancy in the 1970s, supposedly the age of sexual freedom. I even got a copy of *Our Bodies, Ourselves*, which every young woman had at the time, and in there was a lot about abortion but very little about pregnancy.

An interesting aspect of the story is how some of the women in the Heterodoxy Club, who are advocating for women's rights, have a derogatory attitude toward Bridget. Why the contradiction? Did you come across anything in your research that sheds light on this?

The women in the Heterodoxy Club—which was real and the common denominator for famous women of that day—were all wealthy and educated and upper class. There was then, and for decades to come, a casual classism and racism among people who on the other hand were fighting for women's rights or other kinds of social equality. And the Irish, of course, were seen as an inferior race. The parallel between that ethnic prejudice and the prejudice against Italians and blacks was something I wanted to explore.

You say on your website that *The Possibility of You* started out as a historical novel focused on an Irish nanny whose young charge dies in the 1916 polio epidemic. How did it transform into a story set in three different time periods, including the present?

It started out as a historical novel with a much pared-down version of the 1976 Billie story as a framing story. But the framing story never really worked; it just wasn't compelling enough. One early reader said the 1976 story consisted of Billie saying, "And then what did you do, Grandma?" Zzzzzzzz. And so I kept looking for ways to make the framing story more modern and more compelling and also to make the events of 1916 matter more going forward.

What do you most enjoy about writing historical novels? What can you tell us about the one you're currently working on?

This is my first historical novel and I'm hooked. There was a steep learning curve: I remember asking writers I admire like Geraldine Brooks and Jodi Picoult how they knew when to stop researching and start writing, and whether they did all their research before they began. Research some, write some, research some more was the message. And at some point you need to let go of all that great history you've learned and just let the characters live and breathe.

I'm working on two new novels now, both compelling and wrestling for my attention. One is another historical novel, set again in 1916, in the Adirondacks at a great rustic estate owned by a young widow, modeled on Margaret Vanderbilt, whose husband has gone down with the Lusitania. Grief stricken, she travels north to sell the place, only to encounter the amazing bed that the resident woodsman—hunky, naturally—has spent the winter building for her on her late-husband's instructions. As with *The Possibility of You*, there is also a present-day story that parallels the historical tale. The other book is a contemporary novel, funny but I hope also deep, about four characters—two women, two men—searching for happiness in a modern world that promises a lot but often doesn't deliver, at least not in the obvious ways.

Enhance Your Book Club

1. Given that family is a prominent theme in *The Possibility of You*, allow members to invite their mothers, daughters, or other special guests to join the discussion.

2. Have each member research a historical aspect of the book—such as the Comstock Laws, the Heterodoxy Club, the building of the subway tunnel between Manhattan and Brooklyn, the polio epidemic of 1916, or figures like Emma Goldman, Margaret Sanger, and Beatrice Hinkle—and share their findings with the group.

3. Cait and her friend Sam meet up at a "groovy—Sam's word—cocktail lounge . . . made out to look like a soigné lounge in old Saigon, or maybe Shanghai" (pp. 151–52). To set a similar scene for your book club gathering, converse by candlelight and serve Gin-Gin Mules. Here is a recipe for concocting the ginger-flavored drink: www.epicurious .com/recipes/drink/views/Gin-Gin-Mule-232358.

4. To learn more about Pamela Redmond and her writing, visit www.pamelaredmondsatran.com.